"There was no cold demand in his eyes now, only a scalding heat. She felt herself weakening, drawn beneath his spell. She gave a half-hearted sound—nay, not of protest... of surrender."

SAMANTHA JAMES

A Promise Given

AVON BOOKS  NEW YORK

This is a work of fiction. Names, characters, places, and incidents either are the product of the author's imagination or are used fictitiously. Any resemblance to actual events, locales, organizations, or persons, living or dead, is entirely coincidental and beyond the intent of either the author or the publisher.

AVON BOOKS
A division of
The Hearst Corporation
1350 Avenue of the Americas
New York, New York 10019

Copyright © 1998 by Sandra Kleinschmit
Cover art by Max Ginsburg
Inside cover author photo by Glamour Shots
Published by arrangement with the author
Visit our website at **http://www.AvonBooks.com**
Library of Congress Catalog Card Number: 97–93789
ISBN: 0–380–78608–7

First Avon Books Printing: January 1998

AVON TRADEMARK REG. U.S. PAT. OFF. AND IN OTHER COUNTRIES, MARCA REGISTRADA, HECHO EN U.S.A.

Printed in the U.S.A.

WCD   10 9 8 7 6 5 4 3 2 1

Prologue

Scotland
Late 1200's

It was the smothered sound of laughter that drew the lad to the stable. Though he was not yet a man, he was well beyond the point of boyhood. He stood tall for a youth of ten and five—aye, taller than many a man twice his age. There was the wiry promise of vigor and brawn to the proud set of his arms and legs; beneath the kilt he wore, his legs were sturdy and long.

He stood in the doorway for a moment, the curve of his brow wrinkled in concentration, wondering if mayhap his ears had deceived him.

But then a flicker of movement caught his eye—it came from the shadowy corner just beyond a precariously perched pile of hay. A trill of feminine laughter drifted high and bright into the gloom of the murky interior.

He knew that laugh.

The lad blew out a weary sigh. Why wasn't the girl on her knees at the kirk? Her father Duncan would be furious if he knew of her absence—not that he was surprised, the lad decided dryly. "Always into trouble," the lass's father would shout at her.

Aye, and that she was, the lad reflected. For at that very moment he spied her, on her knees in the dirt, along with half a dozen lads from the village.

All eyes were fixed intently upon the pair of dice that bounced to a stop on the ground.

The lass squealed and clapped her hands in delight. "I won again!" She laughed, displaying white, even teeth. In but an instant she was on her feet, bare and small beneath her, her arms flung wide, her skirts worn and whirling as she spun around and around in circles. If she were aware of the avid attention the lads lavished upon her sun-browned ankles and lithe, supple calves, she gave no sign of it.

No beauty was she—nay, not like her sister Margaret. Her hair was the color of flame shot through with glimmers of amber and gold, wavy and thick and untamed. But her eyes were glorious, as clear and bright as verdant fields of green, fringed by lustrous black lashes; within those depths sparkled the essence of spirit and life. As always, in some distant corner of his being he was struck anew by such purity and color . . .

The lad smiled. "But the game is not yet won," he said from his place in the shadows. "I've yet to roll."

The lass whirled. The sudden darkening of those remarkable eyes betrayed her ire at his discovery. She beheld him warily, her regard baleful and silent as he stepped out and approached the group.

The village lads hailed him heartily.

"Ian!"

"Come sit with us!"

"Aye, 'fore this wee lass steals the very clothes from our backs!"

The lad called Ian eyed the small pile of trinkets where the lass had been sitting. A slow smile crept across his lips.

"Cheating again, is she, laddies?"

Her jaw clamped shut. "I do not cheat!" she flared. "And you cannot roll, for you are not part of this game!"

Good-natured grumbling arose.

"Och, come now, Sabrina. Let him roll!" This came from Jeremy, a fair-haired, freckled lad of four and ten.

"Aye!" chimed in another. "What harm is one more roll?"

One boy nudged another. "Perhaps she doesn't wish him to roll because she *is* cheating."

"I am not!" she shouted.

"Then prove it," said another with a sly smile. "Let Ian roll."

Her lips compressed. Her eyes narrowed. "So be it then."

"And what are the stakes?"

"There are none." Her tone was short.

"Ah, but surely there must be something—" He stopped, for a decided gleam had begun to glow in her eyes.

Her chin came up. The makings of a smile tugged at her lips. "Aye. There is," she murmured. "If I win, you must spend the next fortnight with Douglas in the high pasture."

Douglas was her father's chief sheep-tender. He spent most of his days—and aye, his nights as well!— away from the keep and in the company of those woolly four-legged creatures. Och, but it seemed she truly wished to be rid of him!

His own reply was just as prompt—and every bit as firm, though he could barely keep the twitch from his lips. "And if I win, you must kiss Robert." He nodded toward the lad who sat at the very end, a boy of nearly his own age who gazed at her with calf's eyes whenever he thought she was not looking.

He'd startled her. He could hear it in the shrillness of her cry. "Kiss Robert! Whatever for?"

"Because that is the wager. But only if you lose, of course."

Already the shock had faded from her eyes. The lad gazed at her with one dark brow arched high. "Well, Sabrina? Do you accept this promise?"

Her head had lowered. The bright curtain of her hair shielded her expression from him, yet the lad could almost see the turning of her mind—oh, a dangerous thing, that! Then all at once she tossed her head. "That I do, Ian. That I do." She flashed a sunny smile, then bent to retrieve the dice from the ground.

"Nay." The lad stopped her with a word. "We will use Jeremy's."

Jeremy obligingly dug in his pocket for a pair of rough-carved dice, then dropped them into Ian's hands. In turn, Ian passed them to the lass with a flourish. "You may roll first," he said with a faint smile.

She snatched them from his hand. Her eyes lifted briefly toward heaven, then with a deep breath she rubbed them within her palms and threw them across the dirt.

She rolled an eight. Hiding a smile, she gathered them and returned them to Ian. "Your turn," she murmured. She was smiling, clearly pleased with the outcome of her roll.

Without a word Ian squeezed the dice tight in his palm, then released them.

Shouts punctuated the air.

"Look at that! He won!"

"Aye, he won! Ian beat her!"

"Robert, you sow! You get to kiss her!"

All eyes turned to the flame-haired lass. She had risen to her bare feet and stood stiffly erect. Only now the thunder of a hundred storms darkened her eyes to a turbulent blue.

"You are low," Ian pointed out. "You must kiss Robert."

For the first time she looked ready to bolt. The other lads all held their breath. 'Twas Ian who broke the silence. "A promise given is a promise kept," he said very quietly.

By now Robert was on his feet as well, a silly grin on his face. Casting one last arch glance at Ian, the lass marched forward. Her eyes wide open, she leaned forward and pressed her lips to his.

Shouts arose. Emboldened by the other lads' cheers, Robert's hands shot out. He grabbed her waist and snatched her against his chest. He mashed his mouth against hers. His tongue shot out and darted against the closed seam of her lips. Sabrina wrenched herself back as if she'd been burned. "That is disgusting!" she cried.

There were hoots of laughter as she scrubbed the back of her hand across her mouth. The lad who stood watch near the door could not help it; his own laughter joined the others'. She whirled around, her glare encompassing the lot of them. "Begone," she shouted.

The group of boys dispersed from the stable with good-natured grumbling.

But it was on him—the lad who had yet to move from his berth near the doorway—that the fire of her gaze burned hottest.

"You enjoyed that," she accused.

He made no secret of it. "Aye," he agreed.

"Why? You like seeing me humbled? Is that it?"

"Humbled? You?" The very thought made him chuckle anew. "Sabrina, were you ever humbled—by anyone—I do believe God would strike lightning down from the heavens."

She made no reply, but raised her chin so high that he thought with amusement her spine would surely crack. "What are you doing here?" she asked. "Ah, but 'tis to be expected I suppose. You Highlanders are a lazy lot." She stuck out her tongue. "And ye're the worse of all, my fine Highland prince."

The lad was undaunted. "And I might ask the same of you. I'm well aware your father went out hunting at dawn, Sabrina. But were you not to spend the morning on your knees in the kirk, preserving your silence and praying that your tongue be more honeyed in future, in the hope that you would grow to be more like our Blessed Virgin?"

The lass muttered something under her breath. Ian withheld a smile. She had a rash and reckless tongue, of that there was no doubt—'twas the very same that incurred her father's wrath, and subsequent punishment. Also of a certainty, the lass did not flatter him. But this he ignored, and went on lightly, "The dew has not yet left the fields, yet here you were, on your knees throwing dice!" He shook his head, unable to resist teasing her. "A most unholy endeavor, at that."

The set of her chin was mutinous. "What!" she cried. "Think you that you are my keeper?"

"Nay, never that—though mayhap you need one."

His ready reply did little to soothe her.

"I thank the Lord above I was not born the eldest. I feel sorry for Margaret—to think she must someday marry you—a Highlander, yet!"

Ian directed a thankful prayer heavenward that she'd been born the younger, not the elder, for there was a pact between their fathers that he should wed the eldest daughter—Margaret was nothing like Sabrina. Young as she was, Sabrina could be as biting as a bitter east wind. Ah, but she was a bratling. A bonny one, but a bratling nonetheless.

"I bear you no ill will, lass. And indeed, I pray you take comfort in this, for it seems you have won this wager after all. There is no need to wish me well away from here, for I've been summoned home."

She blinked. "Home . . . to the Highlands?"

"My father has determined there is no longer any need for me to foster here at Dunlevy. I will see your father when he is home from the hunt, and then I am off."

He'd startled her. She stared at him, her small mouth parted in shock.

"What! Will you not wish me godspeed?"

At last she blinked. "Aye," she said faintly, and then again: "Oh, aye! May your journey be a swift one."

He noted with wry amusement she did not bid him a *safe* journey. Well, little wonder, for they were ever at odds, it seemed.

He swept her a low, gallant bow. "I pray you remember me long and well, Sabrina, for I remain ever your true and loyal servant."

Small fists knotted at her sides. She stomped her foot. "True? Nay, not to me! Loyal? To thine own end, I daresay."

One shoulder lifted in a shrug. "And what is wrong with that, I ask?"

She stomped her foot.

Ian threw back his head and laughed. He was not surprised, for such was the young lady's temperament. His smile still wide upon his lips, he turned to leave. But before he could take a single step, the sound of her voice stopped him.

"Ian!"

He glanced back at her. "Aye?"

"You won't tell Papa you found me here?"

There was something in her tone, something almost akin to fear. . . .

The lad frowned, faintly puzzled. Sabrina was a wild one. This he knew well and true. And Donald Kincaid was often harsh with the lass, but not cruel. For all that he himself was occasionally irked by her antics, he was not wont to see her punished.

He shook his head. "I won't tell him."

"Do you promise?"

"Aye. I promise."

Her gaze flitted away. When her eyes swung back to him, they seemed to blaze. "Remember," she said almost fiercely, "a promise given is a promise kept."

"I do not forget, lass," he said gently.

A slight incline of her head was her only response. With that she darted past him and flung the door wide. Ian watched as she fled into the misty wood.

What mischief was she off to now?

He smiled, his good humor restored. In the years to come, he had no doubt she would lead some man a merry chase, hither and yon, this bonny wee lass, until the poor man was dizzy and would no doubt not know what whirlwind possessed him.

Oh, but he did not envy that man!

He walked from the barn, whistling a quaint old tune. Praise God he was to wed the elder—Margaret— and not her. Yet he could not help but ponder mildly what would come of Sabrina Kincaid. 'Twas inevitable that their paths would cross again, for he would someday wed her sister. Yet their destiny would never be entwined as one . . .

Or so he thought.

One

The Year of our Lord 1306

It was the last day of summer, and the billowing breeze carried with it the sweet scent of fresh plump roses still abloom.

The courtyard at Dunlevy Keep bustled with activity like a brew bubbling in a pot. Men and horses and animals milled about; chickens zig-zagged across the yard. From around the corner came the clang of battle lances. But inside the great hall an angry shout bounced from the timbered rafters.

"Sabrina! Where is that blasted girl? God's teeth, she is never around when I need her!"

Two of the maids exchanged glances. The younger of the two sprinted toward the flat-topped building that housed the kitchens. Speeding toward the vegetable gardens, she rounded the corner, bracing herself as she came to a halt. An instant later, she lowered her eyes at the sight of her mistress, held fast in the arms of a fair-haired giant.

"Psst," came her whisper of warning, "your father is calling for you, m'lady."

Immediately the young woman sought to wiggle

from his embrace. But the fair-haired giant would have none of it, and merely clasped her tighter.

Even while the lady gloried in his possessiveness, caution reigned supreme. "Jamie," came her urgent whisper, "I must go. 'Tis not wise to keep Papa waiting."

His embrace loosened, though he did not release her. With a ferocious scowl, the blond giant raised his head. "Curse the man," he stated bluntly. "Why does he never call upon Margaret?"

Sabrina Kincaid wrinkled her nose at him. "Margaret has responsibilities as well. No doubt she is already busy with other duties."

Jamie MacDougall's lips thinned. "Och!" He made no secret of his disdain. "The man allows you no peace. He treats you more like a servant than a daughter."

Sabrina's smile wavered. The denial which sprang to the fore would not emerge, though she knew not why. In his own way, she knew her father loved her. And yet . . . she knew also that he blamed her for her mother's death, for it was just after giving birth to her that her poor mother had died.

As if he sensed her distress, Jamie's arms tightened anew. "Faith, but I wish I could wed you now," he said, his voice low and fervent. "By the saints, this very day."

Sabrina tipped her head back so she could see him. A hint of sadness tinged her smile. "As do I. But we both know Papa would never allow it. I am the younger, so Margaret must wed Ian first."

Jamie's arms fell to his sides. "'Tis because I am a MacDougall."

"Nay," she said quickly, though in truth she was

not certain. Her father harbored no fondness for the MacDougall clan. She knew he disapproved of her seeing Jamie; to date, she had discouraged Jamie from asking for her hand, for she already knew her father would refuse. Mayhap when Margaret was wed, he would be more accepting.

"Ian." Jamie practically spat the word. "What keeps him in the Highlands—and away from his bride-to-be?"

Sabrina smoothed the lines from between heavy blond brows. "I do not know," she said with a sigh. "But his father died nearly a year ago. And I heard Papa say there was talk of trouble in his clan."

Jamie scoffed. "Mayhap he does not wish to wed Margaret."

Nay. It could not be so. Oh, at times Margaret's tongue cut deep as any blade; but Margaret was fair as an English rose—as fair as their poor dead mother had been. Sabrina could not conceive of any man who would not wish to claim such beauty for his own.

"Sabrina!"

She started at the nearness of her father's roar. "Go," she pleaded quickly. "Jamie, you must go now!"

A brief hard kiss upon the lips . . . and then he was gone, vaulting nimbly across a low, ivy clad stone fence and into the forest beyond. Sabrina whirled, gathered her skirts in hand, and darted back toward the keep.

Papa's stout form lumbered into view. "Sabrina!" he bellowed, then stopped short as he spied her. He scowled at her. "There you are, girl! Where the devil have you been?"

Sabrina's voice was a trifle breathless. "Checking the vegetable gardens. I daresay we shall have a fine crop of cabbages and leeks to store for winter." Deftly she guided the subject away from her whereabouts. "Did you wish to see me, Papa?"

"Aye!" Duncan Kincaid straightened to his full height. "The MacGregor comes, Sabrina! He comes to Dunlevy this very day!"

"The MacGregor," she echoed blankly, then all at once her heart seemed to stop. Did he mean . . .

"Ian?" she whispered. "Ian is coming?"

"Aye, the very same."

Sabrina swallowed. She was unused to thinking of Ian as the MacGregor. Indeed, she would prefer not to think of that Highland rogue at all!

But she was no longer a child. Though discretion was not in her nature, over the years, she had worked hard to curb her tongue and hold her opinions to herself.

She glanced at Papa. "Does Margaret know?"

"Aye. He has sent word that he wishes to prepare for the marriage. She is in the kirk praying for his safe arrival." He cast her a glance from the corner of his eye. Sabrina didn't miss the full import of that glance; she knew full well he thought she spent too little time in the pursuit of heavenly guidance.

But for once he did not chastise her. "There's much to be done," he said shortly. "There is food to be prepared and rooms to be readied for the MacGregor and his clansmen. See to it, lassie."

Sabrina hurried to obey. Very soon the keep was a buzz of frenzied activity. Within the hour freshly laundered sheets clapped in the breeze, like sails beneath an azure sky. Sabrina sent three maids abovestairs to clean several vacant chambers, then went in search of Margaret.

She found her sister in her chamber, sitting in a straight-backed chair near the window, as if the day had wrought no news whatever of the imminent arrival of her husband-to-be—'twas as if this day were no different than any other.

Sabrina paused from her place near the doorway; Margaret was not yet aware of her presence, nor was the maid Edna. In truth, the two sisters were nothing alike—nay, not in looks or demeanor. Margaret was tall and slender, her face pale and heart-shaped; her eyes shone like vivid blue sapphires. Her blond hair shimmered down her back like glimmering moonlight.

Unbidden, Sabrina's dirt-smudged fingers tugged at the end of the thick red-gold braid that dangled over her shoulder. As a child, Sabrina had longingly wished that she could have been blessed with sleek, lustrous hair like Margaret's instead of her own unruly curls. Indeed, she'd gone through several years where she'd wavered between hurt and resentment that God had seen fit to fashion Margaret in their mother's image—that He had favored her so and thus Margaret had attained their father's unquestionable devotion and love, while she was considered naught but a nuisance—aye, and one who resembled neither father nor mother. But she was not given long to envy, for such was not her way.

Sabrina lingered a moment longer. Her brilliant green gaze drifted over the perfection of her sister's ivory profile. As always, Margaret's façade was one of tranquil serenity. Many a time Margaret had played hostess to her father's guests; all were enraptured by her charm and beauty. Her laughter floated in the air like the lilting notes of a songbird. . . .

Indeed, it was hard to believe that Margaret could

dare speak a harsh word to anyone. Yet Sabrina was well acquainted with the sting of her sister's tongue—and aye, her temper.

Once, some years earlier, she had trod upon the hem of Margaret's new gown, accidentally soiling it with her muddy slippers. Margaret had been furious. With a cry of rage, Margaret had whirled and slapped her face.

Odd, that she should suddenly remember that now, after all this time. . . . She knew Margaret better than anyone. Yet there were also times when Sabrina felt she knew her sister not at all. . . . Still, she was certain her sister would never deliberately hurt a soul on this earth.

Closing the heavy wooden portal, she stepped within. "Well, well," she said cheerily, "'twould seem that you alone have your wits about you this day." She smiled across at her sister, the elder by a year. "'Twould seem a miracle if everyone in Scotland did not hear Papa's bellow that the MacGregor comes, clear to the Highlands and beyond."

Margaret laid her sewing in her lap. "And why should I be all in a dither? 'Tis only Ian."

"Oh, but the MacGregors are fearsome giants," chimed the wide-eyed maid. She paused from her task of stripping the bed of its linens to hastily cross herself. "'Tis said if provoked, they eat their young alive!"

Sabrina bit her lip to keep from laughing aloud. Edna was a shy, superstitious young girl, afraid of her own shadow, but Sabrina loved her dearly.

A mischievous twinkle glinted in her eyes. She pursed her lips, striving for a properly worried expression. "Well, he is, after all, a Highlander. And we all know what barbarians they are. But mayhap that is why Ian was sent as a child to foster here at Dunlevy—to save his clan from extinction."

Edna's eyes nearly popped from her head. She pressed a hand to her rounded bosom. "He has no brothers? No sisters?" she whispered.

Sabrina shook her head. "Nay, not a one. None that survived childhood, at least." It was true. There had been two younger brothers, but they had both died in infancy.

Edna was properly horrified. "Savages! Savages, all of them!" With a great cry she snatched up the dirty linens and fled.

Margaret sighed. "You know," she said dryly, "she will carry that tale to Papa, and it will no doubt have been embellished a good deal by the time he hears it."

The corners of Sabrina's lips crinkled in merriment. "Well, I should hope so. I did try to give a bit of fodder to the imagination."

"But she is right," Margaret mused. "Ian is a giant."

"A giant!" Sabrina's snort was distinctly unladylike. "I think not, Margaret. He was always as skinny as a sapling in winter!"

"Ah, but I'd forgotten. You did not see him when Papa and I journeyed to Edinburgh, did you, Sabrina? His cousin Alasdair was with him, and he, too, has the look of a MacGregor about him. But you had taken ill to your bed, as I recall, and could not travel with us."

Indeed, Sabrina *had* forgotten. Ian's last visit had come several years earlier, but she had missed him. According to Cecilia, the village healer, Sabrina had eaten something rancid—she'd been so sick she could barely raise her head off the pillow for days.

Throughout the afternoon, she'd held thoughts of Ian at bay. But now, now she allowed the memories to fill her mind. The last time she had seen him was years earlier, that day in the stable. A shadow seemed to slip over her, enfolding her in darkness. She could not help the trace of bitterness that seeped through her. He had made a promise . . . a *promise* . . . only to reveal his true nature in the bargain.

Margaret had fixed keen eyes upon her. "I've come to note that you do not care much for Ian, do you? But 'twas not always so, was it?"

Nay, Sabrina nearly cried, for it was true. Though they had played together as brother and sister—and verbally sparred like the very same—deep inside there had been a time when she'd thought of Ian in a way that was anything but sisterly. . . .

Odd, that she should remember it . . . and remember it now. . . .

But all that had changed. And Margaret was looking at her in a way that made her wish she was more adept at hiding her true feelings. Lightly she said, "You need not worry, Margaret. Of course I shall welcome him into the family."

One elegantly shaped golden brow climbed high. "Ah," Margaret said smoothly. "But would you wish another husband for me?"

"Indeed, I've never even thought of such a thing," Sabrina admitted. "This marriage has been arranged for nearly as long as I can remember."

"Yes," Margaret murmured. "Yes, I do suppose there is little point in speculating. The men I'm acquainted with are either clansmen, married, already betrothed, or a trifle too young."

Sabrina's mind had already sped straight to Jamie.

A pang of guilt nipped at her, for she regretted that
Margaret's choice of husband had never been her own
to make. Mayhap it was selfish of her, but she was
eternally grateful that Papa had not made similar efforts to see his youngest daughter betrothed. Yet for
the first time she was given to wonder if Margaret
loved Ian. . . .

It was much later when she was at last able to slip
away. Her steps carried her down a little-used dirt
pathway that wound away from the keep, to a glade
hidden deep in the forest, a place she had always
treasured as her own. There was never anyone about
to disturb her musings, and it was here that she had
come when she tired of Papa's roars of disapproval.

The day's last spears of sunlight burst rich and
golden through the boughs of fir trees which arched
overhead. At the center of her haven was an oval-
shaped pool of clear, glistening water. Feathery-
rimmed ferns grew thick and abundant near the
pool's edge.

The keep seemed a world away. Sabrina sat in the
sweetly scented grass and hugged herself in mounting
excitement. Margaret would soon be married; the
prospect of telling Jamie they might wed sooner than
even *she* had hoped filled her with happiness. She had
tamed the wicked ways of her youth and there was
no reason for Papa to refuse. No doubt he would
count himself well rid of her.

A smile curved the softness of her lips as one small
slipper slid off her foot, followed by its mate. Sabrina
wiggled her toes delightedly, loving the coolness of
the grass against the soles of her feet; she'd always
hated the constraint of footwear. Suddenly feeling
free and carefree as she never could in the company

of others, she loosened her plait and ran small, slender fingers through thick, wavy skeins of amber-gold.

A butterfly skipped across the width of the pond. The surface of the pool was smooth as a bed of freshly fallen snow; the waters glistened invitingly, and she was all at once conscious of the grime of the day's efforts heavy upon her body.

Her fingers crept to the laces of her bodice. Dainty white teeth caught at the flesh of her lower lip. High above, birds perched in the branches chattered to each other. A rabbit scurried through the grass alongside her.

There was no one to see. No one to care. Besides, it wasn't as if she'd never done so before. . . .

Bowing to the lure of temptation, she tugged the hem of her gown high and over her head. A moment later she dove naked into the pool from a narrow, rocky ledge. She gasped at the coolness of the water against her flesh, but she welcomed it wholeheartedly, for the day had been unseasonably warm for spring.

She broke the surface of the water with a breathless little laugh. God, but she loved this place! Here, there was no one to chide her, no one to watch with disapproving eyes, no one to tell her what she should or should not do. Here she was free as never before.

She dove in yet again. Three strokes took her toward the shore. Finding her footing on the sandy bottom, she stood, squeezing the water from her hair. Twisting it into a long rope, she flung it over one bare shoulder, her gaze idly skimming the glade.

Then all at once a strangled cry wedged in her throat. Sheer panic clutched her heart. Alas, she had made a terrible, terrible mistake . . . !

For she was not alone at all.

Two

The chieftain of the clan MacGregor was in the prime of manhood, with muscles hewn like a massive oak tree. Like his father, he stood tall as the mountains, towering over his clansmen. Like his mother, he was sharp of wit and word, the proud set of his shoulders disclosing the glory of his race.

He sat upon his steed, keen gray eyes surveying the valley before him. It was, all in all, a most glorious day. Neither wind nor rain nor fog swept across the rolling hills that surrounded Dunlevy Keep. Ripe fields of gold stretched off to the south and west. Just ahead, the forest was a wild tangle of dark green.

It was almost as if he'd never left . . . as if nothing had changed. . . .

Worn leather creaked as he shifted in his saddle. His cousin Alasdair had ridden on ahead; no doubt he was already at the keep. Ian was anxious for the journey to be at an end. A warm meal, a horn of ale, and a soft bed would do much to ease the ache in his joints.

In all truth, Ian could not say he was fond of Duncan Kincaid, for 'twas his belief that Duncan was a man whose nature was not particularly warm nor wise nor patient. Nor was he always fair or generous. But though the Kincaid was a man ruled by his emotions, he was also a man with strongly held beliefs.

His father David had known the Kincaid in his youth, for his father's mother had kinsmen in the Lowlands—the acquaintance had been carried into adulthood. Ian's father David held that it was important to have allies beyond one's own clan; that was why he'd been sent to foster at Dunlevy as a youth.

And why he and the Kincaid's daughter Margaret had been betrothed as children.

His own father—David—had been a man to command honor and respect. Though he was fierce when challenged, he was neither brutal nor ruthless. Oh, he could thunder and roar and fight like so many of his fellow Scots. Blame and envy were not his way; nor would such be Ian's way. From him, Ian had learned to value honor and pride and strength.

Only once had his father bowed to weakness, to his own needs. Yet in the end, it had cost him his happiness . . .

And aye, his very life.

God's bones, but it seemed a lifetime ago that he'd left this place! A weary bleakness settled into his bones. Much had transpired since he'd left, much that he'd never expected.

He remembered that day well. He'd been anxious to return to the Highlands, to boast and strut his newly acquired knightly skills as all young boys did upon passing one of life's most memorable seasons—from boyhood to manhood.

Instead he'd returned home to find his father remarried. Not that he'd minded, for his mother was long since dead. He had adored his new stepmother, for Fionna was young and gay and the loveliest woman he'd ever laid eyes upon.

Fionna. A faint bitterness crept through him. But now she was dead . . .

And his father as well.

Ian had loved his father dearly. And so it was that he would honor his father's wishes, which was why he returned to Dunlevy. To marry Duncan's eldest daughter Margaret.

Odd, that he felt no kindling of excitement at the prospect of seeing his bride-to-be again, beauteous though she was. In all honesty, he'd never harbored any great affection for Margaret. Indeed, he was surprised that Duncan had not demanded he and Margaret marry long ago. Nay, there had been no haste in marrying, especially since Duncan had not pressed the issue. And so Ian had curbed the restlessness in his soul—and aye, his manly appetite—but he knew that the time had come to honor the agreement.

The hardness of his mouth softened ever so slightly. In all the time he'd been gone, he could not think of Dunlevy without remembering eyes as green as the misty hills that surrounded this place.

A faint smile etched one corner of his mouth. Lord, he almost hated to admit it, but . . . he'd missed the bratling. He'd missed her. . . .

Sabrina.

All at once he found himself beset with memories. He suspected Margaret had altered very little, for he'd seen her but two summers past; no doubt she was as comely as ever. But Sabrina . . .

He'd often marveled that the two were sisters. There was scant resemblance between them; Margaret was blond, as cool and serene as her perfectly formed features and hair, while Sabrina was flame-haired with a mouth that knew not when to close. He nearly laughed aloud as he recalled the time she'd stolen his sword and hacked off her skirts to resemble his kilt. She had then marched full tilt into the hall for the evening meal like the veriest soldier swaggering into battle.

He hadn't been quite so amused then.

Nor had her father been pleased.

A smile of remembrance on his face, Ian nudged his horse forward through the forest. The rich, pungent scent of trees and damp earth filled his senses, yet his mind remained otherwise engaged. What mischief was the imp into these days? Faith, but she had plagued him endlessly with her pranks and her prattle! She'd incited his ire, and on occasion, his sympathy, though he'd never let the little minx know it. Never had he understood why Duncan had let his youngest daughter run wild as she did, dirty and with no regard for authority, save a switch on her behind from her father's hand. He chuckled anew, just thinking about the little witch.

The sound of a sudden splash snared his attention. Curious, he followed the sound toward its source—a small, sparkling pond hidden beneath a leafy green bower.

The splash came again. What he saw brought him up short, for here was a sight that wrenched all thought of the bratling from his mind in aught but the blink of an eye.

Now here was a woman . . . aye, and one who could turn many a man's head—and no doubt had! She walked to a rocky ledge, her body naked in all its splendor, angled slightly away from him. Her hair was a dark, wet rope twined over one shoulder; it hung well past her buttocks.

Ian's mouth grew dry. Why, she might have been a wood nymph sprung from some secret glade solely to pleasure his eyes—and his other senses. Indeed, he'd much rather gaze on this sweetly formed lass than dwell on the troublesome little sprite who had so tormented his youth.

He dismounted, his gaze never leaving her. She was small in stature, yet unusually beguiling. Her skin gleamed with the luster of a pearl. Her breasts were surprisingly full, tipped by rose-hued nipples that peaked hard and tight from the coolness of the water. Below the narrow indentation of her waist, her hips flared in sweet enticement. She raised one hand to her hair, sweeping back an errant lock and displaying the generous curve of one full breast before diving cleanly into the water. She broke the surface with a tiny splash, then swam toward the shore. Rivers of water sluiced from her body as her feet found purchase. She moved forward, coming closer to where he now crouched at the base of a stout oak . . . ever closer.

All that was male within him surged to the fore. Desire unchecked simmered in his veins. Bold gray eyes roamed avid and hot, for she had yet to glean his presence. His mind consumed by blatantly erotic fancies, he longed to attach a face, for the profile she presented foretold a beauty exquisite, a sweetness and youth he could only imagine. All he sought was but a glimpse. Ah, if she would only turn her head. . . .

She did, shaking the water from her hair, her eyes squeezed shut.

Her face was small and oval. Her mouth was damp and dewy, the exact shade of pink as her nipples. The arch of slanted brows lent her a look that was almost elfish. An odd feeling knotted his belly, for she seemed faintly familiar.

Her lashes lifted. Suddenly he felt he'd been struck in the chest with the butt of a lance. He stared into eyes as misty green as ...

As the hills of Dunlevy.

Yet his mind balked. Nay, he thought numbly. It could not be ...

Their eyes locked endlessly. For one horrified moment, neither could move, nor speak.

It was she who broke the spell, and it appeared she had no such lapse where his identity was concerned. She scrambled backward, dropping to her bottom as soon as the water reached her thighs. Swiftly she dragged her knees to her chest and scowled at him.

Little did she realize she still afforded him a most tantalizing view.

"You—you rogue!" she sputtered. "What the devil do you think you're doing?"

He spread his hands wide, feigning affront. "What! I but enjoy the beauty of the day. And indeed"—he gave an exaggerated leer—"there's much to be seen."

He'd shocked her. He could tell by the way her eyes flew wide.

He sighed. "I know you, lass," he remarked mildly. "You're angry."

Her shock had begun to wane. If her glare could have blistered, he would be naught but a pile of ash.

"Of course I'm angry! You were spying on me!"

He gave a slight inclination of his head. "Why, thank you, madam. I'm pleased to note I did not frighten you."

She let loose with a scathing denunciation that left

no doubt as to her opinion of him. Ian paid no heed. Boldly he strode forward. Bending low, he scooped her clothes from the bank and flung them over his shoulder.

Her tirade ceased midstream. "Ian! Wh-what are you doing?" She lurched forward, only to remember her state of undress. She plopped back down in the water.

His gaze lingered on the bareness of her shoulders. Remembering himself, he gave a low, gallant bow. "I but return the favor from so many years ago."

Her face turned the color of the dawn.

He continued. "Surely you've not forgotten the time you watched *me* running naked from the stream, searching all about for my clothes."

Her voice was but a whisper. "You—you knew?"

Ian gave a robust laugh. "I knew, lass, though I was far less amused then than I am now. But I've often wondered . . . did you like what you saw?"

Her eyes flashed. "As I recall, there was little to see," she retorted sweetly.

Ian laughed even more gustily. "No doubt you're right," he agreed good-naturedly. "I was but a lad—a bony one, at that. And coming from a cold stream as it were, no doubt that which you sought to see was but a shriveled little carrot."

His regard dropped to her breasts, hidden behind the shield of her arms. "But you, Sabrina," he said softly, "ah, lass, you've grown a bounty I'd not expected."

"And you are still as insolent as ever!"

"And you, I see, are still the bonny bratling."

He crossed his arms over his chest. "You'd best

come out. Your lips are turning blue. I will act as your maid."

Her mouth opened, then closed. "You will not!" she managed at last.

He braced his legs wide apart and raised a brow.

Thus began a contest of wills. He meant it to be a joke, to tease her, but her regard flamed hotter than a blazing sun in the desert.

"You are a jackass!"

He inclined his head. "Indeed."

"A wretched beast. The most loathsome creature ever to walk this land—"

"I've no objection to waiting all night, if need be." His tone was as smooth as oil.

She fell silent. The minutes dragged, one into another. Her teeth began to chatter. Ian was faintly irritated at her stubbornness when at last she spoke.

"Turn your back."

It spun through his mind to refuse, for her tone was no less than a demand. One dark brow came up. But she must have gleaned his intent, for she made a faint choked sound.

"P-please." She blinked, those brilliant green eyes suspiciously bright.

Ian stared. Tears? From the bonny bratling? He scoffed. Nay, not Sabrina.

He heard the long, ragged breath she drew in. "Ian—"

"Just a moment." His tone was gruff. Abruptly he turned his back. Yet some devil had seized hold of him, for he did not leave, nor did he remove her clothes from his shoulder. Instead he remained where he was.

Behind him, water splashed.

He could feel her directly behind him. Her linen chemise was snatched from his shoulder as if she feared he would turn at any instant. And indeed, he was tempted—mightily tempted. Deep within him, he was startled by that temptation. Yet another part of him was appalled. Oh, he could not deny he enjoyed a beauteous face and form as much as the next man. But this was Sabrina, his bonny bratling. . . .

"All right. I'm finished." Her voice was slightly breathless.

Ian turned, only to behold a stare as frigid as the lochs of the Highlands. *So this is how it would be, eh?* he thought. She was still as feisty as ever.

He whistled to his horse, who was lazily grazing on lush green grass. He gestured grandly as the animal trotted up. "Shall we be off?"

Her chin tipped high. "I cannot return with you."

The challenge in her eye grated. "And why not?"

"'Twould not be proper," she informed him loftily.

"Proper? And when were you ever proper, I ask?"

"'Tis obvious where I've been! What would everyone think? If they knew you'd come upon me n—" All at once she stopped.

His grin was utterly wicked. "Naked?" he supplied.

Her chin snapped shut. "You must go first," was all she would say.

Ian ran a callused fingertip down her nose. She looked as if she'd like to bite it off. "I suppose you're right, lass." But he would have the last word after all, by God. He allowed his gaze to wander, a blatantly thorough inspection of her form, lingering with flagrant interest on her breasts.

Ian couldn't help it. The merest hint of a smile tugged at his lips. He had but one thought. Foolishly, he'd somehow imagined Sabrina still a child. Oh, but he'd been wrong, for there was a difference—a vast difference. Aye, there was grace where before there had been only a gangly clumsiness. A supple ripeness where before had been breasts as flat as a washboard.

"I must say, lass," he drawled. "You've changed. And quite delightfully so."

Her eyes flamed. "Blast you . . . you . . . you vile Highland wretch!"

Ian chuckled as he swung up into the saddle.

She was still sputtering and cursing as he rode off into the forest.

He threw back his head and laughed again. Now this was the Sabrina he knew. He felt a lightness of spirit he'd not felt in ages. God, but it was good to be back.

Three

Sabrina did not share the sentiment.

Back at the keep, she fled to her chamber. There she sank down upon the bed and pressed cool hands to cheeks that were still flushed as if with fever. In all her days, she'd never been so embarrassed. Sweet Mother Mary, if she had to face him again, she would surely wither away in sheer mortification!

The memory rushed through her head again and again, like wind through the trees; it would not be banished. Ian had seen her naked . . . *naked!* 'Twas even more shocking that he had stared at her with wholly unguarded appreciation. Why? she wondered frantically. She was no beauty like Margaret. Or did he but seek to mock her?

Seeking to regain her wits, she pulled up a stool before the fire which burned in the hearth. There she pulled a comb through wavy tresses that were still damp.

She could not help but recall his reminder that she had once seen him naked. Aye, and it was true. While he swam in the stream one day, she had crept forward unnoticed, snatched his clothes, and hidden them in the bushes. While he had searched madly about for

31

his clothing, she had watched from a tree—though she'd never dreamed he'd been aware of her presence! In truth, it was mostly mischief that had spawned the prank. But she had also harbored a young girl's curiosity about what he wore beneath his kilt. And aye, about the nude male form. . . .

Her mind gave her no peace. Why couldn't he have left her alone, to dress in privacy? But alas, he had not, and so he'd left her with no choice. If only she could have waited until darkness fell . . . if only she were not such a coward. . . . But the very thought of making her way back to the keep in the dark made her stomach roil.

The soft line of her lips compressed. Oh, but he had always been a troublesome youth! And now he was a most odious man!

A knock on the door interrupted her reflections. It opened and Margaret stepped within. She frowned at Sabrina's damp, rumpled gown.

"Sabrina, you must dress! Papa expects us belowstairs soon for the evening meal."

"He is here?" Though she already knew the answer, Sabrina could not bring herself to say his name.

"Aye. And his cousin Alasdair arrived this afternoon as well."

"So you've seen him?"

"Aye," Margaret affirmed briskly. "Now come, Sabrina. Hurry and dress."

It was on the tip of her tongue to refuse—to retort that if she never saw Ian the MacGregor again in this lifetime, 'twould not be too soon. Yet Margaret had already opened the chest which held her gowns.

"I *am* dressed," she grumbled.

"You cannot wear that," Margaret tossed over her

shoulder. "It looks like you've been running through the forest."

Perhaps because I have. Sabrina had to stop herself from blurting it aloud.

Margaret turned, a gown in each hand. "Which will you wear, Sabrina? The blue wool?"

Sabrina pulled a face. "Nay, 'tis too hot."

"What, then? The crimson velvet?" Margaret raised the gown high, then made a disapproving sound as she spied a rip in one of the seams. "Sabrina! You've not yet mended this!"

Sabrina shrugged. Margaret was much more suited to such household tasks. She held out her hand. Margaret sighed.

"You will look little better than a beggar!"

Sabrina smiled at her sister. "It matters little what I wear," she teased. "All eyes will be upon you."

Margaret denied it, but Sabrina could see she was pleased. Acknowledging that she could not hide away forever, she dressed as quickly as she was able, then plaited her hair into a single fat braid and let it hang down her back. As the heavy door swung shut behind her, she fell into step behind Margaret. For the merest instant, she envied the smooth, sleek coils wound on each side of Margaret's head.

The sounds of male voices soon reached their ears. Boisterous laughter could be heard coming from the hall. As they drew ever nearer, Sabrina swallowed and sought to ignore the cold lump of dread that lay like a stone in the pit of her belly.

Servants milled about, carrying platters of food to the table in the center of the hall. Thick, fat candles set upon spikes in the walls cast flickering shadows all about. A fire crackled and burned brightly in the hearth. 'Twas there that her father stood between Ian and the man she surmised was his cousin Alasdair. Sabrina's eyes widened. Her father was not a small man, neither in girth nor height, yet he seemed nearly dwarfed by the two Highlanders; they towered over him, making him appear small, almost feeble.

Beside her, Margaret had glided to a halt. Lifting her pointed chin, she cleared her throat.

'Twas all that was needed to divert the attention of the three men.

Margaret smiled and inclined her head in silent greeting.

Sabrina yearned to sink through the floor to the earth below. Instead she took a deep, settling breath while the trio crossed to where they stood.

Ian murmured a greeting to Margaret—and then his gaze fastened on her. "Sabrina! How good to see you again after so many years. You were . . . what? . . . but a wee lass of twelve when last we saw each other, were you not?"

His warm, lilting burr did not fool her. She gritted her teeth, even as she forced her lips into a semblance of a smile.

"Well, if it isn't the MacGregor himself." The bite in her tone was thinly disguised. But by the saints above, she would not humble herself before him.

But when she would have turned away from him toward his cousin, she suddenly found her hand seized in a relentless grip. "Oh, come now," he proclaimed heartily. "Such formality between childhood friends. Will you not bestow on me some token of affection? After all, we've not seen each other these many years."

He mocked her—oh, but he mocked her most cruelly! His brashness sparked the embers of her temper. She opened her mouth, only to catch Papa's scowl of warning.

"Nay? Mayhap later, eh?" His gaze dipped to the rounded neckline of her gown. He smiled. Despite her fury, Sabrina felt her cheeks flame scarlet. "Though I must say, you've blossomed into quite a lovely young lady."

Oh, but she could cheerfully murder the rogue before the night was out! She tugged at her fingers; his grip tightened, as if he would refuse to release her . . . yet in the end he did. And, thank heaven, there was no need to reply, for Margaret laid her hand on his sleeve.

"Ian, you've neglected to introduce Alasdair. He and Sabrina have never met."

"Yes. Well, I'm from the Highlands, you know. We're not known for our manners." His gaze held Sabrina's an instant longer, then he glanced at his cousin. "Alasdair, as you've no doubt guessed, this is Sabrina, Margaret's younger sister. Sabrina, my cousin Alasdair, of the clan MacGregor."

Alasdair clasped her icy cold hands between his. Ian's hair was black as a raven's wing; his cousin's was shades lighter, a rich shade of russet brown. He was not quite as tall as Ian, yet he was nonetheless an imposing figure. Still, she liked the laughter lines that radiated outward from warm, brown eyes.

"Well, I begin to see the way of it"—Alasdair chuckled—"why you were betrothed to Margaret, and not Sabrina. Indeed, mayhap I should stand betwixt the two of you . . . or is it well away from the two of you?"

"There's no need for that, Alasdair." Ian's voice

was mild. "Sabrina and I are truly quite fond of each other. Aren't we, Sabrina?"

She couldn't back down from the challenge in his expression. "Quite," Sabrina managed to agree.

Her eyes said quite the opposite.

Stepping forward, Alasdair clasped her hand between both of his. "Well, I've heard much of you, Sabrina. And contrary to what you may believe, I've found myself quite intrigued by the prospect of meeting you. Aye, and now that I'm here, I'm certainly glad I came." He nodded toward the table. "I believe your father awaits us at table. Shall we?"

Sabrina blinked as he proceeded to lead her away. She had the feeling he'd just paid her a compliment, but flattery seldom came her way.

As usual, Papa took his place at the head of the table. He'd placed Ian to his right, with Margaret next to him. Sabrina sat to Papa's left, with Alasdair beside her. It was disconcerting to find herself directly across from Ian. Though the width of the table separated them, he was far too close. And when his gaze chanced to tangle with hers, she felt herself go hot all over.

Her hands clenched and unclenched in her lap. He'd said she had changed. But he had changed too. He was bigger; beneath the fabric of his tunic, his shoulders stretched wide as the horizon. His massive stature made her stomach quiver oddly. All traces of boyhood had vanished. Nay, no smooth-cheeked scrawny boy was he. Were she to think of a ferocious Highland warrior, her mind would surely have conjured up a man such as this!

She could not help but note the servants' response to the pair. Edna and another maid were helping in the kitchens this night. Both were visibly nervous. Indeed, Edna was trembling as she offered tidbits of venison to Ian from the huge wooden platter she carried. Ian took a steaming haunch, then murmured something to the maid. Sabrina could almost hear her *whoosh* of relief as Edna edged toward her father.

Gathering herself in hand, she turned her attention to his cousin. "Is this your first visit to the Lowlands, Alasdair?"

"Aye, though I vow it will not be the last." A faint mischief sparkled in his brown eyes—at last, a kindred spirit, Sabrina decided with delight.

"You are one of Ian's clansmen?"

"Aye. We're related by blood."

"Oh?" Sabrina eyed him curiously. To her knowledge, Ian had no siblings.

"Aye, my father was brother to Ian's father."

Were it not for Alasdair, the meal would have been endless. Surprisingly, she soon felt herself relaxing, for Alasdair was quite the charmer.

It was while her wine goblet was being refilled that she heard her father address Ian.

"We heard there was some strife in the clan upon the death of your father."

Sabrina's gaze slid to Ian. She was stunned when Ian's expression underwent a lightning transformation. All traces of pleasantness vanished as if it had never been. He was sober and stern and unyielding. She sensed a hardness in him she'd never have suspected . . . or perhaps she was not surprised at all. Indeed, after the mean-spirited trick he'd pulled on her as a child . . . It wasn't so much that he'd made her kiss Robert that long ago day in the stables. That she could have accepted. But he'd told Papa . . .

His voice was like ice, so cold it made her shiver. "Indeed. And precisely what did you hear?"

Duncan balked. Sabrina's chin nearly dropped. Not once in her life had she seen a man who could make her father ill-at-ease—yet she had the unfamiliar sensation Ian was doing exactly that!

"Only that . . . things were not as they were before." Duncan hesitated, spreading his hands. "'Tis only to be expected—the petty squabbles and such over who will succeed as chieftain. 'Tis the Scots way."

There was a slight edge to Ian's smile. "I hope you do not doubt my place as chieftain."

"Nay . . . nay, not a whit!" Duncan was quick to reassure him. "You're known across the land as the fiercest of Highland warriors. And by God, I'd not let my Margaret marry a weakling."

For the longest moment Ian said nothing. His expression was like the face of a stone: impassive, revealing nothing of his thoughts. His head bowed ever so slightly. He brought the tips of his fingers together on the table, tapping them lightly together. Yet when he raised his head, whatever troubled him seemed to have vanished.

He addressed her father. "I've heard rumors that there are supporters of the Red Comyn who live near Dunlevy."

Her father's mouth turned down. "No doubt you mean the MacDougalls. They're kin to the MacDougalls in the Hebrides. They live in the next valley. There's one in particular who forever stirs the pot to boiling . . ."

Sabrina held her breath. Sweet heaven, surely he did not *know* . . . ?

"Jamie . . . that's who 'e is . . . aye, his name is Jamie!"

She very nearly choked on her wine.

Praise the saints, she recovered quickly and no one seemed to notice. By now Papa had warmed to his subject. "For months now the young rascal seeks to rally others to his cause."

Ian tipped his head to the side. "And what is his cause?"

Papa snorted. "To restore the Baliol line to the throne!"

Sabrina's heart sank like a weighted stone.

Across from her, Margaret pursed her lips. "How so?" she murmured. "Baliol fled to Normandy when he surrendered the crown, did he not?"

"Aye," Papa agreed. "But John, lord of Badenoch, the Black Comyn, was once a contender for the throne. He married Baliol's sister and had a son— John, the Red Comyn. As Baliol's nephew, his son John had a double claim to the throne."

Sabrina listened intently to the discussion. Before her birth, Alexander, King of Scots, had died in a fall one stormy spring night. His successor was his three-year-old granddaughter Margaret, Maid of Norway. But when the Maid had died en route to Scotland, Scotland was left with no clear heir to the throne.

Shortly after Alexander's death, several guardians of Scotland were appointed to govern the realm until such time as Margaret ascended her rightful place as queen. But when the child died, various contenders soon appeared to lay claim to the throne. The strongest of these were Robert the Bruce and John de Baliol; both claimed by right of descent from David, Earl of Huntingdon, younger brother of Malcolm IV. King

Edward of England was called upon to settle the matter.

He decided in favor of Baliol, who promptly swore fealty to the English king. After a time, when Edward demanded Baliol—and Scotland—join his invasion of France, Baliol resisted. Instead he formed an alliance with France. King Edward was furious. He laid siege to Dunbar Castle and there defeated the Scots troops. Baliol was then stripped of his crown and exiled in France.

The Red Comyn was gone, too. He'd been killed by Robert the Bruce, grandson of the Bruce who lost the throne to Baliol—struck down by the Bruce in the kirk at Dumfries. From there he'd marched to Scone, where he'd been crowned king. But then the Bruce's army had been defeated by the Earl of Pembroke just months after his coronation. The Bruce had fled . . .

But no one knew where.

"We've lived far too long under the yoke of England," her father said with a scowl. "They are never content with their own. Always and ever they covet what belongs to others—to us! 'Tis time we had a Scots king."

"Ah, but we do," Alasdair chimed in. "When the time is right, the Bruce will come out of hiding and rout the English scourge from our lands."

Sabrina spoke unthinkingly. "But it seems only fair that the Red Comyn's son should assume the throne, for he is great-nephew to Baliol. And Baliol was king first, chosen over Robert Bruce."

"Chosen by an English hand, I would remind you!" her father snarled. "Baliol was naught but an empty cloak from the time he was crowned. He had no mind of his own."

"And what about the Bruce? He cares only that he will be king, and cares little about the good of Scotland."

Duncan glowered at her. "Och! And what would you know of it?"

Sabrina's eyes flickered but she held her ground. "I have ears and my head is not filled with straw, Papa. I am quite capable of making decisions for myself."

"'Tis not the place of a woman to offer an opinion, lassie. Will ye never learn to hold yer tongue?"

Sabrina gazed at him blithely. "It would seem not, Papa." She spoke with demure meekness—when she knew full well she was neither demure nor meek!

He rolled his eyes. "Ye're not so fair as your sister, lassie, but I do not yet despair—though God help the man who takes ye off my hands!"

Her chin came up a notch. "If you imply that no man will have me," she stated levelly, "you are wrong."

Papa's head whipped around. "And what do ye mean by that?" His eyes narrowed suspiciously. Only then did Sabrina realize she might well have gone too far. . . .

His fist crashed down on the table, sending dishes rattling and plates flying. "By God," he exploded, "you'd better not mean that . . . that MacDougall devil Jamie. I told you I'd not have you anywhere near him. He's the devil's own, and I'll not have my daughter seen with a man such as he, I tell ye! Ye can be certain he wants but one thing, daughter, but ye'd best not be givin' it, ye hear?"

Sabrina's lips quivered. His scathing denunciation was like a slap across the face. Always he looked upon her with disfavor . . . always! Caught midway between tears and defiance, she drew a deep, quavering breath. But before she could utter a word, he stopped her cold.

"Nay, say nothing!" he thundered. "You would do well to heed your sister's ways, lassie. She knows a woman's place. Now off and away with ye, girl!"

A scalding shame swept through her body—how like Papa to censure her before Ian and his cousin. But Sabrina was well aware that further argument would gain her nothing. Her father was set in his ways and would not listen, at least not to her, she decided bitterly. Summoning her dignity, she rose without a word and left the hall. Was it her imagination ... or did she feel Ian's gaze drilling into her back like the point of a knife? Oh, no doubt he quite enjoyed her humiliation!

She was pacing the length of her chamber when a knock sounded on the door. Before she could call out that she wished to be alone, the portal swung open and Margaret glided through.

"What?" she asked tiredly. "Have you come to chastise me as well? I pray you, do not."

Margaret paid no heed. "You provoke him."

'Twas plain she referred to Papa. Sabrina sighed and dropped onto the bed. "I say not a word and I provoke him." She could not hide her bitterness. "I am not like you, Margaret," she said with a shake of her head. "I cannot hold my heart within my breast and let none know how I feel—"

"Aye, and all know how you feel, Sabrina. Papa is right. When will you learn to hold your tongue? At times I wonder that you are my sister. Many a time I've thought that surely you must be a changeling— indeed, I often wished it were so!"

Stung by her sister's acid scorn, Sabrina could only stare at Margaret's perfect features, now twisted in a sneer. Her heart cried out. Why must Margaret always be so hurtful?

It was not in Sabrina's nature to be spiteful and mean, no matter the provocation. "I regret that you have felt this way," she said quietly, "for as surely as our mother is dead, we are sisters, sprung from the same womb, the same seed. Never have I regretted it." And it was true. They shared the same mother and father. But alas, they did not share the same heart.

Margaret shrugged but made no reply. After a moment she said, "I've come to tell you 'twas decided that the wedding will take place a sennight hence. You'll assist with the preparations?"

Margaret's tone told her that of course she assumed she would. Sabrina speculated wryly what her sister would have said had she refused. Ah, no doubt she'd have been sternly set on her ear and told to mind her tongue once again.

She inclined her head. "I shall be happy to assist in whatever way I can," she murmured.

Margaret smiled the tiny little smile that conveyed she was well pleased, then withdrew.

Sabrina soon climbed into bed, but sleep did not come easily. Her mind was filled with the news Margaret had just imparted.

A sennight hence, Margaret and Ian would be wed. Man and wife. Aye, she was glad, for it meant that soon she and Jamie could be wed as well. . . .

So what was the odd little pain that knotted her heart when she chanced to think of Margaret wed to Ian?

God above, she did not know.

Four

The wedding preparations began in earnest.

Many a horse and messenger was seen entering and leaving the keep, for Duncan sought to let all those nearby know of the impending marriage of his eldest daughter, that they might join in the celebration.

Ian spent that first night rather troubled, wondering what Duncan had heard about his father's death. That his father had taken his own life was no doubt common knowledge. Did Duncan believe it was because his father was heartbroken over the death of his beautiful young wife? 'Twas a story Ian himself had fostered. Nay. *Nay!* Duncan couldn't possibly know the truth—no one but he knew all that had happened. . . .

Ian was determined to keep it that way. He'd not allow his father's name to be blackened further.

But now that he was back at Dunlevy, he walked the same paths he had as a youth. He slept in the very same chamber. And there dwelled in his mind many a distant memory, some he'd forgotten until now.

He remembered the day a messenger had come to announce that William Wallace sought men to fight the English at Stirling Bridge. He had wanted to charge off to join Wallace's army. He'd been a hot-headed lad, eager to serve his compatriots, eager to practice what he'd spent these past years learning. But Duncan had stopped him. He'd said he would not allow it lest his father David approved.

The battle at Stirling Bridge was fought and won ... he'd been crushed that Wallace's army had triumphed without his able sword hand to lend assistance.

Ian smiled faintly. Faith, but that seemed such a long time ago! But now he had another cause. He'd offered his sword to Robert the Bruce, for 'twas his belief that all must come together under one man if Scotland were to fight off the English scourge once and for all.

As for his nuptials, Ian felt faintly detached from it all. A part of him chafed at the wait, for Ian was not a man to whom patience came easily. But Margaret had insisted she could not be ready in less than a sennight. As the prospective husband, there was little for him to do, and so he spent many an hour riding through the hills, or standing atop the parapet.

At times a sliver of guilt cut through him, for oddly enough, 'twas not his bride-to-be that oft consumed his thoughts ...

It was Sabrina.

He had no answer for this—indeed, more than once he questioned his rationality. His only explanation was that she'd grown into a comely wench. Why that truth would claim his attention, he knew not, for many would have deemed Margaret the fairer of the two. And indeed, he'd bedded women just as comely!

As for Sabrina, she was polite but distant when they chanced to meet. Ian was faintly puzzled. He could have sworn she was angry with him, yet he could think of no reason why it should be so.

Little had changed since they were children. Margaret, for the most part, kept to herself except at mealtimes. More than once, Ian found himself irritated with Duncan, for Duncan still took little notice of his youngest daughter—except when he called upon her to complete some such task, which was rather often. Always the lass was quick to oblige, with nary a complaint or a cross word, though her father kept her on her feet from morning till late eve. Never a word of praise nor approval came her way, either.

He was standing atop the tower wall early one evening when he saw a glint of copper-colored hair in the yard below, a small, slim figure. His eyes homed in like a falcon on its prey. She cast a glance all about her, as if she feared she might be seen. A half-smile curled his lips. So she was sneaking away, was she? Well, he could not blame her. He watched as she ducked into the narrow stair well that led to the tower and wall-walk.

Her footsteps announced her arrival even before he saw her. She hurried along the parapet, her head slightly lowered, her shoulders hunched against the bite of the wind. She stopped midway along the wall, then turned and gazed out toward the forest.

Her hair was long and loose and free. It whipped about her shoulders, a banner of purest flame. Ian caught his breath at the profile she presented. God's teeth, but she was lovelier than she looked from afar. His gaze trickled slowly over finely sculpted ivory features, down the slender grace of her throat. A gust of wind molded her thin gown to her body, outlining breasts that were high and full and ripe. Heat shot through him, like a streak of fire. He must have made some small sound, for she spun around to face him. He'd startled her, he realized.

And so he had.

"Fie!" she cried. "Are you spying on me again? Oh, but 'tis just like you, Ian!" Edna's words tolled anew through Sabrina's mind. "Do you know, 'twas said you were a fearsome giant! But you are as small a man as you were a lad!"

He laughed, damn him—he laughed! "Ah, lass, but you tempt me greatly to prove you wrong. I cannot help but wonder why you ever regard me as if I am the most dire of enemies. We were never enemies as children, were we?"

His tone had softened, turned cajoling. Despite all, she knew he was right. At times there had been an unspoken bond between them, for neither had known the gentle love or warm security of their mothers. Sabrina's had been ripped from her at birth—a fact her father never let her forget, while Ian had lost his mother to sickness at a very young age.

Aye, there had been many a time when he was kind to her. He'd helped her bury her beloved gray kitten that had sickened and died one winter. She'd been crushed . . . but while Margaret had merely shrugged and turned away, it was Ian who offered her comfort.

But all that had changed. Ian had made a promise. . . . *A promise given is a promise kept,* he had said that long ago day in the stable. But he had not honored his promise—he'd told her father she'd been casting dice in the stable when she should have been on her knees in the kirk. It was because of him—and her father's punishment—that she lived in terror of the darkness. Though she despised her weakness, 'twas a fear she had yet to conquer.

But she would not let him know it. Nay, her pride would not allow it. She made no answer. Instead she regarded him warily.

"I begin to see the way of it," he said in a soft lilting burr. "Well, then, it seems I shall have to change that." He paused, then went on lightly. "We've had little opportunity to talk, Sabrina. But you've grown into a lovely young woman. Tell me of your life in the years we've not seen each other."

He had caught her off guard. She knew not what to say. "There's little to tell," she said slowly. Of a certainty she'd never admit to him that despite her angry hurt at his betrayal, she remembered vividly that for a time she had missed him sorely. Many a night after he'd gone she'd cried herself to sleep.

"Well, then, I shall tell you of mine. When I went home to the Highlands, my father was well pleased with the knightly skills I learned under the tutelage of your father. But he insisted my instruction would not be complete—that I would not be a man—until I'd learned to understand the ways of other men as well. So he sent me to France . . ."

Sabrina listened intently as he recounted his travels. Not only had he lived in France, he'd visited Germany and Italy as well. A wistful longing tugged at her heart, for Sabrina had never traveled farther than the next valley. She'd often begged Papa to take her to Edinburgh, but he'd refused. The one time he had relented, she'd fallen ill and been unable to travel.

"How long were you in France?"

"Nearly a year."

She was intensely curious. "And what manly things did you do there?"

"What manly things do you think I did?" His slow-growing grin was utterly wicked, his eyes irreverent.

Comprehension dawned in a flash. Sabrina's cheeks went scarlet. "Bedding scores of women, no doubt." She meant to mock him as he mocked her. Instead her voice came out oddly shaky.

His chuckle was low and deep. "Ah, but I could hardly come to my marriage bed with no idea what to do there. But these are things you should not know about."

"I am not a child," she said stiffly.

An odd expression flitted across his face. "Nay," he agreed slowly. "You are not." He turned away then, gazing down at the yard below where a cart full of hay weaved toward the stable.

Sabrina pointed suddenly. "Look, there is Margaret. But who is with her . . . Alasdair?"

When he made no answer, she glanced at him. His attention was not on the yard below, but on her. Only this time he was not laughing. He looked almost stern.

"Your father was not pleased with you at supper that first eve," he said, "when you spoke out against the Bruce."

"There is nothing about me that pleases Papa." She strived for an airy tone but was not at all certain she succeeded.

He regarded her, his dark head tipped slightly to the side, as if in query. "Do you truly believe the Comyns belong on the throne? Or do you merely wish to disagree with your father for the sake of rebellion?"

Rebellion? Oh, but it was not true! All her life she

had sought to please Papa. A pang swept through her. But alas, she could not. . . .

So how was she to answer? In truth, what she knew of Robert the Bruce and the Comyns, she'd heard from Jamie. Unlike her father, he did not think her so feeble-minded that she could not understand the turmoil of the times.

She lifted her chin. "'Tis just as I told Papa—I have a mind of my own. As for the Bruce, he changes sides as oft as a gale blows from the east. One moment he is Longshanks' ally, the next his enemy."

"That has been true in the past," Ian admitted, "but 'tis my belief he now carries in his heart the good of all Scotland."

Sabrina stopped short of calling him a fool. "His family has had lands in England since the time of the Normans. And he was raised in Longshanks' court," she pointed out. "Methinks he is more English than Scot! And you forget—he murdered the Red Comyn before the high altar in the kirk!"

There! That should silence him. But alas, it did not.

"Comyn let Longshanks know of a plot the Bruce hatched to claim the throne of Scotland. He was barely able to escape with his life. That is why Comyn was killed."

Sabrina was not convinced. "So you say. But mayhap he merely wished to eradicate the other claimant to the throne—the *rightful* claimant."

He rubbed his chin and gave her a long, slow look. "And whose words would those be, I ask?"

For an instant she balked. Yet somehow she managed to state firmly, "Mine!"

"Indeed"—his gaze was cool and assessing—"why, I could almost swear that which you speak sounds very much like . . . like a MacDougall." He paused. "I am most curious, Sabrina. Is Jamie MacDougall tall and fair-haired? And do the two of you sometimes meet in the kitchen garden?"

Sabrina was too stunned to say a word. How could he possibly know. . . . She paled suddenly. God's teeth, did Papa know?

Somewhere she found the courage to face his challenge. "I cannot imagine why you should say such a thing."

"No?" The way he arched a single dark brow lent him the look of the devil. "Then mayhap your faculties are not so keen as you think, Sabrina—for Edna was rather forthcoming about your trysts with the lad."

Edna! Her jaw snapped shut. Why, the rogue had somehow charmed Edna—she who had thought the MacGregor was naught but a monster!

Her chin nudged upward. "And what if I have?"

"Then I would wonder what your father would think of such meetings. For I believe I'm not mistaken when I say he is not fond of the MacDougalls."

The soft line of Sabrina's lips tightened. It would be just like him to discharge her secret to Papa—indeed, if his past behavior were to tell the tale, she could well expect it!

Resentment smoldered within her. Through some miracle she held on to her temper by a hair's breadth. "Papa does not know Jamie as I know him."

His eyes narrowed. He looked as if he wanted to say something. But a chill breeze eddied around them, and Sabrina shivered.

He frowned. "Come," he said gruffly. "It grows cold here." He took her arm and led her toward the narrow stone stairs. He didn't release her until they had descended and stepped within the great hall. It was deserted except for a hound snoring near the hearth.

Just then a servant carried in a platter full of roasted meats. He set it on the table at the far end of the hall. A fragrant aroma drifted toward them, but Sabrina's stomach was churning so that she could not appreciate it.

"Supper will be served soon," he said. "Shall we sit?"

She gave a quick shake of her head, all at once feeling awkward. "I—I believe I shall take a tray in my chamber. I—I'm not feeling well."

It was a lie. Something strange was happening. Her heart was beating like a pagan drum. So near to him like this, all she could think was how big he was. He possessed a raw masculinity that shouted his manhood to the heavens and beyond. Never had she been so aware of any man, even Jamie.

She swallowed, and lifted her eyes. A dark haze shadowed the squareness of his jaw, though 'twas obvious he'd shaved that morning. Her gaze jerked away, only to confront the broad width of his shoulders, covered by a leather jerkin. He wore trews, so tight they outlined every bulging muscle in his legs. She knew not where to look. She knew not what to do. She buried her fists in her skirts, feeling very much like the child she'd claimed she was not.

"Then I'll escort you to your chamber."

"Nay. It's not necessary—"

"Pray do not argue, Sabrina. You are right—you do not look well."

Once again long fingers curled around her elbow.

Do not touch me! she longed to scream. His presence surrounded her like a mantle of darkness and all she could think of was escape. The corridor was filled with shadows, for the candles mounted high on the walls had not yet been lit. She stumbled once. Ian's grip tightened; it was all that prevented her from falling. Their bodies brushed in the darkness. She breathed a sigh of relief when at last they stood before her chamber door.

He released her. But he did not bid her good night as she thought he would. Instead he murmured, "Your father should not have said what he did last eve."

Sabrina blinked. "What did he say?" she asked faintly.

His regard was unsmiling, his expression unreadable. "That you are not so fair as Margaret."

Sabrina's face burned painfully. She took a fortifying breath. "I do not mind. Nor do I envy her. I—I accept her as she is. And I accept what I am as well."

"It was cruel of him." He sounded almost angry. "Nor is it true."

Once again, she knew not what to say, and so she said nothing. But in that ringing silence . . .

His gaze dropped to her mouth.

Sabrina's heart leaped like a frightened doe. He stood so close—'twas verily impossible to breathe.

His head bent low. She couldn't tear her eyes from his mouth. There was a stab of some unknown feeling low in her belly. But he merely ran a fingertip down her cheek.

"Sleep well, bratling," was all he said.

The tender gesture so startled her that she could

scarcely breathe. She did not move for long moments after he turned and walked away.

He had called her lovely. Why? *Why?* Ugly, would have been more like the Ian of old. But it was just as he'd said. She was no longer a child. And—oh, but she could not lie to herself!—Ian was the most handsome man she'd deigned to lay eyes upon. . . .

"We missed you at supper."

Sabrina had glanced up when she heard the door creak open. Margaret stood on the threshold. She beckoned Margaret inside, then quickly sat up from where she had been lying on the bed.

She smiled at Margaret. "Oh, I've no doubt my absence was a welcome respite for all who crave peace and quiet."

"Actually it was rather dull," Margaret complained. "I can't remember a meal so utterly boring."

Sabrina's mind sped straight to Ian. Had *he* missed her too? She caught herself in mid-thought. God in heaven, what was wrong with her?

On impulse, she patted the spot next to her on the blanket. "Come sit," she invited.

Margaret hesitated, then did as she was bid. "I can stay but a moment," she warned. "I am to play chess with Alasdair in the hall."

Sabrina couldn't help but feel wounded. In but a few days, Margaret would be leaving here for the Highlands. Never again would they live together as sisters.

A voice in her mind chided that Margaret would miss her not a whit. Countless times throughout their lives she had approached Margaret—to talk. To sit. To simply share her company. But somehow Margaret had always managed to make her feel unwanted, as if she were naught but an inconvenience. Sabrina loved her sister; she greatly admired her grace and gentility. But the warmth she had sought in her sister was simply not to be, at least not for her, and it had ever been so. A pang of guilt shot through her, for in her childhood she had oft felt far closer to Ian than her own sister. . . .

Ian. Faith, why must he be ever in her mind? His image flashed before her: dark, craggy features, his tall, spare form. Did Margaret find him as handsome as she did?

Margaret sighed. "What is it, Sabrina?" Her tone was impatient.

Sabrina bit her lip. "'Tis nothing," she murmured. Drawing up her knees, she hugged them to her chest.

Margaret grimaced. "I can tell you've something on your mind. Out with it."

Sabrina felt her face grow hot. "'Tis nothing. I've no wish to trouble you further—"

"Tell me, Sabrina." Margaret looked as stern as an old hen.

"All right, then. You see, I was just wondering if he"—she finally decided there was naught she could do but blurt it out—"I wondered if he had . . . had kissed you!"

"Who?" Margaret's tone was sharp.

Sabrina blinked. "Ian." Indeed, who else could she have meant?

Margaret did not look pleased. "Nay," she said shortly.

Sabrina's lips parted. "Never?" she whispered.

"Such things should be done only between husband and wife. And we are not yet husband and wife."

Margaret's voice rapped out; she was obviously affronted by such audacity. "Why do you ask such a thing?"

Why, indeed . . . Because she had wanted to know what it was like to be kissed by Ian . . . because she'd thought he was going to kiss *her*, and she'd wondered what it would be like if he had . . . because she had kissed Jamie and she wanted to know if it was the same. . . .

Oh, but her mind was all amuddle! And all at once she was deeply ashamed that she *had* kissed Jamie, for Margaret made it sound so—so wrong. But was it wrong? She and Jamie would someday be husband and wife. . . .

"I—I don't know," she stammered. Gathering herself well in hand, she summoned a smile. "'Tis just me, Margaret, being silly and fanciful again. Now go and have your game of chess with Alasdair."

Margaret cast her a glance that proclaimed she'd surely lost her mind—and mayhap she had. But already Margaret was gliding toward the door.

"Good night, Sabrina," was all she said.

"Good night, Margaret."

It was a long, long time before Sabrina slipped into the arms of slumber. Before she did, she prayed she might dream of her beloved . . . of Jamie.

Dream she did . . . but not of Jamie. Nay, it was Ian's strong features who flitted through the darkest realm of her mind.

Little did she realize it was much the same in the chamber down the hall.

For Ian, too, sought to fill his mind with visions of the beauty he would soon wed . . .

Instead he dreamed of Sabrina.

* * *

It was early the next afternoon when Edna sought out Sabrina where she was checking stores in the larder.

"My lady," she whispered, then beckoned to her.

Sabrina quickly stowed her keys in the pouch fastened to her gown and hurried to where the maid lurked in the doorway.

"What is it, Edna?"

"Your Jamie wishes to meet you at the pond, my lady," the maid told her. "As soon as you are able."

Sabrina bit her lip. She hated the doubt that crowded her mind, but she was all at once reminded how Edna had revealed to Ian what she would have preferred remain secret.

"Tell no one of this, Edna." Her tone was unusually stern. Within her eyes was a silent warning. "Do you understand?"

Edna's gaze flitted away. "Aye, mum," she said in a tiny voice.

Sabrina squeezed the girl's shoulder to soften the sting. She could not find it in her heart to be angry with her. "You are a dear, Edna," she said softly. "Should anyone ask, you know not where I am."

Edna nodded. Sabrina's steps carried her quickly away. She departed the keep from a little-used entrance next to the stables.

The day was warm and bright, alive with the scents and sounds of late summer. Slivers of sunlight streaked through the treetops high above. The air vibrated with the hum of insects. Birds shrieked to one another, heedless of the visitor below.

At last the pond came into view. Sabrina halted.

The sweep of her gaze scanned the clearing. Where, she wondered, was he . . . ?

A tall figure stepped out from behind a stand of trees, tall and handsome, clad in rough linen shirt and leggings.

"Jamie!"

With a cry, Sabrina picked up her skirts. Her heart-beat quickened as she hurtled toward him. He caught her close. She clung to him and buried her face against his chest, craving the security only his presence could bring . . . needing desperately to drive away the haunting dreams of a dark-visaged face with eyes that glimmered like steel.

Jamie's low voice, grainy-rough with an edge of laughter, rushed past her ear. "With a welcome like this, I do believe I should stay away more often."

A wisp of a smile curled her lips. Suddenly she felt rather foolish indeed. "I missed you."

One thick golden brow hiked upward. "So I gather, lass," he said in his soft burr. "So I gather."

An arm about her shoulders, he led her toward a patch of soft, mossy ground. Jamie sat, then gently urged her down with a tug on her hand.

"I heard the news that Margaret is to be wed to the MacGregor."

Sabrina nodded. "The wedding is planned for to-morrow."

"Good! Then I can ask your father for your hand—" He broke off when he saw her expression. "What is it, love? Our turn will come next, I promise."

Sabrina's gaze had turned cloudy. "Papa may be difficult," she said quietly.

His smile of encouragement vanished. "Because I am a MacDougall," he said flatly.

Never in her life had Sabrina felt so helpless. "Because your family supports the Comyns."

Jamie scowled. "I do not seek to marry *him*. I seek to marry his daughter."

Sabrina laid a hand on his arm. "We will find a way, for I swear, I will not let Papa keep us apart—" She broke off at the expression of guilt that flitted across his ruddy features.

Panic, swift and merciless as an arrow to the heart, swept through her.

"What?" she cried softly. "What is it?"

He clasped both her hands in his much larger ones. The sudden agony she felt was mirrored on his face.

"You know how much I long to make you my bride, Sabrina." His voice was hoarse with all he felt.

Wordlessly she nodded. Her eyes clung to his.

"And you do not doubt that I love you."

She did not. But there was something wrong. She searched his features but could find no answer there. "But what?" she said faintly.

He hesitated. "But we may have to wait a wee bit longer than we hoped. For there is not just the matter of your father's consent—"

"We could run away. To a place where we are not known—"

His voice cut across hers. "I cannot."

Sabrina went very still. "Why not?" she whispered.

There was an endless silence before he spoke. "'Tis said the Bruce will soon return."

An eerie prickling trickled up her spine. Alasdair had predicted the very same the night he and Ian had arrived. Should she tell Jamie? She hesitated, feeling as if she were caught fast in a spider's web with no way to free herself.

"But that has naught to do with us—"

"I cannot abandon my family. My cause. The Bruce cannot remain king. I pray that you will forgive me, but . . . I must leave soon."

Though her heart wrenched, she understood. Oh, there was a part of her that wished she could rage and scream and cry that she might keep him at her side . . . but this was a matter of honor and loyalty.

A matter of duty.

"How soon?" she whispered.

"Two days. I know I should have told you earlier, but I awaited word from my uncle in the Highlands." He hesitated. "Tell me you do not hate me, Sabrina. Promise me you will wait."

Her heart turned over. He was so brave. So torn. Very gently she cradled his face between her palms and gazed into eyes as blue as the bonny sky.

"I will wait," she said softly.

His eyes darkened. "Then let me hold you just once more . . . let me kiss you that I might remember the sweet taste of your lips, that you might be with me evermore. . . ."

With a groan he crushed her against him. Her arms slid up and twined around his neck. She clung to him shamelessly, cherishing the moment, not quite understanding the fierceness of his kiss, but wanting to give him all he sought and more.

The weight of his chest pressed her to the ground. His mouth on hers was hot and potent. One hand slid upward from her waist to just beneath her breast. His thumb raked brazenly across the tip of her breast. Sabrina's heart slammed against her ribs, for this was play in which she had no experience.

She felt his fingers in her hair, loosening her braid.

"Please, love." His words were a hoarse mutter against her lips. "Do not say me nay."

What her answer would have been, she would never know. At precisely that instant, her eyes flicked open; they widened in sheer horror.

For once again, it seemed, she was not alone . . . rather, *they* were not alone.

Ian stood but an arm's length above them.

Five

Somehow she managed to tear her mouth free of Jamie's. Frantically she pushed at his shoulders. "Stop!" she gasped. "Th—there is someone here!"

A curse broke from his lips. He twisted and bounded to his feet, only to come face to face with Ian. "Who the devil are you?" he demanded. He reached for the dirk at his waist.

By now Sabrina had struggled to her feet. She grabbed at his arm. "Jamie, no!" she cried. "'Tis Ian!"

Shock flooded his features. She felt the muscles in his forearm loosen. "Margaret's betrothed?"

"Aye."

This came from Ian; it spun through her mind that never had a single word sounded so ominous.

His mouth was a forbidding, straight line. His jaw was clenched as tight as a babe suckling on its mother's teat. It flooded her mind that he was not just angry. He was furious.

Ian transferred his burning gaze to her face. "I see you are quite recovered."

His voice was heavily laden with mockery. Though it took every ounce of courage she possessed, she refused to back down. Deliberately she slid her other hand around Jamie's elbow. "Jamie and I are to be wed," she informed him loftily.

He laughed, a sound that held no humor. "Indeed. Well, methinks your father was right, Sabrina. This lad"—he spoke the word as an insult—"wants naught but one thing from you."

Beside her, Jamie stiffened. "That is not for you to say—"

"No? My eyes do not lie." Ian made the pronouncement flatly. "I know what I saw. You touched her as no honorable man would touch a woman he seeks as his wife."

So he had seen Jamie's hand on her breast. . . . Mortified, Sabrina wished she could vanish into the air, like the faeries of legends past.

Jamie flushed. "You know nothing. And I will not answer to you—"

"And I demand no answer, though indeed, I should kill you where you stand here and now."

Jamie bristled. He drew himself up to his full height. "I fear no one, least of all you."

"Brave words, lad. But only a fool believes himself invincible." Ian's hand was on his dagger. "However, I am prepared to be generous. Leave. Leave, while I offer you the chance. For I vow I'll allow this tryst to go no further."

Sabrina's heart leaped to her throat. Though Jamie was tall and well-muscled, Ian was broader and outweighed him. Thin-lipped and tense, Ian's shuttered features bespoke a chilling coldness. In a contest between the two, she feared Jamie might well be the loser.

"Go," she pleaded. "I am fine. He will not harm me. There is no point in staying—"

Jamie gave a muffled exclamation. "And leave you with him? Nay, Sabrina—"

Panic swelled in her breast. "Yes! Jamie, please!" she pleaded.

He scowled. "Sabrina—"

With her eyes she implored him. With her lips she beseeched him. "I will have no blood shed because of me. Go. Go now."

Time hung never-ending. She feared he would not listen. Then at last his eyes flickered. His tone conveyed his regret. "Remember I leave two days hence to join the battle to restore the Comyns to the throne. If you need me before then . . ."

"Do what you will . . . what you must." With tremulous lips she smiled. Her heart ached, for she knew not when she might see him again. "And remember, I will be waiting."

His eyes darkened. He dragged her into his arms and pressed a passion-filled kiss on her lips. Sabrina clung to him desperately, caring not that Ian watched.

At last Jamie raised his head. He pressed a finger to her lips, and then he was gone.

Sabrina watched him disappear into the forest. All the while she felt the fire of Ian's gaze upon her. When at last she turned back to him, the heat of it seemed to burn clear inside her.

"Why are you so angry?" she asked daringly. "Because I am with a man? Or because that man is a MacDougall?"

"'Tis very clear your father would not approve of a MacDougall."

"'Tis none of your affair!" she retorted hotly.

His smile was tight. "As your future kinsman, I believe it is."

She glared her ire—but could find no argument within her—save one.

"Jamie loves me."

"He loves what lies between your thighs."

Sabrina's eyes widened at his bluntness. "You are crude!" she gasped. "And you are wrong, for Jamie *does* love me."

He made a sound of disgust. "You mistake love for lust, lady."

Resentment and rage simmered inside her. "I need none such as you to protect my virtue."

"Virtue?" His lip curled. "You have none."

"And who are you to judge? Who are you to know of a woman's wants? Ah, but I forget." She mocked him as he mocked her. "You've been to France and so you know all there is to know of love."

He gazed at her with thinly veiled disapproval. "You are as unmanageable as ever. Your father should have curbed your wildness long ago."

Her eyes narrowed. "How dare you speak to me so!"

"You would dare speak ill of me . . . if I let you."

A sudden burst of recklessness washed over her. "You could not stop me!" she taunted.

Aye, and unwisely. Indeed, oh, so unwisely . . . for all at once he seized her by the shoulders.

He stared down at her, an unmistakable glint in his eye. "Ah," he said softly, "but I do believe I could." He smiled, a smile that sent a chill to every corner of her heart. "I find I'm curious, Sabrina. What wicked ways have you learned as a woman?"

Sabrina suppressed a shiver. She *had* curbed her wickedness. Regardless of what Ian thought, Papa had seen to that.

But she would not yield, not to him. "What would you know of a woman's wants? You may exceed Jamie in years, my Highland prince"—the childhood nickname she'd had for him came ready to the fore, emerging without conscious remembrance; only now it was a jeer, and she tossed her head boldly—"but I daresay Jamie is far more skilled in the arts of pleasing a woman."

Had she known what the insult to his manhood might provoke, she would never have taunted him.

"Ah, but he is just a boy, Sabrina. And he gave to you the kiss of a boy. But this"—his hands tightened on her shoulders—"this is the kiss of a man."

He took her wholly by surprise. Sabrina had no chance to prepare herself. No chance to evade him. He'd said he would not hurt her . . . but one terrifying glimpse of his eyes, glittering and blazing, and she feared she was wrong.

His mouth came down on hers, hard and consuming. He kissed her with ruthless intimacy, parting her lips with the demand of his.

Her hands came up between them. She sought to push him away, but he was as immovable as a pillar of stone. A tiny whimper, a sound of protest, escaped her.

He raised his head. She felt the touch of his eyes like the slash of a swordpoint. "What, Sabrina! Do I rob you of your sport as he robbed you of your virginity?"

His arrogance knew no bounds. "He robbed me of nothing. What he took was mine to give . . . and freely given!"

Time swung away while each tested the resolve they found in the other's eyes. And then he did what she did not expect, not in a thousand years.

His arm clamped hard about her back. He pulled her full and tight against him. They were welded together from breast to belly, the softness of her thighs wedged against his own. Lean fingers tangled in her hair, turning her mouth up to his . . .

He kissed her anew.

Aye, he kissed her anew . . . but now he sought to please where before he'd sought to tame. A little shock went through her, and suddenly Sabrina was seized with a far deeper fear.

His kiss was so very different than Jamie's, she thought with a shiver. Jamie's was sweetly worshipful, while Ian's was heady and persuasive and strangely erotic. Aye, she decided hazily, 'twas so very different . . .

Yet not distasteful.

She struggled against an insidious pleasure. Deep in her heart she was appalled that she could feel such a thing with this man—she was appalled at both of them! She could feel the rhythm of his heart drumming hard against her own. She gave a little moan—of surrender or denial, she knew not which.

Her fingers curled against the soft wool of his plaid. Her lips parted beneath the pressure of his. All thought, all sanity, scattered to the far reaches of the earth. There was only the hot seal of his mouth against hers, hungrily demanding, darkly passionate.

It ended as suddenly as it began. He lifted his head and stared down at her. Sabrina's legs buckled, as if she were without courage or strength. She would have collapsed had he not caught her.

Slowly she brought her head up. Glittering silver eyes rained down on her, but she could read nothing in the depths of his gaze, neither triumph nor elation.

With a stricken sound she broke away from him. This time he made no effort, neither to stop her nor help her. All at once she was shaking so that she could scarcely stand. She pressed a trembling hand to her lips.

"What have you done?" she whispered, and then it was a wrenching cry: "What have you done?"

She spun around and fled toward the keep.

In truth, Ian had no answer.

Nor did he know why he'd kissed her.

He knew only that he'd been angry—angry as never before that her wildness hadn't abated—that she was still the daring little enchantress she'd been as a child. A crimson mist of rage had come over him the instant he'd seen her with Jamie—seen that wretched traitor daring to explore the round swell of her breast.

Nay, he *did* know why he'd kissed her. He'd meant to teach her a lesson—that she could not challenge him without paying the price.

He'd not expected the wave of passion that swelled within him the moment he dragged her into his arms.

He didn't understand the way she had trembled beneath his touch. Oh, she had resisted at first— they'd both been so full of emotion, so full of anger! But his fury had given way to something else, something just as potent . . . just as powerful . . .

And far more dangerous.

For now he knew how she felt beneath his hands, small and delicate and soft, as if she would surely break in two. Yet she was startlingly lithe and firm.

He wanted . . . more.

He wanted . . . what could never be his.

He wanted . . . her.

Sabrina.

He cursed her to the heavens . . . and damned himself thrice as blackly.

It was a long time later when he returned to the keep. He strode into the hall and called for pungent ale. Perched on a wooden stool below a woven tapestry, he drank deeply. The world had just begun to pleasantly recede when the swirl of feminine skirts caught his eye. He stiffened as a form drew near.

But it was only Margaret.

"My lord," she murmured.

Ian spared no greeting, for his mood was not tame. He gave a terse nod and waited.

"I wonder if I might have a word with you."

"What is it?"

She linked her fingers before her, as cool and calm as ever. "I would like to stay on at Dunlevy for several days after the ceremony."

A muscle in his jaw jumped. "No," he said.

Her eyes flickered. "But, my lord, I've many things to—"

He was on his feet in a heartbeat. "No," he said again.

"Ian, I pray you—"

He slammed his fist against the wall. "We leave for Castle MacGregor immediately after the ceremony, Margaret. That is final."

He strode away without a backward glance.

Sleep did not come easily for Sabrina that night. Her mind reeled whene'er she thought of it. . . . Ian had kissed her. He had *kissed* her.

Nay, not just once . . . but twice.

Much to her dismay, she could think of naught else. His kiss had been like fire, his body well muscled and strong . . .

Why it was so, she didn't know. She loved Jamie. They planned to wed as soon as they were able. So why this cursed awareness of Ian as a man, a very handsome man indeed . . . ?

He had changed. He had changed from a gangly youth into a man of stark masculinity. They hadn't always liked each other as children. Though he'd never been one to treat her with scorn, at times there had been an air of haughtiness about him, and it was that which had sometimes led her to provoke him. Certainly she'd never been one to guard her tongue or mind her manners—nay, not then.

So why had he kissed her? Was it her fault? The question played through her mind, an endless litany. Papa had always accused her of being bad. He'd scolded her for not being more like Margaret. Mayhap he was right, and her soul was tainted. Mayhap Ian could not help himself. . . . Nay, he was not to blame. *She* was, for she was as wicked as Papa had always said.

Margaret . . . she cringed inside. How could she face Margaret again after what had happened? Now she knew what shame truly was. She had kissed the man who would be her sister's husband . . .

Sweet Christ . . . and on the eve of her wedding!

It was the raucous sounds of activity belowstairs the next morning that woke her. Sabrina was not surprised, since there had been a flurry of guests arriving these last few days. She had just finished dressing when she heard a knock on the door. In answer to her summons, Edna peeped inside. "My lady, is your sister with you?"

Sabrina was on her knees searching through her trunk for a veil. Her tone was distracted. "Nay, Edna, I've not seen her."

Edna made no reply. When Sabrina glanced up, the girl was still standing there. She looked confused.

Sabrina frowned. "What is it, Edna?"

"My lady . . . her bed has not been slept in."

Sabrina scrambled to her feet. "Are you certain?"

Edna nodded. "Aye. I thought . . . mayhap . . . she spent the night with you . . . this bein' her last night at Dunlevy . . ."

Sabrina shuffled backward through her mind. "I've not seen her since yesterday morn." A prickly unease slithered up her spine; quickly she pushed it aside.

"There must be some explanation," she said crisply. "Surely someone has seen her. Check with the other servants."

But no one had seen her. In the yard a short time later, Papa strode up. "Sabrina, where is your sister?"

Sabrina could not disguise her worry. "I do not know, Papa. Have you seen her this morn?"

"Nay, not since the evening meal last eve." A deep crease appeared between Papa's brows. "'Tis not like her to leave without telling someone of her whereabouts."

"Could she have gone for a walk?"

This came from Ian. He had stepped up behind her without her awareness. Sabrina turned slightly. She had to stop herself from withdrawing abruptly, like a skittish mare. Alasdair was with him. Both wore Highland dress—kilts and plaid. Ian's was secured at the shoulder by a jewel-encrusted brooch.

Papa hesitated. "She always rode when she left the keep."

"Her mount—"

"—is still in the stable." Sabrina could not quite find the courage to meet his gaze directly.

It was soon apparent, Margaret was nowhere to be found. All were called upon to aid, but a search of the keep yielded nothing.

No one had seen her since last eve.

Midmorn, a dozen riders departed the gates. The hiss of whispers from the guests filled the hall. Sabrina paid no heed. As the hours dragged on, she struggled against panic. Where could Margaret have gone? And why did she not return?

All too soon evening prepared to draw its veil over the land. Papa soon rode in. Sabrina leaped up and ran to him, a cry upon her lips. "Papa—"

He shook his head. Her shoulders sagged.

At the table in the hall, he sat with his head propped between his hands. Sabrina's heart went out to him, for his face was worn and haggard. She went to him. Lightly she placed his hands on his shoulders.

"It will be all right, Papa." She sought to reassure him. "She will return—why, no doubt within the hour."

He said nothing. At length he spoke. "Leave me," he said tiredly. "Just . . . leave me be."

Sabrina's hands fell away. She fought back tears. Ah, but she should have known better! He would not want comfort, nay, not from her.

She returned to a bench along the wall, to wait anew. Before long, the sound of horses drifted to her ears. Shouts came from the bailey.

Ian and Alasdair strode through the door. They

stopped short when they saw her father sitting at the table. Sabrina moved toward them, her gaze mutely questioning.

A spasm of pain crossed Alasdair's face. Wordlessly he held out something in his hand.

It was Margaret's mantle, sodden and dripping.

She swallowed. "Wh-what is this?"

Alasdair's voice was very quiet. "We found it near the loch to the east of the keep. It lay upon the rocks near the shore."

The loch? A horrible fear choked her. Her gaze drifted to Ian. His features were lined and drawn. They confirmed her worst suspicion. Blackness rimmed her vision, but she did not lose consciousness—if only she could!

Papa had pushed himself upright. "Nay," he cried. "Nay, it cannot be . . . Margaret! My child!"

Alasdair shook his head. "I'm very sorry, but it appears Margaret has drowned." There was a world of silence. "She is dead, my lord."

Six

Two days later they knew it for certain. One of Margaret's slippers washed up upon the shore of the loch. Only then did Papa allow a funeral mass to be said for his beloved Margaret.

At mass the next day, Sabrina stood in the kirk, still and pale. Ian and Alasdair were on the other side of the aisle. Papa stood next to her.

Though she was wrenched with grief inside, there were no tears. Certainly she and Margaret had never been close; Margaret had always hidden her feelings behind a façade of cool serenity. But Margaret was her only sister and now she was gone.

The mass ended. Father Stewart came forward to offer solace. As he laid a hand upon Papa's shoulder, Papa began to weep. The sound tore into Sabrina's heart like a dagger twisting and turning.

Sabrina longed to comfort him, to offer what solace she could. Yet for what purpose? He would only turn from her, for as always he wanted nothing from her. ... Bitterness welled up in her breast. Why? her heart cried out. Why couldn't he love her as he loved Margaret? Why couldn't he love her just a little? No doubt he wished it was her and not Margaret who had died. . . .

Her breath came fast, then slow. In that moment Sabrina hated herself. Such thoughts were wicked . . . as *she* was wicked. Papa had always said so. And now she knew for certain it was true.

Bile stung her throat. Her insides twisted into a sick, ugly knot. Blindly she began to move through the maze of people gathered in the kirk toward the entrance—most who had come for the wedding had stayed for the funeral. Outside, the day was warm and cloudless. Her steps carried her forward, faster and faster. Before she knew it, she was running—she knew not where nor did she care. Branches stung her cheeks, but she cared not; neither did she hear the shout of her name or the footsteps pounding behind her.

She ran until her lungs burned with fire and she could run no more. Exhausted, she sank to her knees. Her stomach was churning. Specks of black and gray floated before her eyes. Unable to stop herself, she began to retch violently.

She was only dimly aware of someone kneeling beside her, a strong arm sliding about her shoulders, of gentle fingers pulling her hair back.

Her head was still spinning as she saw that it was Ian. He guided her to a fallen log and helped her sit. The stream was nearby. Dimly she heard him dip a cloth into the rushing waters. He returned and sat beside her. He then proceeded to wipe her face and neck. Sabrina turned into the damp coolness gratefully, too weak to thank him.

When he had finished, she forced her eyes open. She braced herself inwardly, for she was certain he might laugh, that he would taunt her anew for her weakness. But he merely stared at her, his expression unreadable. Though she longed to escape, her strength had deserted her.

She averted her face. "You may leave now."

"You are unwell."

Sabrina's throat worked convulsively. "God's blood! Can no one do as I ask?"

"You should not be alone, Sabrina."

She began to rock back and forth. Guilt rode heavy on her heart. "You don't understand," she said dully. "It's my fault she's dead. It's my fault Margaret is dead!"

"No, Sabrina. She fell in the loch and drowned. It was no one's fault. It was an accident."

All at once she felt as if she were flying apart inside. Her breath came jerkily. "He knows what we did, Ian. He knows."

Ian's gaze sharpened. "Who? Your father?"

She shook her head. Her arms came around herself, as if she were chilled to the bone. "Nay," she said faintly. "God. God knows that you . . . that we . . ."

He gave an impatient gesture. "We did nothing! 'Twas a kiss, no more."

"It was wrong," she whispered. She began to shake from head to toe. "He took Margaret to—to punish me. Would that He had taken me now, but He means for me to suffer through all eternity. He will see that I pay for all the evil things I've done."

Ian swore beneath his breath. "Sabrina! You are not evil!"

"Papa said I was. Dear God, he still thinks I am! I remember . . . many a time did he accuse me of being the devil's arm."

"Sabrina, he did not mean it—"

"He did!" she cried. Her eyes were half wild. "And now . . . I see the way he looks at me—he wishes I had died instead of Margaret. And . . . God help me"—her voice broke—"I cannot help but be glad that I yet live." Tears stung her eyes, but she forced herself to go on. "So you see, I am evil. And Margaret died because of my sin. I-I do not blame you, Ian. 'Tis the wickedness in me. I know that you could not help yourself—"

His hands came down on her shoulders. Strong fingers curled around her arms. He shook her until her head fell back and she looked at him, dazed.

Roughly he said, "I kissed you because I wanted it. 'Tis God's truth, Sabrina. *I kissed you because I wanted it.*"

At his declaration, the tears that burned the back of her throat broke loose. Her mouth trembled as she fought to hold them back, but it was no use. A deep, jagged sob escaped, and then another.

Ian could stand it no longer.

Her tears were his undoing. Slowly, his arms crept around her, bringing her close. She turned her face into his neck and wept. Sensing she needed to purge her grief, Ian held her until at last her tears were bled dry. She lay against his chest, limp and drained. In one swift, decisive move, he gathered her in his arms and rose to his feet; that she made no protest as he strode back to the keep was but a sign of how shaken she was.

He paid no heed to the shocked glances that came his way. Just outside Sabrina's chamber, he encountered Edna. The little maid's chin dropped.

"Your mistress is overcome," he said. "Tell me

quick. Do you know a sleeping potion?''

Edna's eyes were all agog, but her head bobbed eagerly up and down. "Cook does," she said quickly. "I'll fetch it for ye."

"That's a good lass." He nodded toward the door. Edna obliged him by opening it, then hurried on her way. Ian smiled dryly as he shouldered the door closed a moment later. If only all women were blessed with the little maid's intuition.

He crossed the floor and lowered her to the bed. She drew her knees to her chest and curled away from him and into herself, her eyes squeezed shut. Ian stood over her, his hands flexing and unflexing. Did she know he was still here? If so, he was surprised she did not demand he leave.

Edna returned shortly, a small cup in her hands. Tiny plumes of steam wafted into the air. "Here, my lord. This should help her sleep. Have her drink all of it."

Ian took it, sniffing gingerly. The brew carried a strange scent he did not recognize, yet it was not unpleasant.

"Sabrina." He spoke her name. The mattress gave beneath his weight as he sat.

Her eyes flicked open. She glanced across her shoulder. He held out the cup.

"This will help you sleep." His tone was quiet but insistent. "All of it, Sabrina."

Her eyes blazed fire for an instant, and he thought she would argue. Instead she turned back to him and extended a hand. She made a face as she sipped it, but she drained the cup before handing it back. With a weary sigh, she leaned back against the pillows. Her eyes stayed upon him, half wary, half watchful.

"There is no need for you to stay," she said after a moment.

"I'll remain until you sleep." He could be just as stubborn as she.

"Nay, not *here*." With a wave of her finger she indicated the room. "I mean . . . here at Dunlevy. There will be no wedding. You should go back to the Highlands."

"I will," he returned politely, "when I am ready."

It wasn't long before the potion took effect. Her lids began to droop. Ian saw her struggling to focus. But just when he was certain she would drift off for good, her eyes snapped open.

She touched him then. A dainty fingertip reached out and traced the outline of his mouth.

Ian had gone very still, both inside and out. For an instant, a curious tension hummed between them. Her eyes, wide and unwavering, collided with his. Ian caught his breath, for they were the color of fresh spring grass moist with morning's dew. He could not help but wonder what went on behind those incredible eyes, for she was careful to reveal nothing of her thoughts. But then, with the very same fingertip, she touched her own lips.

And he knew they shared the very same thought . . . of the very same memory.

Desire cut through him, so strong it was almost a physical pain.

"Sleep," he murmured.

Her lashes swept closed. She turned her head aside, but not before he glimpsed the single tear that squeezed from beneath her closed eyelids.

Some nameless emotion swept through him. He let out a long, uneven breath. He sat there for a long time, listening as her breathing grew deep and even. Her guilt rent him in two. His conscience pricked at him.

Mayhap she was right. He should never have kissed her. It was wrong, for at the time, he was bound to Margaret. And yet, it had happened. And God help him, he didn't regret it. Indeed, some little known sense within him whispered that it was somehow inevitable.

Gently he drew the back of his knuckles across her cheek. Her skin was like the finest silk, her mouth soft and tremulous . . . and vulnerable. It seemed odd to think of Sabrina as vulnerable . . . Sabrina, his feisty bratling. . . .

But she was a woman full grown, and the proof of it lay before his very eyes. Her breasts rose and fell with every breath, offering as temptation sweetly rounded flesh he knew instinctively would fit his hands to perfection. A vision soared high aloft in his mind. He saw her as she'd been that day at the pond, her skin pale and creamy, sleek and glistening. Only now there was a difference—her eyes were full upon him, smoky with longing as she beckoned for him to join her. . . .

He drew a deep, unsteady breath, aching with the need to kiss her anew, to smother the protests he knew would follow and allow his passion free rein. He clamped his jaw tight, battling a rush of molten desire. Reluctantly he drew his hand away, resisting the urge to linger.

He could lie to himself no longer. Since the day he'd first returned, he could scarcely take his eyes from her. He was drawn to her in a way he'd never expected. She possessed a tantalizing enchantment he could not deny. Aye, he enjoyed a lusty tumble with a wench as much as the next man. Were she any other woman, he'd have been tempted to take her, to let his desire run full measure and have done with it once and for all.

But this was Sabrina. *Sabrina*. Not a wench to be used and discarded.

Aye, she was a lovely, desirable woman, and he had no trouble understanding Jamie MacDougall's desire for her. She was too beautiful and tempting for her own good.

And he could no more stay his own desire for her than he could stop the rising of the sun.

Anger tightened in his breast. A dark and bitter tempest brewed within him as he thought of her father. His mouth thinned to a hard, straight line.

What would happen to her? How could he leave her with her father? Duncan looked with disfavor upon his younger daughter, ever and always. He had loved Margaret best. Indeed, Ian wondered harshly if he had *ever* loved Sabrina. The last thing she needed was more guilt heaped upon her head; the wretch would do precisely that. He would crush her spirit—leech the very life from her soul little by little—indeed, he was surprised the bastard hadn't already done so. And she fared little better than a servant—that, too, was something he feared would never change.

A muscle tightened in his jaw. He tapped his fingers together before him, his mind twisting and turning. She was not his responsibility, a voice inside reminded him. He was not beholden to her. He owed her naught . . .

But she had no one else, still another voice chided.

And the issue was no longer clouded by his obligations to Margaret.

The shadows of night poured through the windows when at last Ian rose. Resolve crystallized inside him. He knew what he must do . . .

And why.

Sabrina woke slowly the next morning. Something elusive danced within her brain. She groped for the memory, her mind still befuddled with sleep. She had slept deeply, more deeply than she had for ages—but no wonder. Her mouth was dry as bone, no doubt from the sleeping potion Ian had . . .

Ian. He had brought her here, to her chamber.

She remembered being lifted, borne upward and cradled against solid warmth, and burying her face against his neck—'twas a sensation that was distinctly memorable—and distinctly pleasurable. His scent was clean and woodsy, his skin had been smooth and warm. And later, she remembered him staring down at her. His mouth was set sternly, yet she had sensed he was not angry.

She cringed inside. She had made a fool of herself. She had wept in his arms. And yet—he had not made her feel foolish. He had brought her here, and taken care of her, as no one else had ever done.

I kissed you because I wanted it. Had he truly said that? Or had she only imagined it?

She flung back the coverlet, suddenly impatient. God in heaven, why did it matter? What was wrong with her? Oh, how she wished she could be indifferent to him. Despite her every effort, she could not put him from her mind!

But she would, she vowed . . . aye, this very day!

To her utter consternation, she learned later that morn that Ian had still not yet departed for the Highlands. Silently she fumed. The rogue! She could almost believe he stayed on solely because he knew it would vex her!

It was late that afternoon when she encountered Alasdair lounging on a bench in the great hall. He immediately came to his feet when he saw her.

"Sabrina!" he greeted her. "We missed you at the evening meal. I trust you're feeling better?"

Sabrina felt her cheeks heat. Of course her headlong flight from the kirk must have been noted by all. She summoned a faint smile. "I am fine," she murmured.

His brown eyes softened. "'Tis not to be wondered at," he said kindly. "It has been a trying week."

"That it has," she admitted. There was a small pause. "I've not seen Ian today. Is he preparing for your journey back to the Highlands?" She held her breath and prayed.

Alasdair's broad shoulders lifted in a shrug. "I've no idea," he said cheerfully. "Ian has chosen to keep his plans to himself."

Hmmmph, thought Sabrina. Somehow she was not surprised. "It seems a bit unfair that he keeps you from your kin so long." She eyed Alasdair curiously. "Do you have a wife who awaits you at Castle MacGregor?"

"I fear there's none that will have me," he said with an exaggerated sigh. "All the ladies are smitten with my cousin."

Sabrina smiled, her first genuine smile in days. "Oh, I doubt that. You're a handsome devil," she found herself teasing. "I suspect they all secretly pine for you. Mayhap you need only give your lady of choice some encouragement."

The corners of his eyes crinkled as he chuckled. He took her hand and gave her a gallant bow. "I shall keep that in mind, kind lady."

Just then a door off the hall was flung wide. Startled, Sabrina glanced over to see her father standing in the doorway of the counting room. He was glaring at her.

Hurriedly she dropped her hand from Alasdair's grasp and hid it in her skirts. "Was there something you wished, Papa?"

"Aye." His eyes were snapping. "A word with you, Sabrina."

He did not wait for her but stalked back into the counting room. Sabrina followed him. He strode to the chair behind the long wide table where he sometimes worked during the day. But Sabrina stopped short as she realized they were not alone.

Ian sat in the low-backed chair across from Papa.

Papa indicated the seat next to Ian. "Sit," he commanded.

Sabrina did as she was bid, but she sat on the edge of the chair, her feet poised as if to flee. Her stomach began to churn. Ian—drat his soul!—appeared totally at ease. He even looked rather pleased. . . . All at once she felt distinctly like a lamb being led to slaughter.

Papa wasted no time. "Ian and I have been discussing future plans," he said gruffly.

Plans? Somehow she wasn't quite sure she liked the sound of that. But she nodded politely, tucking her feet beneath her chair.

"As you well know, Ian's father David and I

wished to continue the bond between our clans. That is why Ian was betrothed to Margaret."

"I know, Papa." In all truth, he told her nothing she did not already know. She was uneasy, for it wasn't like him to share such things with her.

Papa's tone was gruff. "Margaret is dead. But as Ian has suggested, there is no reason why David's wishes—and mine—should be put aside. Our clans can still be united." His eyes bore into her. "Do ye understand what I'm tryin' to say, girl?"

Sabrina's heart had begun to hammer. "Nay," she said faintly. Unbidden, her gaze slid to Ian. He was watching her, a slight smile curling his lips—oh, a devil's smile, that!

"What your father is trying to say is this, Sabrina." His tone was as easy as his smile. "I returned to Dunlevy to take a bride . . . and so I shall."

She blinked and stated the obvious. "But—Margaret is dead."

He said nothing. His smile merely widened.

An awful feeling had wedged in her chest. Nervously she moistened her lips. "Who then?" she whispered, knowing the dreaded answer.

There was a screaming rush of silence. "You," he said softly. "You will be my bride."

Seven

Had she been standing, she would surely have fallen to her knees. Her fingers curled around the carved arm of her chair in a death grip. Her ears roared with the pounding of her heart. She could scarcely believe she'd heard aright!

Ian had yet to deliver her of his regard. Oh, but he looked so smug, so sure of himself!

Her lips compressed. Her mind rebelled. "You cannot mean that."

"Oh, but I do," he returned promptly. "And indeed, I will."

Those silver eyes were all agleam. Blast his hide, he was enjoying this!

"You're mad if you think I'll marry you!" she cried.

Her father surged to his feet. "By God, you *will* wed him, Sabrina! You'll do as you're told for once!"

Sabrina turned pleading eyes to him. "Have I no say in this?"

Papa's jaw thrust out. "The matter is already decided!"

This could not be happening. She gave a slight shake of her head, as if to clear it. "Dear God," she said numbly.

"What! Now you pray?" Rage propelled him around the table. He stood directly before her. "I've done my best to put the fear of the Lord into you, all to no avail! Well, now you know you should have prayed when you were a child! Mayhap then you'd not be so disobedient and willful!"

His censure stung, but Sabrina was determined not to show it. Valiantly she raised her chin. "I cannot marry Ian. I am already betrothed to Jamie Mac-Dougall."

"I'll kill him before I'll let you wed that blackguard! Do ye hear me, girl? By God, I'll kill *you*."

And looking at him now, she well believed it. Though she was frightened of his anger, she met his blistering gaze head-on.

"I cannot marry Ian," she repeated doggedly. "I *will* not."

"You will. You will not dishonor me." He jerked her to her feet, his fingers biting deeply into the soft skin of her upper arm.

Sabrina stifled a cry of pain, then raised her head. Her heart leaped fearfully, but she ignored it. Instead she gave a tiny shake of her head. "No, Papa. I will not."

His lips twisted. An expression of such malice crossed his face that she nearly cried out. Then without warning, his hand came up. He struck her viciously across the cheek.

The blow felled her. Sabrina slid to the floor, stunned. Too late she realized she should have expected it. Flecks of white floated before her eyes. Her stomach turned sickeningly.

She didn't hear Ian leap to his feet so suddenly his

chair crashed to the floor. Nor did she see her father draw back his fist for yet another blow.

Steely fingers curled around his thick wrist. "Strike her again, Duncan, and you'll wish you had not."

His tone was all the more deadly for its quiet. Duncan's eyes flickered. His face went from fiery red to ashen gray. Only then did Ian release him.

Duncan stepped back. Gruffly he said, "Margaret would never have been so insolent."

Ian's countenance was rigid. "Sabrina is not Margaret," he said through his teeth. "But you never could see that, could you?"

Duncan blanched anew.

"The wedding will take place tomorrow," Ian said coldly. "See to the arrangements."

Duncan nodded and left the room.

Sabrina was only dimly aware of voices buzzing above her head. She closed her eyes, fighting back nausea, aware of her cheek throbbing like a red-hot brand. But she struggled instinctively when a strong hand descended on her shoulder.

"Stop!" commanded a voice above her. "'Tis only me, Sabrina."

It was Ian. She opened her eyes to discover he knelt beside her. An arm around her shoulders, he pulled her to a sitting position. His expression was grave, his eyes thunder-dark with concern.

Stupid, foolish tears pushed to the surface. Sabrina swallowed them, wanting desperately to succumb to the temptation to lean back against the strong comfort of his embrace. But this was all his fault . . .

Lean fingers traced the broken, puffy skin on her cheekbone. His touch displayed a gentleness that was totally at odds with the sudden flames that leapt in his eyes. He swore a vile oath.

"That bastard. He's struck you before, hasn't he?"

Sabrina did not answer; nor was there any need to. In the instant before her gaze slid away, he saw the truth there.

"You have my word I will not treat you thusly. You will come to no harm by my hand."

Her throat burned, for she was still perilously near tears. She longed to snap that she knew how well and true he kept his promises. "Indeed," she managed unevenly. "And a promise given is a promise kept, is it not?"

An odd look crossed his features. "Aye," he said.

She pushed at his hands, mortified beyond belief that Ian had borne witness to her humiliation. "You need not coddle me," she told him, her voice very low. "I am fine."

He released her immediately, as if he found her suddenly abhorrent. As she stood upright of her own power, she didn't see the way his eyes hardened to stone.

After a moment she regained her bearings. Could Ian be reasoned with? Desperation filled her breast. God above, she had to try.

Slowly she raised her head. If she had to beg, then so be it. "Stop this marriage, Ian. Stop it now while you still can."

He was like a wall of iron. "I will not dishonor my father's memory by disregarding his wishes."

"But he meant for you to marry Margaret, not me!"

"It's you who's blind yourself, Sabrina. It was my father's greatest wish that our clans be allied. Margaret was decided upon simply because she was the elder. But now Margaret is gone."

He made it sound so simple—but simple it was not! Her frustration must have shown, for his gaze seemed to drill into her.

"You are a fool if you think your father will allow you to marry Jamie MacDougall." Baldly he stated his prediction. "Marriages are made for expedience and gain."

Deep in her heart, she knew he was right. But she could not admit it—nay, not to him, not even to herself. "I cannot do this," she said fervently. "Dear God, I cannot!"

"I suggest you ready yourself, Sabrina. Our marriage will take place on the morrow. There is naught you can do to stop it."

No hint of a smile broke the grim line of his lips. He was utterly ruthless, utterly determined. As he spun around, Sabrina felt as if a cold wind had blown across her heart.

She could not help it. Bitter despair descended like a shroud of darkness. Her heart felt trampled, as if trod upon by a thousand hooves. She sank to the floor and wept.

An hour later she was dry-eyed and determined. Her mind flew like clanging swords. If she could somehow get to Jamie, they might escape. He would not yet be gone. She didn't care where they went. She would even live among the cursed English! She cared only that she was far, far away from Ian . . . far enough away that he might never find her.

The evening meal that night lasted an eternity. She could feel Ian's gaze on her, burning and dark. Papa's was thoroughly disapproving. Even Alasdair appeared unusually subdued. If he was surprised by the news that she was to marry his cousin, he said naught. Still, she was nervous. Fervently she prayed she would not reveal herself.

When it was done, she fled to the sanctuary of her chamber. Once there, she gathered some clothing and stuffed it into a small pouch. When she was certain that all in the keep lay abed, she crept through the darkened corridors and out into the bailey. Quietly she saddled the little mare she always rode.

The moon climbed slowly aloft. She was grateful for the light it cast upon the land like a silvery torchlight. If the darkness had been like a thick, oppressive blanket smothering the earth, she might never have ventured forth.

Soon she was skirting the forest, for she possessed not the courage to breach its shadowy depths. She chided herself inwardly, for 'twould take her longer this way. But soon the winds began to blow. The shimmering light from the moon began to fade. A dense bank of clouds began to gather dark and ominous across the sky. Sabrina grew nervous. Her courage began to erode. She jumped at every little sound. Somehow she gathered her wits in hand. She reminded herself that Jamie lived just over the next rise. She could make it. She *had* to.

A leaden mist began to fall. Within minutes it escalated to a downpour. Sabrina shivered, for the air had been warm when she'd left. Foolishly she'd not thought to bring her mantle.

And then it happened. A tremendous light flashed before her. A zigzag of lightning split the sky, as if cast by some mighty hand from above. An ear-splitting blast of thunder roared across the land, followed by a sharp crack that shook the very earth.

Her mare was terrified. Her eyes rolled back in her head. She bolted forward, nearly unseating Sabrina. Sabrina crouched low over the mare's neck, twisting her fingers in the animal's mane, while the mare ran on as if she were being pursued by the devil himself. Branches pelted her face. A startling gust of wind nearly stole her breath. Then the mare lost her footing. With a horrible sense of the inevitable, Sabrina felt herself pitch violently to the right. The mare's mane slipped through her fingers. With a stricken cry, she landed hard upon her back.

She lay there, stunned. Mercifully, she knew instinctively that she was not injured, but it was an instant before she regained both wits and breath. An eerie feeling prickled the hairs on the back of her neck. Slowly she turned her head. Another flash of lightning illuminated the darkness. 'Twas then she realized she was not alone. . . .

Both horse and rider were silhouetted against the backdrop of the storm-ridden sky, cast in silver for that mind-splitting instant. Sabrina's heart seemed to stop, then resumed with thick, dull strokes. For one horrifying, frozen moment she stared, praying she was wrong—hoping it was so. For though he was dark and faceless, his features hidden in shadow, she knew it was he . . .

Ian.

Ian climbed the stairs slowly, his mind preoccupied. The words Sabrina had spoken earlier gnawed at him.
A promise given is a promise kept.
The phrase was almost familiar. Indeed, he could

scarce rid himself of the notion . . . and then remembrance struck. From out of nowhere, some long-forgotten memory leaped out at him.

A promise given is a promise kept, lad.

He had been sitting at his father's knee, staring up at his father's countenance, bearded and intent. Aye, and 'twas not the first time he'd heard those very words, he realized suddenly. Indeed his father David had sought to instill in his son those very same qualities that made him a man of honor.

But it was an odd thing for Sabrina to say, was it not?

Sabrina. The line of Ian's lips grew taut. He could not help it. He was suspicious of her. Throughout the evening meal, she had scarce spoken a word. Rather than the show of spitting defiance he'd expected of her, she had sat with her head bowed low.

Her father had questioned her harshly when she'd first appeared at table. "Do not yet sit!" he had roared at her. "You may join us only if you acknowledge that this marriage between you and Ian will take place on the morrow."

Ian had quirked a brow and fixed his eyes on her like a hunter on its prey. In turn, she'd avoided the touch of his gaze as if she were convinced he had some horrid ague.

"I do," she had whispered.

She had been so accepting. *Too* accepting, Ian decided broodingly. Too . . . meek. It wasn't like her. With every step that carried him toward her chamber, he was more and more convinced of it.

He knocked loudly upon the oaken portal. When no answer came, he called her name.

Still no answer.

Ian did not hesitate whatsoever. He threw open the door and stepped within. His gaze sought the bed that occupied the center of the far wall. The coverlet was mounded in the center of the mattress. He should have been satisfied. Aye, and many a man would have been. . . .

"Sabrina," he said loudly.

The figure beneath the mound of covers did not stir. Ian's eyes narrowed. His booted feet echoed on the floor as he crossed to her. Sharply he spoke her name.

Still no answer.

In one swift move he wrenched the coverlet downward. A muffled curse escaped his lips as he gazed upon two fat pillows which occupied the place where her body should have lain.

"That witch!" he swore.

Three steps carried him through the door and out into the corridor. A quick search of the stables revealed her mare was gone. So she thought to escape, did she? Well, the little witch could try, but she would not succeed.

'Twas that very thought that spurred him on through the darkness, on until at last he found what he sought.

From high atop his mount, he watched her struggle to her feet. She did so with all the dignity of a queen, he noted dimly, admiring her spirit even as he fought to control his anger.

He swung to the ground, then spoke but one command. "Come to me, Sabrina."

Her chin climbed aloft. She spurned him outright. "Come to you?" she cried. "Never!" Even through the dark gray shadows, he could see the sizzle in her eyes.

"Why did you run, Sabrina? Have you lost the

courage you once possessed?" His lip curled. "You are not the Sabrina I once knew."

And this was not the Ian she had once known. His clenched jaw bespoke an anger held tightly in check. The boyish youth she had once known was gone, and in his place was a stranger she did not know—a man who was feared amongst the Scots as the fiercest of warriors.

His tone verily dripped in icy scorn. The night allowed no glimpse of his eyes, yet she knew, with all that she was, that his fury rivaled that of thunder rolling across the earth. Sabrina did not want to admit that, deep within her being, some part of her feared his rage.

When she made no move toward him, he lost patience. Two steps brought him before her. Sabrina gasped as she found herself seized and lifted bodily. There was a brief sensation of weightlessness. The next thing she knew, she was atop his steed. Before she could move, before she could even think, Ian swung up behind her. One iron-thewed arm slid hard about her waist, imprisoning her against the vast expanse of his chest.

She was not prepared for the feel of him, so hard and so warm—so undeniably masculine. A jolt of mingled shock and panic tore through her. She strained away from him, seeking only to distance herself from him—from the disturbing sensation that rushed at her from all sides.

His arm tightened. His voice, low and vibrating, rushed past her ear. "Do not try me, lest I lose patience. I warn you, I'll tolerate no more of your tricks."

As he bent his head, she caught a glimpse of his

eyes. His hold was like his expression, utterly unyielding.

A bleak despair settled round her heart. It seemed
impossible that he had tracked her down, in the night,
in the coming storm. Yet he had, and now she railed
inwardly that Providence chose to deal her such a
cruel blow.

He whirled his horse around. Then with a touch of
spurs they were off toward Dunlevy. They maintained a frigid silence all the way back to the keep.
Despite his warning, Sabrina held herself stiffly away
from him. Her muscles ached from doing so by the
time they reached the stable.

A cold drizzle had begun to fall. Ian leaped to the
ground first, then held out his hands to aid her. Her
features mutinous, Sabrina longed to slap them away.
His eyes chilled, the promise of retribution swift indeed if she dared to deny him, but she cared not that
he knew of her reluctance. Gritting her teeth, she
placed her fingertips lightly on his shoulders as he
swung her to the ground.

He released her at the very instant she turned away,
as if neither could bear to touch the other. But to her
vexation, his fingers wound around her arm as they
started toward the hall.

Sabrina whirled on him furiously. "I know the
way!" she snapped.

His half-smile was maddening. "And so do I, my
dear." He proceeded forward, his stride so rapid she
nearly had to run in order to keep pace with him.

The wind howled eerily as they wound their way
up the stairs; a pummeling rain lashed the walls. Sabrina's pride was sorely chafed by the time they
reached her chamber. Did he truly think her so meek

and biddable that she would bow low before him without question? Well, he would soon discover she was not so tractable!

She wrenched herself free the instant she was inside her chamber. Somehow she was not surprised when he closed the door and deliberately turned back to her. His expression proclaimed his satisfaction.

"So now I am delivered safely back to Dunlevy." Her voice rang out clear as a bell on a sunny summer morn. She damned him with her eyes, even as she damned him with her tongue. "But do you truly think it ends here? Do you truly think it ends now?"

An easy smile rimmed his lips. "Aye," he stated simply, "for on the morrow you will be my bride."

"We are not yet wed," she reminded him through lips that barely moved. "You cannot have what I do not want to give."

"Can't I?" He moved with a lithe quickness that nearly made her cry out. In one swift move, strong arms imprisoned her, snatching her close—closer yet!—so very close she could see the individual flecks of dark gray in his eyes.

Sabrina was stunned to find his smile wiped clean. "You should be glad it was me and not your father who found you."

She shivered. She'd rather be beaten than locked away as he'd done when she was a child. But she was determined that Ian would glimpse no weakness in her.

She raised a brow, haughty and defiant. "What? Now you expect my thanks? I think not!"

His eyes seared her. "Tell me true, Sabrina. Do you truly wish to stay here with your father?" His gaze slid to the bruise that darkened her cheekbone.

She took his meaning immediately. "I need no one to protect me," she flung at him. "Of a certainty I do not need you!"

"You may not need me. But you will have me ... and have me you will"—the twisting of his lips scarcely resembled a smile—"perchance this very night."

Her heart quaked. A feeling of sick dread clutched at her insides. "What do you mean?" she whispered.

His gaze scraped over her, lingering for long, uninterrupted seconds on the mounds of her breasts. Sabrina colored hotly, for it was as if he stripped her naked.

His words fell like blows on her cheeks. "Only this, Sabrina. Make no mistake," he said tightly. "You are mine now, as surely as you will be mine tomorrow. There is none to stop me should I decide that you will be mine here and now."

She gave an impotent cry of rage. "Why? Why do you insist on this marriage?"

"I've told you. I will not dishonor my father's wish to see our clans united."

"But you—you've never liked me!"

The feel of her body against his unleashed a flurry of emotions. His gaze roved over her upturned features. Her cheeks were flushed from exertion. Her lips were the color of ripe summer berries, moist and full. Ian felt the unmistakable surge of desire in his loins.

"I begin to think I liked you too well," he growled. He released her, then gave a curt gesture. "Undress," he ordered.

Sabrina gaped. "You cannot mean to—to . . ." Faith, but she could not even say it.

Ian had no such qualms. "To bed you?"

Her jaw opened and closed. A nod was all she could manage. She was scarcely able to tear her eyes from his face.

He was silent a moment, watching her with a critical detachment. "And if I do? Would you object?"

"Aye!" she cried.

"Why?"

Her mind was spinning. She said the first thing that sprang into her head. "Because we—we are not yet wed!"

He appeared to consider. "True. But what does a single night matter?" His bland calm was somehow more frightening than anything else.

She had no answer and so she said nothing. He folded his arms across his chest, nodding at her gown. A dark brow arched high. "You've yet to do as I ask, Sabrina. I suggest you be quick about it, lest I do it for you."

Sabrina blanched. Looking at him now, she could well believe it. Never had she seen a man so grim with purpose. He was right. There was no escaping him. No escaping her fate. . . .

Her hands were shaking as she brought them to the laces of her gown. It galled her to remove her clothing before him. Twice now—saints above, *twice* now!—he would see her naked. But yet again, he gave her no choice.

Nor did he turn his back as he had that time at the pond. Instead he tormented her with the ceaseless touch of his eyes as he waited for her to obey. Taking in a deep breath, she slid her gown from her shoulders; it pooled around her ankles. Her movements jerky, she reached for the hem of her chemise and tugged it over her head.

Now there was naught to shield her from the restless prowl of those steely gray eyes. Sabrina flushed crimson as his gaze swept her from head to toe. She could detect no approval on his face, nor did she wish any! Indeed, at that moment, she prayed he found her repulsive beyond measure.

But then he smiled, a slow-growing smile that sent panic surging through her anew. She whirled and dove to the bed, yanking the coverlet up to her chin.

Only then did her tardy mind realize what she'd done. She had sought refuge in the very place she wished to avoid—the bed!

Swallowing hard, she raised her head. Her jaw dropped when she saw he was ambling toward the door.

Her fists locked beneath her chin. "Wh-where are you going?"

At the threshold, he turned to face her, then gave a low, mocking bow. "I'll spend the remainder of the night outside your door," he said smoothly.

Sabrina blinked. "But . . . why?"

"Why, you ask?" He gave a short, biting laugh. "Because I do not trust you not to bolt."

Sabrina was silent a moment. He had brought her here, and she'd been certain she would bear the consequences of his rage as surely as she'd ever done her father's. Only now he was doing the one thing she never expected—he was going to leave her alone. Sabrina didn't know whether to laugh or cry.

Instead she did neither. "I—I will not bolt," she said at length, her voice very low. "You have my word. My—my promise." The oath cost her much. But unlike him, she thought bitterly, she would keep it.

His smile did not quite reach his eyes. "You needn't bother, lass. However much you might wish otherwise, I fear I don't find your word particularly reassuring just now."

Sabrina's jaw snapped shut. She glared her ire and struggled to find a suitable retort. But by the time she opened her mouth, he was gone.

That very same night a dark figure slipped unseen from the keep. He rode long and hard to a tiny crofter's hut hidden deep in the forest. He dismounted, then strode to the door. Testing it, he found it open. Throwing it wide, he stepped boldly within.

His gaze veered to the bed pushed against the far wall. "You did not throw the bolt," he stated without preamble.

A soft trill of feminine laughter filled the air. "Why bother? I knew you would come."

"Nonetheless, I do not think it wise that you be so careless."

Moist red lips pouted. "Why? Did not all proceed as planned?"

His frown eased. "Aye," he said with a grating laugh. "But you will not believe what else has happened ... he is to marry Sabrina."

The woman in the bed rose to a sitting position. "What! When?"

"On the morrow," came his reply. "You realize this will make things more difficult."

The woman rose from the bed. Her covers fell away, revealing her naked form beneath.

"Nay," she said with a slow-growing smile. "'Twill only make things more interesting."

"How so?"

Her laugh was gloating. "The two of them? Why, I daresay, they will kill each other! Ha!" Her smile widened. "If only they would! 'Twould save us the trouble."

He was silent a moment. "Will you follow soon?"

"Aye. I must." Her eyes glinted in the firelight. She beckoned him close. "Now come, my lusty stallion. Let us not think of them, but of us." She slipped from the bed, heedless of her nudity. Instead she arched her breasts and touched her nipples with her fingers, a silent invitation.

The man sucked in a harsh breath. She was the lusty one, for no matter how fiercely they coupled, she was ever ready for more. Her dismissal of his worry troubled him no further, for she was a clever one; this he knew well and true.

His rod already stone-hard, he needed no further encouragement. He shed his clothes and moved to join her. But when he reached for her, she stayed him with a hand on his chest and a shake of her head.

Wordlessly she dropped down on her knees before him. And indeed, speech was impossible, for in but an instant her fingers threaded through coarse dark hairs. He groaned as she stroked and explored. And then her mouth was filled with him . . .

Soft, sucking sounds mingled with the man's groan of pleasure.

Ian MacGregor was forgotten.

Eight

S unlight bleached the sky when Sabrina awoke the next morn. At some point during the night, with stark, painful clarity she came to the conclusion that there was naught she could do to stop this marriage. Inside she was secretly devastated that her fate was no longer her own—wearily she acknowledged it had *never* been her own. *You forget*, whispered a voice in her head, *'twas not Margaret's choice either to marry Ian.*

A pang of guilt knifed through her. This was true, she admitted. But Margaret had never been opposed to marrying Ian. She had not loved another. . . .

Just then Edna burst inside. "My lady," she gushed. "Oh, you are still abed! And 'tis your wedding day!" She clucked her disapproval. "Come now, up with you! We must hurry, or you will never be ready by noontide."

Noontide. Despair wrenched at her heart. To Sabrina, it might well have been a pronouncement of her death sentence.

If not for Edna's presence, she would never have summoned the energy to rise from the bed. Edna clapped her hands and several servants carried in the wooden bath. While Sabrina soaked, Edna bustled around the room, readying her clothing.

Edna had laid out her best gown of soft ivory velvet. Sabrina pursed her lips, then shook her head. All at once she felt distinctly mutinous.

"I think I shall wear another," she said briskly. Aware that Edna's eyes had grown wide as the moon, she strode to her chest and plucked out another. Moments later she was clad in coarse brown wool, tattered about the sleeves and hem. It was one she oft wore while assisting the laundress and doing other various chores about the household.

Edna's mouth opened, then closed. She looked utterly perplexed.

Nor did she wear her hair loose and free, as many a bride was wont to do. Instead she pulled it into a single braid, then curled it tightly about her crown. She also shunned the circlet of fresh flowers Edna would have set upon her head. Mayhap it was petty of her, but she would not celebrate this day in any way.

Edna looked ready to cry. Sabrina had no wish to dismay the little maid, so she smiled and gently kissed her on the cheek. "Do not fret, Edna. No one will blame you."

There was a booming knock upon the door. "Out with ye, lassie!" shouted Duncan. "The priest awaits!"

She called to him through the door. "I will be out in a moment, Papa."

"I'll be waiting in the kirk!" he shouted. His footsteps pounded down the passageway.

She had been standing before the small mirror mounted on the wall. As she turned her head, she glimpsed the ugly bruise on her cheekbone. The skin was broken and slightly raised.

Edna touched her sleeve. "My lady," she murmured, "mayhap a bit of powder—"

"Nay." Sabrina spoke with sudden, startling conviction. She squared her shoulders. Her father had done this to her. Let him see it—let all see it—for she would not hide the truth. Forcing a smile, she took a deep breath and patted her hair. For the first time, she began to look forward to what was about to unfold this day.

The kirk was tiny, situated near the northern tower. As Sabrina stepped within, she saw a small group assembled below the altar. It was there that she directed her steps. The soft *pat-pat* of her slippers gave away her presence even before every eye turned to her. She came to a halt. Papa stood just to her left, Ian and Alasdair to her right.

All was quiet as a tomb.

Father Stewart's eyes darted between her and Ian. Papa's gaze was snapping. He looked ready to explode. For an instant, she feared he would do precisely that, and she trembled to think of his rage. On the other hand, Alasdair's expression was precious. At first he was startled. His eyes rounded, but then she noted his struggle to suppress a smile.

Lastly, there was Ian.

He was resplendent in formal Highland dress, his plaid draped crisply over his left shoulder. In one strong hand he held his Highland bonnet, decorated with the MacGregor badge, a lion's head topped by an antique crown. At any other time, she might have deemed him breathtakingly handsome. But now, the corners of his mouth turned down as his eye ran over her. Sabrina secretly rejoiced—her gown displeased him. Oh, no doubt he would have preferred an eager, blushing bride. But he'd wanted this marriage, and by the saints, now he must live with the consequences.

For Sabrina wanted no part of this marriage. She wanted no part of *him*, and she cared not who knew it.

With a boldness she hadn't known she possessed, she lifted her chin. "Shall we proceed?"

Ian gave her a tight smile. "By all means." He held out his arm. Sabrina hesitated a split second, then placed her hand upon it. Beneath her fingertips she could feel the heat emanating from his body. The muscles of his forearm were rigid. Together they stepped before Father Stewart.

The next minutes passed in a haze. For the first time it struck her that from this day forth, she belonged to him—a possession, a pawn. He would not cherish her tenderly, as Jamie would have, she thought with a pang. He would not love her to the heavens and beyond, as Jamie did. She meant nothing to him, nothing at all. He stood next to her, his features set in rigid lines, cold and austere and formidable . . . as endlessly cold and formidable as her life would be from this day on.

A hollow ache pierced her breast. Her heart cried out in anguish. She didn't want this! She wanted love and happiness, a world of it. She longed to run from the kirk, never to return. As if he sensed her every thought, Ian's grip tightened ever so slightly on her hand. Sabrina could not help it—she stole a glance at his profile.

Their eyes collided, steely gray with muted green. It gave her a start to see herself the object of his regard. How long had he been watching her? she wondered almost frantically. His eyes flickered then, and within those crystal clear depths glimmered an unspoken challenge—a challenge her pride could not ignore.

Her spine straightened, stiff as a lance. The remainder of the ceremony proceeded without incident. Sabrina answered her vows in low, clear tones, Ian in an unwavering baritone.

Then it was over. Dazed, Sabrina heard Father pronounce them man and wife. Ian turned to her. A hard arm slid about her back. All at once Sabrina's nerves were wound tight as a spool of yarn. She read his intent in the arrogant curl of his smile. Her lips parted as she would have voiced her denial.

He would not allow it—he *did* not allow it. His arms snatched her close—close! She had one shattering glimpse of his eyes, fiercely aglow, before his mouth came down on hers.

His embrace was stark and plundering and raw, his kiss like a fiery brand—and aye, that's what it was, a proclamation of ownership. She gleaned his triumphant satisfaction in the instant he lifted his lips from hers.

Though Sabrina's cheeks burned painfully, she glared her displeasure. In that moment she almost hated him for his power over her.

Alasdair cleared his throat. He clapped his cousin heartily on the back, then turned to Sabrina. "Now I shall call you cousin as well," he teased.

Somehow she managed a stiff-lipped smile. Back in the great hall, a feast had been prepared. Various kinsmen came up to offer their congratulations. Ian remained at her side—a veritable leech, she decided—his arm locked about her waist. It was all Sabrina could do not to thrust him from her and shout that it was naught but a travesty. He laughed and talked with ease; one might have believed this was an event he'd looked forward to for years.

But mingled with her ire was another, wholly different sensation. Ian was tall and broad, overpowering and overwhelmingly male. He made her feel small and helpless in a way she liked not at all.

She had little appetite, though Ian had no such problem. He ate and drank freely. Seated next to him at the high table, her gaze strayed again and again to his hands. An odd little tremor shot through her. His hands were like his body, long and lean and strong looking. Silky-looking dark hair liberally coated his forearms and the backs of his hands. Sabrina wondered frantically if the same dense hair covered the whole of his body. . . .

Her mind roamed where it would, and there was naught she could do to stop it. For a time last eve she had feared that he would bed her. Then she had voiced her protest that they were not yet wed. But now that obstacle was no more, and he possessed every right to do whatever he wished.

He had seen her naked, aye—but he had never touched. But now he might caress her wherever he pleased—*when*ever he pleased. She swallowed, her mouth dry as dust. She could almost feel the heated strength of his fingers sliding over her body. There was none to stop him; certainly he would never heed her most ardent wish that he leave her be.

Her thoughts were colored with bleakness. She had not given herself to Jamie, but oh! how she wished with all she possessed that she had. Her chest ached with the force of emotion held fast in her breast.

A cold dread seeped along her veins. She had sur-

vived the ceremony . . . how would she survive the
night to come? Her breath came jerkily. She must find
a way to stop him. Somehow . . .

"Are you afraid of me, wife?"

Wife. Sabrina confined her attention to the silver
goblet before her on the table. There was no tenderness in the word—nothing but arrogant mockery. To
him it was naught but a needle to prick her, a taunt
to bring her low.

To her it was naught but a curse.

"Nay." She had to force the sound past the tightness in her throat.

"Then look at me."

His voice was abruptly harsh. Sabrina obeyed unthinkingly, only to regret it immediately. His eyes
were cool and remote. The slant of his mouth was
hard and unsmiling, his jaw square and unyielding.
Her gaze skipped lower, only to note his neck was
thick and corded with muscle. A wiry tangle of hairs
grew wild at the base of his throat. She thought of all
that lay hidden beneath his clothing . . . and shivered
with a fear she'd never before known—a fear of the
unknown.

She lowered her eyes, determined not to reveal any
further weakness. But all at once she was burning inside. A saving anger flowed into her veins. She resented him fiercely for bringing her to this pass. And
she was suddenly consumed with a fervid desire to
wound him, to make him rue the day he wed her.

Dark brows gathered over his nose. "What are you
thinking?" he asked gruffly.

"Methinks you do not want to know," she murmured.

"I do. Now tell me, Sabrina."

Slowly—guilelessly—she met his regard. "If you must know, I was thinking of Jamie."

"Why?" His tone was curt.

"Because he is the one I should have wed." Through stringent effort, she kept the bite from her statement.

"You would do well to forget him. He is no longer a part of your life."

Sabrina's eyes darkened. "I will never forget him. Never." Her voice rang low and fervent.

Ian's fingers shone white on the stem of his goblet. Though he did not speak, she knew she did not imagine his sudden tension.

"Had you wed Margaret," she stated daringly, "you would have wed a woman pure as new-fallen snow." She smiled sweetly. "Does it bother you, Ian, that another man has claimed what now belongs to you? Aye, I can see that it does. Perhaps you should have taken me last night after all," she went on. "Ah, but it was your choice. Still, then you'd have known for certain. Then you could have spared us both." Inside, she held her breath. Indeed, she might still be spared. If he was convinced she had lain with Jamie, he might not want her. An annulment might be obtained . . .

His eyes narrowed. His voice was dangerously quiet. "So you admit you lay with him?"

"Aye," she said recklessly.

He was angry. She could see it in the tightness that suddenly appeared about his mouth. She savored her victory . . .

For it was extremely short-lived.

In one fluid move he surged to his feet. "A kiss," he said suddenly. "I would have from my wife a kiss."

Desperation filled her chest, for his eyes were all agleam. This was not what she expected, not at all! "You can't," she cried. "Not again!"

"I can." Hands curled about her shoulders, he brought her upright. "And by God, I will."

So help him, he did.

He cared not that all those present watched—and cheered. His kiss was not borne of tenderness, or even desire, she thought bitterly. It was a punishment, a stamp of searing possession and they both knew it. Had they been alone, she'd have fought him with all she possessed. Indeed, he allowed no room for struggle. His arms enveloped her. She was crushed against him from head to toe, so tightly she could scarcely breathe.

His mouth was hotly devouring. She could do naught but endure the scouring sweep of his tongue in her mouth. Foolish tears stung her eyes, for Jamie had never kissed her as Ian kissed her now, in this blatant, shocking way. Her heart cried out the injustice, for aye, even in this he mocked her.

By the time he released her, she was weak-kneed and gasping for air. Her fingers were twined in the front of his shirt; it was the only way she could remain standing. But she bowed her head low, for she refused to let him see how shaken she really was.

But he had yet another blow to deliver.

Shouts and whistles broke out as he raised his head. He gave a triumphant salute then glanced down at her. By now Sabrina had recovered sufficiently to regard him with some measure of detachment.

He bent his head low. "'Tis good that you are dressed for travel"—his gaze swept down to indicate her coarse brown wool—"that pleases me, for now there is no need to wait while you change."

Sabrina blinked. "What?" she said faintly. "You are leaving?"

His smile betrayed vast amusement. "Nay, lass. *We* are leaving," he corrected. "It's time I returned to Castle MacGregor."

Panic assailed her. She wasn't yet ready to face the world—*his* world—as his wife. She groped for excuses. "But—what about the celebration? And my things are not yet packed."

"Ah, but they are," he informed her—and with great pleasure, she noted archly. "Edna saw to it. And we've no time for a celebration."

"But—the hour grows late. There are not many hours of daylight left—"

"No matter. We will be that much closer to the Highlands—and home."

He did not fool her. Sabrina knew why he was anxious to depart for the Highlands. He'd not allow her the chance to escape again.

And mayhap he knew that it displeased her to leave so soon . . . which no doubt pleased him immensely!

A slow burn simmered in her veins as he hailed her father and Alasdair. "As soon as the horses are ready, we shall leave."

Duncan clapped his hands and sent a man to alert the stable master.

A scant quarter-hour later, they stood gathered outside the entrance to the great hall. Alasdair was already mounted. He waited near the gates. Though self-pity was not Sabrina's way, tears threatened, hot and burning. She was about to leave the only home she'd ever known, with a man she no longer knew, to depart for a place she'd never been.

The household servants had formed a straggly line before the wide stone stairway. By turn, Sabrina called each by name. She conveyed her thanks for their service and bid them godspeed.

Edna was the last she greeted. The little maid was already sniffling. Her cheeks and nose were berry-red.

Summoning the dregs of a smile, Sabrina touched her shoulder. "Do not cry, Edna," she sought to tease, "else I will, too." She was only half-jesting.

Edna burst into a loud wail. "My lady, I shall miss you dreadfully!"

Sabrina reached out and hugged her fiercely. "And I you," she whispered. "Say a prayer for me now and then, will you, love?"

"Every day," Edna promised. They exchanged one last hug, then Edna fled sobbing into the hall.

Only her father was left. He'd been pacing impatiently while he waited, but now he halted. He drew himself up to his full height. No sign of emotion dwelled in his expression, neither sadness or joy.

Slowly Sabrina gazed up at him. 'Twas a moment fraught with awkwardness. She knew not what to say. She knew not what to do. Despite all, he was her father and she loved him. And now she yearned for some small sign that he returned the sentiment, if only in part.

His eyes flickered. He glanced over her shoulder where Ian stood waiting near his steed. Gruffly he spoke. "I hear your new husband can be a stern, harsh man. I shall pray you are a better wife than daughter."

Sabrina reeled. His words were like a stake through the heart. She felt as if everything inside was crumbling. Oh, but she should have known! she acknowledged with wrenching candor. Her father spared naught for her, no scrap of affection or love.

But little wonder, for she was not his beloved Margaret.

Bravely she swallowed her tears. She armed herself with pride and dignity—for it was all she had left. Perhaps it was all she'd *ever* had.

"May God be with you, Papa," she said clearly. She reached up and kissed his cheek, then strode to her mare. Though her spine was straight as an arrow, inside she was breaking apart.

The next thing she knew, Ian's hands were on her waist as he lifted her to the saddle. She couldn't look at him—she could not! Had he heard her father's heartlessness? She felt naked and exposed. *No*, she prayed. *Please, God, no.* For if he had, her shame would know no bounds.

Seconds later a trio of riders passed through the gates. Sabrina glanced back toward Dunlevy. Sunlight glinted off the nearest tower. Beyond the grand stone walls, fields and forest stretched endlessly green and verdant.

Her eyes grew lonely as the wind.

Margaret was gone, she thought achingly. Papa was lost to her, beyond her reach forever. She was the daughter of a man who shunned her very existence. And now she was wed to a forbidding, cold-eyed stranger.

There was a stark, wrenching pain in her chest. Dunlevy was no longer her home, she realized. Castle MacGregor would *never* be her home. Her life yawned barren and empty before her. . . .

A single, scalding tear slid down her cheek; it

reached clear to her heart. Sabrina wiped it away with the back of her hand.

It was the only tear she shed. The rest of her pain was locked tight in her breast.

Nine

I shall pray you are a better wife than daughter.

God's bones, but it was all Ian could do to stop himself from riding back and throttling Duncan Kincaid with his bare hands. The bastard! he raged blackly. He deserved to rot in hell for his treatment of his daughter. Sabrina was his own seed and still he gave her nary a care. He could neither comprehend nor condone the man's callous disregard of his own kin.

He'd seen the look on her face, the shocked despair, the moist sheen of emerald eyes gone dark with pain. She reminded him of a wounded doe.

Sabrina was well rid of the heartless rogue, he decided with no little amount of disgust. Though from the look of her, he suspected she was not inclined to share the sentiment.

Oh, no hint of hurt shown in her demeanor. Her profile was regal and proud. She sat her mare with straight-backed distinction. But it was what did not show that concerned him far more.

Little conversation passed between the three of them as they rode on to the north, for Ian was intent on journeying as far as they possibly could. He set a steady but not arduous pace. Just after sunset, they stopped at a sparkling little brook to water the horses. It was then he chanced to glimpse Sabrina's shoulders slump tiredly as she reached out to pat her mare's long neck while the animal drank thirstily.

He signaled to Alasdair. "We shall stop here for the night."

"Excellent," Alasdair said cheerfully. "I fear I've gone soft these past days. Half a day in the saddle and I'm worn to the bone!" He glanced at Sabrina. "But here I am, complaining endlessly when you are surely exhausted."

Sabrina flashed a faint smile. "I thank you for your concern, Alasdair. But I assure you, 'tis unnecessary."

Ian dismounted, smoldering inside. Ah, for Alasdair she smiled. For her beloved Jamie she smiled . . . while for her husband she had naught but contempt!

Her smile withered as he stepped to the side of her mare. She stiffened as he reached for her. In some distant part of him, he marveled at the narrow span of her waist. Once on the ground, she would have stepped immediately away if not for the sudden tightening of his hands.

Their eyes met fleetingly as he took her chin beneath his thumb and forefinger. He tilted her cheek ever so slightly, using only the veriest pressure. With the pad of his thumb, he skimmed the bruise there.

His words were meant for her alone. "Does this hurt you?"

Her lashes dropped, shielding her expression from him. "Nay," she said faintly.

Ian frowned. Was it his imagination—or was there a tiny catch in her voice?

He had yet to release his hold on her. "You are certain?"

"Aye. So please just—just leave me be!" She wrenched her face away and spun around, walking swiftly toward the bushes. But in the instant before she turned away, he saw the storm residing in her eyes.

Ian gritted his teeth. So this is how it would be. He hardened his heart and chided himself soundly. He'd forgotten for a moment. It wasn't him she wanted. It was Jamie.

Alasdair set about fetching wood for a fire, while Ian unsaddled the horses and set them to grazing. After that he erected a small tent. He'd brought it along solely for her comfort—nay, that was not right—for Margaret's comfort. It was odd, he reflected soberly, how things had turned out. Never in a thousand years had he thought to return to the Highlands with Sabrina as his bride.

Nor, he decided dryly, had she.

When Sabrina returned from the bushes, she set out the food and ale they'd packed for the journey. Darkness was complete by the time they sat down. For the most part their meal was conducted in silence. What talk there was came mostly from Alasdair, who seemed oblivious to the tension brewing between the newlyweds. Once they were finished, Alasdair yawned hugely and stated his intention to retire for the night. He spread out a blanket on the opposite side of the blazing fire.

Sabrina nodded toward the tent. "Am I to sleep there?"

Ian nodded.

"Good night then." She rose and stepped within the tent.

Rising, he strode to the tent and pushed the flap aside. He ducked within.

Sabrina whirled. "Ian!"

"The very same," he said calmly. His gaze slid down her body. "The gown, wife. Remove it."

Her mouth opened. Her eyes blazed. "Do not cross me, lass," he warned levelly. "Off with it now. And hand it here."

She clenched her fists. "You harbor an unnatural desire to see me naked!"

"You dally, Sabrina. If you do not do it, I shall do it myself."

She paled, but dragged the garment over her shoulders. The instant she stepped out of it, Ian bent and scooped it up, then strode to the flap of the tent. There he turned to look at her.

Clad only in her chemise, she planted her hands on her hips. "Ian! What are you doing? Would you take it from me?"

One word was all he spoke. "Aye."

Her eyes narrowed. "How dare you? Why, I would treasure it always for the memory it would evoke of our wedding day."

Ian gritted his teeth, strode from the tent and threw the offensive garment in the fire.

By now Sabrina was speechless—a state he decided she did not indulge in often enough. He gestured toward the bedding. "Into bed with you, wife."

This time she did not argue, but dove within the pile of blankets. Drawing the edge up beneath her chin, she stared at him with wide green eyes.

Very deliberately Ian sat and removed his boots.

"Ian . . . Wh-what are you doing?"

She was nervous, he decided, taking a perverse pleasure in her wariness. "I should think it would be obvious."

He stretched out beside her. Lacing his hands behind his head, he pillowed his head on his palms.

Her breathing was quick and rapid. "You mean to sleep . . . here?"

Ian turned his head slightly. Coolly he said, "I dislike that wretched braid, wife. Take it out."

The set of her mouth was mutinous, but she did as he asked. When she'd finished, she combed her fingers through the mass of tresses.

It was a mistake, he realized. Her hair now streamed wildly around her shoulders. It hit him like a blow to the belly just how lovely she was. He was unable to stifle a pang of sheer desire.

"I know what you are about, Ian." Her tone was icy. "You do this only to—to humiliate me."

"Och. Come now, Sabrina. Where else would I sleep but with my bride?" His voice rang with false heartiness. "And this our wedding night yet!"

"Ours was no ordinary wedding," she snapped.

"Oh, on that we are agreed. But what if I told you that I see through your ploy?"

"You speak in riddles and I am weary," she announced archly. "May we speak of this later?"

"We may not." He smiled with false civility. If she could be disagreeable, so could he.

"I beg your pardon?"

He turned on his side that he might face her. "I admit, I was taken aback by your choice of wedding gown. You wore it in sheer defiance, Sabrina, and in so doing you showed me that you are still the rebellious child, still the bratling."

Her eyes flashed fire. "I am no such thing—"

"You are," he said harshly. "You wished to make me angry. Perchance you thought I would not lay with you tonight. But you always did like to gamble, didn't you, Sabrina, even as a child? Still"—his smile was frigid—"you took the risk that I might yet take you in anger.

"Then again, if I were to do so, I'd take little pleasure in the act. And you would have but one more reason to despise me. And in truth, such feelings have no place in marriage. Such feelings have no place between *lovers*."

"We are not lovers!"

"Nay," he said softly, "not yet."

Her eyes grew huge. She snatched the blanket to her chest, as if she'd suddenly remembered her state of undress. Ian was both amused—and insulted. Many a lady had called him handsome—and praised his skill at lovemaking. His wife made him feel the veriest toad!

Some devil inside seized hold of him. "I wonder, Sabrina . . . did your Jamie encounter such reluctance when he sought to make you his?"

Her chin came up a notch. "Nay!"

"So you were ever willing, ever eager."

"I was!"

"And how long have you been lovers?"

Her gaze slid away. It took a moment before she answered. "I-I do not remember."

Ian's brows shot up. "You do not know? Come now, Sabrina. Think. When was the first time?"

"Long ago," she said quickly. "So long ago I do not remember."

A vague suspicion began to dance in his head as a most outrageous thought occurred to him ... but no. She'd taunted him outright that she'd lain with another man.

"I see," he murmured. "And have there been others beside Jamie?"

"Nay!" she gasped.

A faint smile curled his lips. "How odd, then, that you do not remember the first time you lay with him. I know I recall *my* first time quite vividly. And indeed, I've heard it said a woman never forgets her first time." He paused. "If you cannot remember the first time, perhaps you remember the last."

"I do," she said stiffly. "'Twas the last time I saw him."

"Ah, when I came upon the two of you at the pond."

"Aye," she said, but her parry was neither swift nor adamant.

"Hmmm." Ian's tone turned thoughtful. "He did not strike me as looking particularly ... pleased. Could it be he found you lacking? Ah, and I was beginning to think I'd gained a bargain—a woman who knew well and true how to please her man!"

She was struck speechless.

He persisted.

"Virgins are such trouble, you see. They know not how to kiss. They know not how to touch. Where to touch"—his voice fell to a seductive murmur—"and when."

There could be no doubt. He'd shocked his lovely bride to her very core.

He sat up. "So tell me, Sabrina. Do you still find me so despicable . . . ?" As he spoke, he reached for her.

She slapped his hand away. The set of her mouth turned mutinous. "I find you more despicable than ever," she hissed. "This may be our wedding night, and I cannot stop you from taking me. Indeed, I will not fight you. But when you do, know that I will be thinking of Jamie. Not you, never you. Because though my body belongs to you, my Highland prince, my heart is forever Jamie's. In my heart, I am wed to him, not you."

Ian surged to his feet. Damn her! he thought viciously. She was ever haughty, ever aloof. By the Virgin Mary, he should have taken her then and there! Aye, he was tempted! But as she stared defiantly up at him, he saw anew the bruise that darkened her cheek. And even while a crimson mist of rage swam before his eyes, he knew he would not touch her. She'd had enough of cruelty, enough of force.

But this was one victory she would not relish.

He reached out and snatched her to her feet. His gaze scraped over her. "Do not think me so smitten that I can see no other," he said through his teeth. "There are many just as fair—and far more willing— than you, *wife*. I will seek comfort where I please, but rest assured, you'll not do the same."

He pulled her crudely into the vice of his thighs. "You are mine, as this is mine," he said tautly, grinding himself against her woman's mound. She gasped, her eyes riveted to his. "You may yearn for your precious Jamie all you wish. But should you act on it— if I find you with him—with *any* man, I vow that day will be his last on this earth. And by the Rood, you'll wish it were yours."

With that he spun around and stalked from the tent. Amazingly, Alasdair snored near the fire, unaware of the furor that had just passed. He strode to the oak tree and dropped to the ground.

Damn her for being beautiful! Damn her for tempting him beyond reason, for invading into his every waking thought like an unwelcome intruder.

He'd been a fool to query her, he reflected blackly, for he'd done naught but arouse his own jealousy. His mood was as vile as her disposition.

Faith, but the wench knew precisely how to prick his hide, to play upon his every weakness. He was of a mind to march back into the tent, spread her thighs and spend his anger in passion. He shouldn't have cared that it wasn't the first time she'd felt the cuff of her father's blow.

But it would be the last, praise God.

With that his seething anger began to cool. He'd frightened her, he realized. She'd cringed away from him, her eyes wide with fear. Well, mayhap that was well and good. Mayhap she'd bide her tongue. Mayhap she would tread warily from now on.

Still, his mood was not easy. Were he to believe her claims, she was not a maid. Indeed, he'd had no doubt she spoke the truth, for she was still wild and willful as the wind. And he'd seen with his own eyes Jamie's hand on her breast.

But Ian was no longer so convinced, and the question tormented him, even as the possibility pleased him—pleased him mightily. He chafed inside. By God, there was only one way to know for certain. But he could not take her unto him here, with Alasdair nearby.

A restless resolve slipped over him. He would wait until they reached the Highlands, until they were home . . .

There she would not find refuge behind scornful denial.

And then he would know the truth.

Sabrina sank to her knees, stung to the core. His glare was endless, dark and ruthless, burning with a fire that seemed to scald her very soul. Her arms crept around herself. How long she huddled there, she knew not.

Her heart still beat with the driving rhythm of a drum. Ian's image swam before her, his features drawn into a rigid mask. He had been so fierce! And he'd been right—she had taken the risk he might take her in anger; that was something she'd not considered. And for one paralyzing moment, she had been convinced he meant to.

A shudder wracked her body. She'd been unwise— aye, and foolishly so!—to taunt him. Ian was no longer the young boy she had teased and challenged so oft. He was, she admitted, a formidable man, a warrior, powerful both in his presence and his strength. It cost her greatly to admit it, but she feared his anger. She had no one to protect her, she realized with a pang, naught but her wits.

Nay, Ian was not a man to trifle with, for indeed, she might well pay the price for her recklessness. Though she liked it not—though she willed it not— her very life was in his hands.

Her mind raced on. Why, the wretch might well

choose to beat her for her insolence! She hated his power over her, yet she sensed he was not a man of idle threats. If she would defy him, she must be prepared to pay the price. And so, she thought bitterly, she must learn to guard her temper . . . and her tongue.

You are wrong, whispered a voice in her mind. *He would never deign to harm you. Indeed, you forget that he defended you against your father.*

Unbidden, Sabrina's fingers crept to the bruise on her cheek. Once again, she felt the whisper of his touch there.

Does this hurt you? he'd asked.

Sabrina released a long, slow breath. His tone had held no malice, his eyes naught but concern. Mayhap she should not have turned from him so, for her behavior had angered him. But she did not want his tenderness, his gentleness, not when he had stripped from her all she ever wanted.

His voice tolled anew through her mind.*Virgins are such trouble, you see. They know not how to kiss. They know not how to touch. Where to touch . . . and when.*

A pondering frown lined the smoothness of her forehead. She lay back down, drawing the blanket up over her shoulders. What had he meant by that? Could it be there was more to lovemaking than she had thought? She had a rudimentary knowledge of the act, given her by Margaret many years ago.

The thought was unsettling—much as *he* was unsettling. Her gaze drifted toward the flap of the tent.

However it had been achieved, she had what she wanted. Her new husband was not in her bed, nor was he likely to be in the future. She wanted none of him. He wanted none of her. She should have been well pleased. . . .

A nearby howl from without nearly sent her scrambling for the entrance. It was only with the most stringent of efforts that she restrained herself. Her gaze darted to and fro. Firelight danced eerily behind the wall of the tent; were it not for its meager light, she might have indeed fled.

In time, she slept. But her sleep was fitful, and she woke in the morning as cross as her husband.

His greeting was spare and cool. "I suggest you hurry, Sabrina. I'm anxious to be off."

Sabrina hurried through her morning ablutions. She would have liked to dally—ah, if only she dared!

The next two days passed much as the first. Ian was determined to make up the distance they'd lost the day they wed, so he set a grueling pace. There was little speech between any of them. Ian was distantly aloof with her. By noonday, Sabrina's back began to ache. Her bottom grew sore, for she was unused to so many hours in the saddle. Early in the evening, they stopped to water the horses.

Sabrina slid from the saddle with Alasdair's assistance. Her legs protested their burden. Hot needles sliced through her calves. Alasdair caught her when it seemed her legs would give way.

Sabrina smiled up at him. "Thank you, cousin."

Alasdair smiled down at her. Unlike Ian's, his eyes were kind and filled with warmth.

"I'm weary of sitting," she said lightly. "Will you walk with me, Alasdair?"

He offered his arm. "If it pleases you, certainly."

She placed her fingertips upon the sleeve of his shirt. As they began to stroll along the edge of the stream, Sabrina could feel Ian's gaze boring into her back, but she paid no heed. She straightened her spine and ignored him as he'd been wont to do to her throughout these past days.

They rounded a bend in the stream. Here the waters flowed bright and inviting. As they stopped, Sabrina glanced at Alasdair. He was eyeing her with a mixture of reserve and something else, something she could not identify.

She tipped her head to the side. "What is it, Alasdair? Is there something you would ask of me?"

He hesitated. "Pray forgive me if I intrude, but I merely wondered ... is all well between you and Ian?"

So he'd noticed the coldness that simmered between herself and Ian. She gave what she hoped was a nonchalant shrug. "Considering the circumstances of our marriage, as well as can be expected, I suppose."

Alasdair touched her shoulder. "If there is aught I can do—"

Sabrina shook her head. "It's too late for that," she found herself confiding. "It's just that ... that Margaret would have made a far better wife to Ian than I. She readily accepted the marriage and—" It was her turn to hesitate, for what could she say?

"And you have not," he finished for her.

Sabrina sighed. Before she knew it, it was tumbling out. "I-I was pledged to another," she admitted. "My father did not know of it—he would not have approved. And so he—"

"He made you wed Ian."

She nodded. All at once she felt perilously near tears.

Alasdair squeezed her shoulder. "I know Ian as no one else knows him. He can be harsh, I know. His father's death changed him, I fear. But do not despair. Oh, I know this will be of little comfort, but sometimes we must make our own opportunity. Give it time, Sabrina. Give it time."

Sabrina's throat was clogged tight. Alasdair was so kind, so sweet. Her heart ached. If she had to marry a man other than Jamie, why couldn't it have been someone like Alasdair?

"You are right," she said, dashing away a tear. "But I am not meek and biddable. And I fear that is the kind of wife Ian wishes. That is why Margaret was so much better suited to him than I."

The makings of a smile had begun to appear, but all at once Alasdair frowned. "Perhaps you are wrong, Sabrina. Mayhap this means nothing, but . . . I once saw Ian and Margaret quarreling."

Sabrina's slender brows shot up. "Truly? What were they arguing about?"

"I could not say. I did not wish to eavesdrop, so I quickly retreated, to leave them in private."

Her spine prickled, as if in warning. "How odd," Sabrina murmured. "I don't recall the two of them ever having a disagreement, even when we were children."

Alasdair looked uncomfortable. "I should have sworn they were arguing, for their voices were raised. But . . . mayhap I was mistaken."

Was he? A sudden, startling chill ran the length of her. All at once she recalled the first kiss they had shared. 'Twas the very next day Margaret was discovered missing . . . God's wounds! Had Ian murdered Margaret in order to marry her?

She dismissed the notion almost the instant it crossed her mind. She was not beautiful like Margaret. Why, the very idea was preposterous!

Just then there was the crunch of stones beneath booted feet. Sabrina raised her head in time to see Ian striding toward them.

"There you are," he said to his cousin. "I thought you might ride ahead and find a place to stay for the night."

Alasdair inclined his head. "Certainly."

Sabrina had gone very still. Her gaze followed Alasdair's departure until he disappeared from sight. Sabrina gathered her skirts in her hands. "If you will excuse me—"

Deliberately he barred her way. "Nay, wife, I will not."

His mockery kindled a ready indignation. But he stood so close she had to crane her neck to see him. "And *why* not?"

"Because I wish to avail myself of your company."

To torment me, more like! The retort stung the tip of her tongue. She had to bite it back.

His gaze had yet to leave her. "You and Alasdair seem to have much in common." His tone was ever so pleasant.

His expression was not.

She ran her tongue over her lips, all at once nervous without quite knowing why. "I am fond of him," she said slowly.

"So I see." His eyes glinted. "Alasdair has a way with the fairer sex. I pray—for both your sakes—he does not trespass where he should not."

Sabrina mocked him openly. "First you warn me

against Jamie. Now Alasdair. What, milord! Could it be you are jealous?"

"You are mine, Sabrina. Your loyalty belongs to me. I'll have it no other way. It will *be* no other way."

"And I am to obey?"

"Aye. I am your husband and you will obey me."

His arrogance knew no bounds. "And of course I have no say in this."

It was his turn to mock her. "Ah, but I forget. You've a mind of your own, don't you, wife?"

Sabrina jerked when his hands suddenly descended on her shoulders.

His laughter grated. "Why so skittish? You are like a mare whose master has not yet ridden her."

Sabrina flushed. Was he being deliberately crude? She did not know.

"I know of but one solution," he went on. "We must begin anew the task of getting to know one another. Now then. Stay with me while I bathe."

It was not a request. It was an order. He released her, only to tug his shirt over his head.

Sabrina gaped. In but an instant he'd turned and shed the rest of his clothing. Was the man mad? She stared at spare, round buttocks as he walked calmly into the stream. When he was halfway across, he turned to face her. Sabrina had already sat down hard upon the bank.

He called to her. "Will you join me, wife?"

Wordlessly she shook her head, unable to do more. The sight of him stole her voice—her very breath. Her stomach quivered oddly.

His chest and belly were matted with dark, curling hair. She stared helplessly where the water lapped at the downward crease of his hips. His back had been to her as he walked away; she had caught nary a glimpse of the part of him that proclaimed his manliness . . . and, oh, but she was surely as wicked as Papa had always claimed . . . her curiosity was such that she wished she had. . . .

Her arms were braced on upraised knees. She licked her lips. Her gaze strayed, only to return. The compulsion to look at him was overwhelming. It was as if some unseen power had caught her in its grasp. His body was a thing of beauty, leanly sculpted with muscle, all raw power and grace.

He turned and cut cleanly through the water in a shallow dive. When he surfaced, he began to swim parallel to the shore. The ripple of muscle in his chest and arms declared his virility with a potency she could not deny.

There was a sudden, swift movement beside her. Sabrina glanced sharply to her right.

Four bearded men stood before her, their clothing muddied and grimy. The air of menace which clung to them was such that it sent terror winging through her veins.

The tallest of them grinned. "Greetings, my lovely one."

Sabrina bounded to her feet. The men spread out so that they circled her. She tried to dart between them. Pawing hands grabbed at her. A rough hand cupped her breast. She lunged away and whirled, only to confront another.

A twisted leer revealed stained, yellowed teeth.

"Ian!" Her scream rent the air, cut off by a hard arm that threatened to crush her ribs as she was snared like an animal in a trap. Something hit her squarely between the shoulder blades. She fell to her knees, dazed. A shout seemed to come from a long distance away. She raised her head just as Ian emerged from the stream.

But one of the men was waiting. Even as she tried to cry out a warning, he brought a wooden club down upon the back of Ian's head.

Ian crumpled forward without a sound.

Ten

She would have run to him, but a meaty hand grasped the back of her neck and held her where she was. Another seized her hands and bound them tightly with a cord of leather. He left a length hanging free. With this he dragged her to her feet.

"A beauty, is she not?" This came from a burly redhead.

"Oh, aye. A man would kill for one such as her, eh?" This came from one who was thin as a sapling in winter, his beard straggly. There was a burst of harsh laughter as their eyes cut to Ian. Sabrina nearly cried out, for she could see a trickle of blood oozing down his temple. Mother of Christ, was he dead?

The men were English, from the sound of it—and reivers, from the look of them. Sabrina's eyes swept frantically all around, searching for Alasdair. But alas, there was no sign of him.

"You are a long way from the border lands," she said clearly. "Go back where you came from and leave us alone!"

"Ah, but we've developed a taste for fair Scottish maidens," chimed the fourth man. He stepped before her and clamped her face between his hands. Hot, wet lips came down on hers.

Sabrina nearly gagged. He smelled of unwashed flesh. His breath was as foul as rancid meat. She tried to wrench away, but he held her firmly. His tongue thrust between her lips. Sabrina reacted instinctively, biting down hard on the offending invader.

A yowl of pain erupted. The man's face contorted into a mask of rage. He drew back his fist to strike her.

"Nay, Henry!" The order came from the tall blond with long, matted hair, the one who had tied her hands.

The man named Henry scowled, but he dropped his fist. "But, Edward, the wench needs a lesson in manners!" He touched a finger to his mouth. It came away bloodstained.

"Yes, but you'll not be the one giving it. I've another purpose in mind for her."

Sabrina's blood ran cold. What purpose? What did he mean?

He gestured to the stout, burly one. "Roland, search their things. They may have jewels hidden."

"Aye, Edward." The burly man scurried to obey.

They tugged her back to the place where Ian had tethered the horses. Roland rummaged through the pouches slung along the animals' flanks. "'Tis mostly woman's clothing," he said disgustedly. "There's nothing of value here except the woman. And the horses."

"And we shall have all."

Sabrina took a deep breath. "Let me go," she said coldly. "Else I promise, you will pay the price."

Edward sneered. "And who will save you? Your noble swain there? He's dead!"

"Nay!" She cried out in heartfelt fervor. "He still lives."

"Was he your husband?"

"Aye! And he—he will hunt you down!"

"I think not, lady."

"He will," she cried. "He wields his sword with the greatest of skill, for he is the mightiest warrior in all Scotland! And he will have your heads for this!"

The four of them laughed uproariously. Sabrina glared her ire. "You bastards," she said feelingly. "You are the scum of the earth, the veriest rodents—"

Edward twined his fingers in her hair and jerked her face to his. "Cease!" he commanded.

Sabrina spit in his face.

For one terrifying instant, she feared it would be her last. His lips drew back over his teeth. Sabrina quaked inwardly, but she was determined not to show it.

Hot breath struck her like a blow. "Your fairness saves you," he hissed through his teeth. "Were it not for that, I would see that you joined your lover there." He stepped back. "Find me something to gag her with," he said tersely. "Then let us be off."

Almost before she could draw breath, a filthy cloth was stuffed into her mouth. She was heaved up onto the saddle before him. Wildly she thrashed, desperate to free herself in whatever way she could. She grabbed his leg and succeeded in nearly unseating him. He swore and stopped the horse. Leaping down, he seized her arm in a bruising grip that nearly wrenched her arm from its socket. Earth and sky spun crazily as he dragged her down.

She was stunned when he loosened the bonds at her wrists, but it was only to jerk them behind her. The cord was wound around her wrists, even tighter than before. She bit back a cry of pain as he gave the cord one last vicious jerk.

She was flung facedown across the saddle this time. How far they traveled, she couldn't say. Each step of the horse drove the air from her lungs so that she could scarcely breathe. When he urged the horse into a gallop, she thought she would surely die.

But her mind was filled with thoughts of Ian—indeed, her only thought was of Ian. She prayed that he yet lived.

Darkness blanketed the land when they stopped. By now it was clear that Edward was their leader. He dragged her from the horse, then rubbed a length of hair between his fingers. Sabrina jerked her head away. She cared not that her glare revealed her every thought. He grinned.

"Ah, a bit more compliant now, eh, wench?"

The others had gathered round. "We can sell the horses," the red-haired one said. "But what about her?"

The thin one clapped a hand to his groin. He undulated wildly. "I've a yearning to poke deep into a Scots honey pot," he said crudely. "A throw of the dice and we'll see who 'as her first."

Sabrina paled.

"Nay, I say!" Edward's glare silenced the lot of them. "The Earl of Northumberland will pay handsomely for a wild one such as her. But not if she's been used by the likes of us." His gaze skipped to Roland. "Put her in the cave where we cannot see her," he growled. "She tempts us all too greatly. And bind her feet as well."

"'Tis good as done," Roland said gruffly.

Sabrina tried to fight, but it was no use. She was still dizzy and sick from the ride. Her struggles were pitiable as he wound a length of cord around her ankles. Picking her up, he dragged her into a cave etched deep into a rocky hill. He left her lying on the damp, cold surface.

She eased to a sitting position, but it was difficult with both hands and feet bound. The cord around her wrists cut into her tender skin, but she had gone beyond pain; her hands were numb.

Panic spiraled within her. She sought desperately to quell it. Her heart began to pound with thick, dull strokes. She strained to see into the darkness, but it was all-encompassing. The interior was black as soot, cold and dank. Her scream was trapped in her throat. She longed to run headlong from the cave. She stumbled upright, that very intention high in her mind, but it was no use. Her feet were bound so that she couldn't walk. She lost her balance and fell heavily, bruising her shoulder.

Hot, burning tears scalded her cheeks. Her shoulders shook with silent sobs. The darkness threatened to smother her, swallow her up in an endless void. She could not think. She could not breathe. Her breath came unevenly, first slow, then fast. Fear clutched her insides. She lost all sense of time and place. It was as if she'd been hurtled back to the time when Papa had locked her away deep in the bowels of the keep.

"You thought I would never know, didn't you? You were to spend the morning on your knees in the kirk, in silence and prayer. Yet where were you? In the stable!"

"Papa," she cried. *"Papa, I beg of you—"*

"'Twill do you no good to beg! Mayhap now you'll obey, lassie!"

"Papa, please. I am sorry, truly I am. I shall do as I'm told, I promise."

"Bah! You are wicked, child. Wicked as sin. You must be punished ..."

The door slammed shut, leaving her in the dark. She sank to the floor. It was Ian who had told him. Ian who had promised he would not ... Oh, she would hate him forever. ...

It was a sound that drew her back to reality. She knew instinctively that a long time had passed. Her eyes snapped open. She shivered and shivered. Even her fingertips were cold. Her mouth was bone-dry from the gag. She fought spiraling fear anew, for the cave was still as black as ever. In time, she told herself, morning would come. She had only to wait. But then *they* would come, the English reivers—an enemy, just as the darkness was her enemy.

Nay. *Nay!* She told herself staunchly that she must remain calm. She would find a way to escape her captors, even if Ian was dead. ...

Ian. Her heart squeezed. A jagged sob caught in her chest. However much she resented this marriage, she did not wish him dead. ...

Shouts drifted on the still night air. The hair on the back of her neck prickled. Something was different. ... A wavering light appeared to her left. She heard shuffling footsteps. A hulking shadow hovered over her. Sabrina blinked, for the light hurt her eyes.

It was Roland. He pulled her up. Sabrina scrambled back as she saw that he wielded a dagger. But he only used it to slice through the cord around her ankles.

"Come," he ordered. "Edward wants you."

She winced as she got to her feet. Pain like shards of steel shot up her legs. Sabrina was half-pushed, half-dragged from the cave. Roland shoved her toward Edward.

A small fire burned, casting its meager light in a small circle. The thin man stood several paces distant from Edward. The fourth was nowhere in sight. The thin man swayed, and it was then the overpowering stench of ale reached her nostrils.

A tall form stepped from the shadows.

It was Ian.

Her heart pounded, this time in sheer relief. Her cry of joy was muffled by the gag.

Above her, Edward spoke. "You are prepared to pay well for the return of your horses. What about the woman?"

Ian spared her nary a glance. "I want the horses, not the woman. Indeed, I'll count myself well rid of her."

Sabrina's eyes flew wide with shock. Clearly Edward was stunned.

"But . . . she said she was your wife."

"And so she is. But I've decided I've no use for a wife."

"Then you've no objection if we sell her to the highest bidder?"

"None at all."

Sabrina made a choked sound of outrage. Edward glanced at her . . .

A mistake that cost him his life.

The light from the fire caught the glint of shiny metal; the next instant found Ian's dagger buried deep in his throat.

The thin man screamed a name. "Bedford!"

"If Bedford is the one who watched over the horses, he'll not be along." Ian's tone was mild. "His dagger lies deep in his breast."

The thin man turned and fled into the darkness.

With a bellow of rage, Roland lumbered toward Ian. Ian sidestepped him easily and seized his head from behind. There was a twist of his hands and then a sickening crack.

Roland slumped to the ground without a sound. His head lay bent at an odd angle from his body.

It was over in a matter of seconds. Sabrina's eyes were huge. The swift efficiency with which he'd dispatched her captors stunned her. She felt a tremor of part admiration, part fear that she had married such a man.

Striding toward her, he tugged the gag from her mouth. Sabrina struggled for speech. "You—you killed them," she managed at last.

"Aye." There was a glint in his eye. "I do, after all, wield my sword with the greatest of skill. For am I not the mightiest warrior in all of Scotland?"

"You—you heard," she gasped. "You . . . you were awake!"

His smile was totally unrepentant. And indeed, Ian was enjoying the moment. His chest swelled with a manly pride. He had saved her and surely she would be obliged to show her gratitude. But her response was not what he'd expected.

Her eyes glowed with a burning hatred. "Why didn't you come sooner? May the devil take you! You could have stopped them . . . They put me in the cave, Ian. They put me in the dark!"

Ian was stunned into silence. Her eyes were wild,

her tone high-pitched and hysterical. She tore into him then, pounding his chest, cursing him, her fists flailing madly.

"Sabrina!" He tried to subdue her, but she possessed a strength borne of fury and something else— something he did not yet comprehend.

"*Sabrina!*" His regard sharpened. A chill prickled the length of his spine.

She gave no sign that she heard, but continued to fight him with all her strength. Ian had no desire to hurt her, but he had no choice. He closed his arms around her and forced her to the ground, pinning her beneath him with the weight of his body. She cried out and twisted beneath him, until at last she had no strength left with which to fight him.

"Sabrina," he said softly.

Her eyes opened, wide and dark with pain. A finger beneath her chin dictated that she look at him. Only then did he glimpse the tear stains on her cheeks.

He spoke quietly, willing her to listen. "Aye," he said again. "I heard you, Sabrina, but I was dazed by the blow. They took our horses. I had to follow on foot. There were four of them and but one of me. The one called Edward . . . I heard what he said and I knew you would not be harmed. So I waited until the one who guarded the horses slept. The other three were in their cups. Had I attempted to rescue you earlier, I might well have been slain. That is why I waited." He paused. "Do you understand?"

She nodded, her lower lip tremulous. Then all at once her face crumpled.

Her fingers twisted into his shirt. "But they put me in the dark," she whispered again. "They put me in the dark!"

The dry sob she gave cut his insides like a knife. She did not weep—indeed, Ian decided grimly, he almost wished she would. Instead she turned her face into his neck and shuddered. Ian gathered her close and rose with sudden decisiveness. He knew that to remain any longer would only prolong her fear.

Within seconds he rode off, his wife cradled in his arms, her mare tethered to his stallion.

The moon had just begun its descent in the sky when he spotted the blaze of a fire just ahead. He rode further and saw Alasdair's gray stallion. He gave thanks to God above that his cousin had chosen to make camp here, rather than riding further to the north and west. Sabrina was limp in his arms, yet some unknown sense told him she had not slept.

Ian reined to a halt. Alasdair rose from his place near the fire. A grin dallied about his mouth as he strode to meet him. "God above, man," he called. "What kept the two of you—or need I ask?"

Ian grimaced. "English reivers. I was struck down shortly after you left. They took Sabrina."

Alasdair's grin faded. His gaze swung sharply to Sabrina. "Sabrina! Are you all right?"

She nodded. "I am fine," she said tonelessly.

Ian swung down and reached for Sabrina. She withdrew the very instant her feet touched the ground. Ian's mouth tightened, but he said nothing. Alasdair had already erected the tent. Ian gestured to it.

"Go along to bed," he suggested. "I'll be along in a moment." His expression rife with quiet contemplation, his gaze did not leave her until she'd disappeared inside the tent.

He turned to Alasdair, who waited tensely. Briefly he told him all that had happened.

Alasdair swore softly. "So one of the ruffians remains at large."

"Aye, but I don't think he'll be back." Ian recalled the way the man had turned tail and run.

"Nonetheless, we'd best not give ourselves away." He turned toward the fire.

Ian stopped him with a word. "Nay, Alasdair. Let it burn."

"But what if he should return? He might bring others—"

"Sabrina is afraid of the dark." He made the explanation curtly. "Let it burn. If the fool returns, we will deal with it."

"As you wish then." Alasdair returned to his bed.

Ian stepped within the tent. Sabrina, he saw, had made no attempt to sleep. She sat huddled with her knees drawn tight to her chest.

Ian lowered himself beside her, close to, but not touching her. Her eyes met his, then quickly shied away. He could see she was embarrassed, but he had to know what prompted her fear of the dark. It was more than just this night, he suspected, much more. Had she disguised it from him apurpose? Perhaps not, for these past nights they had left the fire burn.

His mind quickly spanned the years. "You did not fear the dark as a child," he said aloud.

She made no reply, but merely tightened her arms about her knees.

"I would have an answer, Sabrina."

"I did," she said shortly. "I did fear the dark."

"Nay." He spoke with surety. "I would have remembered."

"Indeed," she stated coolly. "And do you remember the day you left Dunlevy for good to return to the

Highlands? Do you remember the promise you made?"

"I remember that day. You were in the stables, throwing dice. I-I made you kiss Robert." A hint of a smile graced his lips. Then he shook his head. "But I remember no promise—"

"Your memory ill serves you, Ian. 'A promise given is a promise kept,'" she quoted. She looked at him then, a silent accusation simmering in the dark emerald of her eyes. "You said that, Ian. You did!"

Ian had gone very still. "I remember," he recalled slowly. "You were to spend the morn on your knees in the kirk. Instead you were in the stables . . ."

"Aye, and you promised you would not tell my father I was in the stables—that I did not obey. But you told him, Ian. You told him!" The words were fairly flung at him.

"Nay! I did not! By all that is holy, I swear I did not!" Bewildered by her charge, his hands came down on her shoulders. He turned her so that she faced him. She stiffened and would have pulled away, but his grip tightened subtly.

The breath she drew was deep and racking. "He knew," was all she said. "*He knew . . .*"

An awful feeling began to brew in his belly. "He punished you, didn't he?"

She lowered her lids, refusing to look at him. But her lips trembled anew. "Aye," was all she said. "*Aye!*"

Glittering light from the fire outside cast shadows on her pale face. He could still see the telltale streaks of her tears. He cursed himself, even as he demanded the answer he would have.

"What did he do to you, Sabrina? How did your father punish you?"

"He—he dragged me to a tiny chamber deep below the keep." Her lips barely moved as she spoke.

"The gaol?"

She nodded. "It was cold there. There were no windows. No fire. I-I knew not if it was day or night . . ." Her voice began to shake. She stopped, a long pause to lend strength, he suspected.

"How long, Sabrina? How long did he keep you there?"

"Three days," she said with a shudder. "I-I thought he meant to let me die there." She stopped. "Even now I sleep with a fire in the hearth to light my chamber. In summer as well as winter, though all think me daft."

Ian suddenly understood . . . so very much. Her veiled hostility when he'd encountered her again after all these years. She blamed him for this cursed fear of the dark. . . .

"I swear on the grave of my father, I did not tell him, Sabrina." The pitch of his voice was low and fervent. "I did not betray you."

Her eyes closed. She turned her head aside. "It does not matter," she said tonelessly.

Ian released her. She didn't believe him, but there was naught he could do to convince her. He watched as she rolled slowly to her side, presenting him with her back.

Even as his heart went out to her, a rage shook him, a rage as vile as any he'd ever known.

More than ever, he longed to rob Duncan Kincaid of his life . . . as he had robbed his daughter of her innocence.

He stripped, then lay down beside her, an arm cocked behind his head. 'Twas inevitable that his eyes be drawn to his wife. How was he to convince her he'd not betrayed her? Anyone could have carried the truth to her father. One of the lads in the stable. A servant. Yet he knew she would not readily believe him. Faith, but she was stubborn!

Yet he could not deny he admired her spirit. In truth, he'd been furious when she'd entered the kirk for their marriage ceremony, wearing that damnable rag called a gown—like a banner flown proudly into the heat of battle! For the first time he was sorely tempted to laugh. She was bold and brave and . . . and beautiful. And that, too, he knew she would never believe were he to tell her so. She would deny it . . . as she denied him.

Before long, her breathing began to even out. She slept. Ian's mood softened. He prayed the night's ordeal would not haunt her dreams.

But just as he was about to drift off into the netherworld, she began to stir restlessly. She turned on her back. Her breathing hastened. Her head thrashed from side to side. She began to whimper.

Ian reacted without conscious thought. He closed his arms about her form and pulled her against him, pillowing her head on his shoulder. One hand drifted up and down her back in wordless comfort, absently measuring the nip of her waist.

Her eyes opened. He felt the brush of long, dark lashes against his skin. "Ian?" His name was a husky, sleep-warm murmur.

"Here, lass." His voice was a low rumble in his breast. "Go back to sleep." Her hair streamed wildly across his chest, tangled skeins of red and gold. Idly he picked up a silken length and rubbed it between his fingers, marveling at its texture.

She turned into him with a breathy little sigh. Her lashes fluttered shut.

But now Ian lay fully awake. The scent of her was dizzying. He could feel the trickle of her breath on his skin. The soft fullness of her breast pressed into his side, warming him, heating his blood to fire, swelling his rod to an iron pillar. His mind was filled with sensual images and sensations—her legs clasped tight around his buttocks as he lay buried deep and hard within her. Her hair skimming his belly . . . his thighs . . . her mouth soft and open on his skin as she kissed her way down his chest . . . A cold sweat broke out on his brow.

All that stopped him was the sudden trust she yielded, the way she slept in his arms.

But God save his soul, he had to have just a taste . . .

Her mouth was heaven. It clung to his, sweetly yearning. He trailed his fingertips along the neckline of her gown, then strayed within. For the space of a heartbeat, her breast lay warm and pliant in his palm; he teased the tip to quivering erectness. He nearly groaned. His arms convulsed as he fought the need to roll her to her back and let desire rule.

Reluctantly he loosened his embrace. He reminded himself that Alasdair slept just outside. He must wait for the morrow, when Alasdair did not lay near. Aye, tomorrow they would be home, and he could take all the time he wanted. It would but make the moment all the more sweet.

But in the night she turned to him yet again. In the night she yielded all she held back in the cold light of day. . . .

'Twas the longest night he'd ever spent.

Eleven

Sabrina woke alone the next morning, her body stiff and sore from her cramped confinement in the cave. Ian was no longer abed. She could hear his deep voice outside. She'd slept deeply, when she'd not thought to sleep at all. She shivered in remembrance, then sifted slowly through the strand of memories which followed. The sensation of being cocooned in strong, sheltering arms caught the fringes of her mind. . . . Odd, for she could have sworn that firm male lips had dwelt sweet and warm upon hers . . .

She sat up abruptly. Nay. Nay, it wasn't so. *That* she would have remembered.

She rose and stepped outside. The morning was cloudy and damp. A quick glance revealed Ian already saddling the horses. After seeing to her personal needs, she returned to find him waiting for her, ready to depart.

She glanced around curiously. "Where is Alasdair?"

"I sent him on ahead that all might be in readiness for our arrival." There was a small silence. "And also for another reason."

His pause made her uneasy. "What reason?" she murmured.

"My kinsmen expect me to return with Margaret as my bride. This way all will know of Margaret's death—and why I return with you as my bride."

All at once there was a hard knot in the pit of her belly. What would Ian's clansmen think of his new bride? Would they accept her in Margaret's place, or would she be shunned? Besides the fact that she was not the bride they expected, she was a Lowlander, an outsider. Life would be difficult enough without being ostracized. . . . She was suddenly besieged with doubt.

"There is no need to worry," he said quietly.

Too late she realized her distress must have shown. "I am not worried," she denied quickly.

A black brow rose askance, but he made no further comment. Instead he gestured to her mare. "Let us be off."

Sabrina stepped forward so he could help her mount. Her pulse quickened when she laid her hand in his. But all at once he scowled and pushed up the wide sleeve of her gown.

Sabrina glanced down quickly. He was staring at the chafed, red areas where the cords had scraped her tender skin.

She flushed. "'Tis nothing," she said nervously. "I scarcely feel it."

His voice was gruff. "They did naught else to harm you?"

"Nay." To her dismay, there was a slight catch in her voice.

His frown did not ease. His gaze touched on her bruised cheek. "Praise Mary, the bruise is almost gone, else my kinsmen would think I had to beat and bind you before you would wed me."

She very nearly reminded him that while *he* had not, her father had. But something in the tense line of his jaw made her hold her silence. The tender man who had cradled her close might have been naught but a figment of her imagination.

Ian set a hard pace when they departed. Sabrina knew he was anxious to be home. The terrain had begun to change during their second day of travel, when they left the gentle valleys of the Lowlands behind. Craggy mountains reared to the north and west, and they were headed straight into them.

They stopped to rest the horses midmorning. Ian nudged his stallion next to her mare; the animals stood almost chest to chest. He nodded toward the misty peak that loomed just ahead, the summit steeped in clouds.

"Ben Ledi," he said. "Once we are through the pass we are in MacGregor country."

It was a dangerous trail indeed. Sabrina's heart lodged high in her throat as they traversed the narrow mountain pass. Far below, jagged rocks lunged upward, like a giant mouth yawning to reveal gaping teeth. Yet she could not deny there was a kind of stark beauty to the mountains of the Highlands. There lay before her a land of steep valleys, swift and dangerous streams and shimmering, gemlike lochs of sapphire. Yet Sabrina felt a distinct shiver up her spine as they began to descend the valley between the mountains. She felt frail and small here amidst such lonely grandeur.

They pressed on, twisting and turning, rising and plunging with the rhythm of the land. The weather began to turn as well. A row of black clouds began to gather on the horizon. Hours later, Ian reined to a halt. Sabrina sighed and absently pressed a hand to the small of her back to massage away the ache there.

"Sabrina."

The sound of her name drew her attention. Ian lifted a hand and pointed.

"Look there," he murmured.

Sabrina followed the direction of his hand. Rows of cottages crouched next to the roadside, but she paid them no heed. Atop the next ridge a towering castle jutted craggy and harsh, like a huge gray monster lifted from the earth. Square and sprawling, four stone towers loomed in harsh silhouette against the evening sky.

A tremor went through her. "That is Castle MacGregor?"

"Aye." Pride echoed richly in Ian's voice.

She sought to smother her dismay. A heavy weight seemed to gather on her chest. This was no sun-bathed valley like Dunlevy Keep. The castle was dark and imposing . . . much like its master, she thought helplessly.

Ian nudged his mount forward. Sabrina followed.

A wet drizzle began to fall from the leaden sky. A flash of lightning split open the seething mass of clouds. Thunder rolled, an ominous threat.

A tiny little pain stabbed at her. She had but one thought . . .

'Twas indeed a cold, befitting arrival.

But long before they clattered across the draw-bridge, a shout was heard.

"He returns! The MacGregor returns!"

By the time they entered the inner bailey, a crowd

of men had formed a straggly line that soon surrounded them. Sabrina blinked, for surely there must have been a hundred or more. Despite the kilts which bared so much of their legs, a fierce-looking lot they were—soldiers all—of dozens of shapes and sizes, of varying age and rank.

"Is this your bride, Ian?" someone shouted.

All at once he was there beside her, so close their thighs brushed. A lean hand swooped out to capture hers. He raised their joined hands high aloft. "Sabrina," was all he called out. "My bride."

A cheer went up, a cheer so deafening it surely shook the very ground beneath their feet. The next thing she knew, she was plucked from her mare like a hen from its nest . . . by a bearded red-haired giant with shoulders as broad as his sword!

Despite the fact that he looked her up and down brash-as-you-please, he did so with a ready, gap-toothed smile that was somehow engaging. A trifle of her dread departed. She smiled back at him.

"Why, she's just a mite, Ian!"

Ian leaped to the ground with a lightness that betrayed his size. "Ah, but the lass has a bite that would fell even the stoutest of men."

"But not you, eh, Ian?" The giant winked at his chieftain.

"Nay, Fraser. Not I."

What was this? A warning not to cross him? Sabrina's back went straight as a lance. Two pair of eyes collided, one dark green and snapping, the other with a decided glint.

Her smile remained firmly in place. "Indeed," she said airily, "mayhap 'tis time you were aware, husband, that if you thought to marry a lass as spineless as a coward, you should have married elsewhere."

Ian's mouth curled upward, but now there was a slight hardness in his eyes. He clapped a hand on Fraser's shoulder and responded in kind. "You see what I'm about?" he said lightly. "I must be ever on guard, for she wields her tongue with an edge as cutting as a blade."

The giant waggled his brows. "Aye, and as deadly as any man!"

The pair was already striding off. Sabrina silently fumed. What was she to do—entertain his soldiers? As if he'd suddenly remembered her existence, Ian suddenly stopped. He glanced back over his shoulder and said mildly. "Coming, love?"

Love? Sabrina considered placing a well-aimed foot at his behind. Instead she smiled sweetly. "As you wish, my lord."

This time he waited for her to precede him up the wide stone stairway that led into the great hall. Sabrina wondered what he was about. Was he baiting her, kindling her temper? Oh, no doubt he was waiting—hoping!—for her to play the fool before his clansmen in order to show them he was her master!

Well, she would *not* oblige them. She would be gracious and pleasant, no matter the cost.

The great hall was immense. A huge stone fireplace dominated the outer wall. On the far wall a staircase led upward, then disappeared into another wall. Ian had no sooner walked inside than he was surrounded by several men, for it seemed there were urgent matters to attend.

Now that she was on her feet, it struck her how dirty and disheveled she was. She'd not had a bath in several days. She smelled of horse and leather. But now she stood at Ian's elbow, forgotten.

"Ian."

If he heard he gave no sign of it.

She tried hard not to glare. Instead she cleared her throat and tried again.

Still no response.

Straightening her shoulders, she wound her fingers firmly into his shirt and tugged. *"Ian!"*

Three pair of eyes swung to her. The silence that followed was glaring. She hadn't meant to shout; not until then did she realize she had.

But she'd not apologize. She raised her chin and said clearly, "Could someone please show me to my chamber? I should like to unpack. And I'd dearly like a bath."

"Of course." He snapped his fingers. A small, dark-haired maid ran through a tall arched doorway. "This is Mary," he said curtly. "She'll take you abovestairs."

"Good evenin' to ye, mistress." Mary dipped into a shy, awkward curtsey. "If ye'll just come this way . . ."

Sabrina smiled tiredly at the little maid and started after her.

Ian spared her nary a glance. For some reason she could not imagine, Sabrina felt a pinprick of hurt. She told herself staunchly it was simply because she was tired. Besides, she much preferred his indifference to his enmity—even worse, his whole-hearted attention!

The chamber Mary led her to was easily thrice the size of the one she'd occupied at Dunlevy. She gazed longingly at the massive bed across from the window . . . until she noticed the broadsword leaning against the wall next to it.

A prickle of warning went through her. The chamber was Ian's. She knew it with every sense she possessed. Ian did not expect her to share the same chamber—on that she was not mistaken, for he'd made it plain he harbored no desire for her. She turned to tell Mary she'd erred, but two other servants had already followed them in and placed a large wooden bath before the hearth.

She sighed. What did it matter that she bathed here? Ian was busy belowstairs and there was time enough to find her bedchamber later. A quarter hour later, she was leisurely soaking in a warm bath before the fire. Mary was of an age with her, soft-spoken and shy. She reminded her a little of Edna, and the remembrance made Sabrina's throat tighten. A wave of sadness battered her. She would never see Edna again, nor Dunlevy.

Of a certainty she would never see Jamie again. . . .

Rising, she dressed in a clean chemise and light woolen gown Mary had retrieved from her pouch. Mary was brushing her hair dry before the fire when she noticed the girl had started to unpack the rest of her gowns.

Mary noticed the direction of her glance. "Ye needn't worry," the girl said quickly. "I'll have the rest of yer things in the chest there"—with her chin she indicated the chest next to the window—"by the time ye return from supper, my lady."

"Oh, but I won't be sleeping here, so you may as well wait." Sabrina patiently stated the obvious. "I'd hate to put you to more work."

The brush stopped midstroke. Mary gazed at her as if she were daft. "Of course ye will. Where else would ye sleep but with yer husband?"

Sabrina wasn't certain how to explain that not all husbands and wives shared the same bedchamber. She knew her own parents had not, for her father had kept her mother's chamber just as it was the day she'd died. But apparently in Mary's family that wasn't the case. But before she could say a word, there was a knock on the door.

"Supper awaits in the hall, my lady," called a male voice. "My lord asks that you join him."

Her stomach rumbled, reminding her that she was indeed ravenous. Her hands instinctively came up. She began separating the thick tresses in order to braid it.

"Oh, don't bind it, mum," Mary cried softly. "It's lovely just as it is."

Sabrina's hand stilled. She bit her lip and gave a self-conscious laugh. "But Mary—"

"Please, mum. I've never seen hair so thick and glorious in all my days. 'Tis lovely. Truly."

The knock came again, this time more insistently. "My lady?"

Sabrina sighed. "Very well then," she murmured. Mary beamed and rushed to open the door for her. A burly man-at-arms waited to escort her.

In the hall, he pointed to where Ian stood near the hearth, then went on his way. Sabrina paused uncertainly near the foot of the stairs. Ian had his back to her and was busy conversing with one of his men-at-arms.

The scene before her was riotous. Rowdy laughter and voices bounced from the rafters. The hall was jammed with men and women. Sabrina was certain every clansmen from here to the sea had crowded here this night. The scent of roasted meat mingled with the smell of ale.

"You are Sabrina?"

A tall, white-haired man had stopped before her. Though his shoulders were stooped with age and he supported himself with a staff of oak, she had to tilt her head back that she might see his face. His cheeks and brow, she noted, were deeply scored with wrinkles. Eyes like storm clouds swept the length of her—Ian's eyes, she realized.

"Yes"—her tone was slightly breathless—"I am Sabrina."

"I am Uncle Malcolm, brother to Ian's grandfather Fergus." Sunken lips curved into a smile. "Och, but ye are a beauty if ever there was one. Ian is a lucky laddie, to be sure. . . . Welcome to the clan, lass."

Sabrina couldn't help but smile in return. An air of frailty clung to him, yet she could not help but think he must have been a fearsome presence in his youth. "I begin to see where Ian gains his height." She barely reached his shoulder. His burr, she noticed, was thicker than Ian's.

Beneath his plaid, thin shoulders lifted. He gave a wheezing laugh. "Oh, it's in the MacGregor blood, to be sure." Just then a sotted soldier weaved by. He fell, nearly crashing into her. The man managed to rise and stagger off.

Malcolm shook his head. "Ye must forgive us, lass. We are Highlanders, and Highlanders need no excuse to make merry. And now that our chieftain has returned—and with a bride yet . . ." He shook his head. "Now come and join the feast," he invited.

He nodded to the nearest table. Before she knew it, food and drink were placed before her. Malcolm had eased into the seat across from her. "They tell me you are from Dunlevy, eh?"

Sabrina nodded.

"Where Ian fostered," he recalled. A shaggy white brow cocked high. "Then ye must have known Ian when he was a swaggering young lad."

She chuckled. "I did indeed. He used to call me the bonny bratling."

"And she used to call me a Highland prince," said a voice just behind her. "Why is that, do you think, Uncle?"

Sabrina stiffened. Ian proceeded to take the empty place next to her. So he had finally deigned to acknowledge her, had he?

Her earlier vow was forgotten. "I can tell you why, Uncle. Because he possessed the lordly arrogance of a prince"—her barb was swift and smooth—"and still does."

Fraser had seated himself astride the bench next to Malcolm. On hearing her reply, he erupted into laughter. "I do believe this bonny lass has brought you to your knees, Ian! Why, methinks she is just the one to tame the MacGregor!"

Sabrina braved a glance at him. That hard mouth was curved in a smile, but she knew he was piqued.

The night progressed. Ian maintained his place beside her. Sabrina was agonizingly aware of his nearness. His lean thigh stretched beside her own, but little conversation passed between them—not that there was a shortage of well-wishers. Sabrina's head began to spin with names and faces—she prayed she would remember all on the morrow. Many of those, she reflected dryly, would remember little of the night just past.

Unlike his clansmen, Ian ate and drank sparingly, though one of his kinsman boasted how the new chieftain had, at his inauguration, drank a horn of wine to the dregs without falling down.

But her husband was not so unaware of her as she thought.

The fresh, clean scent of her was dizzying. It addled his brain . . . and his senses. He wanted to tangle his fingers in her hair and twist her mouth up to his, claiming its sweetness for his own. All the while he'd tarried here below with his men-at-arms, his mind had been occupied with thoughts of none other. While Kirby gave him an account of the fortnight's events, he'd wanted to say to the devil with duty. He longed to turn, mount the stairs, and crawl into the bath with his bonny bratling. . . .

Would that have shocked his lovely bride? He had his suspicions. And tonight he would know if he was right, by God. If she was indeed a virgin. Tonight . . .

His mouth compressed. He chafed inside, for with him she was as cool and elusive as ever, while beside him she accepted a tender tidbit from a distant cousin. Emboldened, his cousin pulled her up to meet his brother across the hall.

There was scarcely a man in the hall tonight who could tear his eyes from her. With but a look, with naught but a smile, she entranced. She enticed. He scowled, for she touched off a hundred different emotions inside him: jealousy, possessiveness. A brooding darkness slipped over him. He had wed her. Made her his bride. She was his . . .

And his alone.

Music sang out from somewhere. With burning eyes he watched as Fraser pulled her into his arms.

She danced a lilting tune with him, then another . . . Her gown swept high, displaying a flash of shapely leg, a provocative flare of the hips.

The bench scraped loudly against the stone floor. He was across the hall without being aware he'd moved.

Still laughing, she bowed low, then gracefully rose upright. When her gaze tangled with his, her smile slipped away. Her eyes flooded with dismay.

Ian took ice-cold fingers within his grasp. She tried to tug free. He wouldn't allow it. Instead he tucked her hand into the crook of his elbow.

Unaware of the tension between them, Fraser grinned at them both. "You'd best take care of her, man—else I will."

"Aye," said another. "A wife with both beauty and vigor. You must value her greatly!"

"Oh, he values his horses far more than I." Though her tone was light, he could feel her straining not to touch him. "I heard it from his lips. Is that not so, husband?"

"What is this?" Fraser was aghast. "Surely you jest!"

"Nay," said Sabrina. "On our journey here, I was captured by English reivers. Aye, Ian came after me, but he was prepared to pay well for the return of his horses. Indeed, he said he would be well rid of me. 'Tis obvious he meant to let them have me."

So she would embarrass him, would she? He slipped an arm around her waist and brought her close against his side. She would learn not to spar with him.

"Ah, but there was never a chance of that, love. After all, I've yet to claim my husbandly rights."

The gasp she emitted was gratifying.

"Aye," he went on. "Our journey here took four nights and days. Since Alasdair slept little more than an arm's length away . . ." He let the sentence trail off. "So you see, we've yet to spend the night alone."

There was a shout of ribald laughter. "Ye'll never get a wee bairn that way!"

"Fer shame with ye, man!"

"Begone with ye then, or ye're no' the man we thought ye were!"

Ian bore the good-natured ribbing. He glanced at his bride. Her cheeks flared crimson. "Aye," he said with slow deliberation. "'Tis a situation I must remedy . . . and what better time than now?"

With that he swept her from her feet and high into his arms. She did not struggle until he began to ascend the steps and the hall was behind them. When she did, his hold merely tightened.

"Be still!" he hissed.

She went rigid in his arms. Ian's steps carried him swiftly to his chamber. He breached the entrance and closed the door with the heel of his boot.

Slowly he lowered her, sliding her down his body that she might feel his power and strength. The instant her feet touched the floor she backed away.

The tapers in the wall sconces flickered over her form. Her beauty struck him like a blow to the middle. He could hear the sound of her breathing, quick and ragged.

"This—this has gone far enough, Ian." There was a ragged tremor in her voice. "You—you challenged me and I admit, I spoke rashly—"

He shook his head, amused by her bravado, though

it was hardly convincing. "'Tis not your apology I want, Sabrina."

She gave a tiny shake of her head, her eyes both accusing and pleading. "What then, Ian. *What?*"

His gaze roamed her body, lingering on the curve of her breasts beneath soft crimson wool, the narrow span of her hips before returning to her face.

"You," he said softly. "I want you."

She went pale. "What do you mean?" she whispered.

His regard never wavered. "It means you are right where I want you. In my castle. In my chamber. And soon"—a hint of a smile curled his lips—"soon you'll be in my bed."

Twelve

Even while Sabrina was furious that he had announced to all that he would bed her, an icy shock ripped through her. Her head swam dizzily. This could not be happening. It could not . . .

She squeezed her eyes shut and prayed that this was but a dream—a dream from which she might awaken. But alas, when her eyes opened, he was still there, tall and powerful, the width of his shoulders obliterating her view of the door.

She spoke wildly, the first thing that came into her head. "You said you—you did not want me in that way."

"Nay. I said there were others as fair as you." He advanced a step.

She retreated. "And far more willing," she recalled. "So why do you not go find one?"

His eyes seemed to sear her very soul. "I think not. You swore before God to be my wife. You cannot hold me at bay, Sabrina. You cannot hold the night at bay. Very soon," he promised, "there will be nothing between us, not even these words which you parry so long and so well. I'll claim what is mine . . . and I'll claim it now."

"What!" she cried. "Will you gag me like the English reivers did?"

"Nay," he said, his tone almost lazy, "for I can think of another way to silence your lips—a much more pleasurable way"—his gaze fell to her mouth—"for both of us."

Icy fingers of dread crawled up her spine. He was set on this course—set on her!

Desperation filled her breast. "You forget, Ian, you married me only to ally our families. And you would bed me only to—to spite me! To crush my pride, to assert your will over mine!"

He smiled as if he knew her veriest thought . . . her every fear—a smile as black as his heart!

"Ah, now you're the one who forgets, lass—for I meant what I said. You see, I do want it. I want *you*," he said again.

But all at once his voice was harsh. "Now will you come to me willingly, as you said you would the night we wed? Or will you challenge my manhood anew and taunt me with your lover Jamie? Or will you fight me like a vixen and a shrew? 'Tis up to you, Sabrina. But know this. No matter your choice, the outcome will remain the same."

Sabrina's gaze fell upon his hands. They rested now upon his hips, lean and dark and powerful. She pictured those hands against her flesh, binding her to his will. . . .

She swallowed. Her limbs trembled, as if she were ill from fever.

Slowly he circled her. "What is this, lass?" he mused. "Why, I could almost believe you are afraid of me—of this night. Yet I wonder why you should be. Why this strikes me, I cannot say. After all, you're

a woman who is no stranger to a man's possession—
and this from your own lips."

Sabrina looked away. There was that in his tone
which demanded the truth. Oh, but she could almost
believe he knew she'd never lain with Jamie—with
any man. Faith, but he was a devil!

There would be no surcease, Sabrina realized. The
silence ripened, along with her unease.

He stopped before her. The length of two swords
lay between them. He touched her nowhere, yet she
felt him with each and every sense she possessed.

"Well, lass? You've naught to say? Come here,
then."

She went, on shaky legs, praying he would not see
her trembling.

"Come now, lass. You wound me. You make me
feel the most unsightly man in all Scotland."

Both hands were on her shoulders now, disturb-
ingly warm and strong. As he spoke, his gaze roved
over her features, one by one. Sabrina thought hazily
that his expression was oddly hungry. But then his
mouth came down on hers . . .

And then she wasn't thinking at all.

His arms came around her, trapping her fast against
his body. She shuddered, but not with distaste. Aye,
if only it were so!

When at last he raised his head, he was no longer
smiling.

"Undress me, lass." The order came low and tight.

Her eyes flew to his face. "Ian!" His name broke
from her lips, an urgent plea. "I pray you . . . I—I cannot!"

For one mind-splintering moment, she was certain
he would make her. Something blazed across his face,

something she did not fully understand. Then abruptly, a black brow climbed high.

"Very well, then. As before, if you do not do it, I will."

Unbeknownst to her, she clenched her hands before her. God save her soul, but she could not look away as he stripped.

He stood before her, all sleek, sculpted muscle sheathed in bronzed, hair-roughened skin. His shoulders gleamed in the candlelight, hard and smooth. Dense, dark curls matted the whole of his chest and abdomen. Her gaze strayed helplessly lower . . .

Her throat constricted. She wanted to look away, but she couldn't.

Before her very eyes, his staff turned to an iron pike.

Unconsciously she gauged and measured . . . Some small, faint sound escaped. She trembled, convinced a night of horror awaited her.

"What is wrong, Sabrina? You are no innocent. You've surely seen a naked man before. Why, you've seen *me* naked—and of your own free will."

Her gaze jerked back to his face. His smile was unpleasantly lazy.

"Aye," she managed, "but you were just a boy!"

"So I was. And I asked once before if you liked what you saw." There was the tiniest pause. "I would ask again now."

It was true. She *had* wanted to see. And deep inside, there was a part of her that had curiously wondered about the changes manhood had wrought . . .

"I see far more than I wish," she blurted.

One lean hand clamped her shoulder. She jumped. His laughter scraped her nerves raw.

"'Tis your turn now, lass."

He moved so that he stood directly before her, so close she could feel the heat of his body. Cool gray eyes captured hers. Before she knew what he was about, he'd swept her gown from her shoulders. It puddled around her feet. Her chemise followed suit. All too soon she was as naked as he.

The backs of his knuckles trailed across the taut plane of her belly. He smiled.

Sabrina blanched. His gaze was boldly irreverent—it left no part of her untouched. Why, he even gazed at the red-gold fleece between her thighs. Her arms lifted, that she might shield herself.

"Nay, Sabrina." His hands shot out, shackling her wrists to her sides. "There's none to see but mine eyes."

Shame scalded her cheeks. Oh, but he mocked most cruelly. "The very eyes I seek to avoid!" she cried.

His expression grew chill. "The eyes of your husband, I would remind you."

"I need no such reminder!" She wanted to run. To hide. But he had yet to release her.

His mouth thinned. His hold on her wrists relaxed though his tone was laced with steel. "There is no shame in standing before me so."

But there was. A world of it. Something broke inside her then. Her only thought was of escape. She wrenched away and lunged madly for the door.

But alas, he was too quick for her. A long arm snaked out and snared her about the waist. The room whirled giddily as she was spun into his binding hold . . . and high into his arms.

The next thing she knew she was lying on the bed, carried down with the weight of his body.

Never had she been so wretched. Her composure was in tatters, her pride sorely bruised. "Stop this game. You toy with me and well you know it!" She pushed against his shoulder but he was immovable as stone.

His eyes were glittering pinpoints of light. "How so?"

She bit back a strangled sound of anguish. "You—you know!" she choked out.

He loomed above her, his shoulders wide and gleaming like oiled oak. "What, Sabrina? What do I know?"

Sabrina was unable to say a word. She lay beneath him, shaking and spent, her emotions clogged fast within her breast.

Ian's eyes were dark as a Scottish sky in winter. "Tell me true, Sabrina, and tell me now. Did you lay with Jamie?"

She flinched from his angry demand. The air was stifling as he beheld her, his lips ominously thin.

Mutely she shook her head. She could do no more.

"You claimed he'd made you his, when in truth you've lain with no man. You are a maid, aren't you, Sabrina?"

She buried her face against his shoulder. "Aye," she cried brokenly. "Aye!"

The arms around her grew tense, so tense it seemed he might snap her in two.

"Look at me, Sabrina."

His rigid tone compelled compliance. Slowly she raised her head. An endless storm brewed in the fire of his eyes. His regard was almost blistering.

"You think I do this to bring you pain? To punish you?"

"Don't you?" The words were wrenched from her, laden thick with the threat of tears unshed. She could feel his anger clear to the bone. Despite his avowal otherwise, she was certain he was bent on vengeance. She had lied to him and now she would pay the price for her deceit.

"Nay, I do not!" His denial was vehement. "Listen to me, Sabrina, and listen well. I am not like your father. I will not punish you. You will come to no harm at my hand. Ever."

Little by little, the rage began to fade from his features. Yet still his words were no less fierce.

"Aye, I wed you against your will. This I know. This I cannot change, nor would I. You will share my castle, and aye, you will share my bed this night and all others. You will someday be the mother of my sons. You are my wife in name, and soon will you be my wife in deed and spirit as well. But I would not bring you unto me with hurt and pain between us— I *will* not."

She knew what he was saying. She could not evade his possession, the duty of the marriage bed.

"Now. Do you understand this?"

She flushed, aware that something had changed in the way he held her. His hold was no longer angry . . .

But filled with possessiveness.

She nodded, unable to tear her gaze from his. Her hands came out to rest on his forearms, as if to keep him apart, though it was not resistance she intended.

She ran her tongue over her lips. "Ian," she said faintly.

"Aye, lass?"

She was quiveringly aware of his body above hers. There was nowhere she could not feel him, the brand of his skin hard and warm against hers.

"The candle," she said faintly. "Snuff the candle."

He shook his head. "Nay, lass."

She swallowed. "Then must we be . . . naked?"

For an instant he gazed into her eyes; she had the oddest feeling he was wondering if he'd heard her aright. An odd little laugh escaped his lips, a husky, male sound. Sabrina was not certain if she should be angry or relieved.

Then suddenly his laughter ceased. His eyes darkened. He drew back that he might gaze the length of her. There was no cold demand in his eyes now, only a scalding heat that made her tremble anew. Her heart surely stopped in that instant, then seemed to thunder wildly in her breast. No man had ever looked at her so, not even Jamie.

A hand rested possessively on the flare of her hip. "You're beautiful, lass," he said quietly.

His words disarmed her. His look made her shiver both inside and out. A hot ache constricted her throat. The breath she drew was deep and uneven. "Nay," she said haltingly. "Nay, I am not—"

His mouth hovered but a breath above her own. "Would you rather I showed you? No. I can see you don't. But I wish to."

His hand slid down her throat. A thumb beneath her chin urged her mouth up to his.

'Twas a kiss like none other. Slow and deep, almost unbearably sweet. The hunger she tasted in his mouth did but kindle a hunger of her own. She felt herself weakening, drawn beneath his spell. She gave a half-hearted sound—nay, not of protest . . .

Of surrender.

Her breath left her lungs in a long sigh. Her arms crept around his neck as she yielded the promise of her innocence. As if he sensed her capitulation, a lean hand slipped to the rounded flesh of her breast. His fingers now joined in the assault on her senses.

With his hand he circled one swelling mound, first with his fingertips, then his palm. Sabrina's pulse began to race. Her nipples began to swell and ache, even before those devil fingers swept across one dusky peak. Sensation ran rampant through her body, startling sensations never before known. Her low moan echoed in the back of his throat.

But that was only the beginning. His mouth slid with slow heat down the tender cord of her neck. He kissed the madly thrumming pulse at the base of her throat. Her heart plunged into a frenzy, for he did not stop there.

For one mind-splintering instant, his dark head was poised above the swelling fullness. She could feel the moist warmth of his breath there, and then his tongue came out to touch the deep rouge disk. She inhaled raggedly, unable to look away. A stab of divine pleasure shot through her. With naught but his tongue he teased her nipples stiffly erect, first one and then the other. And when he began to gently suck one straining dark peak, she thought she would die of sheer ecstasy. Her breath grew shallow and quick.

She nearly cried out when he drew back. But then his mouth was on hers again. Her lips parted, a wordless invitation. With nary a hesitation, he reclaimed the honeyed interior, his tongue a boldly seeking invader.

Lean fingers traced a shattering trail down the staircase of her ribs. The heel of his palm skimmed the hollow of her belly, back and forth, warmly tormenting. In the back of her mind, she was certain the way he touched her was wanton and scandalous. Surely other people did not do such things. . . . A vague protest formed in her mind. Awash in a dark, forbidden pleasure, it never found voice.

He grew ever more daring.

Sabrina was shocked when his fingertips threaded themselves in the curling thatch that guarded her womanhood. She clutched at the hardness of his shoulders and inhaled sharply.

"Rest easy, lass." He soothed her with a husky murmur, trapping her lips beneath his. Even as his tongue swirled far and deep, his fingers uncurled, sliding deep within those silken curls, seeking her secret cleft.

Her entire body jerked. Her eyes flew wide. She tore her mouth free. "Ian—"

He caught her startled gasp with his lips. "Trust me, lass," he said against her mouth . . . into it. "I vow I'll not hurt you."

His hand was between her thighs now. Insistent. Undaunted. Venturing still further. She shuddered. A restless questing simmered within her. Sweet lord, she thought dazedly, what was he doing? A part of her was shocked by the intimacy. Still another decided vaguely that he knew her body far better than she.

The pads of his fingers brushed soft, feminine flesh. A daring lone finger breached pink, silken folds. And then he touched her—a tiny phalange of flesh—rubbing and circling there, intent on a tormenting foray that robbed her of breath and the last vestige of sanity. Her hips surged upward, in search of the delicious torture. She whimpered helplessly.

Then it happened. Something burst within her, centered there in that place where he staked his claim so fully. Wave after wave of scorching fire spread through her. She felt herself flung high aloft to the very heavens, drifting free of earthly bonds.

When at last she floated back to reality, Ian was on his knees before her. With his own he spread her legs wide. Unbidden, her gaze fell to his staff.

To her untutored eyes, he was enormous. Thick and swollen and rigid.

When he began to lower himself over her, her eyes flew wide. She shook her head, stunned and frightened all at once. "Ian . . . how can you . . . how can I . . ." Even as she faltered, she reached out to push at his shoulders.

He mated their fingers in a burning clasp; they were borne to the bed alongside her head. "Hush, lass. 'Twill be all right." His mouth grazed hers, the wispiest caress. He whispered her name, and within that sound was a plea she did not fully understand. Yet his low intensity sent an odd little quiver all through her.

He kissed her mouth, slow and lingeringly. Conscious thought fled from her mind like the wind across the mountains. Sabrina forgot her fear. Her senses abrim, she forgot everything but the feverish need clamoring within her, the need to be filled as never before. The smooth hard tip of his organ separated damp, pink folds . . .

And then he was with her, deep—deep!—inside her, a shearing blade of lightning.

Sabrina cried out, unprepared for the rending pain. Her voice caught on a half sob. "Ian . . . *Ian!*"

He whispered something. She knew not what. His lips brushed her cheeks, the tender curve of her jaw, the throb of her pulse where it beat so strongly at the base of her throat. Though he did not move, she could feel the straining pressure of him full and snug within her.

His mouth returned to hers. "Do I hurt you?"

His lips were but a breath above hers. Already the hurt had begun to fade. "Nay," she said faintly.

He released the clasp of their fingers, only to snare her hips in his hands. He withdrew slowly, making her catch her breath. Naught but the head of his rod remained within her. She couldn't tear her gaze from his face. His features were rigid and tense, his eyes were burning like silver torches.

Again his swollen shaft pierced deep within her, achingly slow. Sabrina clutched at his shoulders, certain she would be torn asunder. But this time there was no pain. Her body gave unto his, her tender flesh yielding all that he sought . . . and more.

Her eyes half-closed. In the pit of her belly, a heated warmth unfurled. With every heartbeat, flames raced higher and higher along her veins. Her breath grew quick and shallow. She shuddered and raised her hips at the very instant he plunged down. . . .

Their bodies met, again and again. The tempo of his thrusts quickened, until she was certain he touched her very womb. His breath rushed by her ear, harsh and scraping. She sensed him losing control, but she no longer cared, for suddenly she was caught up in the same wild frenzy.

Only moments earlier she'd have deemed it nigh impossible . . . but suddenly she was spinning high aloft, flung into a realm of white-hot release. Dimly she heard herself cry out. She felt both terrified and amazed, for she'd never dreamed she might find such glorious ecstasy in his arms. Above her he gave one last shattering lunge. A shudder shook his body. His scalding release bathed the very gates of her womb with heat and fire.

Slowly she felt the tension seep from his muscles. A wispy caress dwelt upon her cheeks, brushing away the tangle of hair there.

"Are you all right, lass?"

Sabrina could not speak. She could not fault his lovemaking; he'd been a patient, tender teacher.

You will someday be the mother of my sons.

She went utterly still inside. God's wounds, it was unthinkable that she would someday bear his babe. Why, he might even now have planted his seed within her.

She could not help it. Despair crept around her heart, a halo of darkness. She despised herself, the weakness of her flesh. In truth, she had not thought it would come to this—she'd foolishly not allowed herself to believe it. She had taunted Ian that when he took her, 'twould be Jamie in her mind . . . in her heart. But alas, she could scarcely summon his visage in her mind's eye.

He was right. The babe she would someday carry would be Ian's, she acknowledged with bitter bleakness, not Jamie's. She had betrayed Jamie. She had *betrayed* him. And she'd promised she would wait . . .

She should have fought. Protested. Pleaded for mercy, if need be. Yet what would such have done? a silent voice reminded. He'd vowed the outcome would be the same.

'Twas just as he'd said. She was his in name and in deed. But not in spirit—never in spirit . . .

"Sabrina?"

A questioning note lurked in Ian's voice. He raised himself on his elbows.

"Don't!" she cried. "Don't look at me!" She turned

her face aside and shoved at his shoulders, desperate to rid herself of his presence.

He rolled to his side, obliging her. But there was no escaping him. Catching her chin between thumb and forefinger, he forced her eyes to his.

With his thumb, he swiped the moisture from her cheek. "What is this?" he demanded. "Tears? Did I hurt you?"

She swallowed. "Nay," she whispered, for she could not lie.

His expression was black as a sky that foretold an eastern gale—aye, and his eyes were just as ominously forbidding. "Then why these tears?"

Her lips were tremulous. "You do not understand," she said haltingly. "It should have been Jamie. It should have been Jamie—"

"Stop!" he commanded. "By God, I wooed you with far more care than many a man! And you repay me by daring to speak of another with your woman's flesh still wet from my seed! Well, I will not allow it, Sabrina. I will not!"

He leaped from the bed, careless of his nakedness. "You may spend the night alone, Sabrina, alone with your dreams . . . alone in the darkness." His lip curled. "Indeed, that is the way you prefer it, is it not?"

Stunned, Sabrina watched as he snatched his clothing from the floor. She pushed herself upright, scrambling for the sheet to cover her nudity.

"Ian . . . Ian, wait!"

But he did not wait. He *would* not wait.

An instant later the door slammed with such force the walls seemed to shake.

Sabrina collapsed in a flood of bitter tears.

Thirteen

Ian dragged his plaid around his shoulders and shifted to his back. But as he did so, a bristly wad of hay pricked his backside; an unsavory, pungent aroma drifted to his nostrils. Faith, but there would be no sleep for him at all this night! With a grimace, he heaved to his side. His patience was short—along with his temper. Gritting his teeth, he cursed the lovely vixen he'd taken to wife.

This was not, he reflected blackly, how he had envisioned this night. Nay, he'd thought to spend hours tutoring Sabrina in the pleasures of the flesh—and ensuring his own in the bargain. Instead he was here in the stable. No doubt, she was relishing her victory in ousting him from his own bed! Indeed, his only salvation was that no one had seen him depart—there were none to witness the insult to his manhood—and aye, his pride.

Finally, with a sigh he sat up. Broodingly he stared into the darkness. The night air grew cool around him, and before long his anger cooled as well; in its place was a hurt he could not deny.

He felt . . . betrayed. He had wooed his beauteous bride, taken a tender care with her he'd never shown

183

another. And aye, he'd felt her lips tremble beneath his, her body arch into his in sweet surrender. Yet in the end it was Jamie she thought of . . . Jamie she longed for . . . Jamie, blast his hide! . . . and not him.

It was inevitable that his gaze turned toward the keep, toward his chamber. He was tempted, and mightily so, to return to Sabrina. To show her that while her lips might speak of another, her body craved his with a passion that matched his own. Resolve crystallized inside him.

"Ah, Sabrina," he murmured aloud. "You think you are well rid of me, but I promise you, lass, you are not. Savor your victory, my love. For now, I will allow you your distance. But 'tis the last night I will spend here, the *only* night. . . ."

On that note, he finally slept.

A watery trickle of light seeping through the shutters woke Sabrina just after dawn. She'd spent a goodly part of the night tossing and turning. She'd slept little, for she'd never felt so alone! 'Twas most odd, for only now did she realize these past nights whilst Ian slept near, she'd not been so mindful of the shadows that lurked just beyond reach.

And now . . . now though she strived to stow the memory away, she relived the evening's play anew. The feel of his hand running wild over her body, his mouth on her nipples, which even now seemed to swell and tingle. The feathery rush of whispered words on her cheek . . .

Most of all she recalled with scorching remembrance the way his swollen shaft had stretched her woman's flesh, the stunning pressure of him seated to the hilt within her. Drawing her knees to her chest,

she buried her face in the pillow, flooded with a scalding rush of shame.

There was a timid knock upon the door. It opened,
and Mary peeped inside.

"Would ye like a bath, mum?"

Sabrina raised her head, pushing the tumbled
skeins of hair from her face. She was tempted to answer nay and ask the girl to leave her be. But she
could not hide away here in her bedchamber, for such
was not her way.

And she'd not give her new husband the satisfaction!

She smiled at the girl. "Thank you, Mary. I'd like
that very much."

The bath was soon ready and waiting. She dismissed Mary, saying she needed no assistance. As she
lowered herself into the steaming waters, she winced
a little, for she was tender there between her thighs.

The feel of him was still strong about her person.
Sabrina scrubbed furiously to rid herself of his scent,
as if she could rid herself of him! Her mind skipped
ahead to the night to come. Now that he'd made her
his wife in every way, would he do so again? Nay.
Surely not. He'd fulfilled his duty to the marriage bed.

You will share my bed this night and all others.

A voice of stern admonishment resounded in her
brain. He was her husband, the voice chided, and he
had the right to lay with her, no matter how she dis-
liked it.

But you did not dislike it, reminded another.

Her hand stilled. Her throat tightened oddly. He
was right. With silken words he wooed her. With
flaming caresses he swayed her. He had been tender
and slow, and once the pain of his possession had

ebbed, he'd brought her to a wondrous peak of rapture.

She cringed inside. Would Ian mock her with his victory? She despaired the weakness of her flesh, for she'd made it ridiculously easy for him.

The water was cold by the time she arose. 'Twas time to brave the day . . . and her husband as well.

As Sabrina wound her way down the stairs, she did not know what awaited her in the great hall—but it was certainly not what she found.

In the glaring light of day, she saw that cobwebs danced from every corner. A stale odor rose from the rushes strewn about the floor; they were utterly filthy. Several benches had been overturned. A snoring soldier sought sleep there upon the hearth—'twas a wonder his ears had not been singed!

Upon the table the remains of last eve's meal still resided. Even as she watched, a hound leaped upon it and seized a haunch of venison. He sank to his belly, the tidbit between his paws.

Sabrina gaped as a fat little piglet waddled across the floor, grunting and rattling the rushes with his nose. The piglet stopped and did his duty then and there. Her jaw closed with a snap. She vowed the little beastie would be their supper. The stench of ale came to her nostrils . . . and little wonder.

No one greeted her arrival. It seemed the night's celebration had bled through till morn.

Two burly fellows were wrestling on the floor. From the corner came a bray of laughter. Amid shouts of encouragement, they rolled over and over. . . . Directly in their path was a slender figure clad in pale blue wool.

By some miracle they stopped just in time. The pair

stared upward into snapping green eyes. Their jaws slackened. Finally one jammed his elbow into his opponent's ribs.

"Up with ye, man! It's 'er ladyship!"

The pair scrambled to their feet.

Sabrina was secretly appalled. Sternly she looked the pair up and down. "Have you men no duties to attend? None of you?"

The taller of the two wiped a trail of ale from his mouth. "'Twould seem not," he said weakly.

"Then fetch that hound and put him outside. He may share our scraps—but he will not share our table!"

Her gaze shifted to the second man. "You there. What is your name?"

"A-Arthur," he stammered.

"Arthur, fetch that piglet and put him in his pen, and see to it that he and his brothers and sisters remain there. This hall is not a stable."

She glanced around. "Now," she said crisply, "someone tell me where the maids have gone to. This hall needs a thorough cleaning, and I suspect it will not end here."

But before the man could answer, the hall went utterly quiet. The hairs on the back of Sabrina's neck prickled. She knew, even before she finally turned, that Ian stood there.

She felt the stroke of chill gray eyes upon her. Her fingers curled into her palm. When she turned to face him, she longed to sink through the floor to whatever awaited her below. She could read naught from his expression, neither approval nor condemnation. Would he gainsay her authority? she wondered frantically. Would he belittle her before his people?

His gaze flickered away. He addressed himself now to all those who watched their chieftain and his lady.

"I must beg pardon," he called out, "for my wife is a Lowlander and we all know what a peculiar lot they can be. I imagine she'll tolerate no laggards, since I once heard one say that toil is good for the soul. Why, no doubt she'll even make us take baths once a day! But we'll not have war within the household. We can save that for the Campbells, damn their thieving hides!" He glanced around. "You heard her, lads. See to your posts. And be quick about it, now."

Sabrina blinked, unable to believe she'd heard aright. Relief surged within her, for if he had chosen to counter her, she'd never be able to hold her head up again. Well, she would show him that she could be generous as well. She would ignore his needling remark about Lowlanders.

The hall emptied within seconds.

She felt his gaze settle on her. "I trust you do not approve of your new home."

His nearness made her stomach quiver like pudding. "'Tis not that," she said quickly. "'Tis only that it seems very clear this castle has not seen a woman's hand in many a year."

A strange expression flitted across his features. It was gone so quickly she decided it must have been a trick of the light.

"Indeed," she went on, "there is much to be done."

He studied her, his regard so thorough she grew uneasy.

"What? What is it?"

The makings of a smile appeared. "I merely wonder at your sudden penchant for cleanliness. Why, you used to run dirty and barefoot."

"And so did you." Her reply came swift as an arrow.

"So I did, bratling." The word came out sounding very much like an endearment. Sabrina stared, for unless she was mistaken, lazy amusement twinkled in his eyes. What was this? she wondered in amazement. Last night he'd been angry with her; now he regarded her with something akin to—to tender indulgence! Sabrina knew not whether she should be relieved or wary. But before she could question him further, he spoke.

"No matter," he said lightly. "I have the feeling you would ask something of me. So tell me. What is it?"

Gathering her courage, Sabrina pressed on. "I would have your leave to direct the servants. I suspect the entire castle needs a thorough cleaning."

He inclined his head. "'Tis done. I'll see that you are given the keys."

With that he took her arm and assembled the household servants. There he announced to all that she was mistress here; that her commands would be obeyed as surely as his own. The keys were delivered into her hands. The servants scurried away to do her bidding. Sabrina turned to do the same.

A hand on her arm forestalled her.

Ian stood facing her. Something about his expression flung up her guard. Fighting back a wave of anxiety, she lifted her brows.

"Yes?"

"I just wanted you to know"—a smile dallied about his lips—"'tis glad I am to see that the night's pursuits did you no harm. And indeed, I pray that you shall attend all your wifely duties with such... vigor." With that, he released her and turned away.

Sabrina glared her ire. He mocked her. After all he had dared—after all he had done!—he mocked her!

"My lord?" she called after him. Her tone was honeyed.

He half turned, a rakish brow raised high.

She smiled sweetly. "Your stench is most ... . peculiar. Forgive my Lowlander oddities, but"—she wrinkled her delicate nose in disdain—"methinks you need a bath. I pray you will attend to it ... and soon."

To her utter amazement, he winked at her. "Only if you join me, sweet. Only if you join me."

To her horror, Sabrina was speechless. When no rejoinder came his way, he threw back his head and laughed. The arrogant lout, he laughed!

She marched away, yet she could not be angry, for he was not angry. Still, she was determined to put her husband out of her mind. And she succeeded quite well, for indeed, she was so busy she had no time to think of the wretch. Very soon there was not a single pair of idle hands. Sabrina discovered that the servants were not unwilling or lazy. They simply needed someone to direct their efforts, but they were agog when she rolled up her sleeves and joined them in the day's work.

By the end of the day, the laundry shed was overflowing, the tapestries had been taken down from the walls and beaten free of dust. The hall was scrubbed from end to end. Clean rushes were laid on the floor and sprinkled with rosemary.

All in all, Sabrina was pleased with the day's work. Tomorrow she would inspect the kitchen and the castle stores. For now she was exhausted. Ian had ridden out to tend to his business and had not yet returned. She told Mary she was too tired to sup. All she wanted was to go to bed. With luck she would be asleep by the time he was back.

Her leisurely soak eased the ache in her muscles. She had just slipped a long white bedgown over her head when the door creaked open.

It was Ian. In his hands was a tray laden with food and drink.

"You are no doubt tired from all your efforts today," he said smoothly, "and Mary told me you'd not eaten. Am I not a thoughtful husband?"

Sabrina arched a brow. Determined, more like.

"And indeed, since I am anxious to please my wife, I even did as you asked—I bathed while you were busy with your work. My only regret is that you were not here to join me."

Sabrina bit her lip. Oh, but he was a rogue to tease her so!

But now she drew a deep breath. "Does it not bother you that everyone will think that you . . . that we . . ." Her gaze strayed inevitably toward the bed. Her furious blush said all that she could not; and suddenly there was a gleam in Ian's eyes, a gleam that reminded her all too keenly of all that had happened there, in that very bed. . . .

Fragrant aromas wafted in the air. She hadn't been hungry before. Now she was suddenly famished. When Ian slipped the tray onto the table near the fire, she took the chair he offered. Ian declined the food she offered, saying he'd already eaten. But he drank from a goblet of wine, and while the silence that drifted between them was not comfortable, neither was it uncomfortable.

Suddenly some strange mood descended, like a dark cloud dropped from the sky. She was mistress of this huge castle, a role that was to have been Margaret's. Aye, she could run a household. See to it that supplies were laid in for the winter. But she could never replace Margaret, for Margaret would have presided over all with a grace and poise she could never begin to match.

But what of the people of Castle MacGregor? Would they have loved her? Sabrina was all at once reminded . . . though Margaret's air was always that of a lady, her tongue could be caustic indeed.

A vivid memory assailed her. Once, when she was perhaps ten or so, Sabrina had worn a jeweled brooch that had belonged to their mother. On seeing it, Margaret had been livid. She had torn it from Sabrina's shoulder, caring not that she'd ruined Sabrina's gown. Margaret had made her cry. Indeed, Margaret had oft made her cry. . . .

Shame pricked her. What did that matter? Margaret was gone. *Dead.* She would never see her children grow straight and tall. Never feel the golden rays of the sun upon her head . . .

Unknowingly, Sabrina's hands had dropped to her lap. Her gaze had fallen as well. She felt humble and sad and small all at once. But most of all she felt a burning shame at her pettiness.

"What is it, Sabrina? What are you thinking?"

Her lips pressed together. She shook her head. Were even her thoughts not to be her own?

"Tell me, Sabrina. What are you thinking?" Ian's voice jabbed at her, like the point of a dagger.

Slowly she raised her head. "If you must know, I—I was thinking of Margaret."

He sat back, his long fingers toying with the stem of his goblet. "Indeed. Wishing that Margaret were here instead of you? That it was Margaret who lay with me in bed last night?"

Sabrina's eyes blazed. "Aye!" she flared. "For then she would be alive!"

He was silent a moment. "I do not mean to be cruel. But Margaret is gone, Sabrina. And you are very much alive . . . and very much my wife."

"I do not forget." God above, she *could* not forget. "Margaret lies cold in a watery grave, while I lie warm in your bed. Am I not allowed to mourn the loss of my sister?"

"You are. Indeed, 'tis to be expected. But I wonder, Sabrina"—beneath his quiet voice was a note of steel—"do you mourn the loss of your Jamie as well?"

Their eyes locked. "Your words, my lord, not mine."

He swore softly. "You do not fight, yet neither do you yield. I told myself I'd let you be. But then, why should I deny myself what I want? And yet I've no desire to take you unwillingly."

His fingers drummed atop the table. To Sabrina, the sound was like fingernails raking along her spine.

"A wager," he said suddenly. "You were always fond of dice, were you not? Well, I propose a wager. A single throw of the dice by each of us will decide the outcome."

She glanced at him sharply. His smile was dangerous. She liked it not a whit!

"I rolled against you once before—and lost," she reminded him flatly.

"I remember. But I stand just as much chance of losing as you."

This was true, she realized. "And the stakes?"

"That you do not disdain me—nay, not with words.

Not with the touch of your hands, or eyes—that you come to me willingly.''

A voice inside urged caution. She was intrigued despite that. ''What if I win?''

''You spend your nights in solitary comfort.''

But she would be spending her nights alone. In the dark. Uncertainty gnawed at her. And yet . . .

''Will you abide by it?''

His reply was swift and unwavering. ''I will.''

''A promise given is a promise kept, Ian.''

''I'm well aware of that, lass. So. What do you say? Shall we roll the dice?''

Sheer bravado pushed her to her feet. ''Aye,'' she said recklessly.

While Ian went to the cupboard and retrieved a pair of dice, Sabrina sank to her knees upon the floor, tucking her skirts around her. Squatting down on his haunches, he joined her.

His dark brows hiked imperiously, he extended his palm. Within lay the dice. ''You may go first,'' he murmured.

Sabrina nearly snatched them from his hand. Oh, but he was so confident he would win! She cupped them in her hand, directed a quick prayer heavenward . . . and rolled.

Eleven!

She clasped her hands against her breast, nearly chortling her glee. A smile upon her lips, she watched Ian reach for the pair. He rubbed them between his palms . . . and let them drop.

Twelve.

She stared disbelievingly. She had lost to him . . . again.

Ian rose. There was a heartbeat of silence. Eyes

downcast, Sabrina could not bring herself to look at him.

Strong hands curled warmly about her shoulders. He pulled her to her feet.

She could look no higher than the bristly tangle of hairs at the base of his throat.

He didn't mock her with his victory. His words were not at all what she expected. "You kissed Robert that day," he said softly. "Do you remember?"

Her mouth turned down. "Aye. He used his tongue." Her tone turned accusing. "As you did on our wedding day. 'Twas ghastly!"

"You'll not always think so," he predicted. "Besides, there are other things one can do with the tongue—a very skilled French woman taught me that. The French have a way of making love—indeed they have many ways. And . . . how shall I put this? When it comes to making love, the French are connoisseurs."

Sabrina was both curious and appalled. "'Tis sinful to talk about such things. 'Tis sinful to—to do such things!"

A smile curled his lips. "Then may the devil take me, for I intend to do both!"

"If you are so taken with the French way, mayhap you should have married a Frenchwoman!"

His smile widened. "Careful, lass. I could almost believe you're jealous."

"Nay, not jealous. I merely wonder that you—that you wish to bed me again when you clearly find me lacking."

"Not lacking," he corrected. "Merely lacking in experience"—his smile slowly ebbed—"a matter I fully intend to rectify."

There was a ringing silence, and then he said, "Look at me, lass."

It was a quiet demand. Reason scattered in every direction. Sabrina longed to run, yet where could she go that he would not find her?

Swallowing, her gaze trekked slowly upward, only to find herself captured in the hold of his eyes as surely as a rabbit in a snare.

"Put your arms around my neck."

The air was suddenly alive with a thundering tension. His eyes glowed silver, ablaze with some emotion that was oddly exhilarating—yet somehow almost frightening as well. Her stomach knotted. Faith, but when he gazed at her so, she could scarcely think!

She drew a shuddering breath. "Ian—"

"I'll not be swayed, lass." Quiet as his tone was, within was a note of warning. "You said you would come willingly—and so you shall."

Helplessly she obeyed, slipping her arms about his neck, lacing her fingers together that he would not feel her trembling.

His regard had dropped to her mouth. "Excellent," he murmured. "Now part your lips and bring them to mine."

Her pulse skittered wildly, but she did as he said. Her lashes fluttered closed as he kissed her, the contact slow and warm and sensuous. She gave a breathy little sigh, unconsciously molding her body against the rock-hard contours of his.

"More," he invited huskily. Her jaw slackened. In turn he deepened the kiss. Now he explored her mouth with the wanton stroke of his tongue, tracing the ridge of her teeth, the sleek wet interior. The thought spun through her mind that it was not so very unpleasant after all.

The world was spinning when at last he raised his head. "That was not like Robert." The confession spilled forth unbidden before she could stop it.

"I should hope not," he murmured, and then his mouth was on hers again. His kiss was like a drug, luring her into a realm where she could do naught but cling feebly to him—the only rock in a world tipped awry.

She had little recollection of being relieved of her gown. She watched dazedly as Ian filled his hands with the roundness of her breasts. Lazy fingertips traced slow, maddening circles around the boundaries of her nipples. When at last his thumbs raked again and again over tautly straining peaks, she exhaled, a rush of sound.

"That was what you wanted, wasn't it, lass?"

She couldn't deny it. She couldn't deny *him*.

Suddenly he was on his knees before her.

The hot wet cave of his mouth replaced his hands. He sucked first one pink crown and then the other, creating in her belly a rushing torrent of need. Her breath grew quick and shallow.

His hands slid down to her hips. His thumbs rested near, yet not quite touching the golden thatch between her thighs. She felt the heat of his kiss there in the dip of her naval, the ridge of each hipbone. With lips and tongue he blazed a nerve-shattering path down the hollow of her belly, closer and closer to the apex of her thighs.

His mouth brushed reddish-gold fleece.

"Ian!" She caught her breath in shock. His name was a soft cry of confusion.

If he heard, he gave no sign of it. He was intent upon his task.

The grasp of her mind faltered. God's teeth, would he indulge in still more taunting play? Nay. 'Twas unthinkable!

With his thumbs he bared her core. A stab of sheer pleasure shot through her, a dart of fire as he took the gliding exploration of his tongue ever further. With hot, torrid strokes he lashed her quivering bud of sensation, a wantonly erotic caress that ripped the air from her lungs, the strength from her limbs.

She lost the battle to keep hold of her senses. Her fingers curled and uncurled against his shoulders. 'Twas as if she were melting, inside and out. Blindly she clutched at him.

He caught her just as she would have collapsed. She was borne swiftly to the bed. His eyes burning, he divested himself of his garments and crawled over her.

He pulled her full and tight against him. Sabrina was achingly aware of everything about him. Smooth, corded muscles. Hair-roughened skin. The press of her thighs against that part of him that pulsed with a life of its own.

With his fingers he parted damp, weeping folds. He came inside her with a single stroke; she could feel the sleek wet heat of her passage stretch to the limit, but there was no pain. She could feel him—all of him—heat and power, his rigid thickness—encased within her. She couldn't tear her eyes away from the place he possessed so fully. Her belly pressed his. Dark hair mingled with red-gold silken down.

He withdrew, the spear of his sex wet with passion's nectar. The muscles of his buttocks tightened.

His swollen rod pierced deep within her, again and again. With every plunge of his body into hers, heat stormed all through her.

His mouth was on her neck. The curve of her cheek. "Say it," came his dark whisper. "Say my name."

The timbre of his voice was oddly thrilling. He raised his head and stared down at her. Candlelight flickered over his shoulders, awesomely wide. His expression was taut with strain, but his eyes shone with an unmistakable hunger.

Something in her rebelled. He would have her body, aye. But not her heart. Never her heart.

Her lips clamped together. No sound would pass through them. Her eyes squeezed shut, to shut out his need—his image—but even then she could still see the shape of him behind her closed eyelids.

She thought he swore. The rhythm of his hips quickened. Faster and faster, driving almost wildly. And all at once she was caught up in the same frenzy. Dark, forbidden ecstasy exploded inside her. She bit back a cry. Even as she did, his seed spilled hot and thick within her.

Above her, she felt his body relax by subtle degrees. She lay there, stunned by what had happened.

Twice now—twice!—he'd awakened her to a passion she'd not known she was capable of. Her heart cried out the outrage. Why? Why Ian? It was as though he commanded her body, as though he governed the very beat of her heart. She didn't understand it. She didn't understand herself.

But she was too tired to think. Her eyelids grew heavy. No protest found voice when Ian eased to his back and drew her close to his side. Lulled by his warmth, oddly comforted by his strength, she slept.

Fourteen

Not so with the man at her side.

His mood was still dark when he'd risen from his lumpy bed of hay this morn. He'd risen before dawn that all would not know of the discord with his wife. Yet when he'd come upon her this morn, he'd been sorely tempted to laugh, for his soldiers were utterly confounded by her orders.

Nay, he decided anew. He'd not spend the night in the stable again. He'd find a far softer comfort in his bed—and her slender, shapely arms.

Lifting the sheet, he gazed at her. He allowed his regard to wander where it would, savoring the beauty of face and form, with no worry of reproach from his shy, prideful wife.

A powerful swell of possessiveness came over him. It was just as he'd said. She was in his home. His castle. His bed. Now it was real, real as it had not been before.

She was his. His and no other's.

He was pleased with the way she'd embraced her role as mistress of the castle. A twinge of bitterness crept through him. If only she embraced her husband so readily!

Theirs would not be a chaste marriage. This he knew well and true. He would not even try to keep his distance, for he knew he'd fail. She had only to be near and he was stirred beyond reason.

If she needed time to accept their marriage—to accept him as husband—so be it. But he would not deny himself the enjoyment of the marriage bed. It felt so right with Sabrina, right as it would never have been with Margaret.

'Twas fate that had robbed Margaret of her life, he decided. 'Twas fate that led him to Sabrina. Their destinies were entwined as one. He could not fight it. His mood grew suddenly fierce.

Nor could she.

Sabrina woke amidst a flood of sensations. She seemed impossibly warm, though the covers were twisted down around her feet. The reason for that firelike heat suddenly struck her—Ian's hard body lay flush against her own. Her head was pillowed on the sinewy pad of his shoulder. Her hand lay small and white atop the wiry forest on his chest. Her legs were twisted with his, one hairy thigh snug against her own. It was the memory of what lay cradled between those thighs that made her go hot all over, as if she were ill with some dreaded ague.

Her gaze trickled slowly upward, over the strong column of his neck, the squareness of his jaw, shadowed with a day's growth of beard. He was, she thought with an odd little shiver, a most handsome man, both in face and form.

But she froze when she saw that her perusal had not gone unnoticed. Ian's eyes were open.

He moved. With a blunt fingertip, he traced the

shape of her mouth. "So tell me, bratling. Do you still despise me?"

Despise him? Indeed, at that moment, she knew not what she felt! Her heart was in a frenzy. His touch, light though it was, made her quiver anew. Her eyes grazed his, then slid away. "Nay," she whispered helplessly.

A finger beneath her chin, he tipped her face to his. Something blazed in his eyes. His mouth took hers in a deep, unbroken kiss. She could feel the rise of passion in him—aye, feel it in the iron-hard shaft against her belly! Their mouths still fused, he rolled her to her back.

She tore her mouth free. "Ian!" She was aghast. "'Tis daylight!"

"So it is, sweet." He bathed the peak of one breast with the moist heat of his tongue. She trembled to think that he would do to her in the full light of day what was better done in the dark.

"Ian—" Her hands caught at his shoulders, but there was no stopping him . . . and soon she didn't want to. With lips and hands he set about arousing her, stoking the dormant fires within her to blistering flames, his touch as bold and brazen as the man himself.

When at last he parted her thighs, he gazed down at her, his eyes alight with a sweltering passion. His penetration was tormentingly slow; she gasped at the long, torrid friction. He whispered her name, the sound low and strained, bringing her eyes to his face. The cords of his neck were taut. She sensed his restraint as he began the rhythm that would take them both to heaven. But she no longer cared if he was slow and easy. Her nails dug into his back, a wordless plea.

In answer he plunged harder. Deeper. As if he sought her very womb. An exquisite ecstasy seemed to burst inside her. She buried her face against his neck and clung as she was flung high aloft, to the sky and beyond.

Long moments passed before her ragged breathing slowed to normal. Above her, Ian braced himself on his elbows and gazed down at her.

His fingertips were pleasantly rough as he brushed a tangle of hairs from her cheek. "Still so reluctant?" he murmured.

Sabrina willed her anger to come. It would not. But she could not meet his eyes.

"Oh, you can tell yourself that you were meant for another. But there is a bond that draws us together—a bond of desire—a bond I cannot fight. Nor can you." His tone was almost whimsical. "I know you feel it . . . as I feel it. Admit it, Sabrina."

His tone held no malice. No challenge. Not even the veriest hint of triumph.

Her throat closed. Suddenly she was perilously—foolishly—near tears. Was he right? she wondered in alarm. God help her, she didn't know. She knew only that when he touched her, her body seemed not her own. Her *will* seemed not her own.

He sighed. "So be it. But there'll be no other man between us in this bed. Promise me."

She looked at him then. To her confusion, his expression was utterly grave.

She gave a tiny shake of her head. "I—I do not know what you mean."

"I mean only this. I have only to touch you—to look at you—and thoughts of no other dare intrude. It's been this way since the day I returned to Dunlevy." There was a heated rush of silence. "I would ask the same of you."

Jamie. He meant Jamie. Until now, she'd forgotten her careless taunt the night they'd wed. *I cannot stop you from taking me. Indeed, I will not fight you. But when you do, know that I will be thinking of Jamie. Not you, never you.*

"Why?" she said unevenly. "Why would you have my promise?"

"A promise given is a promise kept. I know if you give it, you'll keep it."

For the life of her, she didn't understand why he asked this of her—why it mattered. But he was intent.

And he was right. There *was* something between them. A powerful lure she could neither fight, nor deny.

Nor, it seemed, could he.

She swallowed. "You—you have it," she said haltingly, her voice very low. "You have my promise."

He bestowed on her a gaze so deeply probing she felt it to the marrow of her bones. He must have been satisfied with what he saw there, for he brushed a brief kiss on her lips and arose.

She watched as he strode to the fire and stoked it. Naked as a newborn babe, he crossed the room and washed from the washbasin. His body was so unlike hers, she mused—hard and muscled where she was round and curved. Dark and hairy where she was fair and pale. Yet he was all sleek, supple grace . . .

At that very instant, he glanced over at her. Sabrina blushed fiercely, mortified that she'd been caught staring at him with unabashed curiosity. Not so with Ian—he planted one hand on the ridge of his hip, grinning hugely, as if he could read her mind.

"Why do you blush, Sabrina?"

"You know very well why I blush," she said without thinking. "You are naked!"

He chuckled, a sound that made her think of days gone by . . . lazy, happy days when they were just children.

"As I recall, Sabrina, you once harbored a desire to see me naked."

"And as I told you before, you were just a boy!"

His grin was wicked. "Naught has changed, I assure you." He raised his arms from his sides. "You see? I still have two arms. Two legs—"

"You—you are bigger." This emerged before she thought better of it.

"Indeed. Where?"

"You—you know where!" she blurted. Her gaze strayed where it should not, and then her cheeks burned hot as fire.

He glanced down his body. "Ah," he said knowingly. "Mayhap you are right. Of course being a man, I do like to think that *some* things have changed—"

His tone had turned brash, yet still underscored with a hint of laughter. Sabrina squeezed her eyes shut, groaned, and pulled her pillow over her head. Oh, but he was a brute to torment her so!

The bed dipped; the pillow was plucked from her hands and pushed aside.

"Open your eyes, Sabrina." His tone held no small measure of laughter.

Sabrina opened her eyes and gazed at him, silently pleading that he cease his play.

He was undeterred. A daring finger swept down the arch of her throat, clear to the swell of her breast revealed just above the edge of the blanket. There it traced a shattering path to and fro.

"Why do you chide me so, dear wife? Why, you are naked, too."

Sabrina swallowed. Her mouth was suddenly dry as dust. "Have you no business to attend this morn?"

His laughter was low and husky—and somehow oddly pleasing.

"Your mood is certainly much improved." Her tone was tart, her glare but an abysmal attempt.

"What is this?" he said lightly. "Would you be rid of me, wife? Why, I recall many a time when we were children when you were ever and always at my heels."

Sabrina was silent. Lo, but it was true. Most of the time Margaret had aught to do with her—indeed, Margaret had often scorned her. Her sister had made her feel small and awkward and ugly. As her father, he forever disapproved of her. She was forever fearful of making a mistake and earning his censure.

Only Ian had paid her any heed, though she was aware he felt she was often underfoot. But with Ian she could be herself. She had depended on him. Looked to him for approval. Oh, they had bickered as children were wont to do. But she had felt far closer to him than anyone. But then even that had changed. . . .

Somehow she managed to meet his eyes. "I—I'd forgotten." But it was not so much a matter of forgetting, but not wishing to remember. . . .

"You've not," he said promptly. "Why, you followed me like—like a hound to its prey. Indeed, there was a time I thought you were more than fond of me."

"You were mistaken," she said stiffly.

"Was I?"

His knowing smile was vastly annoying. "As I recall, my lord, you had no time for me."

"That was never true."

"It was. The last year you spent at Dunlevy, you had no patience with me. You were constantly cross with me."

"And there were times I thought you would skewer me through."

There were times she'd wanted to, for he'd teased her unmercifully. Nor had she wanted him to know her true feelings, for he would have laughed at her . . . still, she'd cried many a tear over his distant behavior. She'd masked her hurt with a disdain of her own, vowing that he would never know she'd fancied herself in love with him—nay, not then, and of a certainty, she would not confess such weakness to him now!

"You were curt with me," she said again. "I remember it well."

Something flickered across his features, something she couldn't decipher. "Mayhap you are right," he said with a crooked little smile. "I spent those last months anxious to fight with William Wallace, dreaming of becoming a hero. But your father would not allow it, and I fear he was right. I was but a boy then, a boy who played at being a man." For a moment, a faintly whimsical expression dwelled in his eyes.

He withdrew his hand. "But you are right. I'd best be up and on my way."

He rose and dressed. Sabrina watched, the covers pulled up to her chin. She wondered crazily if she would ever be like him—so carelessly nonchalant about nudity. Never, she decided vehemently. She would never be able to appear naked in his presence and not be thoroughly embarrassed.

To her dismay, he did not leave until she had bathed and dressed as well.

She knew the hour was late when they entered the great hall and found it nearly deserted, save for Fraser. Fraser did not see them, for his back was to them; he was ambling toward the courtyard. Even as they watched, he reached around to scratch his rump.

Sabrina stopped short. Her gaze veered straight to Ian's. A memory leaped out at her, a memory of a time when she and Ian had hidden in the kirk loft after mass one morn. They'd been peering down as the kirk emptied. As soon as he thought himself alone, Father Gilbert had hiked up his robes and scratched his behind. As he heaved an immense sigh of relief, both she and Ian had convulsed into laughter. . . .

Twinkling gray eyes met hers. Her heart turned over, for she saw in him a glimmer of the boy she'd so adored.

Her mind screamed. Sweet Mother of Mary, what was happening? It couldn't. Nay, not again. Not after all these years . . .

He bent his head to hers. "Do you remember, lass, the day we once hid in the kirk loft after mass? As soon as the kirk emptied, Father Gilbert pulled up his—"

"I—I remember." Her tone was breathless.

A smile twitched at Ian's lips. "I could never regard Father in quite the same way after that. 'Twas difficult to think of him as pious and inviolate—and I forever feared that God would strike me dead for such blasphemy."

Strange, that her mind should work as Ian's did, that both recalled the very same memory, at the very same instant; even more strange was that she'd felt that very same way whene'er she chanced to see Father Gilbert, from that day forward.

Just then Uncle Malcolm entered, shuffling toward them.

Ian hailed him with a hearty greeting. "How are you this fine morning, Uncle?"

Uncle Malcolm stopped and looked up. He drew his plaid more tightly about his shoulders. "Fine, but for the chill in m' bones. I daresay we're in for a wee cold spell."

Ian clapped a hand on his uncle's thin shoulder. "I'll have Mary brew some warm spiced wine, Uncle, and see that another blanket is brought to your bed."

Sabrina spoke up. "There's no need for you to trouble yourself, Ian. I can see to it." She smiled at Malcolm, but to her surprise, he looked her up and down as if he'd never seen her before. Sabrina was puzzled. She'd talked to him at length only yesterday afternoon.

"Who be this young lass with ye, Ian?"

Ian slipped an arm around her shoulders. "This is my wife, Sabrina, Uncle. She returned with me from Dunlevy Keep several days ago."

"She did, eh?"

"Aye, Uncle." Ian's tone was one of utter patience.

"Well, ye be a lucky lad then. She's bonny as heather in full bloom."

"That she is, Uncle. That she is."

Sabrina flushed. Did he mock her? She wasn't cer-

tain. The eyes that dwelled upon her were warm as
sunshine—or did she only imagine it? As soon as
Uncle Malcolm turned to mount the stairs, his arm
slid from her shoulders. She felt curiously bereft.

When Malcolm was out of earshot, her gaze sought
Ian's. "He didn't remember me."

He nodded. "'Tis an affliction that comes and goes
like the fog these past few years. Some days his mind
is as sharp as my own. Others he is confused. He
knows where he is, and who he is. And he knows me,
though he sometimes thinks I am my father. And
there have been times when he's forgotten that my
father is dead."

The day set a precedent for the ones which followed. While Sabrina assumed the duties as mistress
of the household, Ian was off tending to affairs as
chieftain.

On the surface, all was well. It appeared Sabrina
was slowly growing accustomed to her role as his
wife. But whene'er their eyes chanced to meet, she
was the first to tear hers away. Ian chafed inside. His
lovely wife did not flinch from his touch, nor did she
resist.

Yet neither did she yield. There was a part of herself
she withheld from him. He wooed her as he had
wooed no other. He was ever patient, when patience
was not his way. He was slow and tender, when desire coursed hot and demanding in his veins. Had she
denied him, he'd never have taken her. But there was
never any need. Her body knew. Her body accepted
him. Oh, he knew he pleased her. She writhed and
twisted beneath him in passion's dance.

But he wanted more.

He wanted to hear his name on her lips; he yearned

to hear her cry out in the throes of her climax. He ached to have her touch him of her own volition. Touch him the way he touched her. . . .

Frustration roiled within him like a storm-tossed sea. They shared their meals together. They shared their warmth during the chill of the night; shared flaming kisses and white-hot caresses. But there was a bridge between them, a bridge he was barred from crossing. She held herself distant from him.

He roused her one morning, for no matter how many times he took her, he wanted her more with every day that passed. But she pretended to be asleep. He persisted, kissing her into wakefulness. But he'd seen the rebellion flare in her eyes, even as her body arched to his.

Would it be like this every time he wanted her? The question plagued him endlessly.

Autumn had long since descended across the land, and with it the advent of winter. There had been trouble with the Campbells of late—they had a penchant for taking what was not their own—but these past days had been quiet. One cloudy afternoon a steady downpour drove his kinsmen and soldiers inside.

He had asked Sabrina to cut his hair. She'd complained oft enough that he looked shaggy as his sheep. So it was that he presented the shears to her with a flourish, seating himself upon a stool before her.

A slender brow rose askance. "Are you certain you trust me?" she asked sweetly. "What if I were to cut off your ear?"

The sweetness of her smile stole the bite from her tone and the darkness from the blackest night.

His eyes glinted. He winked at Fraser and Alasdair,

who sat nearby. "Better my ear than my nether parts."

The others roared. "Ye married a woman of spirit, Ian!" someone shouted.

Sabrina had blushed to the roots of her hair. Though he knew she was sometimes flustered by such bawdiness, she bore it well. He marveled that he had ever thought her experienced in the ways of men. She was an innocent, through and through.

It pleased him to no end.

Now, intent upon the chore at hand, her lovely mouth was pursed. She bent slightly toward him, revealing a tantalizing glimpse of round, swelling flesh. Ian inhaled sharply.

His finger traced the neckline of her gown. "She needs taming, lads, and I'm just the man to do it." In one smooth move, he stood and hoisted her over his shoulder.

She thumped her fists against his back. "Ian! Ian, put me down this instant!"

Their audience erupted with encouraging cheers— and earthy suggestions. His grin was wholly devilish. "I do believe we'll finish this task in private, wife."

In their chamber he sat with her in a chair before the fire, cradling her in his lap.

He brushed his mouth against her cheek, inhaling the fresh, clean scent of her. "Are you angry, lass?"

She sighed. "Ian, you are—impossible." Her charge lacked heat.

"Do I embarrass you, then?"

"Aye," she said promptly.

He loved the way she blushed even now. "Ah, but I am the envy of every man belowstairs."

Her flush deepened. Her gaze flitted away. The tip

of her tongue came out to dampen her lips. "Why do you say such things?" she whispered. "Why?"

Though he did not understand it, he sensed her uncertainty. A finger alongside her jaw, he guided her eyes to his.

"You are beautiful, Sabrina. Beautiful and—"

"Nay," she interrupted. "I am not. Not like Margaret."

"Ah, but I did not choose Margaret. Our fathers arranged the betrothal. As for you, I *did* choose you."

She shook her head. "Only to unite the clans—"

"No." It was his turn to interrupt. "'Twas naught but an excuse to wed you . . . and bed you."

He'd shocked her. He could see it in the way her eyes flew wide.

He gave a self-deprecating little smile. "'Tis true, lass. Oh, I told myself the same as I told you and your father—that I would honor the agreement made between our fathers by marrying you. But it was a lie, Sabrina. I wanted you then—" his smile faded—"and I want you now."

He felt her tremble. His arms tightened. Carrying her to the bed, he laid her down and showed her the truth of all he spoke, breathing into his kiss all the fervent longing held deep in his being.

His reward came when she sighed and slipped slender arms about his neck. "I truly . . . please you?"

His heart leaped. She sounded almost anxious. He rested his forehead against hers. "Like no other."

A faint glimmer entered the dewy green of her eyes. "Ah. And what about the women you left behind in France?"

"All forgotten," he whispered, busily engaged in removing her clothes—and his.

But when he would have slid between her thighs, she stopped him with a finger upon his lips. "You once said there are many ways of making love." Two bright spots of red appeared on her cheeks. "I find I'm curious, my lord . . . is the French way the better way?"

He gave a husky laugh. "I much prefer *my* way."

And with that his arms engulfed her. In one swift move he rolled so that he lay beneath her . . . astride him. He could feel the ridge of his manhood pulsing and erect against her furrowed heat.

She inhaled sharply. Her gaze collided with his, dark and questioning. "Ian! Dear God, how—"

Gently he pushed her to a sitting position. "Your trusty steed awaits," he murmured.

Hands upon her hips, he showed her the way of it. . . . Lifting. Lowering, imbedding himself deep in the sleek velvet of her sheath. Rooted to the hilt inside her, he nearly groaned aloud, for her clinging heat was searing and wet and tight around his throbbing member, melting him with her liquidity.

"Ride me as you will, lass." His voice was low and taut. His hands fell away, dropped to his sides. He watched her, allowing her the freedom to take him as she would.

The rise and fall of her hips was slow at first, almost tentative. He played with the dusky tips of her breasts, leaning forward to taste those budding crests, relishing the way they hardened in his mouth. He watched her eyes go all soft and hazy. He buried his thumb in the soft down between her thighs, seeking her swollen core. He felt the long, shivering breath she drew there where he lay planted so snugly in her depths. And all the while the ritual dance of mating continued, quickening in tempo until conscious thought was but a distant memory, until naught else existed.

Catching her hips, he lunged almost wildly, feeling the burning rise of his seed. Gritting his teeth, his climax exploded inside her, scalding him inside and out. Above him, she collapsed against his chest.

In the aftermath, he eased her to her side and brought her close. Her hair streamed wildly over them both. He'd brought her to pleasure, he knew. But even while the certainty pleased him immensely, he could not ignore the twinge of disappointment which dulled his own satisfaction. Just once, he longed to hear her moan her joy aloud. Just once...

A long time later, while the fire in the hearth burned low and the fire in their loins had cooled to embers, she spoke. "I heard Fraser speak of the Campbells earlier today."

His fingers sifted idly through the length of shimmering, red-gold strands. "Not singing their praises, I hope."

"Hardly." She tilted her head that they might see them. "Are they our enemies, then?"

Our enemies. Ian could not help but note her reference. It pleased him—pleased him mightily.

"They steal our cattle," he said lightly. "We take it back."

"*Take* it back?" A slender brow quirked high. "Steal it back, more like. You Highlanders bow to no law but your own."

He grinned. "That's the way of it here in the Highlands."

Her lips pursed, but he could tell she was not angry. "No wonder you have no peace!"

He brought her hand to her lips and kissed it. "I would much rather have peace between us." His eyes held hers immeasurably.

She made no answer. She *could* not answer, for indeed, Sabrina was caught in a maze and knew not which way to turn—indeed, she knew not where her heart lay!

Ian had only to come near and she was caught in a haze of conflicting emotion. He had only to touch her and she went weak inside. Since the day of their wager, there had been a softening in him. They'd talked and laughed about the days when they were children. She'd been convinced he would never remember, but he did. . . . Did he truly think her beautiful? Nay. Surely not. 'Twas just a trick—a trick to make her bend to his hand—to lure her more easily to his bed. Yet what need was there for tender words and artifice? a voice inside scoffed. She was his wife. 'Twas her duty to lie with him. To tend his hearth and home.

In all truth, she could lie to herself no longer. She was coming to miss Dunlevy less and less. Castle MacGregor, with its stark, austere exterior, was peopled with those who radiated life and warmth and humor.

It was the next afternoon that Sabrina spotted Uncle Malcolm sitting alone near the hearth. His thin shoulders shivered. He scooted his stool nearer the fire.

Her skirts whirled as she spun toward the kitchen. Scant minutes later, she pressed a cup of warm mulled wine into his hands. There were still days he did not know her. She had come to recognize those times, for his eyes were dull and vague.

But this day his regard was almost piercing. He bid her come closer.

Sabrina obliged. "What is it, Uncle?"

He nodded, as if to himself. "You look like her. That's why he married you."

She frowned. "Who, Uncle?"

He misunderstood. "The lad, that's who! He loved her, y'know. All knew it."

The lad. Did he mean Ian? A tingle trickled down her spine. She tried again. "I do not understand, Uncle. Who is it that I resemble? And who was in love?"

He paid no heed. "Aye, there's the look of her about ye," he pronounced. "Ye have the same hair, though yours has more flame . . . She took m' nephew to his grave, y'know." He thumped his staff against the floor. "The Lord may strike me down, but I am glad she is dead, wretched witch! And I thank the lad for sending her to the devil, for that is where she belongs!"

Sabrina blanched. She resembled a dead woman? The thought was eerie. "Who, Uncle? Who is dead?"

He looked at her then. "Fionna!" he stated forcefully.

The old man was in a state, that was keenly evident. With his fragile health, Sabrina decided she dare not press him further. And indeed, she could not help but wonder if perhaps he'd not been rambling a bit. . . .

Alasdair. Alasdair would know.

She found him outside the smith's shed, polishing a dagger. He glanced up when she spoke his name softly.

He stood immediately. "Sabrina! Are you looking for Ian, lass? I'm afraid I've not seen him."

"In truth, I would speak with you." She linked her

fingers before her. "Alasdair, I wondered . . . who is Fionna?"

His smile withered. He looked at her sharply. "Where did you hear her name?"

"Uncle Malcolm."

Alasdair sighed. "He did not tell you then? Ian has not told you." He glanced around, grimaced, then took her hand. "Come. Let us go elsewhere. The battlements, I think . . . yes, the battlements. We'll not be disturbed there."

High above the castle, the battlement was deserted. Sabrina turned to him the instant they were alone.

"Why do I have the feeling I do not want to know?" she wondered aloud.

Alasdair clapped a hand on her shoulder. "'Tis not so bad as all that, Sabrina! I merely thought this a matter best discussed in private."

"Thank you, Alasdair. You—you are very kind. But I am more curious than ever to know about the mysterious Fionna."

"There is nothing mysterious about her, Sabrina." He sighed. "Fionna was wed to David, Ian's father."

"His mother, then—"

He was shaking his head. "Nay. Ian's mother was Lenora. Fionna was David's second wife. They wed when Ian and I were . . . oh, mayhap five-and-ten. She was much younger than David, indeed, not so very many years older than the two of us."

"Uncle said he loved her . . . 'the lad loved her,' " she quoted. She had to force the sound from her throat. "Did he mean Ian?"

Alasdair hesitated. She knew then . . . *she knew.*

Ian had been in love with his stepmother.

There was a painful squeeze of her heart. She

turned and stared out where the wind rippled the treetops. She had to struggle to concentrate on Alasdair's voice.

"I cannot say for certain," he was saying. "Fionna was—an enchantress. Young and lithe. Full of laughter and gaiety." He smiled slightly. "All the lads, myself included, were a wee bit in love with her, I think."

She glanced at him. "Uncle said she was dead."

"Aye. Over a year now."

"He said she took his nephew to his grave." There was a small pause. "What did he mean by that?"

Alasdair looked uncomfortable. "Ian should have told you. But I suppose there is no point in hiding it. Sabrina . . . David took his own life. Ian's father took his own life."

She took a sharp breath. "After Fionna died?"

"Aye. In his grief over her death, he killed himself."

"Alasdair, how did she die? How did Fionna die?"

There was a hollow silence. "She was murdered."

Murdered. Her blood seemed to congeal. "Dear God," she said faintly. "How—"

"Strangled. In her bed."

"But who, Alasdair? Who killed her?"

"The killer was never found."

"Never found!" She was aghast. "Do you mean to say no one had any idea who might have murdered her?"

His gaze flitted away. "There were suspicions, yes. And talk . . ." He paused, then shook his head. "Sabrina, I do not think—"

"Tell me, Alasdair."

The wind was chill, but it was as nothing compared to the chill in her heart. An eerie foreboding prickled her skin. For she knew, even before he spoke, what he would say. . . .

"'Twas Ian who found Fionna," he said quietly. "'Twas whispered he killed her in a jealous rage."

Her lips parted. "No," she whispered. "*No.*"

All at once her heart was pounding heavily. There was a dull buzzing in her ears. Specks flashed in her vision. She blinked to clear her eyes, but it was no use. She flung out a hand, aware that she was falling. She heard a shout, a voice she dimly recognized as Ian's.

She caught but a glimpse of harshly carved features, the burning touch of silver eyes, a mouth relentlessly thin. He was coming toward her! Dimly she heard herself cry out—in terror or in shock, she knew not . . .

All at once strong hands were upon her, bearing her upward.

And then she knew no more.

Shadows of light and dark played upon the earth. Clouds shifted restlessly across the night sky. The wind moaned a wistful song as a lone horseman wound his way up a rocky hillside to the tiny cottage that was perched atop it.

Once there, he entered the cottage. He peered through the darkness.

"Where are you?"

"Here. By the window."

He saw her then, seated on a chair, arms drawn around her legs as she gazed into the distant night.

He made his way over to her. "Why do you not light the candles?"

She gave a throaty laugh. "I am not weak like her. I do not cower in the dark."

Nonetheless, the man stopped to light several candles. The cottage slowly filled with a yellow glow.

He went to her, gazing down at her, at the unfettered glory of hair that tumbled to her waist, a cape of shimmering moonbeams. As always, he was struck by her look of purity. He marveled. Whoever would have guessed . . .

"Are you glad I came?" she whispered.

"You know I am." His eyes burned hotly as he reached for her.

His mouth crushed hers. Within seconds their garments were cast aside and they were naked. A muscle-thewed arm drew her up and into the valley of his groin. His mouth feasted on the arch of her throat; her nails dug into his arms.

"Now," she invited, parting her limbs wide for his entrance. "Come to me now."

She was damp and hot. He turned and swiveled, spreading his legs wide and bracing his back against the wall. His hands filled with succulent white flesh. With a guttural sound deep in his throat, he lifted her and brought her down upon his thickened lance. She screamed with pleasure as he rammed home then and there, writhing upon him in a wild frenzy, as aroused as he.

Again and again he brought her down upon his hardened spear. The very walls seemed to shiver and jump, for this was a mating that was as savage and fierce as a northern gale. She cried out as her pleasure reached its zenith. His breath harsh and rasping, twice more he brought her to climax before reaching the pinnacle himself.

It was hours later that he propped himself up on his elbow beside her in bed.

Trailing his fingers across the tips of her breasts, he spoke. "We do well together, do we not?"

"'Tis because we are much alike, you and I. We share the same heart. The same soul. And there are none who know us for what we are. . . ." Her eyes gleamed. "Do you think they know we have been secretly meeting these many months?"

"How could they? We have hidden it well."

"Yes. I suppose you are right. Now tell me. What news do you bring?"

His laugh was grating. "They torment each other. She watches him when she thinks he will not see her. And his eyes follow her as a hunter follows its prey." He shook his head. "'Tis the strangest thing. I do believe he sees me as a rival."

"Careful, love, or you will make *me* jealous, and that would not be wise."

His smile reflected his satisfaction. "Oh, you need not worry on that score."

"She must die, you know. We cannot take the chance that she might someday discover what we have done. She would not understand." Her lip curled. "Indeed, if she were to divulge our plot, all would be for naught."

"Aye," the man agreed. "Indeed, we can blame her death on him."

The woman smiled. "So tell me . . . does he love her, then?"

The man paused to consider. "I do not know. But he desires her, of that I have no doubt."

"Ah. So he will miss her when she's gone?" The

woman couldn't have sounded more pleased. "Perhaps he will even fall in love with her."

"You may well be right."

"He should never have married her." The woman's laugh was trilling. "'Twill be the death of her."

"Aye, and the end of him." He paused. "I say we do it now."

She shook her head. "Nay," she whispered. "Not yet. We must be patient. It will take time to accomplish what we must."

"I cannot help it. I wish for it to be over and done." His tone had gone brooding.

"As do I. All you have longed for is within your grasp. But we cannot move too fast, or it will arouse suspicion."

The man's jaw clenched hard. He said nothing.

But the woman knew just what to do. She trailed her fingers over the grid of his belly. "It will all be over soon, I promise. And then we will finally be together."

She smiled against his lips. Her fingers found his rod, still wet with his seed—and her own hot nectar.

Within a heartbeat he was stiff and engorged once more.

But only the night heard his cry of pleasure. Only the night heard her scream of ecstasy. And only the night bore witness as they plotted and schemed. . . .

Fifteen

Consciousness returned slowly. Sabrina was hazily aware of the softness of a bed beneath her limbs. The sweep of a hand upon her brow. A deep male voice calling her name.

She opened her eyes, only to stare straight into Ian's darkly handsome face.

Remembrance returned with a shattering rush. *'Twas Ian who found her . . . There were those who said he killed her in a jealous rage.* She lurched upright. But her head seemed to spin and float. She felt wholly out of step.

Above her, Ian swore a vile oath. Hands cupping her shoulders, he guided her back to the pillows.

"Sabrina! What is amiss?"

The gentleness of his hands was in stark contrast to the grimness of his face. His mouth was a thin line. She shook her head, unable to speak.

"Are you ill?"

"Nay," she managed at last.

"Then why did you swoon? As I recall, you're not given to such spells, are you?"

"Nay," she said again. But her stomach was heaving. Nausea rose up in her throat, threatening to

choke her. "I—I do not know. My head feels strange."
She lay a hand on her belly.

"Here, too?"

He covered her hand, where it lay on her belly,
with his own, completely eclipsing hers. Alasdair's
voice spun through her head anew. *She was strangled
in her bed.*

Ian's fingers were lean and dark. She stared—in
fear or fascination, she knew not which. They were
strong, as he was strong. Powerful . . . and potentially
lethal. He had only to reach out, wrap her fingers
around her neck, and the life would be forever
crushed from her . . .

"Sabrina!"

Her eyes climbed to his. His expression was dark
as a thundercloud. It came as a shock to realize he'd
spoken her name twice.

She swallowed. "Yes?"

"I asked if it is your time."

Lord, but she could hardly think. "My time?" she
echoed blankly.

"Aye, your woman's time!"

Belatedly she realized he meant her monthly flux.
"Nay!" she gasped, mortified beyond belief that he
would speak of such a thing.

He rose. "Wait here," he commanded.

As if she would leave, she thought, a tinge of hysteria coloring her thoughts—as if she could! Her head
was pounding, her belly churning. Never in her life
had she felt so miserable!

He wasn't gone long. He returned bearing a small
goblet. Lazy plumes of steam wafted from the ceiling.
When he sat beside her, she detected a faintly minty
odor.

A hard arm slid about her shoulders, bringing her upright. "Drink," was all he said. She drank every last drop of the brew, partly because she was afraid not to, partly because she had no strength to argue. When she was done, she slipped back against the pillows.

Ian remained where he was.

Sabrina was rather vexed. She wished he would leave, that she might recover her wits. 'Twas shock, no doubt, that had caused her to swoon. Embarrassed by her weakness, she opened her mouth to tell him, but all at once it seemed too much effort.

She must have dozed, for when she opened her eyes again, the dusky haze of twilight slanted through the windows.

It appeared Ian had not moved. His head was angled toward her. The lines about his mouth had softened, but there lurked about him an air of tension.

"Better?" The graze of his knuckles skimmed her cheekbone.

She nodded. Slowly she pushed herself to a sitting position, shifting slightly away so that her back rested against the wall.

She didn't notice the way his lips tightened.

"On the battlement, you cried out when you saw me, Sabrina. Even now you seek to hide it, but you cower away from me." His eyes were the color of steel, and just as unyielding. "I would know why."

"You—you were angry." She spoke unthinkingly, the first thing that popped into her head.

"That I was. You were alone with my cousin. Would you have my clansmen whisper that the two of you cuckold me under my very nose?"

She gasped. Indignation spurred her ire. "Why, that is preposterous!"

"Indeed." His tone was cold as a winter wind. "Several saw you approach him. Do you deny you sought him out? Did the two of you plan a secret assignation?"

"A secret . . . but that is ludicrous. 'Twas not that at all! And if we did, we would make certain that all did not see!"

"No? Then why were you with him? Why did the two of you seek to be alone?"

Her chin came up. "There was a *need* to be alone," she stressed.

"Indeed." He had no compunction about confronting her. "Why, pray tell?"

There was no escaping the determined glitter of his eyes. "I needed to speak with him."

"On what matter?"

A mounting fury held her silent. She was not a child to answer his dictates!

"Tell me, Sabrina. Or by the Cross, I'll—"

"You'll what?" Outrage fired her courage. "You'll kill me in a jealous rage the way you killed Fionna?"

She hadn't meant to say that. God's wounds, but she hadn't! Only now it was too late. . . .

His face was a mask of stone. "So. He told you, didn't he? Alasdair told you."

Her anger drained as suddenly as it had erupted. She gestured vaguely. "'Tis not what you think. I—I asked him about her." She faltered. "You see, Uncle said I looked like her. He said you—you married me because I looked like her."

"You are nothing like her. Nothing."

An awful band of tightness crept around her breast. Of course she wasn't. Fionna had been beautiful . . . and yet Ian almost sounded as if he hated her. Her breath came fast, then slow. Her mind veered straight to Margaret. Ian had been the first to find Fionna . . . the last to see Margaret alive. . . . For the span of a heartbeat, the notion winged through her mind that mayhap he'd killed both. . . .

His eyes narrowed. "God's blood! Do not tell me you believe it!"

The breath she drew was deep and shuddering. "I— I do not want to," she whispered.

His jaw clamped tight. "Have I not shown you every care—here in this very bed?"

She couldn't tear her gaze from his face. "Aye," she heard herself say.

"Have I ever hurt you? Laid a hand on you in anger?"

Her eyes clung to his. "Nay," she said faintly.

"Nor would I—not you or any other woman. I despise those who would prey on the weakness of women."

It was true. He'd never laid a hand on her that was anything but tender. True, there was a harshness in him that had not been present as a lad. But was he a murderer? She cringed from a thought too terrible to consider. Nay. She could not believe it. She *would* not.

"I did not kill Fionna," he stated flatly. "You may choose to believe me or not, Sabrina. The choice is yours. I will not beg forgiveness for that which I did not do—not to God and not to you. Nor will I have my own wife going behind my back, whispering about me to another! From now on, if you have questions, come to me, not Alasdair. Do you understand, Sabrina?"

His command prickled her temper. "I did not go behind your back! I went to Alasdair because I thought he would know . . . that he would tell me the truth—''

"And I would not?"

"I—I did not say that!" She floundered. Her heart and mind were all amuddle. In fury and indignation, she jammed her fists against her thighs. "Oh, but you twist my words to suit your own purpose!"

"I do not. I but hear what you speak."

Faith, but he was stubborn! "Then tell me this, Ian. That first night at Dunlevy, I remember Papa said he'd heard there was strife in the clan upon the death of your father. Is this why? Because there were those who thought you murdered Fionna?"

For an instant she was certain he would refuse to answer. His expression was close and guarded, as were the words he now spoke.

"That was but a part of it. Aye, there were a few— but none who dared say so to my face. But if my clansmen believed it true, would I be chieftain? I think not. I admit, 'twas a time of great unrest within the clan. Fionna had been killed. My father's death was unexpected—and came but days afterward."

She longed to ask who killed Fionna, but Ian's features were darkly shuttered. The rigid cast of his jaw discouraged further questions.

Disheartened, she turned away as he disrobed, then crawled into bed beside her.

He made no move to touch her that night. They lay with far more than just distance between them. And it was then that a chilling thought etched itself into her mind. . . .

He'd said for her to come to him with questions. Could it be there was something he did not wish her to know? A truth that others might tell her but he would not? She shivered, recalling the fierceness of his rage when he'd caught her with Jamie. All at once the man she'd married seemed to be a stranger.

Her sleep that night was fitful, not at all restful. She felt she'd just closed her eyes when she dimly heard a knock on the door. The covers shifted; she felt Ian rise. She was only dimly aware of low male voices conversing near the door.

The next thing she knew there was a hand on her shoulder, jarring her into wakefulness.

"Sabrina!"

She winced at the prod of his voice. He was still angry, she decided vaguely. Would it always be so . . . ? She rolled to her side and forced her eyes open.

Ian stood at the bedside, towering over her. He was fully dressed, she noted hazily.

But his features were as grimly forbidding as ever. "I must leave, Sabrina."

She gazed dumbly upward into eyes as gray as the northern skies. "Leave?" she repeated, the huskiness of sleep still clinging to her voice. "To go where?"

"There is trouble elsewhere on my lands." He strapped his sword belt into place.

The fog of sleep lifted, like a curtain being plucked high and away. She pushed the blankets away and sat up, swinging her legs from the bed. The stone was frigid as ice upon her feet, but she paid no heed. "Trouble?" she echoed. "Of what sort?"

He shook his head. "I do not know. I received a message this morn, asking for assistance."

"Is it the Campbells, do you think?"

"In all likelihood." Even as she reached for her clothes, he was striding for the door.

Scant minutes later, Sabrina ran into the bailey.

Above the tower, the ceiling of the sky hung low and threatening, the clouds dark and ominous. The damp air carried with it the bite of the coming winter. In her haste, she'd forgotten a shawl. But her own comfort swiftly fled her mind as she spied the body of mounted men that had assembled. There was such solemn determination about the group that a spark of fear leaped high in her throat. All were heavily armed. Clearly this was no hunting foray.

Ian stood engrossed in conversation with Fraser. Sabrina remained where she'd stopped on the last step, patiently waiting. Ian glanced up once; their eyes touched briefly. She summoned a semblance of a smile, not at all certain she'd succeeded. But at least he knew she was there.

At last he finished. He clapped a hand on Fraser's shoulder then turned and strode for his stallion. In one swift move, he swung up into the saddle. A silent signal from him . . . and the group thundered toward the gate.

Her smile froze. He spared her no kiss, no second glance—not even a good-bye. Raw pain splintered through her. Bleeding inside, she blinked back hot, foolish tears.

Fraser made his way over to her. He did not ride with them, for he'd been charged with staying to protect those here at the castle.

He mistook her tears. His voice reached her gently, all the more painful for it came from such a great, hulking man. "Dinna worry, lass. They go to Kildurn. No doubt they'll be back before dark."

"We can only hope." She struggled to keep the disappointment from her tone, but there was no disguising the wrenching ache in her heart. Before she shamed herself utterly, she turned and ran back into the hall.

In truth, Ian was no less shattered. He was bitterly stung, wounded by her lack of faith. Did Sabrina truly think he had murdered Fionna? It mattered little that his bitch of a stepmother had deserved her fate. He would never harm any woman, no matter the provocation. But he had seen the way she trembled in fear of him, as if he were a monster. Mother of God, in fear of *him!*

His thoughts tormented him. The seed of doubt had been planted. Would she turn from him . . . into his cousin's arms? His mood was black as the mountains that loomed ahead. Oh, but her smile ever abounded for Alasdair and not for him. Never for him. She gazed upon his cousin with sunshine and warmth . . . would she ever deign to look upon him in that way? It rankled that she had sought out Alasdair, and not him, to ask about Fionna. That she trusted Alasdair . . . as she obviously did not trust him.

But the truth of Fionna's death must remain forever hidden. It was a secret he would carry with him to the grave. He had promised himself that . . . and a promise given was a promise kept.

It could be no other way.

They had been riding for perhaps an hour when Alasdair rode up alongside him. Ian gritted his teeth. It was all he could do to speak to his cousin. "What is it?" he asked coolly.

Alasdair's eyes flickered. "I was worried when Sabrina did not come down to supper last eve. How is she?"

"Sabrina is my concern, cousin, not yours."

"And she is my friend," Alasdair said stiffly, "and so I would ask again. Is she well?"

Ian stared straight ahead where the mountains rose sharp and stark against the horizon. "'Tis none of your concern—"

Alasdair's hand shot out and caught his bridle. "We tussled on occasion when we were lads, Ian. It is not like us not to confront our anger. Let us have this out now, shall we?"

His men began to rein in, clustering around them in a half circle. Ian gestured with one hand. "Ride on," he shouted. "We will catch up."

The men dispersed. Once they were alone, Ian's gaze, dark and burning, rested on Alasdair.

"Very well, then," he said curtly. "You had no right to tell her about Fionna."

"Then you should have, cousin."

Ian chafed. Alasdair was right. He *should* have told her, just as he should have known those foolish rumors would come back to haunt him. But it was all in the past, and it was there he'd hoped they would remain.

He met his cousin's gaze head-on. "You are right. It should have come from me, and did not. But was it necessary to tell her that some whispered it was I who murdered her?"

Alasdair did not back down. "She asked how Fionna died, Ian. I knew more questions would follow. It would have come out sooner or later—since you obviously had no intention of telling her, I merely thought it best if it came from me. Have I not always stood at your side—in battle and otherwise?"

Ian was silent. Those who knew him had known he would never use his strength to best one weaker than himself. Indeed, most of his clan had stood behind him, even when the rumor was strongest. In time, it had dwindled away, when those who doubted came to recognize that their new chieftain was a fair and just man.

"You are right," he said finally. "You have always rallied to my side, Alasdair." A little of his tension eased. "Do you know, I was given to wonder if you did not mean to turn Sabrina against me."

Alasdair cocked a brow. "That was why you bid Fraser to stay at the castle, and not me, was it not?"

Ian chuckled. "You know me well, cousin."

"You act like a jealous husband."

"Perchance because I *am* a jealous husband."

"Ah, and I can see why, with a wife as comely as Sabrina." He sighed. "I envy you, Ian."

"You have only to find a woman of your own, Alasdair. If you wish, I shall find you one, lest you be as old as Uncle Malcolm on your wedding night."

"I think I shall do the finding myself, Ian, lest I find myself wed to a hag! Indeed, what makes you think I've not already found my bonny lass? Think that you know me so well?"

They turned their mounts toward the others, slipping into the banter that usually marked their relationship. But while Ian's mood was considerably lightened, it was not to stay so.

They reached their destination in late afternoon, descending into a narrow valley. In summer, Ian knew, there was nowhere more peaceful than this place. Flowers brightened the valley floor; the air was sweetly scented with their perfume. But where before dozens of huts flanked the rushing stream, only a handful remained. And now the acrid odor of smoke burned his nostrils. Silence lay over all like a smothering fog.

Behind him came a collective indrawn breath. "Jesu," one of his men exclaimed. "Who did this?"

Just then a woman emerged from one of the huts. When she saw them, she screamed and began to back away.

"Hold!" someone cried. "We mean you no harm!"

Only when she saw their plaid did she stop. An elder man joined her; a score of others showed their faces as well. Small children clung to their mothers' skirts, their eyes huge and frightened.

Ian was the first to dismount. He raised a hand. "You have naught to fear," he called out. "I am Ian the MacGregor."

The woman ran forward and seized his hands. "I am Donelda. Praise God you are here." The white-haired man stepped up as well. "This is Fergus, my father."

Ian's face was grim. "Fergus. Donelda. What happened here? Who did this?"

The old man shook his head. "We woke in the middle of the night to the smell of fire. A score of men set the torch to all that would burn, then scattered our cattle. Those who tried to stop them were struck down. Donelda lost her husband and eldest son."

One of Ian's men shook a clenched fist. "They were Campbells, weren't they? Those thievin'—"

"They were not." The others had gathered in a half circle around them. "They came in the name of Comyn the Red," someone shouted. "To restore the Comyns to the throne. The rightful rulers. 'Twas their battle cry."

Had this been in retaliation for his support of the

Bruce? The Campbells had pledged their support to the Bruce. In this, at least, they were united. He could not help but think of Jamie MacDougall. . . . Did he have a hand in all this?

"The Bruce, my lord. Ye know him, do ye not?"

Ian nodded. "I do."

"He'll stop these blackguards, won't he?"

Ian hesitated. "Much has happened since summer. The English defeated his army at Methven. Then Comyn's vengeful relatives attacked at Dalry as he attempted passage over Loch Lomond. His party was forced to split up. His wife, daughter Marjorie, and brother Neil were captured at Kildrummy and confined. Neil died as traitor in October. The Bruce was forced into hiding."

Ian paused. "At present I do not know his whereabouts. I have no doubt that soon he will return to set things aright. In the meantime, you need not fear. I will send troops here to protect you and help rebuild."

He stared out where the wind rippled the grasses of the valley. He saw all through a fiery mist of rage. A dark resolve slipped over him. "We will find the fiends who did this." His voice carried with it an edge of steel. "I will not rest until they are found."

Fergus thumped his fist on his chest. "We stand by you, my lord, as we stand by the Bruce."

A young woman, jiggling a babe on her hip, stepped forward. "They rode to the north and east, my lord. I saw them."

Ian strode to his stallion and mounted. A storm swirled within him, roiling and growing stronger by the second. He ripped his sword from its scabbard and raised it high. His eyes blazed with the heat of a lightning bolt.

"To the Bruce! And to vengeance!"

A cheer broke out. Mingling with the thunder of hooves on the earth was a bloodcurdling battle cry.

A single day and night had passed—the longest of her life! Sabrina missed Ian desperately. She felt the pain of separation keenly—that she'd not thought to feel it at all only made it that much harder to bear! She missed the heat of his body next to hers in the dark of the night, the strength of his arms hard about her back, the comfort of his presence—odd that she'd become so quickly accustomed to it!

She bitterly regretted the way they had parted. If she could, she would take back all she had said, all the harshness that passed between them. She told herself he cared naught for her. That it wasn't her he'd wanted, but it made no difference.

She prayed fervently for his safety, for the day he would return.

It was early in the afternoon on the second day when she decided to ride outside the castle. She was too agitated to work, too unsettled to rest.

She was headed toward the stable when she felt a tug on her hand. She glanced down to see a small, dark-haired child beside her.

"Well, hello, there." She smiled down at the girl.

Dark eyes shone brightly. The girl crooked a finger and beckoned her close. Curious, Sabrina knelt down.

"I've a secret," the girl whispered. "A secret I can tell only you."

Sabrina's eyes softened. "Indeed," she murmured. "And what is this secret you can tell only me?"

"A man bid me come to you. He wishes to meet you at the oak tree by the spring. He said to tell no one but you."

Sabrina frowned. Was this a game the child played? She smiled encouragingly at the girl. "Do you remember what this man looked like?"

"He was tall—with hair the color of ripe wheat."

Sabrina's heart leaped. Surely it was not . . .

"What is your name, lass?"

"I am Deanna."

"And where did you meet this man, Deanna?"

"'Twas there, outside the gatehouse, where my sisters and I played."

Sabrina smoothed the child's dark curls. "Thank you, Deanna. 'Twill be our secret, will it not?"

The child's head bobbed. "Aye, mistress."

"Good. Now then, you may go to the kitchens and ask the cook for a jellied tart. Tell them I said 'twould be all right, for we've more than enough for tonight's dinner, and they'd best not shoo you away."

The little girl beamed and ran off, for she'd gained the lady's favor.

Sabrina got to her feet and brushed the mud from her skirts. She decided to forego her ride and walk instead. She headed through the gates, her steps firm and purposeful.

The spring lay not far beyond the castle walls. There was a well within the bailey, but Sabrina had learned that, in summer, the well occasionally ran low and it was necessary to carry water from the spring.

The oak tree came into view, huge and towering, its limbs stripped bare of its leaves. The north side of the trunk was covered in rich, velvet moss.

She halted. A frown creased her forehead, for there

was no one about. She glanced in all directions, wondering if mayhap someone had decided to play a trick on her . . .

Strong fingers wrapped around her arm, whirling her around. Her startled cry died in her throat as she stared upward into a face she'd thought never to see again.

"Jamie," she gasped. "Saints, you frightened the wits out of me!"

In answer he laughed and swept her into his arms. His head swooped down and his lips rested full upon her own. For an instant Sabrina was too stunned to move. Her hands came up between them and she pushed herself away.

His arms fell to his sides. "What is this?" he demanded. "I thought you would be glad to see me, Sabrina."

His censure sent a stab of guilt all through her. "I— I am," she said quickly. "But—you should not be here, Jamie."

"I had to see you. I had to see for myself if it was true—that you'd married him."

Him. Ian. She winced.

"'Tis true," she confided, her voice very low. "I—I am wed to Ian."

His jaw tensed. The pain in his eyes cut her to the quick. The confession was torturous for both of them.

"Why?" His expression was taut and harsh. "Dammit, how could you? He was to marry Margaret—"

"Margaret is dead, Jamie."

Shock flooded his face. "How?"

"She drowned. Her mantle was found near the loch the day they were to wed. We searched and searched"

She gestured vaguely. Her hand fell to her side. "'Twas no use. We found no trace of her."

"And so *you* wed Ian in her place."

She flushed. He made it sound like a condemnation. "I had no choice, Jamie."

For the longest time he said nothing. He stared at her, his angry hurt open and glaring. The silence that lurked between them was as dark and heavy as a moonless night. Then suddenly something changed.

"You are pale and wan, Sabrina. Has he been mistreating you?"

A wisp of a smile curled her lips. She shook her head. "I am fine, Jamie. Truly. He—he treats me well. I spent a restless night, that is all."

Her smile faded. "What about you? Have you joined your uncle in the fight against the Bruce?"

"Aye." He stepped close, his regard somber. His gaze moved over her features, one by one, as if to devour her.

"Come with me, Sabrina." His voice was low and intense. "You need never see him again. We can flee. To France perhaps." He seized her about the waist. "Come with me now—"

She twisted away, evading the hands that reached for her still. "Jamie, please! I—I cannot. I cannot dishonor my father so." *Nor Ian.* But this was best left unsaid. Nor could she stand to *think* what it would be like without Ian. This, too, was left unsaid. . . . Faith, she could scarce admit it even to herself!

"I love you, Sabrina."

The fervor she sensed in him sliced her in two. She despaired her wayward heart. God above, she knew not what she felt! "Do not say that, Jamie! It cannot be—ever!" With her eyes she beseeched him. With her voice she implored him. "Do not make this harder—for either of us, Jamie."

He shook his head. "I cannot let go so easily."

"You must," she began. The drumming sound of footsteps in the muddied lane behind them made them both look up, they'd been alone until then.

Her expression grew harried. "Jamie, please, you must go, for I cannot guarantee your safety if you stay."

In answer he caught her against him. Sabrina did not have the heart to fight him as he took her mouth in a swift, hard kiss.

"I will return," he said when at last he raised his head. His eyes burned bright and intense as a summer sky.

Then he was gone, darting into the forest. Her gaze followed him until he was lost from view.

"Take care, Jamie," she whispered. "Take care . . ."

When she was certain he'd made his escape safely, she turned and walked toward the castle. She despised herself, for she knew she'd hurt him. The burden of her guilt was one she must shoulder for a long time to come. Yet it was just as she'd said. There had been no other choice.

Fraser met her just as she entered the hall. "You need not have worried, Sabrina. They come within the hour."

Her lips parted. "They return? Ian returns?"

He grinned hugely. "Aye."

A joyous relief weakened her knees. Her prayers had been answered. She ran up to the parapet where she could see them from afar. As soon as she spied a group of riders coming down the lane, she hurried down into the bailey to wait.

Before long the soldiers galloped through the gate. Sabrina searched the riders one by one, but there was no sign of Ian.

Then she heard a shout. "Hurry! We need help here!"

Her gaze fixed in horror on the last straggling group to enter. A man's body was draped across the saddle of one horse. Another horse carried two others. Fraser and several others ran forward to lift the first body down. Her heart lurched, for it seemed she had prayed for naught.

The man was none other than Ian.

Sixteen

"Lay him there."

Sabrina nodded toward the bed, then hurried to whisk back the sheet. Her heart was pounding so that she could scarcely breathe; that she could muster speech was a miracle.

Two of his soldiers deposited him on the mattress. "We did what we could," one of the men said quickly, "but he wouldna stop bleeding."

"When was he wounded?" The question came from Fraser.

"This morn." Alasdair had just walked through the door. It was he who answered.

"What happened?"

"When we arrived at Kildurn, we found nearly all of the huts burned to the ground."

Fraser erupted into a curse. "Those blackguard Campbells—"

"Not the Campbells, nor a band of reivers," Alasdair said grimly. His gaze slid to Sabrina. "Comyn supporters."

Sabrina reeled. She felt his cold displeasure like the prick of a knife. Jamie's image vaulted into her mind. Dear God, he'd joined forces with his uncle. But was this what he was about? She felt suddenly sick.

But he had been here, she reminded herself. He couldn't have been a part of this raid.

"We went after the raiders, and caught up to them this morn. They won't be raiding MacGregor land anymore, but we lost two men," Alasdair went on. "Pray God we don't lose Ian as well."

While he recounted the battle, Sabrina stepped to the bedside. Sheer willpower prevented her from crying out. Ian's face was bleached of all color, as pale as moonlight. His shirt and plaid were soaked in blood. His eyes were closed, shadowed so darkly they lay like blots of dark ink against his cheeks.

"Have ye knowledge of healing, Sabrina?" Fraser's eyes sought hers.

Hers were wide and frightened. "A bit. My father was hurt in skirmishes now and then."

Fraser stepped up beside her. "Let's just see what we have here, eh?"

Together they stripped him of his clothing. Sabrina was hazily aware that Alasdair and the others had left them alone. Sensing her embarrassment, Fraser quickly flipped the edge of the sheet over his loins. But his torso, front and back, was smeared in blood—most of it still bright and crimson.

He lay so still and white. And there was so much blood. She pressed ice-cold fingers to her lips and swayed, certain he was dead after all. . . .

Fraser slid a steadying arm around her. "Keep yer head about ye, lass. It may not be as bad as it looks. Besides"—he slanted her a lopsided smile—"I need ye to tell this dim-witted fool what to do."

Mary had already slipped into the chamber with basins of hot water and clean linen cloths. Sabrina be-

gan the task of wiping him clean, instinctively aware
her touch would be gentler than Fraser's. Her stomach
heaved once as the blood-soaked pile of cloths heaped
ever higher, but she ignored it. Twice Ian moaned,
once when Fraser rolled him to his side so she could
reach his back; the other when she touched his left
shoulder. Both times nearly sent her screaming from
the room.

At last she was finished. Together she and Fraser
surveyed the damage. There was a ragged, gaping
hole in his left shoulder, adjacent to his armpit, still
another between his ribs. The whole of his left shoulder and side was one monstrous bruise.

Blood still welled from both wounds, thick and
dark. Fraser murmured that the one in his shoulder
was from a sword, the other from a dagger.

"Praise God 'tis not his sword arm," he added.

"We must bind the wounds tightly so the bleeding
stops, Fraser. Then they must be sewn closed."

They bound long, linen strips tightly around his
shoulder and side. Fraser looked horrified as she insisted he pull it tighter, but he did as she asked. It
seemed an eternity passed before the bleeding eased.

Her hands were shaking as she threaded her needle. It took three attempts to pull the thread through
the eye, but at last she was ready. After cleansing the
wounds anew, she began to work.

Her first stab through his flesh sent a jolt through
her entire body, but Ian moved nary a muscle. The
second was easier, but it was nonetheless a slow,
painstaking task bringing the edges of the jagged
wounds together. Sabrina worked as quickly as she
dared, giving a hearty prayer of thanks that Ian did
not awaken.

Her lungs were burning by the time she'd finished. She breathed a deep-seated sigh of relief and glanced at Fraser. "There. 'Tis done."

Ian's lashes lifted. All the strength seemed to ebb from his limbs. Sabrina stared straight into eyes the color of a clear mountain stream. 'Twas then she heard his voice, more breath than sound. "You enjoyed that, didn't you, bratling?" As if the effort was more than he could bear, his eyes slid closed.

Sabrina couldn't help it. She buried her face in her hands and cried.

He did not wake for three days.

Fever set in the following day, giving her and Fraser the fright of their lives. Never had she seen a man so leeched of color! Sabrina bathed him endlessly with cool water, for his skin was as hot as fire. He thrashed so restlessly Fraser was forced to hold him down. Both watched the wounds carefully for any sign of poisons.

The next day he was still ill with fever. Though now he only twitched restlessly, the rise and fall of his chest was quick and shallow. Time and again she bent her head close to assure herself that he yet lived. Fraser brought food and drink, but her appetite was scant. She did not leave the chamber, for she was possessed of the notion that if she left, he would surely die.

On the third day, exhausted and numb, she pulled up a stool beside the bed. Color had begun to seep back into his skin, and he appeared to be resting better. Though she tried to stop it, several times she felt her eyelids drooping. Finally she let them close. She would rest, if only for a moment . . .

It was a slight tug on her scalp that woke her.

Opening her eyes, she saw lean fingers threading through the tangled silk of her hair where it streamed over the bed. The sight jolted her upright. He was awake—Ian was awake!

She laid a hand on his forehead. His skin was cool to the touch. "The fever is gone, praise God," she breathed. "How do you feel?"

"Like I've done battle with Satan himself—and lost." His voice was as hoarse and raspy as stale rushes.

Her smile was tremulous. His features were gaunt, but his eyes were alert though tired.

He raised a hand. The back of his knuckles grazed her cheek. "I dreamed that you cried for me, bratling."

His whisper sped straight to her heart. She rubbed her cheek against his hand. "You left without saying good-bye." That was not what she'd meant to say, but now that she had, the sharpness of remembrance tore at her breast. Her throat grew hot and aching. "Ian, when I first saw you . . . I—I thought you were dead!"

The glimmer of a smile tugged at his lips. "Ah. And did you rejoice on thinking yourself a widow?"

"Nay!" Sudden, startling tears swamped her vision. She ducked her head that he might not see. "I—I would never wish you dead, Ian. Never!"

Her fervency wiped the smile clean from his lips.

And all at once her emotions lay scattered like leaves before a scouring wind. She felt . . . what she'd never thought to feel for this man. There was a painful catch at the corner of her heart. Ah, but did she dare trust her feelings? She'd been so very certain she was in love with Jamie—but she'd felt nothing when he'd kissed her, neither pleasure nor displeasure.

Did she love Ian?

She knew not.

She *dared* not.

His fingers still lay within hers, there on the coverlet between them. She started to draw her hand away, but his grip tightened, surprisingly strong despite his malaise.

His gaze captured hers. "I did not dream it, did I?"

Her eyes clung to his. She could not look away. Something flickered in those clear gray depths, something that made her tremble inside. With her seated, gazing down at him, she should have held the advantage. Yet never had she felt so vulnerable and exposed!

Her lips parted. "Nay," she heard herself say.

All at once the air between them grew close and heated. He whispered her name, and laced within the sound was an intensity she'd never before heard. He started to rise, his intention obvious.

Her eyes flew wide in alarm. She pushed him back with a hand on his chest. "Ian, no! You must be still!"

The effort made him growl with frustration. "Damnation!" he swore. "I am weak as a mewling kitten." He grimaced. "Help me to rise, Sabrina. There's much to be done. I must send soldiers and supplies back to the village—"

"'Tis already done! Alasdair has seen to it." Her emotions well in hand now, she got to her feet, planting her hands on her hips. "If you would gain your strength back, you must rest—and do as I say."

He glared at her.

She smiled sweetly.

There was grumbling as he drank the broth she fetched for him. He was in the mood for something far more hearty. On the morrow, she promised, if he continued to improve.

She slept on a pallet near the bed where she'd spent the last few nights . . . and woke to find him waiting—somewhat impatiently—for food to break his fast.

Despite the fact that he lay in bed, there was no denying the aura of masculine power that clung to him. There was an odd little quiver in her belly. Her fingers tingled with the urge to travel over his skin, to feel for herself that it was as smooth and hard as it looked.

After he'd finished eating, she decided it was time to change his bandages. The wounds looked better, she decided. She applied a healing salve and rewrapped them in clean linen strips; she balanced a hand against his chest while she did his shoulder. A shiver went through her, for her hand looked dainty and fair against the dark, hair-roughened landscape of his chest.

She could feel the weight of his gaze on her as she worked. She braved a glance at his face—no mockery dwelled there, but his scrutiny was oddly intense . . . and wholly disturbing. Why did he stare at her so? she wondered frantically. Did he compare her with Margaret? With Fionna? The thought was like a dagger twisting inside her, but she betrayed none of her turmoil.

"I begin to see why the English wear armor," she said lightly.

His hands had come out to close on her waist. Their warmth burned clear through her gown.

A roguish brow arose. "Weaklings, all," he proclaimed brashly, "for am I not the mightiest warrior in all Scotland?"

"I believe you are the *luckiest* warrior in all Scotland."

The laughter faded from his features. His eyes pierced hers for the space of a heartbeat. "Aye," he said quietly, "that I am."

His hands had yet to release her. A curious tension hummed between them. Sabrina floundered, for she knew not what to say. Ian opened his mouth; she sensed he was about to speak, but whatever it was, she would never know. The spell was broken by a knock on the door.

Fraser strode in wearing a huge grin. "I told the lass here ye would be fine," he announced, "but she dinna believe me. She fretted and stewed like a hen with wee chicks."

"Did she now?"

"That she did," Fraser proclaimed. "Do ye know not once did she leave yer side? Nay, not once! Why, I daresay she is a veritable saint!"

Sabrina blushed and turned aside. This time Ian said nothing, but she felt the touch of his eyes on her profile as surely as she'd felt the touch of his hand on her cheek last eve.

Ian was anxious to be up and about. Though Sabrina protested most vehemently, her objections were turned aside by the two men. An arm about his waist, Fraser got him to his feet. A few turns about the chamber and he was exhausted. He fell back into bed, cursing at his lack of strength. She very nearly chided him for pushing himself so hard, but held her tongue. Nonetheless, he insisted on rising every few hours. Oddly, he *did* seem stronger every time he arose.

He dozed off and on throughout the day and evening. When darkness laid its covering full upon the earth, Sabrina crept across the floor to prepare for bed. The day had been long and tiring, but the awful fear that had clutched at her these past days had fled. For the first time she knew that Fraser was right— that Ian would heal and be as strong as ever.

Though she longed for the comfort of a long, hot bath, she would not risk waking Ian. Instead she warmed water over the fire and poured it into a basin. As she lowered the ewer to the table, her head began to spin. Spots danced before her eyes, and the floor seemed to tilt sharply to and fro. Gripping the edge of the table, she fought to remain standing. Mercifully, the world righted itself.

She expelled a long, slow breath. Since the day Ian had been so angry when he saw her with Alasdair, she'd had at least one such spell a day—it was unlike her to feel so poorly of a sudden. She'd told herself it was fatigue, for this time while she'd been tending Ian had been fraught with worry. But she was beginning to wonder if the cause were something far different. . . .

Stripping away her clothes, she laid them aside. She scrubbed herself quickly, for the night air was cool against her naked skin.

Little did she realize the feast offered up for hungry, avid eyes that watched from across the room as she loosened her hair. Slender arms lifted those redgold tresses high and away from her shoulders; they fell down her back, a rippling waterfall of fire and honey. She bent and skimmed a wet linen cloth up and down the length of her legs. The bounce and sway of rouge-tipped breasts made Ian's mouth water with a yearning hunger that had naught to do with food.

Her gaze skipped back over her shoulder. Their eyes locked for a long, heart-stopping moment. She drew a white linen bedgown over her head, her movements shy and almost clumsy, for now she knew he surveyed her every move.

Noiselessly she glided across the floor to sit before the fire. She pulled the brush through her hair until it was free of tangles, then set it aside. Tugging it over her shoulder, with her fingers she started to separate it into three long ropes.

Only then did he speak. "Leave it," he said quietly.

Puzzled, Sabrina turned to gaze at him questioningly.

He smiled slightly. "Your hair is lovely, sweet. 'Tis a shame to see it plaited and bound."

Sweet. Her heart squeezed painfully. 'Twas the first time he'd called her thusly. Did he mean it? Or was it but a slip of the tongue—an endearment spoken in idle remark . . .

Spoken . . . but not from the heart.

He extended a hand. "Come here."

"In a moment." She dallied overlong, spreading the glowing embers with a poker, throwing a chunk of wood onto the fire and watching the sizzle of sparks spray upward.

"Sabrina." There was that in his tone which bespoke a subtle warning.

Hauling in a fortifying breath, she went, on legs that weren't entirely steady.

As she reached the bedside, strong fingers closed around hers, drawing her down upon the bed. Sabrina could not help it. She stared in fascination at the hand which imprisoned hers, resting there upon her thigh. His fingers were so much bigger than her own, lean and dark and supple. She recalled anew the tauntingly erotic play of those long fingers around the tips of her breasts, the hollow of her belly, and aye— there at the joinder of her thighs, the place that even now grew warm and tingly in remembrance.

"Now then. You will not sleep upon that wretched pallet again."

It was an order, as arrogant and imperious as ever. Her eyes flashed up to his. She bristled. "And where am I to sleep, then?"

"Where else would you sleep but with your husband?"

"But your shoulder—"

"—is doing quite well, thanks to your care. And indeed"—his smile was brazen—"I will rest much better with my wife beside me."

Her tone was stern. "Ian, you are in no condition to . . . to . . ." To her horror, she grew flustered, unable to put into words the act that even now loomed high aloft in her mind.

"To what?" His expression was innocence itself.

Oh, but he was horrid to do this to her! "To—to partake of . . . of any pleasure!"

There was a devil's glint in those crystalline eyes. "And what pleasure might that be, lass?" He trailed a finger down her bare arm, sending shivers of delight all through her.

"The pleasures of the flesh!" she blurted.

"Ah, but would the pleasure be all mine?" His gaze now dwelled on her lips. His voice grew as soft as thistle-down. "Would it, sweet?"

Sabrina's heart was thudding so hard she feared it would crash through her chest at any moment. "You know it would not," she said helplessly.

His eyes darkened. "Lie with me."

She inhaled sharply. He pressed a finger against the fullness of her lips. "Nay, not in the way that you think. I would hold you, sweet. I promise, that is all."

Sabrina was helpless against such tender persuasion. She slipped into bed beside him, careful not to jostle him, nestling herself against his hard length. His arm came around her and she pillowed her head against the smooth hollow of his shoulder.

For a long time there was no sound in the room but the crackle and hiss of the fire. Her tresses streamed across the width of his chest. With his free hand he lifted a ribbon of hair and brought it to his lips.

"Beautiful," he murmured again.

Sabrina flushed self-consciously. "When I was young," she said softly, "I used to wish for smooth, golden hair like Margaret's—hair the color of wheat. I remember once," she confided, "before you came to foster with us, I took the shears and cut it. Margaret laughed. Papa was furious. But I—I thought it might grow back like Margaret's."

His arm tightened. "I am glad it did not. I much prefer yours. 'Tis like living fire." He was silent for a moment. "You need not compare yourself with Margaret. You are as fair as she. Don't you know that?"

Sabrina had gone very quiet. "But Papa—"

"—was blind to your beauty," he finished almost harshly. "All he could see was Margaret."

Despite his praise, a squall of uncertainty blustered in her chest. "Alasdair said"—her voice was very small—"that Fionna was very beautiful."

At the mention of Fionna, she felt the sudden tension that invaded him. She thought he might refuse to answer. Instead he said gruffly, "Aye. She was."

Despair like a clamp seized her heart. No wonder he'd been smitten with her.

She didn't realize she'd spoken aloud until he gave a bitter laugh. "Smitten? Hardly. Though I've no doubt Fionna believed every man was smitten with her."

"So you did not . . . love her?"

"Nay!"

His vehemence was convincing . . . almost. "And you did not marry me because I—I resemble her?" She held her breath and waited.

His fingers caught at her chin and brought her eyes to his. "As I recall, you are of a size with Fionna and she had hair of flame, but the resemblance ends there—despite what Uncle may say, I do not think you look like her. For you see, Sabrina, her beauty was deadly, her charm poison. My father knew not that she betrayed him with other men. He loved her, but I most assuredly did not. I found her selfish and vain. In short, Sabrina, she was a witch, and if I thought you were anything like her, I would never have married you."

Sabrina bit her lip. She wanted desperately to believe him. And yet . . . "But you thought I lay with Jamie."

"That I did."

"Yet still you married me."

"Aye. Because I wanted you, Sabrina. I wanted you then, and I want you now. That is something that will never change."

A gossamer tendril of hope curled within her. "Truly?"

A rakish brow arose. "Do you doubt me, lass?"

It was then she realized . . . it was not him she

doubted, but herself. Her ability to hold him, to believe that he might truly want her for herself . . .

"Nay," she whispered, and knew it for the truth.

"Good. Nonetheless, I'm not averse to a bit of persuasion."

Though she protested anew that he was ill, he kissed away her protests. Her doubts . . . and her fears. He kissed her, long and lingeringly, as if he were starving—as indeed he was. He kissed her again and again until her arms crept around his neck and she yielded all he sought with a tiny little moan of surrender. Reluctantly he broke away, resting his forehead against hers.

His fingers fell to the hem of her gown. "Might we do away with this?" he whispered. "I would hold you—all of you."

His meaning did not go unheralded. She sat up and whisked the bedgown over her head. It fluttered to the floor, forgotten, as he raised himself on an elbow. Greedily he charted the unblemished flesh that lay open to his gaze. Though she pinkened to the roots of her hair, she did not stop him from looking his fill. Though his loins felt near to bursting, Ian would not go against his word. Besides, he sensed that she was exhausted from her care of him.

Pulling her to his uninjured side, he kissed her forehead and bid her good night.

But sleep did not come immediately. He held her within his embrace, enjoying the rise and fall of her breasts against his ribs, the trickle of her breath across his bare chest.

She was not so unaware of him as she would pretend, he decided—and aye, as he had been convinced. These past few days had told the tale only too well.

He recalled the delicate sweep of a hand on his brow. The way she twitched the sheet into place just so. The gentleness with which she changed his bandages. He envisioned anew the tears that shone brilliant in her eyes when he'd first awakened; her smile, watery but blindingly sweet.

A fierce swell of contentment rose like a tide within him. It was more than just the pleasure she brought to him in his bed, though she stirred him as no other woman had . . . as no other woman *would.* It was more than the fire lit in his loins, the fire in his heart. He'd sensed her apprehension at coming to his castle and assuming the role of wife. But she faced all with a brave determination that earned his admiration, and aye, his respect. Oh, she was still feisty as ever, for she was a woman of spirit and pride, a woman of strength.

And she was his. *His.*

There was a newfound peace between them in the sennight that followed. His recovery was swift, for he was young and well-conditioned. His left shoulder was a trifle stiff, but he knew it would pass.

One morning he announced his intention to spend the day fishing. She startled him by asking if she might accompany him.

"'Tis an arduous climb," he told her, "too rocky for horses."

Her chin tipped, as he'd known it would.

"I am up to it," she declared staunchly.

He smothered a smile, for he'd known that would be her reply.

They set out. Silence settled between them, but it was not an uncomfortable silence. In many places the path upward to the mountain loch was narrow and twisting; they could not walk side by side. Sabrina followed behind, lithe and sure-footed. She slipped once, sending a shower of rocks down the cavernous slope. Ian turned immediately and caught hold of her hand, bringing her to his side.

"I am fine," she said breathlessly.

"Good. 'Tis not far now."

Ever mindful of her safety, he slowed his pace a bit.

As he predicted, it wasn't long before the pathway delivered them to their destination.

A small loch lay nestled in a tiny meadow just below the ledge where they stood. Sapphire waters glistened smoothly. High above, wheeling shafts of sunlight chased away the low-hanging clouds, bouncing off the craggy peaks that loomed in the distance. There was no fog to mar the beauty of the granite mountains, austere and barren though they were, and indeed, it was a sight that never failed to move him deeply.

Beside him, Sabrina caught her breath.

He turned. Did she feel what he did, this—this oneness with the land? He wanted her to, he realized. He wanted it quite badly.

He eyed her closely. "'Tis not like Dunlevy Glen, is it?"

"Nay." She gazed off where earth and sky seemed to meet and meld. "'Tis just as beautiful," she mused softly, "though in a very different way."

His chest filled with pride. Her answer pleased him—it pleased him mightily. "Come," he said, reaching for her hand.

Together they descended to the shores of the loch. Ian spread a blanket to blot out the cold from the

mossy embankment, and it was there they sat. The
next hour was spent lazily fishing.

After a time, Sabrina plucked her long sapling pole
from the waters and laid it aside. To whit, neither of
them had any luck in catching the loch's residents.

Ian felt her gaze touch on his bare legs beneath his
kilt.

"Are you not cold?" she ventured after a bit.

"Aye. Come warm me, wench."

He dropped his pole and reached for her. She
evaded his hands and leaped lightly to her feet.

"I'm famished," she announced.

"So am I."

She ignored his leer and marched over to the pouch
that contained their noonday meal. Ian sighed and
moved to join her. She tore off a tidbit of the roast
lamb they'd supped on last eve and offered it to him.

He did not pluck it from her hand. Instead he
curled his fingers around her wrist and brought her
hand to his lips, taking the tidbit in this way. His
mouth closed around her fingers, clear to her knuckles, sucking the last bit of succulent juice from her
skin.

Her eyes widened. "A tasty morsel, I see." Her
voice was as unsteady as his heart.

"Indeed," he murmured. But now his gaze was on
her lips. A floodtide of desire shot through him. He
ached to plunder the velvet softness of her mouth. He
leaned closer, inhaling the fragrance of her hair. She
wore no coif, nor had she confined her honeyed
tresses in the braid she usually wore. It was loose and
unbound, tumbling over her shoulders and down her
back. Had she worn it thusly for him?

He reached for her, and this time she did not dance

away. Pulling her close, he availed himself of lips sweetly upturned to his, seeking the moist interior of her mouth with the eager glide of his tongue, glorying in the unguarded innocence of her offering. She tasted of honey and roses—of breathless surrender—and all at once his loins surged. He kissed the curve of her cheek, the tender place below her jaw where her pulse thrummed wildly, before returning to smile against her lips.

"More than a morsel," he whispered suggestively. "I daresay, a veritable feast."

He loved the way her eyes opened, heavy-lidded and smoky, to gaze straight into his. The tip of her tongue came out to moisten her lips.

"Ian," she said faintly. "The others will be disappointed if we fail to catch our supper."

"To the devil with the others." He shifted so she could feel the pulsing steel between his legs.

She blinked. "Ian," she gasped.

His laugh was husky. "Why so reluctant, sweet? I was not wounded *there*." Her nearness heated his blood to boiling. He kissed her again, letting her feel the throb of his manhood. But when he started to press her back, she brought her fingers to his lips.

"Nay," she said with a tiny shake of her head. "Let me."

She set her palm to his chest, pushing him back slightly. He leaned back, long legs outstretched before him, the bulk of his weight braced on his hands.

Her green eyes shone with a faintly teasing gleam. "You cannot touch, Ian. Remember that, my Highland prince."

Ian's heart began to thud. Waiting, anxious, a trifle

puzzled, he allowed her to do what she would, for this was a side of her he'd yet to see.

Lifting her skirts, she straddled his body. Then her hands were on the hem of his kilt . . . her furrowed cove brushed his rigid shaft. He inhaled sharply, feeling near to bursting the constraints of his flesh.

The fight to keep his hands at his sides was the hardest battle he'd ever fought—but he yielded with pleasure. An undulating twist of slender, curvaceous hips . . . and the part of him that swelled taut with need of her was imprisoned to the hilt within her tight, velvet sheath.

Impaled on the turgid thickness of his shaft, she gazed down at him with eyes the color of new spring grass. "Aye," she said breathlessly, "an arduous climb indeed."

Immersed in a crimson haze of pleasure, Ian closed his eyes. She was so hot. So smooth, melting him to his very soul.

Her hips lifted. Her secret valley lay poised on the very tip of him.

His eyes opened, shearing directly into hers. "Take me, sweet." His voice was low and vibrating. He could barely summon the strength to speak. "Take me now."

God above, she did. Churning. Straining. Pumping until he thought he would surely die of ecstasy. He gritted his teeth and sought to hold back, but it was no use.

A muffled groan tore from his chest. He caught her hips in his hands while she rode him with wild frenzy, caught up in the same torrent of emotion as he. He shuddered, spilling his seed hotly within her. At the same instant, he felt the rhythmic stroke of her silken channel tighten again and again. He caught her as she gave a low moan and collapsed against him in a wild tangle of limbs.

Her head was buried in the hollow of his shoulder. It was a long, long time before his breathing returned to normal. He trailed his fingers up and down her spine as she expelled a long, pent-up sigh. The memory of her wanton abandon made him smile.

For that was something he'd *never* expected.

All in all, there was little fishing to be done throughout the afternoon. . . .

'Twas a day well spent.

Seventeen

The next days remained relatively quiet. Winter dropped its cloak upon the Highlands, bringing with it a damp, icy chill. Black branches stood stark and naked against an endless gray sky, while the jagged peaks of the mountains stood coated in their wintry armor of white.

Within the castle, spirits were ever jovial as always. The clan MacGregor filled their days with laughter and their nights with food and drink. And as the days sped by, Sabrina could no longer hide from the truth.

She was with child.

She was neither naïve nor stupid. She knew the signs—by her calculations, it must have happened the very first time they'd lain together. Her last monthly course had been at Dunlevy, but there were other subtle signs of the changes within her. Her dizzy spells had begun to lessen, but her breasts were swollen and tender. A peculiar sickness had begun to plague her in the mornings of late, she who was sick but rarely. Ian had not noticed; she was usually still abed when he rose.

There was a growing thread of closeness between them, but Sabrina did not delude herself. All was still

tentative and new between them. She could not help
it; she was reluctant to divulge the news of her condition for fear of jeopardizing their newfound peace.

But Ian was a man of many moods. At times he
was distant and remote; it was as if he were half a
world away. She was well aware of the thunder of
discontent that rumbled across the land, just as she
knew he remained staunch in his support of the
Bruce. It was Fraser who told her Ian was certain the
raid on the village was a warning to those who stood
behind the Bruce. Was it this which preyed so pon-
derously on his mind? She did not know, for whenever she sought to query him, he replied that naught
was amiss.

She watched him one day as he led his stallion from
the stable. A small lad tugged on the trews he wore,
for it was bitterly cold this day. Ian glanced down,
then went on bended knee to speak with the boy. He
laughed and said something; the boy's head bobbed
furiously. He straightened, then lifted the lad high
into his saddle. Gathering the reins, he led boy and
beast across the length of the bailey and back again.
Even from where she surveyed the pair from her
chamber window, she could see the child beaming.
When Ian at last swung him to the ground, he gently
cupped the back of the boy's head before watching
him run off. 'Twas a tender—and telling—gesture.

Her hand crept to her belly, to the slight roundness
that had even now begun to swell, for she was some
three months gone. She must tell him, and soon. Before long it would be obvious to all.

An odd little pain gripped her heart. Ian had once
stated she would bear his sons. But would he truly
welcome a babe? Though perhaps the better question

was this . . . would he welcome *her* babe? She hated
the doubts that blistered her mind and heart. Did he
regret marrying her? Would he have preferred another as the mother of his child? Margaret, mayhap?
Or Fionna? Perhaps she was wicked—as wicked as
Papa had always accused. She despised her pettiness,
for she was jealous of a dead woman—nay, not one
but two!

A shiver went through her. She wondered anew
who had killed Fionna. . . .

She sighed, chiding herself for her foolishness.
There was work to be done and she had best be about
her business.

It was time for the monthly replenishment of the
kitchen herbs and spices. Since these were a precious,
costly commodity, they were relegated sparingly and
kept hidden away in a locked cabinet. But the cabinet
was in a storeroom deep in the bowels of the castle
where it was cool—silly though it was, it was a place
that made her distinctly uneasy. For that very reason
Sabrina had resolved to have the items moved elsewhere. But alas, the chore escaped her attention except for these times when they were needed.

She descended the roughly carved stone steps that
dipped below the level of the ground. In her hand
was a fat, stubby candle. The passageway was long
and narrow, drafty and cold, seeming to end in darkness.

Her footsteps seemed overly loud . . . or was there
an echo? She spun around and halted. A tingle of unease crept up her spine. Did someone follow? She
searched the shadows but saw nothing.

Again she moved forward . . . again that slithering
sound behind her.

She whirled. But there was nothing. No one was there. . . .

Taking a deep breath, she steadied her nerves. She quickened her pace to match the beat of her heart. She told herself it was just her imagination, but she could not banish the flicker of disquiet within her. The storeroom was just ahead. She would gather the herbs and spices and be gone from this place.

Again that shuffle behind her.

She whirled. "Who's there?" she called.

The sharp echo of her own voice reached back to her.

The skin on the back of her neck prickled eerily. There was a sudden tension, a curious chill, but she told herself she was being foolish. Unlocking the storeroom, she swept inside and went straight to the cabinet. But her hands were clumsy, and she dropped the keys. They skittered across the floor, and it was then she saw what had escaped her notice until now— an iron ring attached to a narrow door in the wall, scarcely wider than her person, bolted shut by an oak timber. It vaulted through her mind that it must be a trapdoor of some sort. . . .

Then it happened.

There was a stunning blow dealt to her shoulders. She cried out, in pain and shock. Her candle fell to the floor, then sputtered and went out. In the mind-splitting instant afforded her, she saw booted feet . . . a gloved hand reached for the iron ring in the wall— she heard it ripped from its hinges. Then hard hands were on her shoulders. She was thrust into a gaping hole.

She tumbled inside, landing hard on her shoulder. The door slammed shut; the bolt was jammed home.

Pounding footsteps resounded, then faded to nothingness.

Her heart bounded. Conscious of a throbbing in her shoulder, her head whipped in both directions. She blinked, rubbed at her eyes, and opened them, straining desperately to see, seeking some semblance of light, no matter how meager. A frisson of sheer terror blossomed in her being—there was none. God above, she'd been cast into a pit of utter darkness, a darkness so complete she could see nothing.

A sick dread wound its way into her belly. Someone had cast her into this horrid place. Who? Dear God, *who?* And why? To punish her?

Icy fingers plied their way along her spine. A scream rose in her throat. She bit it back. She had to keep her wits about her. Stunned and trembling and afraid, she got to her feet and felt her way about. The room was tiny, scarcely four steps in length, half that in width. The walls were made of stone. Scraping the toe of her slipper, she felt dirt beneath her feet.

She cringed. What vile creatures might lurk here? Her neck arched. Raising her hands, she touched the walls, moving haltingly until she encountered the outline of the door.

She pounded with her fists. "Help me!" she screamed. "Someone help me!"

Panic erupted. Fear nourished the frenzy to escape. She hammered at the door with all her strength, screaming until her throat was raw. Her coif came undone. Her hair fell out from the force of her blows. She could hear the tearing rasp of her breath, the rampant thunder of her heart jolting her entire body.

But no one heard. No one came. No one cared. . . .

Time passed. Was it minutes—or hours? She felt

she was flying apart inside. It was as if she'd been hurtled back into her childhood. She knew not if it was day or night. The cold seemed to reach up and surround her, like a shroud of death. It seeped within her very bones.

It was like being buried alive.... The walls were closing in on her, the ceiling coming closer ... ever closer. If only she could wake and find it was but a dream....

"Ian!" she cried. "*Ian!*" Terror coursed through her veins. Tears ran down her cheeks. She clawed at the door with her hands. Splinters ripped her flesh, but she cared not.

Ian did not come. He would never come, she realized. She would die here. Alone. Alone in the dark ...

Her chest heaved. A dry sob tore from her throat. In despair she slid helplessly down the wall and curled up in a tight little ball.

Ian returned from the hunt, a stag in tow. Shouts went up as the others saw his quarry.

"We'll have a merry feast this night!"

"Aye, this night and many others!"

Ian grinned broadly. He crossed the hall, a lively spring in his step.

"Is my wife abovestairs?" He posed the question to the maid who had just descended.

The girl shook her head. "Nay, my lord. I've not seen her in quite some while."

Nor, he soon discovered, had anyone else. Ian dared not give voice to the question that leaped to the fore. Had she fled? Nay, he thought. *Nay!* Mayhap she was not blissfully happy, but she was content. She did not spurn his touch, nor his longing.

And her mount was in the stable. His smile had long since vanished. Where the devil was she?

In the kitchens, unbeknownst to those who searched for the castle's mistress, the cook had bid one of her helpers fetch wine from the storeroom below.

"And ye'd best be quick about it, laddie!" she warned sternly.

"Aye, mum." The boy's tone was airy, for he well knew the cook blustered and raged, but in truth she was a pudding-heart. She'd raised the switch to his behind but once, then cried when the deed was done.

The boy was ambling down the long corridor when he suddenly became aware of an odd sound . . . like that of a faint tapping. Startled, he stopped short.

The sound came again.

The lad swallowed and crept forward. He'd heard no tales of Castle MacGregor being haunted, but this did not mean 'twasn't so. Why, not long ago his aunt had been chased by a dark, cowled figure with demon claws at the very stroke of midnight. Why, even now he shivered at the gruesome reminder.

The tapping came again . . . and this time he fancied there was a scream that curdled his very blood.

With nary a second thought, he turned and ran back up the steps as fast as his legs would carry him.

The cook, just coming from the kitchens, caught him by the scruff of his collar.

"Why do ye run, lad? And where be the wine ye were to fetch?"

The lad summoned his dignity—and his courage. "I'll not return there," he vowed. "There be ghosts down there!"

"Och," the cook scoffed. "Ye be listenin' to your

auntie too much. Do ye not know she's overly fond
of 'er spirits?"

"And it be spirits that dwell below," the boy coun-
tered, his eyes huge.

"Ye're a laggard," she accused. "Now be off with
ye and do what ye're told—"

"Wait," interrupted a voice from behind.

The pair turned to find the master filling the doorway behind them.

His gaze was fixed on the boy. "What did you
hear?" he asked the lad.

The lad shook his head. "I canna say for certain,
but there was a sound like this." He thumped the
door frame with his fist. "And then there was a
scream! Upon my word, my lord, 'twas a ghost—"

Before he'd even finished, Ian had spun around and
was heading for the stairs that led below. He beckoned Fraser, who snatched a torch from the wall
sconce. His steps carried him to the first storeroom.
He looked inside, but there was naught to see or hear.

The second storeroom was just beyond. Again he
entered, with Fraser just behind. Both men held very
still. Waiting. Listening.

At length Fraser shook his head. "The lad imagined
it—"

Ian held up a hand, a gesture that silenced his
friend. And then they both heard it, a faint sound . . .
like the mewling of a wounded animal.

"What the devil—" Fraser began.

Ian paid no mind. He traced the perimeter of the
walls. He spoke, almost to himself. "There was a
chamber here long ago . . . it was used as a storeroom
for summer's crops when I was young . . . I'd almost

forgotten it . . . Yes. *Yes!* Here it is!" He threw the bolt and wrenched the door wide.

The chamber was pitch black. "Fraser, the torch! I cannot see. . . ."

He nearly stumbled over her. She was sobbing softly, curled up tightly on the floor, her knees to her chest.

"Sabrina!" He dropped to his knees and gathered her into his arms. She opened her eyes and stared at him. He touched her cheeks. Her skin was ice-cold, her eyes glazed over with tears. "Jesu," he breathed. He was up and on his feet in a surge of power.

She turned her face into his shoulder and clung to him.

Ian strode to their chamber, taking the stairs two at a time.

Once there, he set her on her feet, keeping an arm about her lest she fall. She stood of her own power, but there was a glazed, sightless look in her eye that chilled him to the marrow of his bones. Tears still slipped down her cheeks. She had yet to speak. She was trembling so violently—whether with fear or cold, he knew not—that her teeth chattered.

He spoke her name. She gazed at him, yet he had the oddest feeling it was not him she saw. It was as if her mind had gone elsewhere.

He set his hands to her shoulders and gave her a gentle shake. "Sabrina, look at me! Are you all right?"

Her eyes clung to his. She nodded; he sensed it was all she could manage for now.

His hands fell lower. It was all he could do to pry her arms from across her breasts. He sucked in a harsh breath when he saw her palms. Her flesh was torn and bloodied, her nails broken and torn.

In two strides he was at the door, throwing it open and calling for a basin of warm water. Mary scurried to obey. When she returned, he took it and put it on a small table near the fire.

Sabrina had yet to move. She stood like a stone statue in the center of the chamber. Ian led her to the table and bade her sit. There he dipped a linen cloth into the water and gently began to cleanse her palms. As he worked, he glanced up at her.

"Can you tell me what happened?"

She shuddered. The breath that filled her lungs was deep and racking. "I went below to fetch herbs and spices for the cook. In the passageway I heard footsteps."

"Someone followed you?"

"Aye. But when I turned there was no one there."

Ian's mind worked furiously. Why would someone follow her?

She had seen the pucker of his frown. "What!" she cried out in outrage. "You do not believe me? Begone, then, damn you! I—I do not need you, Ian! Do you hear? I need nothing from you!"

She lurched upward and would have darted away but he caught her by the shoulders and brought her near.

"I will not leave you, Sabrina, not when the demons of the dark haunt you still. But there is only one way in—and one way out." He searched her face. "Are you sure you saw nothing?"

"There was someone there, I tell you . . . I was struck from behind . . . and I saw booted feet before I was pitched within that horrid room!"

It was strange. Very strange. In truth, he did not doubt her, but he would not feed her fright any further, for her fear was very real. To be locked in that room would have been frightening for anyone. To Sabrina, alone in the dark—dear God, it must have been a nightmare.

And indeed, she was shivering again almost violently.

"I believe you," he said quietly. Turning her palms upward, he kissed them in turn. He saw the tears that sprang to her eyes, saw the way she swallowed. Quickly he eased her clothing from her, relieved himself of his, and lifted her into bed.

He slipped in beside her, heaping a mound of covers over them both. There he drew her against his length and warmed her with the heat of his flesh. Yet even when her skin burned warm as his, she shook and shook. It came to him then that this was a chill that came from within.

His arms tightened. "Shhh," he whispered. "You are safe now, Sabrina."

She made a faint, choked sound. "It was horrible, Ian"—her voice quavered—"just like before, when Papa locked me away and I feared he would never let me out. *Just like before.*"

"I know." His throat grew achingly tight. "But I'll let no harm come to you, sweet. This I promise. By God, this I vow."

"Don't leave me, Ian. Don't leave me."

Her plea tore at his heart. "I won't leave you, sweet. I'm here." He laced his fingers through hers and brought their joined hands to his lips.

He knew she was still half-frightened out of her wits. He held her close, willing his strength into her. In time, her shivering ceased. She retreated into the

only place she could find sanctuary . . . the haven of
sleep.

Not so with Ian. Sabrina was right. This was no
accident. Someone had been there. Someone had
locked her in that room. It could have been anyone,
anyone who knew the castle. Servants. Kinsmen.

Yet why would anyone harm her? Or wish to
frighten her? Was there evil afoot at Castle Mac-
Gregor?

His blood ran cold at the thought.

His resolve hardened. He'd sworn he would protect
her, and so he would.

If need be, with his very life.

It was not a restful sleep that Sabrina fell into. Nay,
for her sleep was plagued with dreams. Visions that
came and went, sneaking like the shadowed moon
behind the clouds.

She saw herself, running down the passageway
again, reliving that instant when she'd been pitched
headlong into darkness. And she remembered the
moment when the door had been thrown open. Did
the darkness play tricks with her mind? Or had she
conjured up his image out of desperate longing?

Nay. It was Ian's voice. Ian's touch. Ian's hands. A
terrifying notion uncurled within her . . . Ian. Her sav-
ior? Or her tormentor?

Alasdair's voice whispered anew. *'Twas Ian who
found Fionna.*

And it was Ian who had found Margaret's cloak.
Ian who had found *her*. . . .

Was it he who had locked her inside?

In her dream, clouds shifted and cleared. He was
there again. Her husband. Her lover. He extended his

hands and grasped her own, lifting her. Only there was blood on his hands, dark and crimson. Blood that even now mingled with hers. She screamed and screamed and sought to run past him. But he was there, his footsteps pounding after her. And his hands were upon her, staining her with blood . . .

"Sabrina!"

She woke with a start, a scream curdled in her throat. For a long time she lay there gasping, wrestling with the tumult that churned inside her. And all the while she felt the heat of his lips on her brow, and then his hands, smoothing away damp tendrils of hair. The glow of the fire revealed his features as he leaned over her, etched with concern. There was no blood, only warmth and a tenderness that made her ache inside.

She lay very still, listening to the throb of his heart, steady and reassuring, beneath her ear. Despite the storm that blustered and brewed within her, she took comfort from the sheltering protection of his embrace.

"Ian," she whispered.

His fingers traced the shell-like shape of her ear, a wispy caress. "What, love?"

Love. Her heart squeezed. Was she his love? If only she knew. If only . . .

The question spilled from her lips before she could stop it. "Who killed Fionna?"

He stiffened. She felt his displeasure, like a spear through the breast.

His tone was cold as a wintry morn. "I did not kill her. I thought we'd settled that."

She swallowed. "I—I know that. But—"

"Good." He cut her off abruptly. "Now if you please, 'tis a subject I prefer not to discuss again."

He still held her, but there was a difference now. Though his manner was not harsh, his warmth was gone. A hollow emptiness welled up inside her. Chastened and subdued, her mind twisted and turned where it would, with no hope of stopping it. There was no ease for her troubled soul, no respite from the unknown.

But Ian knew. He *knew* who killed Fionna. She sensed it with all that she possessed. Yet why would he refuse to tell her unless he had something to hide?

He was a man of secrets—secrets he refused to share with her. And he alone knew her fear of the dark. God help her, she was falling in love with him. Were his arms a haven . . . or was he a murderer?

She feared him—what he might very well be.

But foolishly, she loved him far more.

Eighteen

Sabrina woke feeling incredibly drained, utterly weary. It was all she could do to rise and bathe. Mary eyed her oddly. It flitted across her mind that mayhap the little maid had guessed her condition, but Mary said nothing.

Belowstairs, the hall was nearly deserted. Glancing outside towards the bailey, she noted it seemed much more quiet than usual.

Uncle Malcolm was sitting near the fire, his plaid draped over his shoulders to warm him.

"Good morning, Uncle," she greeted. His eyes, so like Ian's, were clear this morn.

"And good morning to you, Sabrina." He hailed her with a smile.

"Have you seen Ian this morning, Uncle?"

"Aye, lass. Word came that several farms in the next valley were attacked last eve."

"Attacked! By whom?"

He shook his head. "I know not, lass."

Sabrina bit her lip. Her mind sped straight to Jamie. "Was anyone hurt?"

"I know very little, lass. But Fraser seems to think 'twas done by those tied to the Comyns."

Sabrina's eyes clouded over. On impulse she knelt down before him. "You've seen the passage of many years, Uncle," she murmured. "What rightful ruler do you believe belongs on Scotland's throne?"

Gnarled fingers smoothed the folds of his kilt. "I do not know the Bruce—I know only what Ian has told me of him. Ian believes that the Bruce can bring peace to this land, while I believe my nephew possesses a wisdom that far exceeds his youth." He sighed. "But we cannot continue to fight amongst our own. We must seek peace lest all Scotland be torn apart. That will never happen unless we stand behind one man."

"And you believe that man is the Bruce." It was a statement, not a question.

Malcolm nodded. "Aye, lass. I do."

His words stayed with her throughout the morn. For the first time, Sabrina began to truly understand the tumult that swept over the land like a pestilence. More and more she had begun to think she'd been wrong to judge so hastily, for of late she had heard much talk of the Bruce. Indeed, it seemed he was not the selfish tyrant she'd thought.

But the Scots were a proud breed, and none would give in so easily. Men would die; their women would weep, their children would grow up fatherless. What would be gained by fighting against each other? All that would be left behind was a legacy of pain and hatred, passed on from father to son.

Her mind thus engaged, she almost did not see the little girl who approached her. She smiled absently at the child, then realized she knew her.

"Deanna!" she exclaimed. "How are you, lass?"

Deanna beamed up at her, then beckoned her close. Sabrina obligingly bent over.

"The man bid me come to you again, mistress. He said that he must see you. He said to ask that you go to the same place."

Sabrina's heart leaped. Jamie. She meant Jamie.

She squeezed the child's shoulder. "Thank you, sweeting."

When the girl had left, she cast a quick glance around to make certain she was unobserved. Then she strode through the gates toward the spring.

He was standing near the oak tree when she approached. A wide smile lit up his features as he saw her.

"Sabrina! You came! I knew you would!"

Though her heart was glad he had remained safe and unharmed, she could not share the warmth reflected in his eyes. "Jamie, you should not be here! 'Tis dangerous!"

His gaze roved over her face. "I would brave Satan himself for just the sight of you, Sabrina."

Sabrina made a sound of frustration. "Jamie, I beg you, do not say such things! Need I remind you I am married to Ian?"

His smile withered. "He still lives? I heard he was wounded."

"Aye, he still lives." She drew a sharp breath. "How did you know of the attack on him?"

He did not want to tell her. She could see it in the way he refused to meet her gaze head-on.

"Tell me, Jamie."

"My cousin was among those who attacked his men," he said at last. "He was one of the few who escaped."

Sabrina was horrified. "Jamie! A village was burned to the ground! Was he part of that, too?"

"Aye." His tone was grudging.

Her lips tightened. "There were men killed! And young boys, too! Many were left without homes!"

His gaze flickered. "I regret that there must be bloodshed. But there is no other way, Sabrina. The Bruce cannot be allowed to rule Scotland." His lip curled. "Indeed, he is a coward, for he has yet to show his face again."

"Perhaps he is dead."

"He is not," Jamie declared flatly. "We have spies who know he is not." His eyes darkened. "But I would not argue with you over this, Sabrina. I must be off. But I was near and—and I had to see you and know that you are well."

She took a deep breath. "I—I am." Her heart was aching inside. She had not seen it before, but . . . they were alike, Jamie and Ian. Both were unswerving in their loyalty—their beliefs, as staunch as ever.

She had changed, she realized almost sadly. She still cared deeply about Jamie. Indeed, there was a part of her that would always love him, the sweet promise of youth they had shared. Her heart twisted in her breast, for she was torn as never before, as she prayed she would never be torn again.

She could not tell him that she loved Ian. She could not hurt him. But now it was time to stand behind her husband. For she had her child to think of . . . *their* child.

Lightly she touched his arm. "You will continue your fight, won't you?"

A glimmer of a smile touched his lips. "To the death," he said softly.

A tremor went through her. "Then I must ask you something, Jamie. I—I would ask that should you ever encounter Ian, you will not raise your blade against him."

"You ask much," he said quietly.

She drew a tremulous breath. "I ask what I must."

Something flared in his eyes, something that nearly made her cry out. 'Twas as if he saw into her very soul . . . saw and knew . . .

"I will not."

Her throat ached so that she could scarcely speak. "Do you swear?"

"Aye," he said, his tone very low. "I swear."

Tears flooded her eyes. Her voice caught on a half-sob. "Jamie," she whispered. "Please do not hate me."

"Hate you?" For the space of a heartbeat, the care-free youth she had fallen in love with was back. Laughter lit his eyes to a brilliant blue. He smiled, that crooked half-smile that never failed to seize hold of her heart.

He shook his head. "How could I hate you?" His tone was soft, almost whimsical. He stepped close, taking her hand and bringing it to his lips. "I love you, Sabrina. *I love you.*"

'Twas a declaration more breath than sound. Time stood still as she was drawn into his arms for one last, fleeting kiss.

When she opened her eyes, he was gone.

"Good-bye, Jamie," she whispered.

An awful despair rode heavy on her heart as she returned to the castle. But all else was forgotten when she saw that Ian and his men had returned. She found him in their chamber, freshly bathed and just pulling his shirt over his head. She paused, drinking in the sight of him, for deep within her had been the unnamed fear that, like before, he might return wounded.

He turned when he spied her standing there. "Sabrina, there you are!" He crossed to her, taking both her hands in his.

"I wanted to be here when you awoke, but I could not."

"I know," she said quickly. "Uncle Malcolm told me where you were."

He gazed at her solemnly. "How are you?"

She flushed, touched by his concern. "I am fine."

He squeezed her fingers. "That is good." He turned to where a tray of food rested on the table. Reaching for ale, he drank deeply, then set it aside.

"I thought you would be here when we returned," he remarked. "Where were you?"

Panic flared, swift and merciless. Did he know she'd been with Jamie? Nay. He couldn't possibly. "I was restless," she returned breathlessly. "I walked to the spring and back."

He frowned. "You should not walk alone, Sabrina. 'Tis not safe, especially now."

Her gaze sharpened. "Why? You've yet to tell me what happened. Has there been more bloodshed?"

"Not this time." His tone turned grim. "But it was just as before. Raiders who came in the name of the Comyns. They burned a dozen huts but no one was hurt."

"Praise God," she breathed.

Ian made no answer. Instead he moved to stand near the fire. Strong hands clasped behind his back, he stared into the dancing flames.

Puzzled, she stepped behind him. "Ian?" she queried. "Is something troubling you?"

"I think you do not wish to know." He spoke without looking at her.

Sabrina stared at the broad lines of his back. His shoulders were ramrod straight. A tingle of unease trickled up her spine. His manner had cooled, and she could not stifle a pinprick of hurt.

"Of course I do," she murmured.

"Very well. Several of the raiders were Mac-Dougalls."

Jamie. Mother of Christ, it had to be! Oh, but she should have known . . . !

Ian had turned to face her, and now that he had, she wished he had not!

Nervously she wet her lips. "Are you certain?"

"Oh, there is no mistake." His voice took on a degree of coldness. "Indeed, when we ran to ground the men who attacked Kildurn, we learned there were several who had only just fled. I am given to wonder if one of them chanced to be Jamie MacDougall—"

"No," she said.

Three strides brought him before her. "No?" he repeated.

Sabrina clasped her hands together before her to still their trembling. She gazed down at the floor, feeling the stab of his eyes on her profile.

"Sabrina," he said tightly. "What did you mean by that?"

Somehow she managed to raise her head. "I mean only this. Jamie could not have been one of the men that fled Kildurn that morn."

Ian's eyes narrowed. "How?" he demanded. "How can you know this?"

Her mouth grew dry. "Because he was here"— there was a stinging rush of silence—"with me."

The words fell between them with the weight of a boulder.

The silence which followed was brutal. Indeed, she almost thought he hadn't heard. . . . But then he cursed, a curse so blistering she nearly clapped her hands over her ears that she might not hear. But far more frightening was the rigid cast of his features.

"Here at Castle MacGregor?"

His voice was almost deadly quiet. He stared so accusingly she longed to shrivel up and fade away. "Aye," she said quickly. "But it was not what you think—"

"Lady, you do not begin to know what I think!"

A saving anger flowed into her veins. "Oh, but I do. You think I betrayed you—as Fionna betrayed your father. But it was not like that at all. He'd heard of our marriage and came to—to see if it was true. I met him at—at the spring."

She could almost see the doubt that crowded his being.

"You met him. And did you attend him with the same wifely vigor that you attend me?"

She stiffened. "What do you mean?"

"Did you lay with him?"

She gasped. "I did not! You profess to know me," she challenged indignantly, "but you know me not at all if that is what you believe!"

"And what about now? You saw him again, didn't you? This very day. That's where you were when I returned—with him!"

All at once Sabrina was outraged, so outraged she was shaking with it. "What is this, Ian? You would have me trust in you—believe that you did not kill Fionna—when in turn you have no faith in me?"

His jaw clamped shut. "And what reason have I to believe you? You had no wish to marry me—indeed, you fled the very prospect! You shun me at every turn."

Their eyes locked in what was surely the longest moment of her life. All the fight drained from her as suddenly as it had erupted.

The breath she drew was deep and racking. "Once. Once I did. But not now, Ian. *Not now.*" She spoke with the fervency of a prayer. She gazed at him, caring naught that all she felt lay naked in her eyes.

But he refused to listen. He refused to see . . .

His condemning silence was brutal, his posture inflexible. But in the instant before he spun around, she glimpsed in his eyes an implacable purpose that chilled her to the bone. He was abrim with a rage darker than any she'd ever known.

Flying after him, she caught his hand and fell to her knees. "Ian, no! You cannot go after him. You cannot kill him! For if you do, you will kill a part of me, too."

His lip curled. "You appeal so bountifully, Sabrina. Do you love him so much then?"

"I—I do not love him, I swear!" Her voice caught painfully. "But still I—I could never forgive you, Ian."

She could feel the tightly leashed tension that constricted his body. Fighting a mounting despair, she waited. Waited endlessly for what the moment would bring. . . .

He jerked his hand away. But there was that in his tone which was terrible to hear. "I will not seek him out, Sabrina. I will not kill him. Not now. But should I find him on my lands again I make no promises."

He left her then, slamming the door behind him.

Sabrina at last gave in to the burning rush of tears.

She didn't go down to supper that night. It was late when Ian finally sought their bed. He neither spoke nor touched her, and 'twas like a dagger in the heart, for never had she craved his touch more! A wave of sheer desolation swept over her. She longed desperately to mend this breach between them, but she feared he would only set her aside.

And that was the one thing she could not endure right now.

It was near dawn before she was able to sleep. It seemed she had just closed her eyes when a hand on her shoulder shook her awake.

"Sabrina."

Her mind dull and sleep-fogged, she opened her eyes. It was a moment before she realized Ian towered over her. His expression was rigidly controlled, his eyes icily distant. Her heart plunged. He was still angry.

"I must go." He turned and reached for his sword, sliding it into its scabbard. That sleek hiss of sound wrenched her jarringly awake.

She raised herself on an elbow, pushing the heavy fall of hair from her face. "Go," she repeated. "Go where?"

"I've received word that the Bruce prepares an army to fight Longshanks. I ride to meet his forces at Carrick."

Longshanks. The English king. A flicker of fear arrowed straight to her heart.

"How long will you be gone?"

He shook his head. "I know not."

Three strides took him to the door. There he turned. Sabrina's mind was still reeling.

"Remember," was all he said. "Go nowhere alone."

And then he was gone.

Sabrina leaned back against the pillows, fighting a crushing pain in her chest. What must she do to convince him of the truth—that she no longer loved Jamie? But once again, he was leaving, and the chasm between them was leagues wide. Yet even if he were not, her pride would not allow her to cast her heart at his feet, for he would surely trample it. Aye, for he neither wanted nor needed her love. . . .

Nor did he love her in return.

But deep inside, deep inside was the terror that he might never return.

And suddenly she remembered . . .

She had yet to tell him about the babe.

All that lay bitter and unresolved between them was forgotten. She dare not guess what his reaction would be, be it gladness or dismay. But she couldn't let him leave, not without knowing.

In that moment, she forgot all—that her feet were bare, and she was dressed only in her bedgown. She raced down the stairs, through the hall, and out into the daylight.

In the center of the bailey a body of men and horses stood ready and waiting for their leader. As she burst outside, Ian was just taking the reins from a stableboy.

"Ian!"

A fierce wind caught her hair, sending it rippling behind her like a silken banner of flame. She stopped, crying his name again and praying the sound would not be carried away.

He heard. The gaze he transferred to her was far from pleased, however. He crossed to where she awaited, his expression fierce.

"Sabrina! What madness is this? Inside with you now, before—"

Her hands were on his lips, halting his tirade.

Through some miracle she found the words she so desperately needed—and the courage to say them. "Ian, I pray you . . . be careful. I would have you return and—and see your son."

He looked utterly blank. "My s—"

Comprehension struck. He inhaled sharply. Shock flitted across his features, even as his gaze slid down her body, as if to seek confirmation.

"When?" was all he said. "When will it come?"

"I cannot be sure, but . . . I think midsummer."

He looked completely torn. The cords in his throat went taut. "Jesu!" he exploded. A hand came out to gently touch her hair. "Sabrina, I—I cannot stay. Yet how can I go?" A look of utter determination tightened his features. "You need not worry. I will return."

To her shame, tears glazed her vision. She gave a choked half-sob. "Promise me, Ian. *Promise me.*"

His expression softened. "I promise, lass."

He kissed her then—kissed her fiercely!—wrapping his arms about her back and lifting her clear from her feet. Sabrina cared not that others watched. She clung to him shamelessly and returned in full measure all he sought and more.

They were both breathless when at last they broke apart. Catching her hands, he brought them to his lips for one last kiss.

And then he was gone.

Nineteen

In the weeks that followed, Ian wondered if his beauteous wife knew at what cost he left her. Her tears that morn he departed sent joy leaping high as the mountains within him, even as he was plunged into the depths of despair at knowing he must go.

From the very first time he'd seen her again, she had ensnared him. His heart. His mind. His every sense. She was mistress of his heart, captor of his soul. Though other men betrayed their wives, his temptations were not swayed, for Ian was well aware he would find no pleasure in another woman's arms.

Nightly she came to him. Naked and sinuous, with hair of fire and kisses of flame, luring him ever deeper within a lair of sweet seduction. In his dreams, she gave to him, all bare silken limbs. He saw her as she leaned over him, her hair dancing across his belly ... and lower, there where the pulsebeat of desire thrummed hard and aching ... And then it was his turn. With lips and tongue he tasted her flesh. Lingering. Driving her half-wild until she shattered in his arms and echoed his desire, crying out her need of him. In his dreams she surrendered as never before, and he was lost, drowning in the heat of her passion.

Aye, she haunted his dreams, the loneliness of the night, his every waking moment. He craved her heart . . . but did she give it elsewhere? He possessed her body, but would she ever be truly his?

Jealousy ate at his insides like a slow poison, for there was still much that lay between them, he acknowledged wearily. It had crossed his mind that the babe she carried might not be his, but such doubts were ruthlessly swept aside. She swore she did not love Jamie MacDougall, yet everything within him warned that even were it so—if she did not love him, then she still cared deeply.

Was he a fool to believe the babe she carried was his—not Jamie's? Despite the doubts that sometimes blistered his mind, there was no denying the truth— she had come to him a maid. And if the babe were expected midsummer, she must have conceived when first they lay together.

He chafed with every day that kept him from home—from her!—but he had pledged his sword to the Bruce and he was a man of his word. And in truth, the Bruce needed him now as never before, for it seemed the English troops were everywhere. The Bruce's army was small; the English numbered far more, and so they sought to strike and plunder and ambush those smaller factions and thus defeat the whole. But that was not all, for the Comyn supporters and kin were ever a thorn in their side—they would not cease their goal of seeing the Bruce toppled from the throne.

Ian prayed daily that he would not fall in battle. Feelings against the English ran high, and the Bruce was more determined than ever to keep the English from Scottish soil.

Ian wanted nothing more than peace—peace for the land he so loved. Peace within his castle and upon his lands, and time with his wife and his child, time spent contentedly basking before the blaze of the fire.

But he feared for Sabrina, for he'd not forgotten that someone had locked her away. But who? And why? Was it an accident? It did not seem likely, he admitted. Was it possible she was in danger of her life? All these questions and more plagued him endlessly, which was why he'd left her with Fraser, for he knew his friend would protect her life with his own.

The emerald green of spring had begun to spread full across the land when several chieftains from the north decided to lend their favor—and troops—to rally behind the Bruce. At last Ian was able to make his way back to Castle MacGregor.

Shouts went up from the tower one afternoon as he and his men approached. Several men set their heels to the flanks of their mounts and galloped toward the gates. Ian brought up the rear, though in truth he was in no less haste to be home once more.

Inside the hall, he smiled and nodded and laughed and spoke, but all the while his eyes restlessly searched the growing crowd for his wife. Then he spied a small, slight figure hurrying in from the kitchens.

Sabrina.

Their eyes caught. Surprise widened hers—surprise and something that made his heart fly and soar amongst the clouds. A slow-growing smile graced those sweetly curved lips, a smile so dazzling and pure he felt blinded. A surge of pride and fierce possessiveness swelled within his breast.

The sounds around them faded into nothingness.

'Twas as if they alone occupied the world. . . .

Her feet carried her slowly forward, one before the other, then faster and faster until she was running.

He caught her up against his chest—close against his heart—for it was there that she dwelled. Now and evermore.

Their lips met and clung, a long, blissful exchange of tender emotion, at once rousing both satisfaction and yearning within him. A loud guffaw from the corner reminded him anew that they were not alone. Reluctantly he released her mouth.

Both her hands tenderly imprisoned within his, he stepped back. He gazed the length of her, his regard long and hungry and avid and making no effort to hide it. A smile curled his lips, for there was a new ripeness to her figure. Her breasts were full and plump, and her belly was unmistakably round; yet still she was lovely beyond measure.

Two bright spots came to her cheeks. "Ian! You should not look at me so!"

All at once he felt a lightness in spirit he'd not felt in ages. "And why not?" he found himself teasing. "All who know me can attest that I've ever an eye for a fair maid."

She glanced about, making certain that no one heard. "Come now," she protested. "I am hardly a maid."

"Ah, but you are most certainly fair." He tucked her hand into the crook of his elbow. Though she protested anew, he could tell she was well pleased.

It was a time for celebrating, for all those who had left with him had returned safely. There was feasting and dancing and laughter aplenty long into the evening hours. Sabrina sat at his side, telling him of all that had transpired in his absence. He was most relieved to learn there had been no further disturbing episodes. Mayhap he'd been wrong. Mayhap she'd been locked in the chamber belowstairs by some bizarre accident. Though how such could happen, he was indeed puzzled.

Just then a curious hound thrust his cold snout beneath the back side of Fraser's kilt. With a cry Fraser leaped high in the air, his expression stunned.

Everyone roared.

Fraser whirled, his features ferocious. "Begone, you mongrel!" he shouted at the offending beast.

The hound had dropped to his belly. He laid his muzzle on outstretched paws. Turning huge, sorrowful eyes upward, he howled mournfully.

Even Fraser's outrage turned to laughter.

Ian's eyes had shifted to his wife's lovely profile, as if to memorize her every feature. "'Tis good to see you smile," he said softly.

"And 'tis good that you are home," she returned.

Her words reminded him that he had yet to be alone with his wife, and it was indeed his most fervent wish. Getting to his feet, he feigned a huge yawn.

"I fear it has been a long, tiring day," he called out, "and having spent many a night on the cold hard ground, I look forward to spending this night in the warmth of my own bed."

"And the warmth of your lady's arms!" someone proclaimed heartily.

"Aye, and that too!" Ian grinned widely. Turning to Sabrina, he extended his hand and tugged her to her feet. Together they left the hall.

Once they were alone in their chamber, he drew her to the chair before the hearth, where a welcoming fire cast out light and warmth. Seated with her snug in his embrace, he gave a fervid prayer of thanksgiving that God had seen fit to bring him safely home again. He was a most contented husband, and before long he would be a father as well. And though he ached to make love to his wife, just now it was enough to hold her, to feel the softness of her body against his, the fragrant scent of her hair . . . all that was far dearer to him than he had ever imagined.

But all at once she ducked her head. He frowned. "What is it?" he murmured. "What is amiss?"

Her lashes lowered, shielding her gaze from him. With her fingers she plucked at the folds of his shirt. "Ian . . . I—I almost dreaded the day you would return, for I was certain you would doubt me . . ."

"Doubt you?" He was puzzled. "How?"

He felt the deep breath she took. "When you left, we had no chance to speak of—of the babe . . . I thought you might think that . . . 'twas Jamie's babe I carried."

Now was not the time to confess that he had indeed.

"But it is not, Ian . . . and I know not how to convince you . . ."

Ian studied the small fingers curled within his, feeling how she trembled.

"You need not convince me," he told her, and God above, all at once it was true. Whatever had existed between her and Jamie—what still might exist—he knew she would not lie. Deceit was simply not in her nature.

A finger beneath her chin, he guided her eyes to his. "Listen to me, sweet, and listen well. I know that there were angry words between us then, but I do not forget that you were a maid when you came to me as my bride. And despite your feelings for Jamie—whatever they were, whatever they are now—you are my wife, and I do not believe you would forsake the vows you made before God so easily."

He paused. His gaze delved deep into hers. "Once I asked that you trust in me, that you not doubt me. And indeed, I would ask no less of myself than I ask of you. But this I must know. You will soon bear my child, Sabrina, and there was a time when I believe you'd have been most horrified by the prospect." He paused. "But what of now?"

For an instant, the wispiest of smiles had grazed her lips, but now her smile waned. Her eyes grew cloudy. She said nothing.

Ian stiffened. He would have put her from him, but she stopped him, placing her hands on his forearms.

"Nay, Ian, nay!" she cried softly. "'Tis not what you think!"

"Then tell me that I may know." There was no give in his voice.

Her eyes clung to his. "I—I am glad of the child. Truly. Though I admit, it happens far sooner than I anticipated. And . . . oh, I know 'tis foolish of me, but . . . I am . . ." She gave a half-sob. "I am afraid!"

"Afraid!" He was stunned. "Why?"

She shivered. "My mother died in childbed."

His arms closed around her. A wave of fierce protectiveness swept over him. He kissed her, tasting the fear of vulnerability.

"I'm sorry. I'd forgotten. But you are young and healthy, Sabrina. And there is no reason to believe that all will not go well, is there?" Almost fearfully he searched her face.

She shook her head. "The sickness that plagued me in the mornings is much better. And I've seen the midwife in the village. She says I am healthy and the babe as well."

"This is good news, is it not?" For some reason, she still appeared troubled.

"Aye," she confided, then hesitated. "You will think me silly, but . . . when my time comes, I—I wish it could be different! Mary is a dearling, but . . . if only Margaret were here, I—I would not feel so alone!"

In truth, Ian had little experience with childbirth. Still, he was not so inconsiderate that he could not understand her feelings. She had no mother to confide in, no one to share her fears. She no longer had a sister, or any other woman she was truly close to.

He offered what comfort he could. "You will not be alone, Sabrina. I will be with you."

Her eyes darkened. "You may well be with the Bruce, so I beg you, do not make promises you cannot keep."

He remained staunch. "'Tis a promise I intend to keep."

And indeed, Sabrina prayed he would, for she wanted him with her. Today. Tomorrow.

Always.

With his palm he cupped her cheek. His gaze never wavered from hers as he murmured, "I missed you, sweet."

His words made her heart catch. His eyes were not cold as stone, but shimmered with a warmth she was almost afraid to believe in.

These last weeks had been torture. She had missed him—missed him dreadfully! But now he was home and—and his eyes were tender and suddenly a chorus sang in her heart as never before.

Her smile was tremulous. "And I you, Ian. I cannot tell you how much—"

"Ah. Mayhap you could show me then. Indeed"—his crooked smile made her heart turn over—"I should welcome it."

It was an invitation Sabrina could not deny. Lightly her fingers framed his face. Her thumbs rested on the plane of his cheeks. Beneath her fingers she could feel the pleasant roughness of his beard. A quiver tore through her. He was so very, very handsome. . . . Her fingertips moved, the veriest caress.

Gathering her courage, she kissed his mouth. As she did, one strong hand slid up to cup the nape of her neck. Her eyes fluttered shut and she sighed, a wispy sound that conveyed her pleasure in the moment—and in him. Her arms stole about his neck. She felt him smile against her mouth, a smile she was given to return in full measure. Timidly her tongue touched his, deepening the contact, twining with his in a wantonly erotic mating that made her heartbeat clamor and reminded her all too keenly how long it had been since he'd made love to her.

He made a sound low in his throat, and now the pressure of his mouth was sweetly fierce and no longer hers to control. But saints above, she cared not, for she gloried in the pressure of his arm tight about her back. In one swift move she was lifted and borne to the bed.

In an instant he was beside her. He kissed her anew, feasting on her mouth as if he were starved . . . as indeed they both were. One blunted fingertip skimmed the delicate sweep of her collarbone. Boldly he dipped within her bodice, claiming the ripeness of her breast. Her nipples tightened and tingled. She arched helplessly into his hand.

Slowly, reluctantly, he released her mouth. Sabrina watched as he rose to his feet beside the bed. She couldn't tear her gaze away as he stripped away his clothing, his form bathed in the hazy glow of the fire. He was all power and grace, his shoulders gleaming bronze and smooth in the firelight, his frame forged of iron.

He quickened before her very eyes.

Her mouth was suddenly as dry as parchment. His intent was obvious, but she was suddenly overwhelmingly conscious of the changes these past weeks had wrought on her own body. Her waist had thickened, her breasts were as full as melons, and she felt swollen and ungainly. Of a certainty she did not feel pretty or enticing!

Though she did not stop him, her fingers fluttered above his. But when all that remained was her shift, she took a deep breath.

"Ian," she whispered, "must we be . . . naked?"

A black brow climbed high. "You asked that the very first time, lass." His grin was utterly wicked. "'Tis how it's best done . . . or do you forget so soon?"

Sabrina could not look at him. She could not.

Slowly his grin faded. One lean hand came to rest on her shoulder. Quietly he said, "You need not be shy before me, sweet."

"'Tis not that," she said unevenly. "'Tis just that I am . . . different," she finished lamely.

His gaze was steady on hers. "Different," he repeated. "How so, love?"

Love. Her heart squeezed. Oh, why couldn't he understand? She floundered, her throat achingly tight.

"Ian," she said helplessly, "I—I know that you are
not blind. I am no longer slim and—"

His fingers on her lips, he stopped her speech. "You
think I do not desire you?"

Sabrina nodded, perilously near tears. "I—I do not
feel . . . desirable," she blurted.

His eyes softened. "Listen to me, sweet. You are as
beautiful now as you have ever been." He shook his
head and now it seemed that he was the one at a loss
for words. "How can I say this. . . . You possess an
allure—a feminine enticement that makes me quiver
like a youth."

Solemnly intent, he splayed his fingers wide across
the hard mound of her tummy. "I desire you as ever
before, Sabrina . . . nay, *more*, for the sight of my son
rounding your belly swells my chest with pride—and
fills my heart to bursting." His tone was low and
husky; it sent a tremor all through her. "I want you,
sweet. I want you as I want no other—as I have *never*
wanted another."

His declaration was all she needed to hear—all she
had yearned for. With a half-strangled sob, she
wrapped her arms around his neck and gave him her
lips, giddy with relief. And when at last she was as
naked as he, she offered no protest.

Stretching out beside her, he caught at her hand,
drawing it down over the iron-hard grid of his belly.
With unfaltering guidance he curled her fingers
around his burning shaft, filling her palm with himself.

"You once said I was as small a man as I was a
lad." There was the veriest trace of laughter in his
voice. "Is that still true, lass?"

Her heart pounded so hard it seemed to jolt her entire body. "I think not," she said faintly.

His eyes darkened. "Touch me, sweet." Raw need vibrated in his voice. *"Touch me."*

And touch him she did. She touched him as she had never done before . . . touched him as she had always longed to do. Though she was shocked at her own brazenness, she did not retreat. His size and breadth made her tremble, for he was rigid and thick, massive and hot in her palm. Stunned at the contrast she encountered, her fingers skimmed daintily over the velvet-arched tip of him, then clasped him anew.

He swelled still further.

A heady sense of power came over her. Guided by instinct alone, she slid her hand up and down . . . up and down in a motion that seemed to drive him half-wild.

"That's the way, sweet. Christ, you make me burn, both inside and out!" His whisper was low and strained. One more pass and his hips bucked wildly.

His hand clamped her. "Enough!" he said thickly. "Else I will spill myself here and now."

But now it was his turn.

His eyes silver-bright and passion-glazed, he eased her back against the pillows. With the pads of his thumbs he traced circles around the dark, straining tips of her breasts. With a groan she caught at his head, guiding it down to where she most wanted his kiss. . . . With a rumble of laughter deep in his chest, he gave her what she yearned for, painting her nipples with the wanton lash of his tongue, leaving them shiny and wet and tautly erect.

His hand drifted lower, embedding themselves in the tight curls between her thighs. With his thumb he teased the tight bud of pleasure nestled within deep pink folds.

A lone finger stretched high and deep. Sabrina moaned as a hot, piercing ache shot through her middle. Another joined its mate. . . . Blistering flames shot through her at the brand of his fingers high and tight and deep inside her. All the while his thumb never ceased its tormenting foray, dipping and circling and rubbing that quivering bud. She whimpered, feeling the tears her body wept, sleek and damp on his fingertips, writhing against him and crying out her need.

He kissed her, then, and the ravenous hunger she tasted in his mouth sent her spiraling anew. He levered himself over her, his knees spreading her wide. Enflamed almost past bearing, she clutched at him.

He braced himself above her, his features tense and strained. She touched the rugged hollows of his cheeks, traced the curve of his mouth that brought such rapture. Her fingers trailed over the binding tightness of his shoulders, loving the feel of bulging muscle encased in sleek, smooth skin.

Their eyes met and held, and she saw in his the same soul-shattering desire.

'Twas at that very instant he came inside her. His mouth sealed hers. His shaft filled her, until she was abrim with him, so deep he touched her very womb . . .

And seared her very soul.

'Twas a joining that shook her as never before—a union not only of the flesh, but of the spirit, a melding of souls. With aching tenderness he claimed her, and she could not withhold a moan of sheer joy.

Her nails dug into his arms. "Ian," she cried softly. "*Ian!*"

With a groan he crushed her to him. Their hips met again and again, a wild, burning frenzy. When she reached for him again, their hands locked. She arched her hips as his churned wildly, to take all he could give and more. Her pleasure crested, a burst of exquisite ecstacy. She felt her body tighten and contract, convulsing around swollen flesh, over and over. And then she was flung high aloft, as if she were floating, free of earthly bonds. Above her, Ian shuddered, a scant heartbeat before he exploded inside her, a scalding release that drenched her womb in fire.

When the winds of passion had calmed, he propped himself on his elbows and kissed her, a kiss of infinite sweetness.

'Twas then that the babe saw fit to make his presence known—aye, and felt! He thumped within her, there where her belly still pressed his father's.

Ian's eyes widened, with shock or fear, she knew not. He shifted to his side in a lightning move that made her smile. "Sabrina," he breathed. "Was that . . . ?"

She chuckled. "Aye," she said, and now it was she who took his hand and shaped it against her. With the pressure of her own, she kept his hand anchored beneath hers, that he might feel his son move as she did. As if the babe knew exactly what his father craved, he moved again, a great, rolling movement.

Ian's slow smile thrilled her to her very toes. He did not snatch his hand away, but kept it there as if entranced.

"What do you think?" he mused. "Lad or lassie?"

She smiled. "Do you have a preference, then?"

"Nay," he said huskily. "As long as you and the babe are well."

His answer pleased her as nothing else could have. "We will have a son, I think," she murmured sleepily. "Aye, a son." She nestled against his shoulder as he slipped an arm beneath her and pulled her near. Exhausted, she soon slept.

Ian's expression was tender as he kissed the place where their child lay nestled within her. Weaving their fingers together anew, he let them rest on the swell of her belly.

'Twas not long before he joined her in slumber.

Twenty

Deep in the mist-shrouded Highlands, spring mellowed the land, bringing the hills and mountains alive in a pageantry of color. Sabrina welcomed it gladly, for she was tired of the stark barrenness of winter. The days grew longer and summer approached; even as the heather bloomed purple and rich, life burgeoned within her.

She and Mary spent much of their time sewing for the bairn, but Sabrina oft grew tired of sitting. She walked down to the village and back, sometimes to the sapphire waters of the loch just beyond the west wall. Though Ian frowned, he did not stop her, for always she walked with Mary and never alone. The day she'd been locked in belowstairs was no longer so frightening. Though she had yet to find an explanation for how it had happened, no longer did she feel as if danger lurked beyond the next corner.

Ian. The very thought of him made her heart pound. He was tender and ever mindful of her condition; indeed, she could almost believe he *did* love her. . . . He seemed pleased about the babe, and for that she was glad. And there was concern about her well-being. Secretly she yearned for more . . . words of love mayhap? Yet none had passed his lips. She chided herself, for that was too much to expect. If he was concerned, 'twas as much for his unborn son's welfare as her own. And so she held her own feelings close in check . . .

For she was not wont to give love where it was not wanted.

And though many was the time where they had talked long into the night, she sensed there was still much he withheld from her. At times he was distant and absent-minded, yet he did not speak of what troubled him—if anything. On several more occasions she sought to query him about Fionna—who might have murdered her and why. . . .

He stiffened immediately, and left her in no doubt he would not speak of it. Sabrina could not help it— she was secretly shattered that he refused to share this part of himself with her. And it was at those times that she painfully reminded herself there was yet another part of him he would *never* share with her . . .

His heart.

In late May he left again to join the Bruce. Sabrina was proud of herself, for she wished him well and bid him good-bye with nary a tear. 'Twas only later, in the solitude of the night, in the emptiness of her bed—*their* bed—that the tears fell.

She was in the hall one afternoon several weeks later planning the next week's menu when Uncle Malcolm shuffled inside from the bailey.

"He comes," the old man announced.

Sabrina glanced up. She had come to love him dearly, though it was just as Ian had said: one never knew from one day to the next where his mind dwelled—past or present.

She tipped her head to the side. "Who, Uncle?"

"Yer husband, lassie! Why else would I be tellin' ye?"

Her gaze sharpened. His eyes were clear as a rushing mountain stream.

Her heart lurched. Ian, she realized dazedly. Ian was coming! Her quill dropped to the table, forgotten. She got to her feet with as much haste as her belly would allow.

But she was barely standing when the echo of hoofbeats thundered outside. Sabrina's hand went to her hair. It was loose about her shoulders and back the way Ian liked it, but she hadn't combed through it since early morn. And her gown was faded and worn . . . Oh, but what was the use in fretting? She was fat and clumsy and hardly the picture of prettiness!

And then he was there, striding through the entrance, every bit the bold chieftain, so very handsome he stole her breath. His gaze swept the hall as if he searched for someone. His gaze lit upon her and he stopped. Sabrina wanted to pinch herself that she might know she was not dreaming, for there was warmth and pleasure reflected in those clear gray eyes, eyes that seemed to speak to her alone.

Then he was there before her, his hands on her waist. He kissed her long and sweetly and Sabrina was quite, quite certain she stood at heaven's door.

When at last he drew back, one corner of his mouth curled up in an odd smile.

"I have something for you, wife."

Sabrina blinked. "What? A gift?"

He ran a finger down her nose. "Not precisely."

She pretended to pout. "What then?" In truth she was curious beyond measure.

His grin was utterly irresistible—and wholly irrepressible. He did not answer, but instead turned and beckoned toward the doorway.

And then Sabrina could only stare numbly, convinced her eyes deceived her.

"Edna," she said, stunned, and then it was a cry of delight: "Edna!"

Edna, her little maid from Dunlevy, raced toward her. The two embraced, alternately laughing and crying.

Finally Sabrina drew back, shaking her head. "Edna, I cannot believe you are here! How long can you stay?"

"Oh, I'll be stayin' a very long while, m'lady." Edna was beaming. "A very long while indeed"—a bubbling laugh escaped—"for I daresay, I'll be callin' Castle MacGregor my home!"

Ian had watched the scene unfold with an indulgent little smile. Sabrina turned toward him and slid her hand within his, too choked up to speak. Her heart stood still. He had done this, she realized dazedly, for her. *For her.*

His caring and concern was her undoing. Her smile grew misty. "Thank you," she whispered when at last she was able. Naked emotion surely shone on her face, but she cared not.

Ian carried her hand to his lips, his gaze never wavering from her own. "'Twas my pleasure, sweet."

Over the next few hours, Sabrina was a trifle nervous that Mary might resent Edna's arrival. But she reassured Mary that her place was not being usurped at all. Indeed, she hoped that Mary would be nurse to the babe, for she had seen how good Mary was with the children in the village.

Mary's eyes lit up. "Oh, but I do love the wee ones," she said excitedly. "I suppose 'tis because I'm the eldest of twelve. But I—I should like that very much indeed, my lady."

"It is settled then," Sabrina said firmly. "You will be the babe's nurse."

It was later, as she and Ian had retired for the night, that she told Ian the news. "You do not mind, do you? That Mary will act as nurse?"

"Of course not. I think Mary is a fine choice." He paused, drawing her into his arms and nestling her close against his length.

"Are you happy then that Edna is here?"

She smiled against the hard curve of his shoulder. "Aye. Though I admit, of a certainty I never expected to see Edna here at Castle MacGregor." She paused. "Were you near Dunlevy with the Bruce?"

"Aye. I left him near Perth. I had to pass directly by Dunlevy, so I stayed the night there. 'Twas then that the idea came to me, for I know that it has been lonely for you here." His tone had grown quiet. "And I thought it might be easier when the babe comes if you had someone dear and familiar with you."

But I am not lonely when you are here, she longed to cry. Yet something held her back. Instead she murmured, "Hmmm. Did Papa mind that you wished to steal away one of his servants?"

Ian chuckled, the sound low and pleasing to her ears. "That he did. But you have far more need of Edna than he, and so I told him."

It was Sabrina's turn to grow quiet. She'd written to tell her father the news that she and Ian expected a child midsummer, but she'd had no response—indeed, she'd had no word from him in all the time she'd been gone from Dunlevy.

She steeled herself against a pinprick of hurt. "Tell me," she said lightly. "How was Papa?"

"He is well."

"Good." The veriest pause. "And did he ask after me?"

"Aye," Ian said quickly. But there was something in his tone, something that warned her all was not right.

And Sabrina knew the truth.

Despite her most stringent effort, a huge lump clogged her throat. There was a sharp, knifelike twinge in her chest. Carefully she eased from him and slipped from their bed.

Her steps carried her unknowingly to the window. There she opened the shutters and gazed out into the darkness. In that moment, her heart was as barren and empty as the night.

She scolded herself fiercely. It had been a foolish question—she knew that now, for aye, she'd already known Ian's answer even before he spoke. Everything within her cried out the heartache. When she had lived with her father he had no use for her . . .

And now it seemed he had even less.

Suddenly she felt the sweep of powerful arms come around her from behind, the rush of warm breath across her temple.

"Come back to bed, Sabrina."

Sabrina did not move. "I wrote and told him about the babe," she said tonelessly. "He did not answer." She could not hide her bitterness. "He does not care."

"He is a fool, Sabrina. A blind, old fool. He cannot change. He *will* not change."

"He would have cared were the babe Margaret's." Her voice was very small. She shivered. "All my life I have felt . . . as if I were unworthy, Ian."

Ian's arms tightened. "It is not you who is unworthy, sweet. 'Tis he who is unworthy of you."

Sabrina made no answer. A hollow ache welled up inside her.

She did not know that her bleakness tore into Ian's heart like a blade from breast to belly. There was an odd tightening in his chest. She was so strong, yet she did not know it.

"Your father is a fool," he said gruffly. "You are not alone—you are never alone. There are those here who care for you greatly, Sabrina."

But what about him? she wondered achingly. Did *he* care? Despair wrenched at her insides. The breath she drew was deep and painful. Why couldn't he love her . . . just a little?

The babe kicked then, reminding her that if she could not have him, then at least she would have this—his child. It was a bond neither could deny nor break. She prayed that their child—their son—would be born safe and healthy.

Ian had felt the movement as well. His hand moved, molding the roundness of her belly where their child nestled. "It will not be long," he whispered. "Are you still afraid, sweet?"

"A little," she admitted. Her heart bleeding, she blinked back a stinging rush of tears and turned into his arms.

"Hold me, Ian. Please . . . hold me."

Strong arms wrapped around her, bringing her shaking body close. He lifted her and bore her to the bed where he drew her close and tight against his side. Sabrina burrowed against him, craving his nearness as never before. She was suddenly terrified—not just of the birth, but something else. She was all at once seized by an ominous foreboding, something she could not put a name to, yet so powerful she could not put it aside.

"Sabrina! What is this? You are trembling!"

"'Tis nothing," she managed, burying her face against the smooth satin of his shoulder. He was so kind, so gentle, and his concern tied her heart in knots. She rubbed her cheek against his skin, loving the musky scent of him, the hardness of his arms tight about her form.

Her hair was a wild tangle across his bare chest. With his hand he stroked the silken cloud of her hair, over and over. She felt the brush of firm lips against her forehead, her cheeks, the line of her jaw. He held her with such tenderness she clung to him all the harder, taking what comfort she could in the sheltering protection of his embrace.

In time, her shaking subsided. She slept.

In all truth, Mary was well pleased at the prospect of being nurse to her ladyship's bairn, for she'd always had a liking for wee ones. Her mistress was generous and sweet, and she could imagine no greater privilege than to be granted the duty of watching over the child.

Anxious to share her news with Thomas, the smithy's son, Mary departed the castle for the village. They were not yet wed, but it was her fondest hope that Thomas would soon ask her. Her steps light, humming a merry little tune, she hurried down the rutted lane. High above, the moon played hide and

seek within silvery clouds. She paused, gazing upward. It seemed to wink down at her, full and bright
and shining its light across the heavens.

Her thoughts grew dreamy. She hugged herself and
sighed, her smile broad. If all went as she hoped, in
time she might someday cradle a bairn of her own.

Footfalls sounded behind her. Mary stopped and
turned.

"Hello?" she called. "Is someone there?"

She tipped her head to the side. No answer was
forthcoming. But a form appeared, seeming to glide
from the shadows behind her, dark and faceless.

Mary's smile withered. A chill ran over her skin.

She whirled and ran as if the devil himself were at
her heels. And perhaps it was, for in an instant crushing hands were upon her and she was hurtled to the
ground.

"Say farewell to Castle MacGregor," said a raspy
voice above her. "I fear you've seen the last of it."

Before she could cry out, she was dealt a stunning
blow to the head.

The world went black.

Her presence was missed the very next morning.

Sabrina had the servants check every corner of the
castle, while Ian sent his men to search the village and
area nearby.

In the hall, Edna wrung her hands. "'Tis my fault,"
she wailed. "Oh, I know it is. I did not mean to usurp
her place, truly I did not!"

"Of course you didn't." Sabrina soothed her. "And
in truth, I do not think that is the case at all!"

It was true—Sabrina did not. A shiver went all

through her. She couldn't banish the gnawing disquiet within her.

It was late when Ian came to bed that night, for he had been out searching all day with his men.

"Do you think she ran away because Edna came?" he asked.

"The thought has occurred to me," Sabrina admitted. "But she was sweet on Thomas, the smithy's son. Indeed, she confided to me only a few days ago that she was certain he meant to ask for her hand soon."

Ian's features were troubled. "The lad is frantic," he murmured. "I sent him to check with her family in the next valley."

But alas, Thomas's journey was for naught; Mary's family had not seen her. Sabrina's worries climbed. Her fears multiplied. Something terrible had happened to Mary. She knew it with all she possessed. . . .

She was right.

Mary's mantle was found on the shores of the loch the very next morn.

Sabrina was sick inside. A chill seized her and she made her way to her chamber. But there was an elusive tug on her memory.

"Just like Margaret," she whispered aloud. *Just like Margaret.* . . .

She could not help it. Her blood ran cold. Her mind sped straight to Ian. Nay, she thought. It could not possibly be . . . Ian had been with her that night. She had slept in his arms the night through, she was certain of it. Or could he have left her after all . . . ?

A shadow of melancholy was cast over all. The air about the castle was quiet and subdued. No longer were spirits bright and gay. It was as if a dark, oppressive cloud had descended over Castle MacGregor.

The truth eluded all, like a path that twisted and turned but led nowhere. Ian, too, was distant and remote. Sabrina wavered between fear and the desperate hope that it couldn't possibly be true—Ian could not have murdered Fionna. Or Margaret. Or Mary . . .

Or had he?

It was Alasdair who reluctantly confided that the villagers had begun to talk.

It was midafternoon. They were alone in the hall, for Ian had gone out hunting.

"I tell you because I fear it will soon reach your ears, Sabrina." He shook his head, his handsome features unusually grave. "And I thought it better if it came from me."

Sabrina eased down on a bench. "What do they say, Alasdair?"

"They whisper that Mary no doubt lies dead at the bottom of the loch. They say—" He stopped, his expression uncomfortable. His eyes flickered. "Bear in mind, Sabrina, this is not what I think. 'Tis only what is being said."

She smiled faintly. "I understand, Alasdair. There is no need to spare me. Please go on."

"They say that first Fionna was murdered. And now there is talk that mayhap Margaret's death was no accident. Now Mary is missing. And they wonder—"

"They wonder who will be next," Sabrina finished for him. Lowering her head, she rubbed the ache that throbbed between her brows. "Tell me, Alasdair. Do they think Ian is responsible?"

Ian neither confirmed nor denied it—nor was there a need to. "You must understand, Sabrina. First his

stepmother was murdered. Then his intended died."
His tone was apologetic.

"And what do you think?"

His reluctance was obvious. "As God is my witness," he stated quietly, "I know not what to think.
Yet at times I wonder the very same. Since the death
of his father David, Ian is . . . different somehow.
Harder. More brooding." A twinge of pain flitted
across his face. "May God forgive me, it seems . . . oh,
I know not how to say this! It seems my cousin is not
the same man he once was."

But was he the man who had murdered Fionna?
Mary? Perhaps even Margaret. That was the question. . . .

Nay. *Nay*. Not Ian. *Not Ian*. She could not believe
it. She *would* not believe it.

But someone had murdered Fionna. Had the same
someone murdered poor Mary?

She shivered.

Alasdair dropped down on one knee before her. He
took her hands within his.

"You're frightened, aren't you?"

"Aye," she admitted.

"Do not be. I shall have extra sentries posted
throughout the castle, during the day as well as
night."

With an effort Sabrina summoned a faint smile.
"Thank you, Alasdair. You are a dearling. But if you
do not mind, I think I'd like to be alone for a time."

"Of course not, Sabrina. But should you ever need
someone to confide in—"

"I shall think of you," she said softly.

He brought one hand to her lips before departing.
Sabrina watched him stride through the door into the

bailey. He was so sweet. So very charming. Indeed, she was surprised that some young maid had not fallen madly in love with him.

That very same day Uncle Malcolm had taken ill to his bed. Before long Sabrina went abovestairs to check on him. Even before she reached his chamber she could hear his rattling cough. Quickly she summoned Edna and asked that she prepare a warm brew to ease his cough.

At his bedside, Sabrina pressed a hand to his furrowed brow. His skin was hot and fevered. Gathering a linen cloth and basin of water, she began to bathe his forehead. He leaned into the coolness of the cloth almost gratefully. He murmured something.

Sabrina bent close. "What is it, Uncle? I cannot hear you."

His eyes opened. Before Sabrina could utter a word, his features underwent a lightning transformation. He grabbed the cloth from her and threw it aside. He flailed an arm. The basin went flying, spraying water everywhere.

"You are wicked," he gasped. "I saw you in the garden with him. I saw you!" Weak as he was, his voice rang with accusation. "You like the blade between his thighs—and there lies the proof!" He gestured toward her belly. "I've seen you with others as well . . . David will rue the day he wed you. By the Cross, he should never have wed you!"

David. Shocked and confused, it was a moment before Sabrina's tardy mind made the connection. He must think she was Fionna.

"Uncle. Uncle, it is I . . . Sabrina. Not Fionna. Do you hear? I am Sabrina, not Fionna!"

His eyes were wild. "I know who you are. I know *what* you are!"

It was into this chaotic scene that Edna entered, carrying a steaming goblet on a tray. Malcolm saw her and cried out. "Help me, lass. Don't let her near me!" He stretched out his arms and pleaded. "Don't let her near me!"

Sabrina was already at Edna's side. "He does not know me, Edna. Please, give it to him if he will take it. Then find a maid to come sit with him."

All at once it was just too much—the strain on her nerves was more than she could bear. First Alasdair's suspicion—and now this. Tears blinding her vision, she ran clumsily from the chamber.

She stopped near the top of the narrow stairway. Her lungs were burning. Her breath came in jagged bursts. She bent slightly to ease the ache in her side.

Even as an eerie prickling tightened her skin, it happened.

There was a touch between her shoulder blades, and then she was tumbling down the narrow, twisting stairway.

A strangled cry tore from her throat. She flung out a hand, landing heavily on her arm. A jarring pain tore through her wrist, but she'd managed to stop her headlong fall.

For several moments she was too dazed to move. Someone had pushed her. *Someone had pushed her!*

She lurched to her feet and reclimbed the stairs. By the time she reached the passageway, it was empty. There was no one in sight.

Too winded to give chase, she sank down to the floor. Her left wrist throbbed mercilessly. She cradled it in her hand, inhaling rapidly, her senses all awhirl.

Footsteps drew near. Her head jerked up and twisted toward the sound.

It was Ian.

All her fears came rushing to the fore. A staggering dread ripped through her. It was Ian who had discovered Fionna. It was Ian who had last seen Margaret alive. And now he was the first one she saw. . . . And all was well when Ian was gone with the Bruce. . . . His name bounced off the walls of her mind. *Ian, Ian, Ian.* Was she wrong? Was he a madman?

His steps quickened as he closed the distance between them.

"Sabrina! God's teeth . . . is it the babe?" He dropped down beside her.

Instinctively she scrambled back against the wall. Oh, but his tone held just the right amount of anxiety. She flung up an elbow, as if to ward him off.

"Nay," she shrieked. "Do not touch me!"

"Sabrina, what nonsense is this! You have naught to fear from me and well you know it!"

"Do I? Someone pushed me down the stairs!" Her voice took on a note of hysteria. "No doubt I was meant to—to die! Yet who do I come upon but you! When you are gone, all is well. Yet when you return, these—these terrible things happen!"

His jaw clenched. He swore a vile oath. Pushing her hands aside, he grasped her arms and pulled her to her feet. He did not release her, but stared down at her, gray eyes ablaze.

"It was not I, Sabrina. Do you hear me? It was not I!"

"So you say! But what about Fionna, Ian?"

His features were terrible to behold. He said nothing.

"You see? And what about Margaret?"

"Margaret's death might well have been an accident."

"And it might well not!" she cried. "So tell me, Ian. Will I be like Fionna? Murdered in my own bed? By the same hand?"

He shook her. "Stop this, Sabrina! I tell you, I had nothing to do with her death!"

There was a stifling heaviness in her chest. Her face was pale and ashen. Her hands shook as though she were ill with some palsy. "Then who did?"

His eyes cleaved directly into hers. "God above, it was not me."

"Then who, Ian? You know," she cried wildly. "I know it. You know who killed Fionna, don't you? You know!"

His eyes squeezed shut. Turned his face upward— to the heavens?—as if he fought some tremendous, inner battle. When they opened, they were filled with such darkness and pain she nearly cried out.

"Aye," he whispered, and then there was a heartbeat of silence. "It was my father."

Twenty-one

Sabrina had no conscious recollection of going into their chamber. The next thing she knew she was sitting on the bed. Instead of sitting beside her, Ian prowled restlessly around the room.

She was numb. "Your father," she said faintly. "Your father killed Fionna?"

He stopped. His hands balled at his sides, he nodded.

Dazed, Sabrina shook her head. "I—I thought he was wildly in love with her—"

"He was. Indeed, he worshiped her."

"Then why would he kill her?"

He was silent for a moment. "He discovered she'd been with another man."

She should have known, she realized. Uncle Malcolm's words vibrated all through her. *You are wicked . . . You like the blade between his thighs . . . David will rue the day he wed you. By the Cross, he should never have wed you!* And he'd once said that Fionna took his nephew to his grave.

Slowly she said, "It had happened before, hadn't it?"

Ian's features were lined and drawn. "Aye."

Sabrina wet her lips. "I asked you once if you loved her, Ian. I know what you said. But I—I would ask again now."

His eyes flashed. "I did not love her. *Ever*," he emphasized. "Oh, I know all believe it was so. But it was not." He gave a harsh laugh. "Aye, I thought she was beautiful, for she was. But during my eighteenth summer she made it plain, she would welcome me into her bed. 'Twas then I discovered what she really was: a faithless, lying bitch. Selfish and vain." His denunciation was scathing. "I was appalled that she would think I would lie with her—my father's wife—my stepmother! She was furious that I spurned her. Indeed, I believe she was the one who spread it about that I was smitten with her. But I soon discovered that had I relented, I'd have not been the first—nor the last."

"And your father never knew?"

"She managed to keep it from him. And no man who succumbed would dare tell my father. I tolerated her only for my father's sake."

Her eyes were steady on his face. "What happened the day you found her?"

He moved, finally, to sit by her, his face shuttered from all expression. "The door to her chamber was jammed. I was summoned by one of the maids. When I opened it, I saw her lying there." He paused. "She'd been strangled with her own veil. At first I thought it might have been a jealous lover who killed her. I dreaded telling my father, for I knew how he loved her . . . when I told him, he spoke not a word. Nary a sound. He merely turned away. . . . I remember thinking how odd it was, that he displayed no hint of sorrow. Nor did he cry out in anguish. But there was a desolate emptiness in his eyes . . . he shut himself away and would see no one. I thought it was grief, for he did not even attend her funeral mass. But I knew he could not go on like this. I entered his chamber"—there was a betraying catch in his voice—"but I was too late. I found him as he lay gasping his last . . ."

Ian's eyes squeezed shut. The muscles of his throat worked. Sabrina's heart twisted, for she knew then at what cost he told her.

Her own throat grew tight. Her hand slipped within his.

"That moment will live on within me forever, for I knew that he was dying. He beckoned me close and told me . . . He'd returned home early that evening— earlier than Fionna expected. The scent of lovemaking was musky in the air, and on her person. And he'd seen a man in the passageway just before he entered . . ."

"So that was when he discovered she'd been unfaithful?" Sabrina held her breath and waited.

"Aye. He confronted her and she admitted it." His mouth twisted. "Indeed, she taunted him with her faithlessness. He said something snapped within him. He was crazed with rage and jealousy"—there was a pulsebeat of silence—"and in that rage he killed her."

Sabrina listened with aching heart. "But he could not live with himself, could he? That is why he took his own life?"

"Aye," he said heavily. "'Twas a burden he could not bear—a guilt he could not live with."

This, then, was the secret that Ian had been hiding. For Ian was not a man capable of murder—faith, but she regretted that the notion had ever crossed her mind! The talk that Ian had murdered Fionna was just that—talk. Ian would not dishonor his father by revealing that David had killed Fionna. He had protected his father's honor . . .

At the cost of his own.

Her heart went out to him, for his pain was etched deeply into his features. Slipping her hands around his waist, she pressed her head against his chest.

His arms closed slowly about her. "May God forgive me," he whispered into the soft cloud of her hair, "I do not regret that Fionna is dead. But I will despise myself forever, Sabrina, for if I had only gone to my father earlier, I might have spared him taking his own life. And now I—I tremble to think he is barred from the gates of Heaven forever for taking the life of another, and his own as well. I pray you do not think ill of him, for despite this sin, he was a brave, virtuous man."

All at once her eyes were abrim with tears. His heartache was her own. Her throat clogged with emotion; she drew back slightly so that she could see him. "You cannot blame yourself, Ian. Despite what the church tells us, I do not believe that God is such a harsh judge. Nor do I believe your father burns in Hell. And I make you a promise here and now, Ian. What you have told me will not pass my lips. No one will ever know the truth of who killed Fionna."

His eyes darkened. He reached for her anew, burying his face in the curve of her neck; this time his embrace was tinged with desperation. How long they stayed like that, the beats of their hearts as one, she did not know.

It was impossible not to notice when a sudden tension constricted the arms that held her. Troubled, she gazed up at him.

"What, Ian? What is it?"

His expression was shadowed. "What about you? Are you all right?" His fingertips went to her injured wrist.

Until this moment, she'd forgotten it. "I will be fine," she murmured, her smile shaky.

His regard was darkly intent. "Are you certain you were pushed?"

She shivered, feeling the chill of remembrance all through her. "I—I think so." Her eyes grew cloudy. "Do you think Mary is dead?"

"I do not know. But I have an awful feeling she may well be." Something fleeting crossed his face, something she couldn't discern. "But it occurs to me that someone wishes you—or everyone—to believe I am responsible for pushing you down the stairs."

Her skin went cold. "And for locking me in the dark?"

"Aye." His tone was as grim as his expression.

Thoroughly unnerved, she stared at him. "You think I was not meant to die?"

"I do not know. At the same time, mayhap that was the intent after all. . . ." He spoke, as if to himself. An icy coldness gripped her, for he was in deadly earnest.

Suddenly he framed her face in his hands. "I know only this. It may not be safe for you here. Perhaps it would be best if I sent you back to Dunlevy—"

"Ian, nay! Nay, I will not go!"

"I want you alive and unharmed, Sabrina. God help me, if anything should happen to you, I would never forgive myself!"

"And what about the babe? You said you would be

with me when he is born! You—you promised!" Perhaps it was unfair, but she could not help but lay the burden at his feet. Her cry was both a plea and an accusation. "Did you lie then?"

Though his jaw was taut, his gaze avoided hers. "Nay," he answered. "But I did not know the danger you might be in."

"And we may well be wrong about everything, for indeed, why would anyone wish me dead?" Her hands went to her middle. "Besides, I cannot travel. My time is too near, or would you have your son born in some field between here and Dunlevy?"

In the end, it was this which won out. "This is true," he admitted with a grimace. With a touch of familiar arrogance, he pulled her close against his side. "But you must have a care and guard yourself closely, Sabrina. Go nowhere alone—"

"Yes. Yes, I know." Secretly she breathed a sigh of relief.

"When I am gone, make certain Edna is with you. And when I am near, you must stay close by my side."

She nuzzled her cheek against the hard curve of his shoulder, thinking that would not be difficult at all. Nay, not at all. "Gladly, my Highland prince," she murmured. "Gladly."

Over a month earlier Ian had received the news that Robert the Bruce had soundly defeated the English troops at Loudon Hill in Ayrshire. Now, in the midst of summer, came still more news. Longshanks, it seemed, had been furious. In retaliation the English had put together an army, determined to crush the Scottish upstarts once and for all. But Longshanks had fallen ill and died on the march northward.

"His son, now Edward II," Ian noted dryly at table that evening, "decided it more prudent not to engage in battle. Instead he turned tail and retreated south."

"He feared our mighty Scots blades!" someone shouted.

One corner of Ian's mouth curled upward. "And we all know why—an English sword is no match for a Scots blade."

"What will happen now?" Sabrina asked later that evening when they were alone.

Ian was quietly pensive. "There is every chance the fighting has not yet ended. England refuses to recognize the Bruce as sovereign, though there is talk that Longshanks' son Edward is not the king his father was. As for the Bruce, he must continue to rally those to his side. And I fear his blood feud with the Comyns and their kin is not yet over."

Gently she touched his arm. What she had to say was painful, yet she knew it must be said.

"I know you have cause to doubt me, Ian, but I have come to realize that you are right. That the good of all Scotland is at stake. Robert the Bruce has done much to accomplish what many thought impossible in our land—to unite enemies one against the other against a common foe—the English."

His gaze sharpened, boring into her as if he sought to see into her very soul. Then with a hand he cupped her cheek. "It pleases me to hear you say that, sweet. It pleases me greatly."

The next few days passed unremarkably. Sabrina lifted her braid from where it lay on her nape. The afternoon was hot, and the babe was a weight that grew heavier with every hour that passed. She could not endure the day without stopping to rest every afternoon.

But there would be no rest for her on this day. She had barely lain down than there came a great hue and cry from the bailey. She rushed to the window.

"Raiders! They come this way!"

Ian heard it too and headed straight for the stable and his horse. Seconds later he was galloping through the gates in a whirlwind of dust. The pounding of hooves filled his ears, for a half a dozen other soldiers gave chase, and it was these he joined. He recognized at least three who belonged to the Bruce's own guard.

The raiders were just ahead—three of them, all told. One of them veered off to the right, toward the forest. Ian followed swiftly. From the corner of his eye, he saw the other two raiders separate, one to the north, one to the west. Clever they were, for their chances of escape increased tenfold by splitting up.

His eyes narrowed. Hunched over the neck of his stallion, he spurred the animal even faster. His quarry had disappeared within a copse of trees. Cursing vividly, Ian slowed to a trot. His head swiveled all around him, searching for any sign of movement.

Suddenly he straightened. Even as his senses screamed a warning, there was a mighty blow to his back. Unable to save his seat, he tumbled to the ground, landing in a pile of leaves. He lay stunned for an instant, the smell of damp earth assailing his nostrils, the breath driven from his lungs. The moment he was able, he rolled to his back, instinctively reaching for the dagger hidden inside his boot. An errant shaft of sunlight caught the glint of shiny steel, and then the dagger was tumbling high and away, end over end, to land far distant in a swirl of fallen leaves.

"I think not," drawled a voice from directly above him. Two booted feet planted themselves on either side of him.

Grimacing, Ian beheld his attacker.

Dear God, it was Jamie MacDougall.

The shock of recognition flared in both their eyes.

Jamie's sword was raised high, poised for the death blow he would render. A hundred things flooded Ian's mind in that instant, for he knew the end was at hand—the fever of battle flared high and bright in the ice-blue eyes that glittered down upon him.

But the blow never came. Time hung never-ending.

Ian bared his teeth. "Just do it," he grated out. "Do it and be done with it!"

Abruptly Jamie lowered his sword. "I cannot kill you," he said tautly.

Ian sucked in a harsh breath. "What the devil—"

Jamie's jaw thrust out. "I will not kill you," he said again. "I *cannot* kill you."

Hoarse shouts drifted on the breeze.

In a heartbeat Ian was on his feet, his mind turning frantically. He made no move to go for his sword. Instead he whistled for his mount. The horse glanced up from where he was grazing on the bushes, then trotted over.

Ian inhaled a stinging lungful of air. "Give me your dagger," he said tightly.

Jamie remained motionless. Shaggy brows drew together over the bridge of his nose.

"For God's sake, man, give me your dagger! I will tell the others you wounded me."

A dawning enlightenment flickered in those brilliant blue eyes. The other man reached for a long-necked dagger and tossed it to him.

Ian caught it. Without hesitation he plunged it deep into his left shoulder, feeling it rip through cloth and muscle and flesh.

He gritted his teeth against a rolling wave of pain. "Go," he urged tautly. "Take my horse and go. Go now!"

The pain was intense now. He sank to his knees, aware of a rustle of movement. His eyes squeezed shut. He prayed that Jamie would hurry. . . .

The thunder of riders shook the earth. "Not so fast now, laddie!" came a shout.

Ian swayed. His heart sank as blue eyes met gray. God above, he had tried. But it was too late. . . .

The Bruce himself was among the men who rode in to the village a short time later.

And it was the Bruce himself who passed sentence. Jamie MacDougall was to hang at dawn.

It was while Fraser bandaged his wound that Ian pondered how he was to tell Sabrina.

The door creaked on its hinges. A whisper of skirts and the sweet scent of lavender announced her presence.

She came straight to the chair where he sat. Ian did not see the silent, questioning glance bestowed on Fraser. Fraser offered a reassuring smile.

"He will heal quickly this time, lass." With a low bow he left husband and wife alone.

There was a protracted silence. No words passed between them. Ian felt the touch of her eyes on his profile.

His insides coiled. What was she thinking? Ah, no

doubt she blamed him. No doubt she condemned him.

He could not look at her as he spoke. "It was not I who captured him, Sabrina."

Tensely he waited . . . waited endlessly it seemed. Then he felt the veriest touch skim the linen bandages that circled his shoulder.

"Did he do this?"

Her voice was more breath than sound. Ian shook his head. How it happened no longer mattered. Later he would tell her the truth. Later . . .

He heard her sigh, a skittering rush of relief.

Slowly Ian raised his head—meeting her gaze was the hardest thing he'd ever done. He would far rather be deep in the thick of battle than here now, in this room.

"The Bruce has passed sentence," he said very quietly. "He is to hang at dawn."

Her eyes filled with tears.

Ian's heart squeezed.

She sank down on her knees before him. Her head bowed low. Her hands came out to clutch at his. When at last she raised her face to him, her lips were quivering.

"Please, Ian. You cannot let him die. You cannot!"

"He is guarded by a dozen men, Sabrina. I risk my own neck if I free him." Everything inside him tightened into a knot. His mood was suddenly black. But mayhap she didn't care, he thought bitterly. Mayhap she preferred his own death to Jamie's. Aye, for Jamie was the one she loved . . .

"I—I would not ask that of you. But Ian, you could go to the Bruce. Plead for his life. I—I know the Bruce will not free him, but must he die? Ian, I beg you . . .

you are the only one who can save him now . . . the only one . . ." The threat of spilled tears bled through to her voice.

Ian had offered the Bruce and his party chambers for the night. Even now, they awaited him below-stairs.

Ian could not help it. If he refused, she might well despise him for the remainder of their days. Yet nei-ther was it wise for him to make an enemy of the Bruce by asking that he spare Jamie's life.

His silence was stifling . . . for both of them.

Sabrina gave a choked little cry. "What, Ian! You cannot? Or *will* not?"

Slowly he rose to his full height. He pulled his hand from her grasp. Sabrina remained where she was on her knees, her features imploring.

"Very well. I will ask. But I warn you, Sabrina, I hold out little hope that the Bruce will relent."

Gratitude flooded her eyes. "I . . . thank you, Ian." Her lips quivered. "*Thank you.*"

Ian departed, saying nothing. He could not, for a world of turmoil resided in his breast. He was not a man without compassion, yet at this moment, a dark cloud of bitterness had slipped over him. He could not help but wonder . . . if *he* were the one destined to hang at dawn, would his lovely wife have begged for *his* life?

He had no answer, and the knowledge was like a stake through the heart.

He supped with the Bruce, awaiting the right mo-ment. As they ate, he could not help but think that Edward of England might well regret engaging a man such as Robert the Bruce, for the Bruce was a man of powerful presence—and relentless determination.

When the last dish had been offered and served, Robert dismissed his men and turned to him.

"Something is troubling you, Ian."

Ian smiled faintly. "Aye, sire. There is no point in dallying longer." His smile faded. "It concerns the prisoner, Jamie MacDougall."

"What of him?"

"I pray you'll not hold this against me, sire, for in no way do I question your judgment. And I pray you'll not question my loyalty, for it is ever yours."

Robert clapped a hand on his shoulder. "You've fought for me long and well, Ian, and I'll not forget that. So speak plainly, man."

"Very well, sire. My wife Sabrina is a Lowlander, from the clan Kincaid. She and Jamie MacDougall were once very nearly betrothed. She deeply regrets that he must die. For her sake, I do not ask that you free him, but that you spare his life."

"The MacDougalls have been a thorn in my side for many a month, Ian."

"I am aware of that, sire. Were it not for the tender feelings of my wife, I would not ask."

Robert nodded. Leaning back, he stared into the wavering light of the candle and stroked his bearded chin.

Finally he shook his head. "I do not consider your request lightly, Ian. But I cannot rule with a weak hand. If I show myself to be feeble and indecisive, I will ever be perceived as such. If I am to be Scotland's leader, defender of the land, defender of its people— then I must govern as one. If my enemies within my own borders—the Comyns and the MacDougalls— see that they will be dealt with harshly, perhaps they will realize further insurrection is futile." His tone was very grave. "My decision stands. Jamie Mac-Dougall will hang at dawn."

With that, Robert bid him good night. Ian sat, his mood as heavy as his heart. The minutes dragged, one into another.

A faint sound alerted him to another presence. He glanced up and saw Sabrina standing there, one hand on the roundness of her belly. Outwardly she was calm, yet Ian was not deceived. Mutely she gazed at him, her eyes wide and dark and questioning.

Ian's throat was raw. The words would not come. His expression as frozen as his tongue, he gave a single shake of his head.

She stared at him, her skin bloodless. Her lips formed a silent "no" . . .

Ian was on his feet before he knew it. When he would have reached for her, she spun away with a dry sob . . . a cry that resounded in the very chambers of his soul.

His hand fell to his side. He watched her flee up the stairs, chiding himself bitterly. He did not follow, for he knew she would want no comfort from him. Nay, she wanted nothing from him . . .

He felt like slamming his fist through the wall. Instead he made his way toward the hearth. His shoulders slumped as if he were old as the stars.

It was there he spent the night.

The shrillness of a cock's cry heralded a new day.

A crowd of onlookers had already begun to gather below the bluff where the gallows had been erected. A long rope dangled from the crossbeam.

In their excitement, no one noticed the woman, heavily laden with child; with head bowed low and downcast eyes she made her way to the edge of the crowd.

"Let it begin!" came a strident call.

A heavy-jowled man gleefully rubbed his hands together. "Aye, let's get on with it!" he shouted. "On with the hanging of the traitor!"

"Aye," chimed in another. "'Tis dawn and we await!"

A gentle morning breeze washed away the last traces of the night's mist. The eastern sky was streaked with pale pink and amber-gold. Beyond, the mountains rose in jagged splendor.

'Twould be a beautiful, glorious day. . . .

Sabrina's insides twisted. The villagers' lust for what was about to take place made her sick at heart, sick to the depths of her being. Yet she could not hate them. To them, Jamie MacDougall was not a flesh-and-blood man, a man they had known and touched, laughed with and trusted . . .

He was but a symbol of the enemy, a traitor to the man who now stood as their king.

"Here he comes!" someone shouted.

Aye, and there he was, towering over his gaoler by half a head. His tawny hair glinted in the sunlight, a halo of gold. Though his hands were bound behind his back, he neither cowered nor faltered. His step was bold and sure; the set of his shoulders, noble and straight; the angle of his head, brave and proud.

He faced death as he had faced life. Undaunted and fearless.

Her heart cried out. Jamie, she thought piercingly. Oh, Jamie . . . may God be with you. . . .

He stepped upon the stool. The noose was draped around his neck; she could almost feel the hemp rough against her skin. She could feel the sun warm upon her face, the morning breeze fresh with dew swirling all about. Overhead the sky was a deep shade of blue.

Aye, she thought achingly. A wondrous day . . .

A priest stepped forward, bestowing a last blessing. He retreated, and a hooded executioner took his place. He asked if the victim had any last words.

Jamie's gaze swept the crowd. "Aye!" he shouted. "Long live Scotland!"

Sabrina's heart was throbbing. Her teeth dug into her lip; she could feel the taste of her own blood. The crowd had gone silent, a hush that seemed to spread across the entire world.

The stool was kicked away. She heard the sound—'twas like the slash of a swordpoint ripping through her . . .

His body jerked. To the right of her someone sneered, "Look at the laddie dance now!"

The cheers of the onlookers blurred. Her insides churned. Nausea roiled up within her like a boiling sea.

She had little awareness of the tall spare figure that had suddenly appeared beside her. Ian's expression was wild. A taut arm encircled her shoulder. He sought to press her face against his chest.

"Do not look," he cried hoarsely. "*Do not look!*"

She fought him. She fought him with all of her strength, though she made no sound. Her head twisted. Her gaze, huge and unblinking, was transfixed on the gallows.

At last he succeeded in turning her face into his shoulder, but in the very next heartbeat, Jamie ceased his struggle . . .

A roar went up from the crowd.

He felt the rush of air she expelled . . . as if her last breath had left her, too.

Ian could have screamed his pain aloud.

She turned her face into his neck. She made nary a sound, but he felt the scalding wetness of tears against his skin . . . tears that rent him in two.

He bent and swept her high in his arms. "Move aside!" he shouted. "Move aside!"

Twenty-two

She made no outcry—would that she had! Would that she had cried. Raged. Screamed . . .

She was far stronger than he realized. Far stronger than he dreamed . . .

For she only clung to him, her fingers twisted in the front of his shirt. He could feel the great jagged breaths she drew.

In their chamber he went straight to the bed. The instant his embrace loosened, she curled away from him and averted her face. "Leave me," she said in a choked little voice. "Please leave me."

Ian stiffened. His mouth thinned to a hard, straight line. His hands curled into fists at his sides. Her dismissal cut bone deep. He was suddenly seething. *Damn her*, he thought furiously. Damn her for turning from him! She would share nothing with him, not even her pain.

He whirled and strode from the room.

In the hall he found solace in a horn of ale.

It was a long time later that a shadow fell over him. He glanced up to see Uncle Malcolm standing above him.

He gestured to the bench across from him. "Sit, Uncle."

The old man obliged, but he peered at him oddly.

Not knowing what to say, Ian murmured, "'Tis good to see you risen from your sickbed, Uncle."

"Ye're the one looks like ye should be on a sickbed, lad. Or is it a sickness of the heart that afflicts ye?"

Ian smiled slightly. Ah, but the old man's sight was a trifle too keen at times.

"The man captured by the Bruce's troops yesterday—Jamie MacDougall—was hung this morn, Uncle." His tone was very quiet. "None are privy to this . . . but Jamie and Sabrina once planned to wed."

Shaggy brows shot upward. "They did!" He frowned suddenly. "And the lass is sad now, eh?"

"To be sure, Uncle." The ale had loosened his tongue, Ian thought vaguely. "She still loves him."

"Nae, lad, ye're wrong."

"'Tis true, Uncle—"

Malcolm thumped his fist on the table. "Can ye not see for yersel', lad? Are ye blind, then?"

Ian's lips twisted. "What is to see, Uncle? She is abovestairs even now, grieving for the man she loves."

Malcolm glowered at his nephew. "And mayhap she but grieves for a friend now lost. What is wrong with that, I ask? Ye're the one she loves, lad. And it's with yer wife ye should be, not here swilling ale like the young fool ye are!"

Out of respect for his elder, Ian said nothing. Yet he could not help but reflect derisively that Malcolm was the one whose sight failed him, for Ian knew his wife wanted no part of him.

"Her lass—the girl Edna—told me when I sickened

that Sabrina tended me one day. 'Tis strange, for when first she came here I thought how much like Fionna she was. And aye, Edna told me I shouted and raged at her that day, for I was convinced it was Fionna who tended me. I remember it not, but indeed, whole days go by that I dinna remember." The old man's gaze grew intent. "But she is not like Fionna, and if anyone should know it, 'tis you, lad, for you are not the fool your father was." He glared at him. "Or mayhap ye are, if ye dinna know she loves ye!"

Uncle Malcolm departed, leaving him to his thoughts—and his ale. And it must have been the ale that made him wonder . . . was Uncle right? Did Sabrina love him? Or was it naught but an old man's whimsy?

The next thing he knew, he was standing at the door of his chamber. With one hand he eased it open and peered inside, but Sabrina did not lie abed, as he expected. Instead she stood in the center of the chamber, her expression confused. She was gazing down at her gown, which clung wetly to the outline of her legs.

Slowly her head turned. But just as she saw him, her eyes flew wide. One hand crept to her belly. She bent slightly, her lovely features twisting in a grimace.

"Ian," she gasped, "your son is coming."

For an instant he stood stock-still. His heart seemed to beat in slow-motion. The babe, he realized dumbly. The babe was coming . . .

He bolted for the passageway. "Edna," he bellowed, "send for the midwife!"

He rushed back to Sabrina. Her frightened expression pierced him to the quick. Before he could reach her, Edna rushed in. "I sent Marcus for the midwife!"

she cried. As only a woman could, in but an instant she'd taken charge of the situation. "Here, my lady, let me get you a dry gown and then we must get you back to bed."

Ian stood by, feeling awkward and bungling. When Sabrina was installed in bed once more, he went to her and snared her hand. Her fingers lay ice-cold in his.

Seeking to reassure her, he asked if she wished him to stay.

"Stay! Nay," she gasped out. "Nay! Go!"

His smile froze. "As you wish," he said tautly.

His elbows braced on the table, his posture wooden, he resumed his place in the hall . . . and called for more ale.

Alasdair and several others joined him, but he was not inclined to talk. He sat in silence, his spirits darkly somber and brooding.

In her he'd found all he sought, all he ever wanted, all he'd never known he wanted . . . only to lose her anew to Jamie. Oh, he'd thought she had come to care for him, but aye, it was Jamie she loved. Ever and always . . .

But it was *his* child she carried beneath her heart.

He slammed down his ale, a sizzle of anger heating his blood. His jaw thrust out. By God, he would not be barred from his son's birth—the child was his, too!

His mood fierce, he took the stairs two at a time.

The door crashed open. He swayed slightly, filling the doorway, catching his hands on the frame to steady himself. Edna gasped but said nothing.

Meredith the midwife, red-cheeked and capable, planted her hands on cabbage-round hips. "A birthing is no place for a man," she snapped, "be he chieftain or otherwise! Now out with ye!"

An arrogant black brow climbed high. "This is my castle, lady, and I'll not be ousted from any part of it!"

Her mouth turned down. "Then be silent and do not interfere!" she advised blackly.

Ian scowled at her, but he paid no heed. Four strides took him to the bedside. The sight he confronted there nearly brought him to his knees.

Sabrina lay against the pillows, looking small and frail, her skin as pale as bleached linen. Her chest rose and fell in quick, shallow pants. As he scraped a chair next to the bedside, her lashes fluttered open.

"Ian," she whispered. "You should not be here."

His heart contracted. The emerald green of her eyes was the only splash of color in her face.

"Ah," he said gravely. "But I promised you I would. And a promise given is a promise kept, is it not?"

She tried to smile, but her smile turned to a spasm of pain as she was wrenched by a contraction. Her gasp turned to a low moan by the time it ended.

Ian leaned forward. He reached for a linen cloth draped over the side of a basin, wiping the sweat from her brow.

"Do not hold your breath, sweet," he murmured. "It but makes the pain worse." He knew it was so, not only from his own experience, but from tending those who had suffered wounds in battle. Laying the cloth aside, his hands locked around hers, warm and reassuring.

"Here, sweet, take my hands." He spoke with calm

encouragement. "The next time the pain comes, squeeze as hard as you like."

Meredith glanced at Edna in startled surprise. Could it be this man would not be a hindrance after all?

He had no sooner finished speaking than another contraction knotted her womb. They were coming closer and closer, almost constant now. Though she did not scream, her lips were torn and bloodied as she held her pain tight inside. Ian was shaken to the depths of his being; he considered for the first time that he might lose her, for he could not imagine she could endure such pain and survive.

His face was pale as he whispered encouragement. He could see her weakening, her strength waning, squeezing her breath from her. Yet her labor grew ever intense, ever more painful. Another spasm gripped her, longer and harder than all that had gone before. When it ebbed, she fell back against the pillows, limp and exhausted.

Trying to hide his fear from Sabrina, he turned shocked eyes at Meredith. "God's teeth! Will it never be over?" It was a prayer, a plea.

Stationed at the end of the bed, Meredith peered beneath the sheet. To his amazement, she gave a wheezing laugh. "Oh, but you worry for naught, my lord! Even now, the head appears!" To Sabrina she urged, "There now, lass, 'tis almost done. The next time you must push hard, for yer babe is suddenly most anxious to arrive!"

Anxious? Ian shook his head, dazed. There was none more anxious than he—except mayhap Sabrina—and both for the pain to merely be at an end!

He did not know that a colossal pressure had built

there between her legs. A racking pain fringed the world with blackness. Though she tried to withhold it, a cry of anguish broke from her lips.

Ian went white. His grip on her hands was fierce. "Sabrina—" he began raggedly.

But then she heard Meredith's voice, sharply commanding: "Aye, that's the way, lass! Bear down, for your babe is almost here!"

Summoning her last vestige of strength, Sabrina lowered her head. She was only half-aware of Ian beside her, grim-visaged and unsmiling. Squeezing her eyes shut, she arched her back and strained mightily. Her nails dug into his palms.

The babe slid from her. In the next instant, a high, wavering cry filled the air. Sabrina collapsed back upon the pillows, so weak she was shaking from it.

Ian rose, numb as never before. He could only comprehend that it was over, that Sabrina was all right, that he'd not lost her.

There was a tug on his elbow. Edna stood there, beaming. "A beauty, my lord!" She gave a half-sob. "Aye, a beauty!" She pressed a swaddled bundle into the curve of his elbow.

Dazed, Ian looked down. He beheld a solemn little face with miniature little brows set over a wee nose. There was not an abundance of hair, but what was there was dark as midnight—dark as his own.

He swallowed. A rush of emotion poured through him, making him tremble. Christ, to think that it had once crossed his mind the babe might not be his. . . .

He unwrapped the swaddling that he might peer at the child more closely, and then he could only stare in utter amazement.

"Ian . . . Ian, please . . ."

Sabrina gazed at him imploringly. Deep circles shadowed her eyes, but he could see she longed to see the babe. He moved to the bedside, sitting so that she might see for herself the wondrous miracle they'd created.

She sniffed. An expression of horror flitted across her features. "Ian, you are . . . sotted!"

He chuckled. "That I am, sweet. But not so sotted that I cannot tell lad from lassie!"

Her lips parted. "What!" she said faintly. "You mean—"

"The son you were so certain you carried, sweet . . . is not a son at all!"

"A girl!" she cried out in distress. "Oh, but I was so sure we would have a son!"

Just then the babe let out a wail.

Ian laughed gustily. Sabrina turned pleading eyes to his. "Ian, may I . . . hold her?"

His eyes softened. He twisted slightly, then with his free arm lifted her so that she rested against him. He eased his precious bundle into her waiting arms.

"Aye," he said softly, "a wee bonny bratling. . . ." He bent and pressed his lips to the soft down on that tiny little head.

Tears sprang to her eyes, for there was a father's pride in that telling caress. Her hand stole to the swaddling, and she uncovered that tiny little body that she might see for herself. A sigh of contentment shook her, and she smiled, a bright golden smile that sent joy winging all through him.

"Oh, Ian, she is sweet, isn't she?"

"Aye," he said huskily. "That she is." His arms engulfed both mother and daughter, cradling them both, for they were more precious to him than life itself. A powerful tide of emotion surged within his chest, but alas, his joy was tinged with a bittersweet pain. He was struck by a bitter irony.

Aye, she smiled now, but what of the days to come? Jamie MacDougall was dead. And their child had been born on the day he'd been robbed of his life. Would she ever forgive him? Would she ever forget...?

His arms tightened. A fierce possessiveness swept over him. She had to. She *had* to. For she was his wife. His *wife*...

And if it took him forever, he would make her love him.

The days that followed were far from easy. Sabrina regained her strength quickly, and for that she was heartily glad. But there were times when a melancholy sadness slipped over her and it was all she could do to shake free of it.

It was at those times that she thought most of Jamie. She mourned him deeply, and raged that Providence had been so cruel—to steal away his chance at life and happiness. Were it not for the babe, her days would have been unbearable. She saw Ian only at mealtimes, for since the babe's birth, he had taken to sleeping in a chamber down the hall. His manner was polite and restrained, but the intimacy was gone.

They had named the babe Elizabeth—Ian had taken to calling her his bonny little Beth. He took pleasure in his daughter, for he came to see her daily, holding her and laughing softly as she puckered her rosebud mouth or lifted tiny dark brows over eyes he predicted would be green as her mother's. An unguarded tenderness lurked in his own at those times, a tenderness that both filled her with joy and made her ache inside.

Her memory of Elizabeth's birth was one she would hold inside her forever—oh, not because of the pain, for that was quickly forgotten. Nay, she would hold in her heart forever the way Ian had cradled her close, both her and the babe. Oh, but he had been so tender and sweet, and it was the most wondrous moment of her life.

And now . . . now she wanted it all back, but she knew not how. . . . She missed their closeness, the warmth of his body against her own in the dead of night; the steady drone of his heart beneath her ear, and everything within her cried out her heartache. What had happened? Why was he so distant and remote?

A fortnight later, she lifted a fretting infant from the cradle at the foot of the bed. "Oh, there, now," she soothed with a half-laugh. "Are you so impatient then for your supper?"

Easing herself down in a chair near the hearth, she opened her gown. She gave a laugh when the babe greedily latched onto her nipple; her cries ceased. Elizabeth was a hearty eater—as her mother could attest!—and her little body had already begun to fill out. Her little cheeks were plump and round, her belly firm. Sabrina had shunned the services of a wet nurse; she could imagine no greater thrill than cuddling the wee form of her child and holding her close.

Crooning softly, she gazed out the open window. The day had been hot, almost stifling, and she welcomed the cooling breeze that eddied within. The purple haze of twilight spread across the sky.

Elizabeth waved a fist high in the air, suckling noisily. Sabrina captured it and brought it to her lips, smiling as she kissed those tiny knuckles.

The door creaked. Sabrina glanced up just as Ian strode within.

He stopped short when he saw her. No hint of his thoughts dwelled in his expression. "Forgive me," he said briefly. "I should have knocked."

She shook her head. "There is no need," she said softly. "This is your chamber."

For a moment he stood utterly still, so still she thought he hadn't heard. His gaze was riveted on the generous expanse of an ivory, blue-veined breast that lay revealed to him. Sabrina felt her cheeks pinken, for this was the first time he'd come upon her when she'd been nursing Elizabeth. But she did not cover herself. Indeed, his unwavering regard made her pulse quicken.

Quivering both inside and out, she gave what she hoped was an encouraging smile. Only then did he drag his eyes away.

"I—I must go," he muttered.

Fear and longing and an endless yearning swept through her. The need to touch him was over-whelming. She longed to run her fingers over the raspy hardness of his jaw, to feel his arms strong and tight around her back. She ached with the need to be close to him once more.

Her eyes clung to his. Summoning all her courage, she wet her lips. "Ian, you—you need not leave."

He gestured curtly. "I've other matters to attend to."

Her smile wavered. "Ian, please . . . can we not talk?"

"Later, Sabrina. Not now."

His tone was almost harsh. There was no hint of warmth in his features, only that shuttered look she had come to dread.

Do not do this, she longed to cry. *Oh, don't you see that I need you? I need you now, Ian. Forever and always. . . .*

But he was already striding through the door.

Sabrina was suddenly shattered inside, her heart abrim with pain. *I love him*, she thought helplessly. *I love him so.* And suddenly nothing else mattered but that he know it.

Quickly she laid the babe back in her cradle and raced to the door. But Ian was gone, the echo of his footsteps in the passageway already fading.

Elizabeth wailed, for she had not yet finished with her meal.

Tears misted Sabrina's vision, but she refused to despair. She raced back to the cradle and snatched up Elizabeth, bringing her to her breast, her tears mingling with that of the babe's.

Later, she resolved. Later she would tell Ian. Tell him that she loved him and—and pray that in time he might come to love her in return, if only as the mother of his child.

But Elizabeth was fretful, and it took her some while to rock her to sleep. With Elizabeth finally snug in her cradle, she bade Edna stay with the babe, then went in search of him.

She had just stepped into the passageway when a voice hailed her.

"Sabrina!"

It was Alasdair. "Alasdair," she began breathlessly, "have you seen Ian?"

"Aye," he nodded. "Indeed, I've a message for you.

He bade me find you and ask that you meet him on the battlements of the north tower."

The battlements? It spun through her mind that it was an odd place. . . . Yet perhaps not so odd. Nay, it was perfect. They could be alone there, and undisturbed. They could talk without being overheard, or waking Elizabeth.

She squeezed his arm. "Thank you, Alasdair."

She hurried toward the tower stairs. She was breathless by the time she reached the last step. Her heart was bounding, afraid and anxious all at once, yet eager to have it over and done. And yet she was almost terrified, for what if Ian spurned her? No. *No*. It would not happen. She would not even think of such . . .

The tower was deserted when she stepped outside. A chill went through her, for it was already dark. She should have thought to bring a candle with her.

Just as the thought spun through her mind, the yellow glow of a torch appeared. Sabrina's heart leaped. But the words she would have spoken caught halfway up her throat.

For it was not Ian who slipped from the shadows . . .

It was Margaret.

Twenty-three

It wasn't long before Ian mounted the stairs once again. Shame pricked him deeply, for he knew not what had possessed him to leave Sabrina as he had. His mouth thinned with self-derision. He was a coward—a coward!

But there was a deeper truth to be faced. He could not hide from it. A painful band of tightness crept around his chest. If it was Jamie she still loved, then so be it. Mayhap, in time, she would forget him. For no matter what, she was his wife. She shared his home and hearth. She had borne his child, and God willing, there would someday be others. He could not imagine life without his flame-haired enchantress. It would be barren and cold . . . no life at all.

Fool! taunted a voice in his head. Was it any wonder that she wanted naught to do with him? He had stolen her away from Dunlevy, from all she held near and dear—from her beloved Jamie. He'd wed her—aye, and bedded her—and all because she'd roused in him a passion that blazed as never before. He'd wanted her. He'd been determined to have her . . . and so he had. Her wishes had played no part in his plans, for selfishly he had thought only of himself.

And mayhap he was still as selfish as ever. For he could not lose her. He could not give her up.

Her melancholy tore at his insides, and he knew not how to approach her. Out of deference for her grief and the arrival of the babe, he had slept elsewhere this past fortnight. But he felt like a stranger—and in his own home yet!—wholly out of step, uncertain which way to turn. Mayhap it was arrogance, but it was not a feeling he was accustomed to.

They could not go on as they were, he thought tautly. He must face her . . . and face her now. He wanted to be back in her bed—*their* bed. He wanted a place in her heart . . .

For he'd yielded his own long, long ago.

Such was the bend of his mind as he entered his chamber for the second time within the hour. A quick glance revealed that Beth was sleeping soundly in her cradle. But it was Edna, not Sabrina, who rose from a chair when he stepped within.

"Where is your mistress, Edna?"

Edna was startled. "Why, I thought she was with you, my lord."

Ian shook his head. "I've not seen her since I left here an hour past."

Edna looked puzzled. "She fetched me to stay with Elizabeth. But just as she left, I heard your cousin say he had a message for her—from you."

"From me!" Ian was taken aback. "But I sent no message." His eyes narrowed. "Is that all?" he demanded.

"I believe he said you asked that she meet you at the north tower—the battlements, I think."

Ian had gone very still. A flicker of disquiet took root within him. Alasdair . . . this was strange, strange indeed. And he did not like it—nay, not a whit!

He grasped Edna's shoulders. "Are you certain?"

Edna had begun to look frightened. "I can be no more certain, my lord." She took a deep breath. "My lord, what is amiss? Is she all right?"

Ian's expression was grim. He whirled and retraced his steps. "Let us hope so," he said over his shoulder. "But say a prayer for her, Edna—and me as well."

Sabrina's heart was frozen. Her mind reeled. Margaret had drowned! Why wasn't she dead?

"What is this, Sabrina? Have you no greeting to spare for your own sister?"

Sabrina stared, convinced her eyes deceived her, yet knowing it was not so. No ghost was this, but a flesh-and-blood woman, a woman who, to all appearances, had been hale and hearty and whole these many months. Her hair gleamed smooth and golden, touched with moonglow. Her gown flowed about her slender form, gauzy white.

Speech was an art she seemed to have lost. "Margaret," she managed at last. "Margaret, how can this be . . . we all thought you dead!" She stopped, shaking her head, as if it was too much to take in, as indeed it was! Suddenly all her questions were rushing out, tripping her tongue. She was elated. She was furious. Faith, but she was all amuddle!

"Margaret, what do you here . . . where have you been all this time? What about Papa . . . does he know you are alive?"

"Nay, sister. No one knows. None but the three of us." Margaret's gaze slipped beyond her.

Sabrina turned slightly. Alasdair stood behind her, his eyes glinting.

Comprehension washed through her. *The three of us.* Herself, Margaret . . . and Alasdair.

A shiver touched her spine. Something was wrong, she realized. Something was horribly, horribly wrong.

Margaret's smile was laced with something she did not understand. But the glitter in her eye . . . Sabrina went cold to the tips of her fingers.

Alasdair moved a step closer.

All at once she felt trapped—trapped with no way out, for Alasdair stood between her and the stairs.

"Margaret, never say . . . never say you pretended to be dead!"

Margaret just laughed, a sound that chilled Sabrina's blood. She was terrified anew, but this time for a far different reason. Instinct warned she should not show it.

"Margaret . . . Dear God, how could you do this to Papa? He was heartbroken when he thought you died. He loved you so—"

"Aye, he loved me. He loved me far more than you, sister."

Her tone was laced with malice.

Sabrina swallowed. "I—I am well aware of that. But there was never a day that I bore you any ill will. Never did it stop me from loving you—never."

"You were ever a pudding heart, Sabrina." Margaret made it sound like a curse.

Sabrina had gone very pale. "Why?" she asked, her voice very low. "Why would you do this?"

"'Tis very simple, sister. You see, I had no desire to marry Ian. I knew it for certain when Alasdair came with him to Edinburgh." She paused. "You remember that, don't you, sweeting? You could not accompany us—'twas really remarkably easy, making you ill—a bit of chickweed in your tea."

Sabrina was shocked. "You did that? You deliberately made me ill that I could not travel?"

"Papa did not want you there anyway. Why should you bother?"

Margaret smiled snidely. Sabrina was beginning to understand. . . .

"Pray go on," she said quietly. "What happened in Edinburgh?"

Margaret's smile took in Alasdair, who blew her a kiss from his fingertips. "Alasdair and I became lovers," she proclaimed airily. "Though none knew it, we saw each other many times these past few years. And when Ian came to Dunlevy to claim me for his bride . . . well, I knew then what must be done."

"You determined not to marry Ian, didn't you?"

Margaret's blue eyes opened wide. "Why, Sabrina, mayhap you are more clever than I knew."

Sabrina's nails dug into her palms. "It was you who locked me in that horrid chamber belowstairs, wasn't it?"

"Nay, love. That was Alasdair."

Sabrina trembled. "Why? *Why?*"

"That was not planned, nay, not at first, for we did not know that you would marry Ian. But when the two of you wed, we decided that you would have to go, for you were in the way. We could not take the chance that you might someday discover what we'd done. And it all fell into place so perfectly. We had only to bide our time, for Fionna's murder had already blackened Ian's name once. When I 'died,' Alasdair had only to plant questions in your mind about my death. Was it an accident . . . or no? We had only to sow the seed, that mayhap Ian had a hand in both those deaths." She gloated. "Oh, but it was all so easy—and so very enjoyable."

Sabrina's gaze slid to Alasdair. "I trusted you, Alasdair," she said through lips that barely moved. "I—I was fond of you! I thought you were so charming! But all the time your words were just lies. . . . It was you who pushed me down the stairs, wasn't it?"

"I knew not if you would die." He shrugged. "If we were lucky . . . either way, there was Ian to blame."

"And what about Mary? Where is she?" Sabrina's throat was bone dry. "Never say you murdered her, too!"

It was Margaret who answered. "Nay. We did not, though I did consider it. Mary, my dear sister, is now in the service of the chieftain of the clan Lindsay, a man who is friend to Alasdair."

Alasdair again. The villagers' talk about Fionna. And Margaret . . . it was he who began the rumors, to make Ian look guilty. He had been manipulating her all along. . . .

"You planned to blame Ian for Mary's disappearance, too, didn't you?"

"Aye, we did." Margaret smiled. "Percival Lindsay believes that Ian lusted after Mary, and that is why Alasdair sought to remove her from his grasp." She smiled. "Indeed, Mary has served her purpose well, for the villagers—aye, and others—are convinced the poor girl lies dead at the bottom of the loch. And poor Mary believes that Ian is to blame for her departure."

Sabrina's stomach was churning. "You have Alasdair, Margaret. That is what you wanted, isn't it? Why must you besmirch Ian's name?"

"That is simple, dear sister. Alasdair has no love for his cousin, and that is why we went to such trouble to smear his name. We have no desire to see Ian regarded as a saint. Nay, we much prefer that Ian's name be cursed by all."

Sabrina took a deep racking breath. "What has happened to you, Margaret? What has happened?"

"Oh, I've been as I've always been, sister. You simply did not see it. It was I who told Papa you were throwing dice in the stable with the village boys, when you should have been in the kirk on your knees. Of course I did not know that Papa would lock you away. And of course I did not know that you would fear the dark ever after. Oh, but I did enjoy that!" Margaret's eyes gleamed. "You really were a devilish child, Sabrina—can you imagine?—gambling instead of praying!"

Devilish? Nay, Sabrina thought faintly. But the devil was in her sister. Her sister was the cunning mastermind of these awful deeds. Her sister, so fair and beauteous, was evil and twisted . . . she had no compunction about murder. Margaret still held the torch, spilling light all about her. All in white, she looked ethereal and angelic and breathtakingly beautiful . . . but her hands, so soft and white, would soon be stained with blood . . .

Her blood. Sabrina's.

For Sabrina knew then, she knew it with a certainty that precluded all else, that she was to die. The two of them would murder her.

Her lungs burned with every breath. "You will kill Ian, too, when I am gone, won't you?"

"Oh, aye. Then Alasdair can take his place as chieftain of the clan, for he has always despised Ian, you know. As for your child, my dear niece Elizabeth, do not fret, Sabrina. I shall make a good mother to her."

The thought of Margaret's tainted hands on her babe filled her with outrage.

"How, Margaret? All think you dead."

Margaret smirked. "Ah, I neglected to tell you that, didn't I? Once Alasdair is installed as chieftain, I shall reappear. I shall tell how Ian struck me on the head and threw me in the waters of the loch. But though I was stunned, I was not dead. Nay, instead I managed to swim from his sight and hide. I wandered, and fell . . . but when I awoke, I remembered naught, not even my name or where I lived.

"Aye," she boasted, "I shall tell how a kind traveler took me in these many months, until one day I chanced to remember who I was—that I was to wed Ian. But poor Ian is dead, and so I may as well wed Alasdair instead. . . . No, you say? Och, but it could easily happen," she crowed triumphantly, "for I heard just such a tale of a man in England."

God above, she was mad—Margaret was mad, yet so very, very clever.

"But come now." Margaret's smirk vanished. "We've dallied long enough." Her sister stared at her with burning hatred that seemed to scorch her very soul.

She beckoned to Alasdair.

Alasdair stepped forward. His teeth pulled over his lips in a feral smile.

In his hands was a length of rope.

"Your body will be found in the morn, sweet Sabrina," he said softly.

Sabrina swallowed. Terror engulfed her, but she knew she must keep her wits about her.

"A pity, I shall tell everyone. But of course we all know who is to blame—"

"Aye," injected a hard male voice. "We do indeed."

Sabrina gasped. Ian stepped from the shadows, not three steps behind Alasdair.

Alasdair whirled. "You!" he spat. Then suddenly a brow arched slyly. "Tell me, cousin. Did you hear? Do you know—"

"I heard." Ian's voice was deadly quiet, his jaw rigid. "I know."

"Ah, cousin, but there is still more yet. You see, it was your father who killed Fionna. I always knew that it was he—and I know why. I saw him, you see—and he saw me that night. Why, I had barely slipped from her bed . . . What!" he taunted. "You did not know it was I with Fionna that night? Oh, a tasty morsel, she was, your stepmother."

Ian's hands balled into fists at his sides. Sheer rage flamed in his eyes. "You bastard," he said from between clenched teeth. "You bastard!"

The rope was flung aside. A dagger suddenly appeared in Alasdair's hand.

"What? Will you kill me, cousin?" His laugh was chilling. He beckoned with it. The blade caught the torchlight as it arced through the air. "Come then. Come now."

But he did not wait. He charged, his weapon raised high for Ian's throat. Sabrina cried out, for no doubt Ian was unarmed—usually he donned sword and dagger only when he left the keep. But she'd forgotten, he was a warrior, quick and fleet with every sense attuned to the veriest danger. He ducked and whirled; Alasdair bared his teeth and barreled toward him anew.

Again Ian eluded him, retreating backward. Sabrina knew then he sought to get Alasdair away from her, to save her from danger. It spun through her mind that never had a man been more splendid and mighty, more valiant and brave.

She was only half aware that Margaret had come to stand near. Margaret turned to her, goading and triumphant.

"Take heart, sister," she hissed. "Ian is weak, as you are weak. Alasdair will kill him, and then we will kill you."

It was all Sabrina could do not to slap the smile from Margaret's face. Her eyes flashed. "We shall see," was all she said. "We shall see."

And all at once it was Ian who was the aggressor, all supple grace and latent power. An iron fist struck low in the belly brought Alasdair to his knees. But Alasdair's arms shot out and in the next instant he'd brought Ian down atop him. They struggled, rolling and twisting. Then they disappeared into the shadows, lost from view.

A harsh, guttural cry split the night, carried on the wind, high and away . . .

Then there was silence.

Endless, horrible silence.

Sabrina could not stand it. The fear that tore through her turned her veins to ice. She stretched out her hands and stumbled forward.

"Ian . . . Ian!"

His name was a sound of anguish, a fervent prayer. Then suddenly he was there, tall and strong and powerful, striding toward her. She threw herself against him, desperate to reassure herself that he yet lived.

"Ian . . . is Alasdair—"

"Dead."

They'd both forgotten about Margaret, who now screeched like a creature from hell.

"You wretch!" Foul, vile curses poured from her lips. "He is dead . . . dead!" Enraged, she launched herself at Ian.

But she still held the torch . . . did it slip from her grasp . . . or did she fling it to her feet . . . ? Yet it did not matter, for the flames had caught the hem of her gown, licking upward . . .

A curdling scream filled the air. Margaret clawed at her breast. Ablaze in flames, that fiery figure pitched herself over the curtain wall.

It lasted forever . . . it was over in but an instant.

For Sabrina, it was too much. Her mind recoiled in horror.

Her body went limp. She slumped against Ian in a dead faint.

Twenty-four

A voice called to her, luring her from the dark void into which she'd fallen. She was in her bed, for she could feel the softness of the mattress beneath her. Gentle fingertips traced the smoothness of her cheek. Sabrina turned her face into the caress, for she'd have known the touch of those lean, strong hands anywhere.

But all too soon, the horror of remembrance battered her. She sat up with a strangled gasp. Ian's features swam before her, his eyes rimmed with concern.

"Margaret—" she choked out.

"She's dead, love." His voice was very quiet. "Take comfort from knowing she is where she wished to be, with Alasdair, wherever that may be."

Sabrina could not help it. She shuddered.

Immediately Ian's arms encircled her, pulling her close. Held fast against him, her trembling gradually subsided.

She drew back and peered anxiously toward the end of the bed. "Is Elizabeth—"

He smiled slightly. "She is fine, Sabrina."

But Sabrina needed the assurance only the sight of her child could provide. Her eyes mutely begging his understanding, she slipped from his arms. A glance revealed he spoke the truth. Elizabeth slept soundly, her cheek plumped out beneath her, her miniature rump stuck high in the air. Sabrina smiled slightly as the infant let out a bubbly sigh.

Ian remained where he was, seated on the edge of the bed, his expression grave. His eyes snared hers, and he held out his hand.

Sabrina inhaled raggedly. All at once she felt inexplicably shy. Three steps brought her within reach, and she held out her own.

Their fingertips touched. His hand curled warmly about her own, drawing her down beside him. Unable to look away, she watched as he weaved his fingers through hers, strong and tight, reassuring despite the tempest still swirling inside her.

Her gaze slid away. "All this time," she murmured, "Margaret was alive. I—I still cannot believe it. . . . I—I hate to say it, but . . . I almost think she hated me, even when we were children. I—I am ashamed to say, I—I did not know whether to believe you when you said you did not tell Papa I was in the stable throwing dice that long ago day. But she was the one who told him, and not once did I consider it might have been Margaret."

"I know, sweet. I heard."

All at once Sabrina's eyes were swimming with tears. Biting her lip hard, she ducked her head, her emotions all ajumble.

"Sabrina! What is this?"

But she only wept the harder, her tears hot and scalding.

Awkwardly he touched her shoulder. "Sabrina," he said helplessly, "I know this is hard. So much has happened. There has been so much death . . ."

Her dry, jagged sob was like a knife turning in his breast. "'Tis not that!"

He slipped a hand between the fall of her hair, watchful and waiting. "What then?"

Suddenly she turned blindly into his chest. "'Tis you!"

He drew her close, snug within the protective binding of his arms. "Me! Sabrina, I—"

"I cannot stop myself from thinking . . . what if it had been you instead of Alasdair?" She buried her face against the side of his neck. "Ian, if you had died—" Her voice broke. She could not go on, for the thought was unbearable.

Ian went utterly still. There was something in the way she spoke . . .

His thumb beneath her chin, he urged her face to his. He stared into misty green eyes, afraid to breathe, even more afraid to hope. . . .

"Would you have mourned me?" he whispered.

Her eyes cleaved to his. "Aye," she said in a strangled voice, and then again: "Aye! Oh, Ian, I—I love you," she cried. Suddenly it was all rushing out, like a dam bursting within her, and there was naught she could do to withhold it. "I love you so! I—I think I fell in love with you long, long ago, when you were just a boy. . . ."

In that instant, his heart surely stopped beating. It resumed with thick, heavy strokes.

He swallowed. "What about Jamie?" It was his turn to falter. "Sabrina, I thought you loved him. When he died, you turned from me."

Her eyes darkened. "Ian, I was confused and sick at heart . . . but never did it change what I felt for you.

And ... oh, please do not hate me! but I so wish that he could have lived on, for he had so much life in him, so much to give ..."

"Sabrina, there is something I must tell you. Something you must know. He could have slain me, sweet. He stood over me with his sword held high, but then he lowered it, when he might easily have been done with me and escaped!"

Sabrina stared. A tremor of shock went through her. Ian felt that *he* should have died. There was no need for him to say it aloud. With utter certainty she knew it.

Her throat aching, she wrapped her arms around his neck and clung.

His pain was vivid as a bloodstain. "I would have saved him if I could. But he lowered his sword and stood there, and said that he could not kill me—that he *would* not kill me. I bade him give me his dagger, and stabbed it in my shoulder, then called my stallion that he might flee. Only by then the Bruce's men were there ..." His voice grew ragged. "I tried to save him, Sabrina. Christ, I—I tried!"

His cheek rested against hers; it wasn't until their tears mingled that she realized he was crying, too. She felt him swallow, struggling for control.

"You cannot blame yourself, Ian," she said softly. "Mayhap it was God's will that Jamie should die, that you might live. For as surely as He watches over us from above, I know that even if I could, I would not change the outcome of that day."

Tears standing high and bright in her eyes, she smiled achingly. "Aye," she said huskily, "I would far rather have you beside me"—she pressed a finger to his lips—"this day and every other."

Her heartfelt confession shook him to the core. Ian felt his heart turn over.

He caught her fingers in his and pressed a kiss to her palm, capturing her eyes with his own.

"I love you, Sabrina."

Her breath caught. Her gaze searched his. "Truly?" she whispered.

"Mmmm." He drew her close. His mouth grazed hers. He smiled against her lips. "I love you, sweet."

Her heart fluttered, then soared. "And I love you, Ian. But I would know"—a faint twinkle had begun to dance in her eyes—"do you promise to love me forever, my Highland prince?"

He rested his forehead against hers. "I do so most heartily, lass. And a promise given is a promise kept, as you well know." He smiled. "Indeed, it's a promise I'll have no trouble keeping."

Epilogue

Sunlight poured from an azure sky, lighting jagged, granite peaks to silver. The waters of the tiny mountain loch glimmered like a jewel, while a warm summer breeze rippled the surface.

Nearly three summers had passed since that tragic night on the battlements, and yet the healing had begun that very eve.

Seated on a blanket beneath the shade of a towering boulder, Sabrina looked on as father chased daughter round the glen, a soft smile on her lips. Squeals of delight filled the air as Elizabeth was snatched high in her father's arms.

The pair had started toward her. Sabrina's heart turned over as two small hands came out to frame lean, dark cheeks.

"I want a kiss, Papa," came the childish demand.

There was a flash of white teeth. "A kiss! And why should I," Ian teased, "for you are a wee bonny bratling."

A giggle floated into the air. "But I am *your* bonny bratling!" came the childish retort. Shiny red lips puckered.

"Aye, my lassie, that you are. And you are as irresistible as your mama!" With that he smacked a loud and noisy kiss upon his daughter's lips. Elizabeth gave a high-pitched shriek, but puckered up for yet another. Her father obliged her, then deposited the little girl on the blanket next to her brother.

Pushing himself up on chubby forearms, her brother grinned at her. Perched on all fours, his knees tucked up beneath him, he rocked back and forth.

Elizabeth promptly turned emerald-green eyes up to her father. "I want a sister!" she announced.

"Do you now?" He reached for her, pulling her into his lap. "Then you must have a nap, my dove."

As her mother could have predicted, Elizabeth started to pout, then abruptly stopped. Long, black curls tumbled over her father's arm as she gazed up at him solemnly.

"If I nap, Papa, will my sister be here when I awake?"

Ian chuckled. "Nay, love, not that soon. And I fear I must have your mother's help on that score."

Elizabeth clasped chubby hands together before her. "Mama!" she implored. "Will you help Papa?"

Sabrina's mouth twitched. There was not a mother in the world who could resist such a plea. Her eyes caught Ian's; a decided gleam had appeared in his and one dark brow arched in utterly wicked amusement. Her cheeks turned pink, for there was no mistaking his meaning. His gaze roved her face. The hot flare of passion and possessiveness she glimpsed there thrilled her to her toes. There would be no objections from her—nay, not a one. Indeed, the very thought made her tremble with longing.

"I suppose I could be persuaded to, love." She wagged a finger. "But you must take a nap, dearest.

And then your papa and I shall see what we can do."

Satisfied with the answer, Elizabeth wiggled from Ian's arms, lay down beside him and was soon fast asleep. Ian fixed covetous eyes toward his wife. A slow smile spread across his face, but at that very instant his son let out a howl of protest. The babe's face crumpled and he turned woeful eyes toward his mother.

Ian scooped up the fretting infant. "I know what you want, lad," he said with a sigh, "and I must say, I envy you your feast."

Sabrina had already bared her breast, for she knew the babe was hungry. Ian dropped to his knees and delivered their son into her waiting arms; the baby turned his head, wasting no time availing himself of his nourishment. Ian laughed at his eagerness. Bending low, he kissed the crown of the babe's head; then, turning ever so slightly, he pressed his mouth to the sweet ivory flesh that nourished his son. Sabrina's breath caught. Her fingers came up to curl in the dark hair that grew low on his nape, the veriest caress.

No words passed between them as Ian stretched out beside her, and indeed, none were needed. They were each content in the moment, content with the world . . . aye, and most assuredly . . . with each other.

The babe suckled noisily. Sabrina traced the arch of one dark brow. Unbidden, her mind traveled back to the night he was born. It was snowy and blustery and bitterly cold, and as the pains grew more intense, she bemoaned the fact that her child had chosen just such a wintry night to make his entrance into the world.

Meredith the midwife had delivered him, with assistance from Edna and Mary, who was once again back at Castle MacGregor. Again to Meredith's utter disbelief, the babe's father was present throughout, there at her side.

And again, it was Ian who eased their son into her outstretched arms, the proudest of smiles gracing his lips.

"Look, sweet," he said with a laugh. "Look what we have here."

"Aye"—her voice caught midway between laughter and tears—"another wee Highland prince!"

Together they counted fingers and toes and proclaimed him the handsomest lad ever born. It was then, held snug in her husband's embrace, that she tipped her head to the side.

"What shall we call him, Ian? What shall we name our son?"

He was silent for the longest time. One dark hand toyed idly with the babe's, so strong, yet so very, very gentle. And then he said something she never dreamed she might hear. . . .

"Methinks we should call him Jamie."

Sabrina stared. Her lips parted. Her throat aching, she touched his sleeve. Her eyes clung to his.

"But I thought . . . Ian, I thought you . . . that he . . ." Words failed her. "Why?" was all she could ask. "Why?"

"'Tis very simple, really. He gave me my life, Sabrina, when he could have taken it just as easily. 'Tis a debt I cannot repay, and yet I owe him . . . so very much . . . my very breath. And now, to name my son for him . . . it seems such a small thing . . . and yet it seems the very least I can do." The faintest of smiles grazed his lips. "I would name my son for a man of honor, a man of deeply held beliefs . . . that is, if it would please you."

Her hand slipped within his. His fingers closed around hers warm and strong.

Sabrina's heart spilled over, and so did her eyes. "It would please me," she said shakily. "It would please me very much." She smiled through her tears. "Our son will be named for a man of honor . . . but it's from his father he will learn the true meaning of honor and respect."

He brought her fingers to his lips. "Then Jamie it shall be," he whispered, his gaze holding hers.

Such tenderness filled her heart that she thought it would surely burst. In that moment, she was certain she could not love him more.

Yet she did, with every day that passed, with every hour. And she knew it would ever be so.

So it was that their son was named Jamie.

It was but a scant month later that Sabrina's father appeared at Castle MacGregor to see his grandson. She had seen him but once before since her marriage to Ian, when Duncan Kincaid had come to visit when Elizabeth was nearly a year old. And though the distance between them was still there, Sabrina still loved him.

Though she'd written to him on several occasions after Elizabeth's birth, she hadn't divulged the truth of how Margaret had really died. Her father still believed she had drowned that long ago day near Dunlevy.

It was better that way, Sabrina decided, and Ian agreed.

Nor did the dark hold any fear for Sabrina. It had gradually slipped away, little by little, until it was no more. And now, the dark held only sultry promises and vibrant whispers . . . and blistering passion untold.

Just then strong hands slipped beneath the precious bundle at her breast. Jamie's mouth had slipped away from her nipple; his eyes were closed, his lashes casting long shadows on his cheeks. Ian gently laid him next to his sister, then silently rose and held out his hand to his wife. Sabrina did not hesitate, but laid her hand within his and allowed him to pull her to her feet.

With a nod he indicated the rock where they had first made love with such wild abandon—a place that had seen many such encounters thereafter.

A roguish brow climbed high. "Do we dare . . . ?" he whispered.

"We do," she said promptly, for now that both children slumbered peacefully, it was time for their parents to turn their attention to each other.

Ian pulled her into the sheltering harbor of his embrace. "Ah, but you always were a brave, bold lass."

Emerald green eyes sparkled up at him. "Never did you mind before this," she reminded him. As they sank to the ground, nimble, daring fingers stole their way beneath his kilt, finding and seeking and stroking.

He groaned his pleasure. "And I do not mind now." He pulled her astride him. "That's the way, sweet. Now. Yes. Now . . ."

It was a long time later when they both tumbled down from that pinnacle of bliss. Ian laughed softly when she collapsed atop him. Ian carried her back to the blanket and lay down beside her. Propping himself up on an elbow, he gazed at her, such unguarded tenderness on his expression that Sabrina felt like melting.

A blunted fingertip came out to trace the fullness of her lower lip.

"Do you love me, lass?"

She trapped his hand against his cheek, her heart in her eyes. "Immensely."

"And do you promise to love me forever?"

She twined her arms around his neck and pulled his head down. "I do," she whispered against his lips . . . into his heart. "I promise to love you, and only you"— she smiled—"forever and always."

And aye, she did.